The Horseman's Graves

The
HORSEMAN'S
GRAVES

Jacqueline Baker

HARPERCOLLINS PUBLISHERS LTD
A PHYLLIS BRUCE BOOK

A Phyllis Bruce Book, published by HarperCollins Publishers Ltd

HarperCollins books may be purchased for educational, business,
or sales promotional use through our Special Markets Department.

HarperCollins Publishers Ltd
2 Bloor Street East, 20th Floor
Toronto, Ontario, Canada
M4W 1A8

www.harpercollins.ca

Library and Archives Canada Cataloguing in Publication

Baker, Jacqueline
The horseman's graves: a novel / Jacqueline Baker.

"A Phyllis Bruce book".
ISBN-13: 978-0-00-200836-5
ISBN-10: 0-00-200836-X

I. Title.
PS8553.A3793H67 2007   C813'.6   C2007-900579-9

Design by Sharon Kish

Printed and bound in the United States
HC 9 8 7 6 5 4 3 2 1

For my mother,
and in memory of my grandfather,
and all the gentle hearts before them.

KNOCHENFELD

ONE

They had always been haunted, those hills. The place where the dead walk. But by the time Leo Krauss arrived with his parents and gape-eyed siblings in 1909 (travelling from the stinking though venerable port of Odessa by polluted steamer to Montreal and then west by train and west by cart and west on mules and, finally, when the mules lay wasted in the dust, west on foot across a land searing under the heat of a prairie sun), the ghosts that had once walked the hills had vanished, or were, at least, imperceptible to those already burdened by the past of another country. Now, it was life the newcomers travelled toward, not death. A big clean dome of pure sky. Infinite, unfettered space. A new start. Death was behind them; here, a life could be resurrected.

Leo's father, Old Krauss—Gustav was his Christian name, though it had been some time since anyone had used it—whether by lack of prudence or enterprise or by sheer perversity took up his homestead in the worst possible corner of that parched, sifting region known as Palliser's Triangle, a supposedly hostile and uninhabitable extension of the American Desert. Though there was better land available, Old Krauss settled himself and his family on a hundred and sixty pitiable acres tucked right up against the Sand Hills, toward the richer land bordering the river, but not of it. He might have taken comfort in the mere fact of its proximity, that good, dark gumbo land, as though it might some-how—by erosion or osmosis—creep over into his own; but the truth was Old Krauss neither needed nor gave comfort.

"Mean as crossed rattlers, those Krausses," that's what people said about them.

"Mean in the old country, mean over here."

"That's how meanness is."

"Can't shake that kind of thing out of the blood," was what they said.

And it did appear to be bred into Krausses, the same as their straight black hair and those pinched dark eyes set into colour-less faces, "like two pissholes in the snow," people said. Flat-out mean: to others, and to their own.

Old Krauss would come into town sometimes, to the café or the grocery or the post office, and laugh to the other men, as if sharing a joke: "Yah, you should have seen," he would say. "She made it halfway down the road this time, she must be getting faster."

It was his wife he was talking about, old Ida, his senior by at least five years. At first, no one knew what he meant. Then Pius Schoff happened to stop by the Krauss place one day just as Old Krauss was on his way into town.

"By God," Pius said later, "I never would have believed it if I hadn't seen it with my own eyes."

But Old Krauss had done nothing out of the ordinary, only what he always did: hitched up his wagon in the barn where Ida could not see, and then cracked the reins and shot from the doors and straight down the road, Ida out of the house and running after him hollering until they—mule, cart, man and wife—were just a receding cloud of dust in the distance and Pius still stand-ing in the yard staring after them. It was Old Krauss's joke on his wife. Often, when she needed her few things from town, she would drag the big wooden table over so that she could stand by the window next to the door—with her washing or her canning or her cooking—one eye fixed on the barn. But Old Krauss must have been blessed with a kind of perverse second-sight that allowed him to predict the precise moment his wife would turn away, and off he'd shoot across the prairies, sometimes with young Leo and perhaps one or two of the other children on the seat beside him, staring back at their mother with those dark, implacable eyes and a look on their faces that suggested neither shame nor even comprehension.

Nor would Old Krauss run Ida's errands in town for her—"What business of mine?" he would say—and so if she heard the wagon she would be forced to drop what she was doing and chase after him. If she caught up, he'd slow down a little, not stop, but slow down, perhaps just so that he might have a good laugh at her trying to jump in. If she didn't catch up to the wagon, as was most often the case, or did but was unable to hoist herself into it, she would be left to return home and do without whatever it was she needed or else to walk the six miles to town, no matter the weather or the season, and hope, at least, for a ride home.

Often, in the middle of winter, Old Krauss would pull his wagon up in front of the grocery and holler to someone, anyone, on the street, "No time for a coat, eh?" and jab his thumb to where Ida sat next to him, nearly dead from the cold and clutching over her ears and neck the black woollen headscarf she wore around the house, her hands bare and raw, eyes streaming wet from the wind, and for comfort only the black beaded rosary she always kept wrapped around her fist. How she didn't die from exposure, no one knew.

Once a week at least Old Krauss could be heard bragging to the other men, usually in Wing's where they met for coffee and Old Krauss there at every opportunity, sitting all day if he could manage, bragging about how he'd made Ida run, as if it were something extraordinarily funny, as if they all shared in the joke, never noticing how the men bent their heads over their cups or simply got up and left, and only Wing with his coffeepot and his dishtowel who would even acknowledge him, smiling and nodding but quite possibly thinking the same thing everyone else was: that Old Krauss was a prize SOB if ever there was one. Old Krauss would sit there all day drinking Wing's coffee and never paying a red cent—that is how the men put it, not a red cent—and Wing too polite or too afraid himself to say anything. Because that was one thing about Old Krauss: if someone ever crossed him, if he ever thought someone had crossed him, they had better watch their backs, or at least that's what he claimed, managing to sound convincing enough for them to believe him. Most of the time he was harmless enough, too stupid and too lazy for any of his plans to work: elaborate, impossible plans. He would spend all his time chewing over his grudge, imagining the satisfaction of besting whoever had wronged him, though never actually putting a plan into action. But harmless most of the time is hardly better than harmless none of the time, since no one could predict when Old Krauss was harmless and when he was not.

———

That first spring after Krausses arrived, the old man went out— no one knew where—and got a dog, an enormous, woolly coated, whitish thing with a tongue that perpetually lolled from its huge mouth and that quickly developed a taste for the neighbours' chickens. It would roam the countryside at night wreaking havoc on the henhouses, sometimes not even eating what it killed, just killing for the sake of killing.

At first coyotes were blamed. But one night Mrs. Arlen Gebler, awake with a bout of stomach upset, spotted what looked to be a large sheep hightailing it out of her yard with one of her best layers clamped firmly in its jaws. Mrs. Arlen Gebler, no fool, knew what she had seen. Word spread. It wasn't long before half the

countryside was laying a bead on the poor beast, just waiting with
their shotguns; to protect their chickens, they all said—"Yah, and
what about the children? Today it's just chickens, but tomorrow?"—but really just because it was Old Krauss's dog, and so
guilty of much by association. Some even tried to bait the animal,
just to have the pleasure of shooting him. Not that Old Krauss
would have cared one way or another about the dog. He treated it
no better and no worse than anything else in his possession. It was
always running around half-starved and sore from beatings. It was
no great wonder the animal had taken to killing chickens, it was so
hungry. The problem was, it had acquired a taste for blood.

It was Pius Schoff who finally got him, and Pius as good a man
as ever there was. But Pius had a thing about Old Krauss.

"May God forgive me," he would say, shaking his head, "but
I hope that sonofabitch rots in hell," shocking all who heard him.
They'd never known Pius to say a word against anyone.

But Schoffs were Krausses' nearest neighbours, and Old Krauss
always borrowing one thing and another and never returning anything, or returning things considerably more worn than when
he'd borrowed them. Sometimes he did not even ask for what he
took, just walked over and took what he needed whether anyone
was home or not. And Old Krauss's gaunt and phlegmatic cattle,
when he had any, always over in Pius's pasture, and the Krauss
children into Mrs. Schoff's garden ("And it's not that they take
the food," she said, "God knows they need it and they're welcome, but they stomp all over everything and break the stalks and
leave nothing"), and tormenting the Schoff kids, worse still since
that afternoon when the eldest Schoff boy—Stolanus—coming
upon Leo and one of his younger brothers beating a stray calf
cruelly with willow switches, turned the switches upon the beaters
until they wept, an act for which Stolanus was to hang his head
later in shame before his father, and for which the older Krausses
exacted revenge upon the Schoff children at every opportunity,
though they had beaten Leo and the younger brother as well for

their tears. And then, too, being neighbours, Pius saw and heard more of what went on there between Old Krauss and Ida, and the children, also, and so maybe he had more reason to feel as he did about Old Krauss.

So, though he hated to do it, Pius shot that dog one morning while the eldest boy, Stolanus, stood watching, and when the big dog dropped in the dust with an air of astonishing finality, Pius lowered the shotgun and, after a moment, said to his son, "Well. That's one of his at least out of its misery."

But afterwards, when father and son stood together over the big dog's body, wondering what to do—whether to cart it over to Old Krauss or just to bury it—Pius felt kind of sorry he'd done it at all.

"Poor beast," he said, and, handing the shotgun to his son, he crouched and tried to hoist the dog up into his arms, but he could not, and he struggled there in the dust, the dog's huge head rolling heavily. When the son moved to help him, Pius waved the boy away.

"I shot him," he said, grimly. "I'll do it."

And so Stolanus stood and watched as his father hefted the huge animal up and across his chest, and when he saw his father was heading out toward the shelterbelt, he went to the barn and exchanged the shotgun for a spade.

Pius was sitting winded on a cottonwood stump with the dog at his feet when Stolanus entered the trees. Without speaking, the boy bent and stabbed at the cracked earth.

"I shot him," Pius said, rising and reaching for the spade.

Stolanus did not look up. "I watched you," he said, and kept digging.

When the last stone had been laid to keep the coyotes away, they replaced the spade in the barn and stopped at the pump to wash the blood and dirt from their hands and then they walked over to Krausses' together.

Halfway there the boy said, "Do we have to?"

He did not really expect an answer, and he did not get one. Just a slight lifting of the shoulders, a resigned curl at the corners of the mouth. And so they walked on in silence, their boots thumping softly in the dust.

———

No one was home. Pius knocked a third time and then said to Stolanus, "I guess Ida was quick today," though neither of them laughed.

Pius opened the door a crack. "Yah, hello?" he called. "Anyone home?"

But there was only the creak of the door on its hinge. Pius sighed, feeling relieved in spite of his good intentions, and reached into his shirt pocket for a bit of paper and the stub end of a pencil. Quickly, he wrote Old Krauss a note—*I shot your dog*—and was about to add an apology and a signature when Stolanus, leaning against the open screen door, looking inside the darkened kitchen with not a little curiosity, said, "Papa."

Stolanus pointed at a spot on the floor just inside the door. There lay what appeared to be the new harness Pius had brought back just a few days previous from Maple Creek, to where they made a six-day journey south by wagon twice a year for supplies. Pius stepped inside and picked it up. It was cut and frayed where someone had been after it with a knife, for God knows what reason, but sure enough, it was theirs. Pius dropped the harness in disgust. He took up the pencil again and added to the note, *Keep off my goddamned property you sonofabitch or by God you'll get the same.* Then signed his name, left the harness and walked home, his boy at his heels.

That evening, Pius was sitting with his family at the supper table over a particularly sweet ham, wondering if perhaps he shouldn't have left that note after all, wondering if it was too late to ride over after supper and get rid of it, thinking it was a very stupid thing he had written and wondering what on earth had possessed him, when the door swung open and in walked Old Krauss, just the way he always would walk in on people, not even bothering to knock. Pius started up from the table, feeling guilty and ashamed and just a little bit scared all at once, but before he could speak, Old Krauss held out the piece of paper Pius had written on and said, "Yah, someone left me a note, but I can't read. What does it say?"

———

Pius may or may not have read the note to him, he may or may not have warned Old Krauss off his property, but one way or another Old Krauss found out Pius had shot his dog. He began to brag around town, how he, Gustav Krauss, was going to show that so-and-so that he, Gustav Krauss, was not to be meddled with. Of course, it never amounted to anything. It never did with Old Krauss. Or almost never. There was some rumour, some story about how in the old country Old Krauss's father had somehow crossed an uncle of Pius's, though neither Old Krauss nor Pius would speak of it, and speculation tended to favour an unexpected pregnancy in one of Pius's older cousins, which resulted in bloodshed, though no one could provide any details, and the story seemed to balloon with each telling until in the end it seemed that Old Krauss's father had been guilty of more than common promiscuity, that his offences had included rape, murder; that somehow young Pius had been involved in the retaliation; that they had carried their grudge with them from the old country to the new. In some tellings, the trouble between Krausses and Schoffs in the old country predated even Pius and Gustav. The old folks told how Pius's father's second-cousin-once-removed's neck had been slit over a little matter of a stray hog, Gustav's father the one generally suspected, though nothing was ever proven. No one knew for certain, but the speculation was enough: Old Krauss, stupid though he was, was born of dangerous men, and who was to say he could not be just as dangerous, worse even—dangerous in the rash and unpredictable way that only the truly stupid can be.

And there did seem to be more than the usual dislike between Pius Schoff and Old Krauss, seemed always to have been, almost as soon as Old Krauss had turned up and, perversely, set down roots on the land adjacent to Schoff's. It was as if the bad blood had crossed the ocean along with the grief and hopes and hand-carved rosaries, and Old Krauss meant to keep it there.

It all made Pius more than a little nervous, as if he had, with the trouble about the harness, reopened an old and darkly festering wound. He began to sleep with the .22 tucked snugly beneath his side of the bed he shared with his wife, a habit which, she confessed, made her uneasy.

"You don't think Old Krauss would really do anything," Mrs. Schoff would always say, "would he?"

"Ach," Pius would reply, and shake his head, "better to be safe than sorry."

One night, Mrs. Schoff turned to her husband. "If you had to," she said, "would you shoot him even?"

Pius thought a while.

"I'd rather not," he finally said.

———

That June, when Pius's prized cattle dog had a litter of pups, he packed up the best two in a crate to take over to Old Krauss, a peace offering, and Mrs. Schoff said to her husband, "Well, you might as well save those dogs the trouble and take our chickens, too."

But Pius just shrugged as if to say, *If he is our cross to bear, bear it we must, and be glad it is no worse.* He never again approached Old Krauss about anything, though things continued to go missing from his yard, more often than before, as if to goad, and the Krauss kids continued to lay beatings at every opportunity upon the Schoff kids. Pius nevertheless advised his children to avoid Krausses, which they did, and to walk away from a fight, which they did not. And when Pius went to town, the other men said to him slyly, "I see you're grazing Krauss's stock again."

"Hell of a good neighbour."

"Yah, that's for sure, that's a real Christian there."

"Love thy neighbour, eh, Schoff?"

When they said that, Pius just smiled a hard little smile and said not a word. Of course, everyone was careful never to say anything to Old Krauss or even within his hearing, because, like Pius, they were not willing to bet on what he was or was not capable of as far as sheer meanness and spite went. And from the way he treated his wife, well.

Old Ida never saw fifty. "Wear out a wife faster than a plow, that's for damn sure," that's what the old folks used to say about Krausses, the ones who had known them in the old country, though not trying to be funny, or coarse either, just stating a fact. Of course, Old Krauss was the first to condemn laziness in others, that old human foible, hating most in others what one hates most in oneself. Though Old Krauss would never have admitted as much, could never have, cursed as he was with the blind stupidity of the self-righteous. He reminded many of that old saying, *Wer es nicht im Kopf hat, muss es in den Beinen haben.* He who hasn't got it in his head has to have it in his legs. But Old Krauss had nothing in the head, and nothing in the legs. Ida did all the work around their place, trying to keep the children fed and in some kind of clothing. The children were expected to work, too, though they all turned out just as lazy as Old Krauss. But he was fond of bragging that he expected his children to work, and they damn well worked, that is how he put it. He would boast how the last child out the door and back to work after mealtime got a swift boot in the arse, just for being last. That much was true. The old man took his own plate and stood by the door, waiting for them, and all the children bolting their food, hardly bothering to chew, the little ones crying already, barely able to eat but so hungry they couldn't help themselves, crying and choking on each mouthful, knowing it would be one of them who would take the blow, which was, if all accounts could be trusted, not delivered lightly. It was really no great wonder Leo turned out as he did. To hell in a handbasket, every last one of them.

"Sure enough," they would say around town in later years, "sure enough, Old Krauss made those kids what they are, just like his own father made him what he is. If not by blood, then by example."

Two

Leo was the only one of the Krauss children to remain on the family farm at the edge of the Sand Hills. The others, the ones who lived, left as soon as they were able. A sister east of Fox Valley was the nearest, having married a man much like her father, as sometimes seems to happen. (This same sister would, many years later, begin but not finish piecing together a family history of sorts, her notes discovered and burned—after her premature death from liver disease—by her own eldest daughter, a nurse from Medicine Hat only too happy to keep her Krauss blood a secret.) All the rest were long gone by the time the old man breathed his last on a stifling day in late August of the summer of 1917 and Leo took over the farm, if it could be called as much. Some of the others came home for the funeral, not out of grief or respect or even propriety, but only to take whatever rubbish was worth the taking and good riddance.

Leo—it must have been Leo—arranged to have a family photograph taken around the pine coffin with Old Krauss stretched out there between them looking just as miserable as he ever did when alive. God knows what made Leo do it, have that photograph taken, but he did it sure enough. Then, after all was said and done and Leo's brothers and sisters had crawled back to whatever holes they'd crawled out of and Leo was settled in the old farmhouse, shack really, all but empty now since his siblings had picked over it like a swarm of army worms on ripe barley, Leo nailed that photograph up right over the kitchen table, maybe out of some latent sentimentality, maybe as a reminder of what sort of blood it was that ran in his own veins, or maybe just to convince himself that the old bastard really was dead and gone. Either way, Leo—he was barely a man then, not yet twenty, as far as anyone could figure—lived out there eight long months with nothing but that photograph of his dead father for company and none of the neighbours in much of a hurry to make a friend of him.

That first winter, Leo might have died for all anyone knew. Old Pius Schoff—who, of anyone, would have been the one to look in on Leo—had been gone a few years, Mrs. Schoff following not too far behind, and so now Leo's nearest neighbour was Pius's eldest son, Stolanus, and his young wife, Helen, and they could not have cared less what Leo did or did not do, especially now, wrapped up in their own troubles: their only child—a little boy—badly hurt in a farming accident the very day Old Krauss was buried. And so they had nothing to do with Leo, or anyone for that matter.

Now and then, one of the other neighbours, for reasons best known to them, would suggest that it wouldn't be out of line to take a ride over and see if Leo was all right out there by himself, but with no one willing to be the one to do so, the uneasy memory of Old Krauss still too fresh in everyone's mind.

So they forgot about Leo, more or less, until the spring, when he emerged from that house like something lain dormant, emerged shrunken and thinner than anyone remembered, as if his bones jutted just short of breaking skin and those two flat black eyes sunk even deeper, but with a kind of fuzziness—and this was the strange thing—a kind of indistinctness about him, in spite of his edges. Indistinct in a way that made people squint up their eyes when they looked at him, as if it was not Leo but their own eyesight that was faulty. He emerged from that shack one bright Sunday morning in spring, wearing a dark suit far too short in the arms and legs, making him appear taller, and with his black hair combed straight across his head, and the bright crocuses dotting the field beyond the yard and a bit of snow still banked up bluely against the north side of the barn, and he hitched up Gus's bony old mule to Gus's bony old wagon and he drove through that blinding spring sunshine over to the little country church at Johnsborough parish, and there, while everyone stood gaping in the yard, he climbed down from the wagon and nodded to the left and to the right and grinned blackly and said, "Good day to you, God bless you, good morning," just as if he had done so without fail every Sunday of his life.

It was not only the appearance of Leo Krauss that made everyone stop and stare, but where he'd chosen to appear. Ida had been the only Krauss ever to attend church (when the weather was good enough that she might walk, or when one of her neighbours thought to—dared to—offer a ride). Neither Old Krauss nor the children ever accompanied her, whether because Ida preferred it or because Old Krauss forbade it, no one was ever certain, though when Old Krauss would happen to run into Father Rieger in town and Father Rieger would invariably ask, *Gustav, when will we see you in church?,* Old Krauss would invariably reply, *Wenn des Papstes Arsch blümt,* when the Pope's ass blooms. He loathed religion in general and Catholics in particular. Cannibals, he called them. Perhaps some principle kept him from church, or possibly something from his shady past, but many suspected it was, again, simply his laziness.

"Ach," he would say, "all those rules. Don't eat meat on Friday. Fast before Communion. Don't take the Lord's name in vain. Good God, a man would marry a goat if that old *Mottenschitter* over there in Rome said to do so. And the *opa norsch* we have here (meaning Father Rieger), they would all shit in their own pants and call it due penance to please him."

Sometimes the older Krauss boys, perhaps at their father's instigation, would ride over to Johnsborough Sunday mornings and throw snowballs or small rocks or even chunks of frozen cow shit at the church windows during Mass and once, on Lenten Friday, a small fish they'd caught in the river, over and over against the window nearest the altar, while Father, who, liking to stray from what he felt was a too-confining Latin Mass, carried on stoically, advising his parishioners that God was angry, yes, angry, and that sin could only be atoned for by the shedding of innocent blood, that God in His wrath and anger had sent Jesus to be punished in their sinful stead, saying (at which point he raised his voice in order to be heard above the fish thumping against the window) of the Lenten fast, "In the words of Matthew, do not look sombre as the hypocrites do, for they disfigure their sinful faces to show men they are fasting until, until, fasting . . . is . . . it's to put oil on your head and, sinning . . ." Then, reddening, he lapsed into the Nicene Creed, stammering, "*Credo in unum . . . in unum Deum, Patrem omnipotentem, factorem . . . factorem . . .*" at which point he finally slammed the Book shut and flew down the aisle and out the front doors, bellowing after the boys as they rode away laughing and hooting across the muddy spring fields.

One All Hallows' Eve, they almost burned the whole place down, and Father Rieger into the bargain (no one ever did discover what Father was doing there in the middle of the night, but it was not for them to question the cloth), and the youngest of the Krauss boys, who had, for whatever reason, been abandoned by his elder brothers, was left standing in the yard snot-nosed and bawling while Father Rieger flapped back and forth between the well and the fire. Of course, the Krauss boys denied it, in spite of their young brother's presence at the scene of the crime, but everyone knew it had been them. No one but a Krauss would have braved the cemetery there—any cemetery—at night without a rosary and fifteen of his boldest friends.

So on that spring morning when Leo stepped through the church doors and dipped his fingers in the urn and crossed himself just as natural as if he'd done it every day of his life, more than just a few heads turned and stared in disbelief. He strode up the aisle, genuflected, yes, genuflected, and edged into a pew, not at the back of the church as one might expect, but right there in front, right behind the prim row of nuns who had ridden out in a wagon from the convent on the edge of town, as they did on Sundays and special Holy Days. He nodded to this person and that as he knelt and then he bent his head piously over his folded hands while everyone stared in shock and outrage at him and then at one another, and Mother Superior—Sister Benedicta—who sat directly in front of Leo, turning and giving him a long, pale stare, as if he were Lucifer himself, and someone in the back of the church muttering, "*Gott im Himmel,* but now I've seen it all."

Of course, they had not seen it all, not yet, not by far, for when Father Rieger delivered the Communion Rite and broke the bread and ate of the body and blood of Christ, and when Kaspar and Remigius Fitz, the altar boys, roused themselves long enough to ring their little golden bell, and when Ludmila Baumgarten, seated at the piano, rose to lead the *Agnus Dei,* and everyone filed up for Communion, Leo Krauss—having never, as far as anyone knew, made a good confession, made any kind of confession at all—without a glimmer of hesitation took his place in line, head bowed, arms folded across his chest, moving in that slow, aimless way he always had of moving, as if his very leanness slowed him where another man would be slowed by weight. More than just laziness; it was as if he was afraid to get where he was going.

When he stepped to the front of the line and the altar boys looked at him and then at each other, Father Rieger seemed suspended in time, standing with the Host pinched dryly between his fingers before Leo's closed eyes and open mouth. Father, too, looked to the right and to the left, as if someone might tell him what to do. But everyone just stared back at him, Mother Superior narrowing her eyes ever so slightly and drumming her gnawed fingers against the hymnal in her lap.

And, so, his face all flushed up above his collar, Father said between clenched teeth, *"Corpus Domini nostri Jesu Christi custodiat animam tuam in vitam aeternam,"* and much to everyone's disbelief moved to put the wafer on Leo's tongue.

It is difficult to say what exactly happened next, whether it was Leo who made an unexpected move or whether Father simply dropped it, but that little wafer went fluttering to the floor while everyone gasped and watched it fall, almost in slow motion, as if it were a cottonwood leaf blown down by the wind, and someone behind Leo making a motion to grab it, but missing, and all the commotion then, someone jostling Remigius Fitz, who sloshed the goblet of wine he held onto Kaspar's white surplice, and Father saying, "Please, please, everyone, a moment," and Leo just standing there calmly while everyone searched the floor, saying, "Where is it? Where did it go? It's disappeared," and Ludmila Baumgarten standing up from her piano bench to announce, "A miracle," and all the shuffling and confusion then, until Leo slowly lifted his big old boot, and there the wafer lay, crushed as a stale biscuit, and no one knowing what to do.

Eventually, Leo bent and brushed the crumbs into the palm of his hand and said, "But it's still good, not?"

Then he popped it into his mouth, dabbed the crumbs from his lips and walked back to his pew, kneeling there as if nothing out of the ordinary had happened.

Afterwards, after Leo had climbed back into his wagon and driven away in the same placid and unhurried manner in which he'd arrived, the more superstitious of the congregation stood around in that unbelievable sunshine and talked darkly of what it all could mean, what kind of misfortune Leo had brought down upon himself, upon them all, what wrath of God. There were those for whom it always seemed to be doom of some kind, Ludmila Baumgarten first among them. And they talked, too, of that strangeness about him—Leo—that fuzziness, and wondered if perhaps he had begun drinking.

In fact, Leo had begun drinking, had even begun making his own liquor with his father's old still and the stunted potatoes he grew on the south side of the shack, with the intention of making a business of it. Unfortunately, Leo drank the stuff as quickly as he could make it. But Leo was fortunate in that he was one of those drunks who hid it well, at least at first, and so, though many suspected, no one had absolute proof.

———

In time, Leo's presence in church became so familiar that no one even bothered to question it. There were other things to move on to: the rumour that the youngest Heironimus Schmitt girl—the fat one, not the pretty one—was to have a baby, and no one as yet claiming title of father; Mike Weiser's new Ford motorcar; plans for a community threshing that fall; and, of course, the seeding. And so Leo came and went pretty much unremarked all summer, nodding and greeting and otherwise keeping to himself, while his fields lay fallow and choked with weeds. Apart from church, no one saw him, not in town, not in the country. It seemed as if he had settled into a quiet life of solitary, impoverished bachelorhood, and that perhaps he would be no trouble to the community after all, having risen above his history and his blood.

Then, one frosty Saturday evening around the middle of October, Leo turned up quite unexpectedly at one of the neighbours'. Balzar and Ottilia Hech, who had known Leo's father, were dead by then and their eldest son Roy had taken over the farm, and he was sitting there at the kitchen table playing cards with his sons while his wife and daughters pinched dough into crusts and stirred the big pot of apples stewing with cinnamon and nutmeg on the stove and the smaller children played horsey on the floor and begged morsels of dough. A knock came at the door and little Mary ran to open it and there with the huge night at his back stood Leo Krauss, dressed in that same cramped suit with his hat held in his hands and his hair combed particularly neatly across his head with something that stunk to high heaven ("Lard," Roy's wife Esther said later. "I'd bet my life on it, and none too fresh, either.")

Little Mary just stood there staring and Roy looked to the doorway in surprise and with a creeping feeling of apprehension and said, "Well, Mary, what are you thinking? Let him in once," and the little girl stepped away from the door and Leo entered and was offered a chair at the table and he took it. The cards were collected and put away and then everyone sat there at the table exchanging puzzled looks and speaking little, and Esther Hech peeking out of the corner of her eye now and then from where she stood at the counter helping her daughters place the latticed dough across the sliced and sugared apples.

Roy sat with his hands folded, waiting for Leo to state his business, wondering what in God's name he could want, and was just about to ask, against all propriety and good judgment, *Well, Leo, what can we do for you?* when Leo abruptly nodded, rose from the table, stuck his hat on his head, thanked them, blessed them and disappeared out the door, into his wagon and down the dark road.

After a moment of perplexed silence, Esther said, without conviction, "We could have given him coffee at least."

Roy just shrugged, wondering to himself why, since Leo had done nothing to warrant it, he felt that creeping unease in his belly.

At church the following morning, Roy learned that, after leaving his place, Leo had continued on down the road, to the next neighbour's, and then on to the next and the next, until around midnight when everybody figured he must have gone home at last (or else to Stolanus Schoff's, they said, and they snorted and shook their heads at the impossibility of that). But it was a mystery what exactly Leo could have meant by it all.

The more sensible among them said, "Ach, he's just lonely. It's the company he's after, and can you blame him?"

And so it went, Saturday after Saturday, always the same thing, coming and sitting wordlessly and then without warning taking his leave, until around the end of November when the middle Brunhauer girl noticed that as Leo sat at the kitchen table with her father and brothers, it was her he was looking at, watching her with a greasy kind of look—that is how she put it, a greasy look—as she went back and forth between the table and the counter, fetching coffee or kuchen. When she noticed, she stood stock-still in the middle of the kitchen and dropped a full pan of plum kuchen, her favourite, right there where she stood and burst into tears.

Her mother bustled around her, cleaning up the mess, saying, "Tilda, what is the matter with you, have you lost your mind?"

And Leo just sitting, watching it all.

After he had gone, Tilda, her face flushed up in shame and humiliation, told her mother. ("A greasy look," she said, and shivered and began to cry again.)

Tilda's mother's face darkened, just for an instant, and then she said quickly, "Nonsense, but really you can be a stupid girl," and Heinrich, Tilda's youngest brother, sang,

"Not long ago it rained,
The roof's still dripping wet;
I used to have a sweetheart,
I wish I had him yet,"

for which he was given a good smack on his backside and sent crying to bed and Tilda after him for her foolishness.

But at her first opportunity, Tilda's mother told the other mothers what Tilda had told her ("a greasy look, yes, that is what she said"), and the mothers raised their eyebrows and told the fathers, who lowered theirs. Soon it was clear to them just what Leo was up to. He was looking for company, all right, and in a hurry, with the prospect of another long winter staring him blank in the face.

————

But things would not move quickly for Leo. He carried on that way through December and into January, courting—without actually seeming to court—the neighbour girls, first this one, then that. Every Saturday night he'd slick back that hair that refused to stay slicked and put on his suit and take his old wagon and his old mule and ride over to one of the neighbours' and sit at their kitchen table and leer at the girls (how had they not noticed it before?) and wait to be offered a drink. For a while, at first anyway, they would pour him out a whisky, perhaps out of some confused sense of helplessness and propriety and good-will, or maybe because they were missing a drink themselves and could not drink without offering him one as well. Either way, it did not last long, that forced hospitality, once they discovered how quickly and easily he dispensed with their liquor. Soon they poured him black coffee instead, and then, when he sat there (glancing peevishly at his untouched cup) so long that most of the family would have gone to bed, the unfortunate girl he had come to court weeping hotly into her pillow from shame and outrage (it had become somewhat of a joke around the parish, one in which the teenage boys—the ones without eligible sisters—took particular delight), leaving only the father and one or two of the older sons sitting and yawning into their hands at the table, they finally ceased pouring even the coffee.

Then, Leo started turning up drunk. It was difficult to tell at first, he carried it pretty well, but his decorum soon began to dissolve until he would just pull into the yard behind his gassy mule and sit there in the blasting snow, shouting from the wagon for Caroline or Amalia or Saraphina or whomever he'd come to court (not always getting the name right). Everyone in the house would do their best to ignore him, going about their business, until eventually someone would say, "What, and will we let him freeze out there?" And no one at first either answering the question or moving to let Leo in, until finally someone would get up and open the door and shout, "Well, don't sit there and yell, you *dummkopf*, come in if you want to come in."

And so he would come in, stagger in sometimes, and the men would prop him up at the table and try to feed him strong coffee and cajole him, rather roughly, into some semblance of sobriety, out of neighbourliness and necessity, but how those fathers and brothers wanted to kill him. Sometimes he would pass out right there at the kitchen table, or be close to it, and everyone so sick of him that the men would just toss him over their shoulders and carry him out to the wagon, tie up the reins and give the old mule an especially hearty swat, thinking, *He will make it home or he won't and it's no skin off my arse either way.*

After a while, people stopped opening their doors to him and instead let him sit out there in his wagon in the subzero night, hollering, until in the end he gave up and went home. And still he showed up every Sunday morning at church like clockwork, nodding to the left and to the right, just as though he hadn't seen any of them since the previous Sunday. And that infuriated the men most of all. They wanted nothing to do with Leo, but they did not want to be ignored by him either.

"What," they would say, "he sits and drinks my liquor and ogles my daughters and come Sunday he nods at me like he's the goddamned Pope?"

And it was true. There Leo was, Sunday morning, with a kind of affected dignity so absurd that it should have been funny, they should have laughed at him, but instead they were insulted by it. There was something infuriating in the way Leo behaved, as if he did not know exactly what kind of a horse's ass he was. Leo could have been tolerated, forgiven even, possibly, if at least he would show some humility, some shame. If only he would show that he knew how low he was. He was a Krauss, after all, a Krauss, for God's sake.

And yet, Sunday morning, there he would be, as if he were above them, and every week take Communion with a soul they could only assume was as black as his teeth with sin. It was enough to drive them mad.

So they locked their doors to him, and when he sat in their yards and hollered for their daughters, and the mothers, out of exasperation, finally said, "Oh, for God's sake, let him in once, all the neighbours can hear," the fathers said darkly, "He can sit there until our cows shit flowers, that sonofabitch will not drink at my table again."

———

When Leo finally realized no doors would open for him and he grew weary of spending his Saturday nights freezing in his wagon, he stayed home. He stayed home Saturday and he stayed home Sunday, and at first everyone was relieved, elated even.

"Good," they said, "let him sit in that shack of his. Let him rot there."

But soon his absence became more of an outrage than his presence had ever been, as if he stayed away just so they would notice, and wonder about it, in spite of themselves. Even the girls wondered—though they would have admitted it to no one—whether he had found himself a woman after all (and wondered, too, in spite of themselves, who that woman was and if she was prettier than they), and hoped that he had, so as to put an end to their own shame and mortification.

So after months of suffering bitterly his presence, they found themselves having to suffer his absence.

"Ach," some said, "be glad he is out of our hair. Be glad it has not come to some trouble."

But others—the Ludmila Baumgarten crowd—began to talk. What should be done? They were Christians, not? And what if he was sick out there? What if he'd drunk himself dead? Someone should take a ride out there, but who? Father Rieger, not present at the time, was selected, unanimously.

"After all," Ludmila pointed out, "what is the church for if not to look to the low and the fallen?"

"Why, Father would be offended if we did not ask him."

"It would be an insult."

"An affront to God and clergy."

"No, we would not place ourselves above the cloth."

That is how they put it to Father Reiger, too, in spite of those who thought well enough should be left alone, and so, the following Saturday, Father bundled up grudgingly in his buffalo-skin coat and headed for Leo's, his eyes stinging in the frigid wind. Halfway there he saw a wagon approaching and he lifted his hand to wave.

It was Leo, dressed in his everlasting suit and with several blankets tied cape-like around his shoulders (it had never occurred to any of them that Leo did not own a coat), and one around his head, over his hat, babushka-style.

"Leo," Father said, when Leo had pulled his wagon alongside Father's horse. "I was just coming to see you."

Leo's teeth clacked. "Well," he said, "here I am, then."

And Father, flustered at the best of times, said, "But where are you going? I had wanted to have a talk with you."

Leo said, "About what?"

And Father said, "Why, about the salvation of your soul."

Leo shrugged and shivered and said, "It's not my soul that needs tending, Father. But you know about that as well as I."

And with a nod and a chuck of the reins, Leo left Father—whose cheeks flamed in spite of the cold—there in the middle of the road, which was slowly sifting over with snow, and he drove on into town, down the main street, past the post office and the bank and the Chinese laundry, past Wing's with its smell of grease and coffee and soya sauce, its pink door still gleaming warmly with the last of the February light, past the hardware and the livery, past the brown Protestant church set well back from the street behind a row of leafless caragana bushes softened by a light dusting of snow, past the town office and Stednick's Dry Goods and the grey two-storey house from which Doc Hamilton had briefly run his practice before returning permanently to the greener pastures of Ontario, abandoning his cats to live and breed among the castoff furniture that still graced, eerily, the parlour and bedrooms and kitchen, past the tall, stiff, white-planked Catholic church of St. Michael's built the previous summer by the town parish, past the lumber yard, the sweet smell of sawdust lingering well into winter, past the red-brick convent of the Sisters of St. Ursula with its neatly shovelled drive and the warm yellow lights in all its several immaculate windows, and on to the Catholic community hall just outside of town, where he pulled his wagon up and sat waiting in the cold and the gathering dark, listening to the dry hiss of snow blowing now and then across the bare and frozen earth around him, shivering and stomping his feet, waiting almost an hour until, at last, the first wagons began to arrive for the social that night in honour of St. Valentine's Day.

Finally, the doors of the hall were thrown open and he could see into the blaze of light, the hall done up in pink and red crepe-paper streamers with white paper doilies and red cut-out hearts the girls had made, and all of them in their prettiest dresses with the snow coming down on their hair as they walked from the wagons and Leo just sitting there under his cloak of old blankets, rubbing his bare hands together painfully in the cold.

Everyone was surprised to see him, of course, though they tried not to show it, and the girls secretly horrified, each one certain he was there for her.

Leo lost little time in making a nuisance of himself, to the single girls and some of the married as well, and the poor, quiet

Eichert sisters whose well-meaning mother had told them, "If I ever hear you refused someone a dance, it will be the last time you go," kept on their feet by him all night, one after the other, as he lurched them around the hall, the bottle of liquor he kept in his jacket pocket thumping against them so that they complained of bruises on their hipbones. The Eichert girls left well before midnight, out of frustration and humiliation and plain exhaustion, and the rest of the girls, bolstered by sips from the bottles in their companions' own jackets, turned their backs when Leo approached them, or laughed in his face, or said unkinder things, the way it often builds, one feeling cockier than the next, trying to outdo each other in boldness, impressing their companions, until Leo just took a chair and sat in a corner by the cloakroom, watching and waiting until the last dance was played and everyone thumped the tables and stomped their feet and sang,

"The Sweep-out, the Sweep-out,
Now the girls are going home.
And had they wanted to be good,
They'd have been home long ago."

Leo was the last to leave, sitting there in his chair by the cloakroom, and everyone laughing and brushing past him to get their coats, just as if he wasn't.

And so when Mike Weiser, on hall duty that night, finally said, "Leo, I'll be locking up in a minute," he said it gently, for he felt a bit sorry for Leo, sitting there in that chair at the back of the emptied and echoing hall. Mike was a widower and knew better than the others the miseries of being alone. So he stopped and leaned on his broom and said lightly, "Ach, Leo, women, who needs them?"

Leo just blinked at him a moment and then he said, "I do."

Then he sighed and nodded, stuck his hat on his head and his blankets on top of that, and walked out into the February night where that sorry old mule stood waiting for him, cloaked now in snow, and the wagon, too, and he did not bother to brush off either the mule or the seat, he just climbed up and sat and clucked the white mule into motion and drove that long dark road home to his farm, and Mike stood there in the snow and watched him go and thought, for the first time, that maybe they'd misjudged Leo, had been too hard on him, the sins of the father and all that. Mike thought maybe, just maybe, Leo did have a heart there after all. Even if it was fed and pumped by Krauss blood, it was still a heart and he was still a man, not?

THREE

T hat very night, after the St. Valentine's social, Mike Weiser stoked up his coal stove and sat down at the kitchen table he'd built for his wife, God rest her soul, with his own hands shortly after their marriage, and by the light of a gleaming kerosene lantern wrote a letter to this dead wife's spinster sister down in North Dakota. He wrote, *Dear Miss Marian Dunhauer*, and then, *Dear Miss Dunhauer*, and finally,

> *Dear Marian,*
>
> *You and I both know what it is to be alone. Come and be my wife and I will always treat you good. I have already one full section and some pasture besides for the cows, they are good beef cows and so you will not have to do so much milking as I know you do at home with your father's Jerseys that are not even good for eating, only if you stew them. There is chickens and sows and I will get a new boar come spring. There is crabapple trees that are good producers. I think you would be happy here and not lonely. It is a good farm and Eugenia—the dead sister—Eugenia kept a nice house. Some of the windows are stained-glass.*

Then he added quickly, *If it is not too much of a shock for you, come as soon as you get this letter.*

And so dear Miss Marian Dunhauer did, by God, she came less than three weeks later with a hand-me-down trousseau packed in a small steamer trunk that her parents had brought over from the old country—and with her youngest sister, a sweet but simple-minded girl, of whom she had custody—and Mike and Marian were married in a small ceremony at Johnsborough with the younger sister serving as bridesmaid and they lived together in the house with stained-glass windows.

The younger sister, Cecilia, lived with them. She must have been about sixteen, though she seemed younger. She helped around the house, taking particular delight in polishing the stained-glass windows; she would tend to them daily, though they hardly needed it, saving each pane for that moment in the day when the sun shone most directly upon it, rubbing away with an expression on her face of sheer wonder. It made people smile to see her.

To look at Cecilia you wouldn't know there was anything wrong with her at all, that is what everyone said, but, as Mike pointed out, she didn't talk so good and she didn't listen so good (sometimes, in the middle of a conversation, she would begin to hum and rock and smile to herself in such an easy, self-assured way that it made the speaker wonder if they had said something crazy themselves).

But the main thing about Cecilia was she hated to be left alone. That's what Mike said was hard, the girl could not be left alone, not for an instant, or she would start to howl and lash at anything within reach, curtains, bedding, furniture, crockery; she wouldn't follow whoever was leaving, or go find whoever had left, she would just sit and howl and lash out, just like a baby. She even slept on a little cot in Mike and Marian's bedroom and several times during the night she would get up and walk over to the bed in the dark and reach out her little hand and touch their faces just to make sure they were there and then return to her own cot and sleep again. Sometimes, on nights when there was no moon, she could not find their faces and her frantic patting at the pillows and whimperings would wake Mike and he would quickly reach out to find her hand and guide it to his own face and then to Marian's, and then she would be all right and they could go back to sleep.

Mike said it wasn't him but his wife who suggested the girl might be happier in a home of her own, with a husband and children to care for.

Unfortunately, no man around would have the girl, and her as pretty as anything—all pink and golden—and a harder worker you never saw. She'd work just as happy as a lark from sunup to sundown so long as someone was always with her. But, should she find herself alone for an instant, you could hear her for miles around on a calm day. If Marian needed to use the outhouse, she had to take Cecilia with her. And Mike would, too, if Marian was not around. He'd prop the outhouse door open just enough so that she could see him from where she stood outside, at a reasonable distance. Or, if he insisted upon closing the door, as he sometimes did, he would leave one hand stuck out through the crack so that Cecilia could hold it while he, well . . . it wasn't hard to imagine how Mike must have felt. And it was understandable that the young men kept away from her, as they did.

When it became clear there would be no suitors, Mike and Marian considered sending her to the nuns at the convent on the edge of town, the good sisters of St. Ursula. But then they foresaw difficulties—the solitary prayers, the bathing—no, it would not do, after all.

And so Cecilia continued to live with Mike and Marian, going wherever they went like a little shadow, from room to room, house to barn, outhouse to chicken coop, and they had pretty much resigned themselves that was how it was to be.

Until one day a courter finally came.

When Leo stepped into Mike and Marian's kitchen and said, "I come to make an offer," they did not at first know what he was talking about. When it became clear it was not a what but a who he was referring to, they both balked at the idea. Cecilia sat there with them at the kitchen table smiling, her blue eyes watering prettily over a bowl of spring onions she was trimming for supper. Mike and Marian lost no time in turning Leo out, and in no uncertain terms. Then, as Mike stood in the doorway fuming, watching Leo ride off in his wagon, he remembered that night of the St. Valentine's social and how Leo had looked stepping out into that snow, and he said to himself, "But maybe he is not so bad after all. Maybe it is just a woman he needs." He remembered those long evenings alone in his house before Marian had come, with nothing but the ticking of the mantel clock and the wind outside and the stained-glass windows black with the night that could not have been any darker and the fields that could not have stretched any farther on every side of him. And so he said, "Let the girl decide."

The girl decided. The following week Leo and Cecilia were married at the little church at Johnsborough with full Nuptial Mass and Benediction (though everyone thought Mike must have had something to do with that, since they could not believe Father would allow it without some incentive and God knows the church could always use a little extra money). Cecilia wore a dress sewed for her by Marian, white, patterned with sprigs of flowers and with a row of covered buttons all down the front; a wreath of wild roses in her hair. As they stood before the altar, Cecilia reached up and plucked one of the pink blossoms and tucked it into the buttonhole in Leo's old suit, causing Father Rieger to pause and scowl down upon them just before the first notes of the recessional hymn, led by Ludmila Baumgarten, rang out, and, though she could not help but roll her eyes and make sour grimaces, Ludmila sang,

"Happiness and God's best blessing
Descends on you from Heaven above.
May love be with you on your way,
The peace of God around you.

Let no discord mar the peace
Of lasting pious tenderness,
For through peace upon this earth
Your life's joy will be renewed."

Many in attendance that day thought Mike wrong, immoral even, not for the bribery, but for allowing the marriage at all. And, Marian, what could she be thinking? Still others, mostly the men, declared that a lousy husband was better than no husband at all. And it was supposed, too, among this same group, that women weren't so eager to be alone, that they wanted a husband, children, a home of their own, and Cecilia presumably no different from the rest when it came right down to it. Maybe she felt lucky anyone had been interested at all. Or maybe she didn't think much about it. Or—and this was what they found really hard to swallow—maybe she saw something in Leo that none of the rest of them could; maybe—was it possible?—surely not—could it be she even loved him? Who was to say, maybe Leo and Cecilia were a match after all.

"Yah," people said, nodding and shrugging, "even a crooked pot has got a lid, not?"

Either way, Leo and Cecilia were married and settled into Leo's little shack that June. Cecilia worked hard, scouring the walls and floor and ceiling of the shack with boiling water and lye, sewing neatly trimmed curtains with mismatched fabric from Marian's endless sewing supplies and rubbing the cheap windows with a soft cloth until they gleamed brightly. She quickly got to know her neighbours (though not Schoffs—Helen and Stolanus and their boy—who still kept to themselves) riding over with Leo, who would sit in the wagon and trim his fingernails with a paring knife while she visited with the women in their front yards and sipped at their coffee sweetened with a little condensed milk, if they had it, and smiled and nodded and made a friend of everyone she met, they could not help themselves, no matter what they thought of Leo.

————

Apart from Schoffs, Krausses' nearest neighbours were Art and Ma Reis (her name was Hady though everyone called her Ma, not because of any particular maternalness—though she had borne twelve children—but simply because that is what she insisted they call her, and when Ma insisted upon a thing, people generally complied). Ma was a force to be reckoned with, didn't like to take things lying down, as she said, and she quickly made Cecilia Krauss her business, walking over across the fields nearly once a week to have coffee with Cecilia and, as she said, to see which way the wind blew.

If it was gossip Ma was after, she could find only good things to say of Cecilia, and if there was nothing good to say of Leo, there was certainly nothing bad either. In fact, the little yard that had once swarmed with scabbed and snot-nosed Krausses scrabbling among the garbage now seemed quiet and neat and peaceful. Cecilia made it so. Though it was already the end of June, she borrowed seeds from Ma Reis and other neighbour women and put in enormous flowerbeds around the porch of the little shack, digging in buckets of chicken manure and eggshells and coffee grounds and vegetable peelings for the sweet peas and daisies and larkspur and bachelor's buttons and peonies and sunflowers, and she planted every kind of marigold in the old coffee and tobacco tins she found littering the house and yard and set them up all along the porch railing and down the rickety steps, and made paths with them, to the barn and the chicken coop and the outhouse, and ringed those buildings around with her flower tins, too, hundreds of them. And though Ma Reis and the others told her it was too late to plant, that she was wasting her time, and though they smiled and rolled their eyes and shook their heads, all those flowers blossomed like crazy, in pinks and blues and yellows and reds and oranges and violets, as if by magic, even the hundreds of marigolds in their tins (and the women said, "But for God's sake, why doesn't she just plant them in the dirt?" and they shook their heads again and said, "Well, that's Cecilia"). She put in an enormous garden out back—carrots and corn and beets and turnips, potatoes (this in addition to Leo's own patch reserved for the rotgut liquor he would brew come September), kohlrabi and tomatoes and radishes and rhubarb, garlic and green onions and white onions and yellow onions, squash and pumpkins, melons and cucumbers, raspberries and blackcurrants and strawberries (these last three courtesy of the teenage girls who "worked out" for the English families and brought home cuttings wrapped in wet rags to their mothers only to be scolded by them for their dishonesty), sweet green peas, waxy yellow beans, dillweed and chamomile and parsley and two kinds of lettuce, everything she could think of to plant—and everything bloomed and flourished under her touch. Even Leo, it seemed—Ma Reis had to admit—looked brighter and cleaner, had put on some much-needed weight and lost that blurry sunken look everyone had noticed when he'd finally emerged from the shack after Old Krauss died.

Leo was always with Cecilia—where else was he to go?—sitting on the porch watching her weed the flowerbeds, or haul water from the well to the garden, or chop at the hard earth there with her hoe and scatter the manure she raked and bucketed and carried over from the chicken coop; or waiting at the kitchen table while she stirred big pans of plump *dampfnudeln* she served to him steaming hot with cinnamon and bowls of stewed plums or crabapples, or watching as she neatly hacked the heads off chickens with a little axe and then strung them up to bleed while she boiled vats of water into which she would plunge them before plucking out their feathers by the fistful. They seemed to have a little money then, most likely Cecilia's, or maybe money Mike had given them to set up house with, and Cecilia replaced her buttoned wedding dress with a pretty blue dress that she sewed herself and that matched exactly the shade of her eyes, and she wore it every Sunday. They rode together in Leo's wagon over to Johnsborough and knelt together and took Communion together, and everyone shaking their heads in wonder, thinking, *So maybe Leo has changed after all,* or else, *Give it time, you will see.*

By August, Cecilia was pregnant, but still she worked tirelessly all through September, putting up in preserves what she and Leo did not eat fresh from the garden, pickling cucumbers and beans and carrots and beets, canning rhubarb and tomatoes and crabapples left over from the neighbours' trees, making jams and syrups and jellies from chokecherries and saskatoons she and Leo picked out in the Sand Hills, until her fingertips were stained deeply blue and the very air around that old place smelled of dill and garlic and vinegar and sugar. There were so many jars and bottles, people wondered how they would ever eat it all. Though it was still too hot to store any of the jars in the house, Cecilia had begun to line the north-facing porch wall with them, from floor to ceiling ("Well," some of the neighbour women remarked to each other, "let's just hope she has the good sense to bring those in before it freezes"), and when there was no more room on the porch, she began to stack her jars in the barn, and they all looked just as pretty as anything, especially there on the porch, glittering like jewels when a bit of light hit them, red and orange, purple and green and yellow, as if the entire front of the house was made of the most intricate stained glass.

And each time they emptied a bottle or jar, Cecilia washed it and polished it on the nearly white apron of bleached sacking she always wore over her dress, rubbing and rubbing the glass until it gleamed, and then she tied a length of string or binder twine around the mouth of it and carried it out to the big cottonwood tree that grew in front of the house and tied it to one of the branches.

"But, Cecilia," Ma Reis said to her in amazement, "you will need those bottles."

Cecilia did not seem to care. When there were enough of them, they tinkled together musically in the wind and Cecilia clapped her hands in delight. The women who came by to visit exchanged a look that was meant to say, "Wait until the next big wind comes up, then they'll tinkle all right," and, "What silliness, what a waste of good bottles."

But when the next big wind rose and swirled the earth up from the fields in tight funnels and set all the buildings creaking and whipped and bent the trees, the jars did not crash against each other and shatter, but only tinkled more loudly, and the women were amazed and said, "It doesn't make sense, that tree must catch some shelter somehow, maybe from the house," and, "Wait until the wind changes direction," and, "Such a waste. All those good jars. I guess they have money to throw away."

And, though the wind changed, though it rose and fell and rose again, and blasted and eased and blasted, though it piled the soil up in drifts along fencelines and nearly sucked the eyeballs from the heads of the beasts in the fields, Cecilia's jars never did break, not a single one.

Leo began to find little coloured bottles for her, too, out at the nuisance grounds where they would sometimes drive on calm evenings, Cecilia sitting in the wagon, with her mending propped gently against her waxing belly, Leo scavenging the growing mounds of refuse for the rare blue and green and amber medicine bottles the English people—the Smiths and Bells and Martins who raised their vast herds of cattle on the best grazing land along the river and who occasionally hired the young German girls as live-in housekeepers good enough to wash their soiled under-clothes but not to catch the eyes of their sons (though this could not always be avoided, in spite of their efforts, and often the girls would have to be dismissed without pay or honour, as the English women put it)—sometimes discarded there.

Cecilia would wash these bottles, too, and shine them on her apron and hang them from the cottonwood branches among the clear jars.

"Listen," she would say to Leo, "how they sound different from the clear jars. Listen how the blue ones sound blue, and the amber ones amber, and the green ones green. All a different sound." And then she would stand there listening and smiling until nightfall, when Leo would go inside and she would follow him.

———

No one saw much of them once winter set in, not even Ma Reis, who in recent years had become increasingly sensitive to the cold and spent much of her time in mending or sewing in front of the blazing coal stove. Leo and Cecilia were seen only at church on Sundays, without fail, where they continued to sit in the second row behind the good sisters from the convent, who would often smile at pretty Cecilia—who could resist her?—and then frown vaguely at Leo as they slid into their seats (some of them, the older ones, still remembered having taught Leo and his siblings on the blessedly rare days they came to school).

After Christmas, people began to remark how tired Cecilia looked.

"Ach," the older women said, "that's how it is with the first. She'll get used to it." And then went on to tell how they had prevailed through their own more difficult pregnancies, and then they all agreed, "But these young ones, they don't make them like they used to. So fragile."

Late in April, Leo and Cecilia missed two Sunday services in a row and, as Ma Reis had been laid up with the rheumatism, everyone asked Mike Weiser how the newlyweds were doing.

"I wish I knew," Mike told them. "We were over twice last week and both times the doors locked and no light."

"Didn't you knock?" they asked.

"Do you think I am stupid?" he said irritably. "Of course I knocked. Either they were not home or they did not answer."

The following Sunday, Leo pulled into the churchyard as usual, with Cecilia by his side. But when she climbed down from the wagon, Cecilia was clearly no longer pregnant and she held what appeared to be a baby swathed several times over in an old patchwork quilt cut up into swaddling blankets.

"But did she have it alone?" the women speculated.

"Did she call the braucha?"

"Was anyone with her?"

"With those two, who even knows if that's a baby in there."

Eventually, Mike and Marian arrived, with Art and Ma Reis coming in behind them, and stepping down from the wagons they all spotted Cecilia juggling the thick bundle against her bosom. It was not difficult to see, by the looks on their faces, that they had not known, either. Marian straightened her skirt and hesitated and glanced toward where the women stood staring and clucking. It was Ma Reis who took charge.

"Cecilia," she said, firmly, walking toward her, and everyone holding their breaths to hear but not really needing to since Ma Reis spoke loud enough that everyone *could* hear, "Cecilia, that baby is bundled much too warmly."

And, taking the baby, she stripped off five layers, chucked the little thing under the chin and handed it back.

FOUR

So they had begun their family, Leo and Cecilia; Cecilia did all the work and Leo did not leave her alone for a moment, and somehow good fortune smiled down upon whatever Cecilia touched. They continued to have children, pretty blue-eyed children born in the spring, as if she and Leo were on the same cycle as the cows in the fields. They continued to take their young brood to church each Sunday, and everything continued to flourish. Leo's ego certainly did. He strutted around more outrageous than ever. Cecilia, though, continued to look tired.

Then one spring following a couple years of exceptional harvests and prosperity, work was begun on a new church closer to the Sand Hills, where there was a greater concentration of parishoners, a church twice the size of the old country church at Johnsborough parish, and with vaulted ceilings and a dizzying spire that outdid even St. Michael's built in town by the wealthier Catholic merchants there. The countryside buzzed with the excitement of it. The frame went up quickly and the men had just begun work on the roof when the marble statue Father Rieger had ordered to grace the new cemetery arrived on a wagonload of supplies from Maple Creek seventy miles to the south. They unpacked the seven-foot monument of Jesus, hands outspread, eyes cast eternally to the heavens. It was truly impressive (and, further, exceeded by at least six inches the statue of the Virgin Mary in the front gardens at the Ursuline convent, a point which Father Rieger was quick to make within hearing of Mother Superior, "Not that it matters," he added, humbly, "for we are all together in the Lord, are we not?").

Father insisted the statue be erected the very next Saturday. The women baked kuchen and strudle and brewed big pots of coffee, and Ludmila Baumgarten offered to play hymns ("Anything to get out of working," the women said), and Father Rieger himself came forward to break ground and dig the first spadeful of dirt for the hole in which they would sink the base of the monument. Father raised the spade in both hands and heaved it into the ground only to have it clang painfully beneath his palms.

Everyone chuckled and shook their heads and agreed, "But this land is not easy even on a priest."

Father rubbed his palms discreetly against his cassock, moved his spade and dug again, only to have the same thing happen, and again and again, until he waved his stinging hands and passed the spade to Lucius Haag, who happened to be standing nearest him, saying tightly, "I put the work of God into your hands," and everyone clapped and cheered and Lucius began to dig.

It took only a few spadefuls of dirt before Lucius stopped, scratched at the soil with the blade and said uneasily, "But, what is that, there?" He pointed with the spade to where he had uncovered what appeared to be long smooth stones of an unusually white hue.

"Ach," someone said, "some animal bones. Toss them over there on a pile. I'll haul them away in my wagon."

Lucius did, digging up and tossing bones to the side and making generally good progress, and everyone standing and chatting and sipping at coffee and watching him. Then he found the skull.

Poor old Lucius, a harmless souser, that is what people said about him, three sheets to the wind on a calm day, held the thing up and was about to say, *Now what kind of cockeyed animal would you say this was, anyway?* when it dawned on him.

"Jesus Christ Almighty," he breathed, and dropped it in the dirt.

At first they wanted to move the whole church. They said it was tainted ground. Some were worried what might come of having disturbed the dead.

"God help us," they said, and crossed themselves, and thumbed their rosaries. "It must be moved."

Father Rieger must have talked some sense into them, or somebody did, and they moved the cemetery instead, to the west side rather than the east, where it would get the setting sun if not the rising. And they put the bones back into the hole they'd been dug from, tentatively, trying not to touch them except with spades, and they covered those bones up and prayed over them and sprinkled holy water and then tried to pretend they hadn't ever been found. But, by the end of that afternoon, though the sign at the gate would still read THE CHURCH OF SAINTS PETER AND PAUL, Knochenfeld it had become.

The roof was on the church within a couple of weeks. Everyone pitched in, everyone but Leo. No one really cared, just as happy that he stayed away, he was still such a thorn in everyone's side, in spite of Cecilia, the way he came striding into Mass so pious and superior. Or, if anyone did ask him to come out and help, he would say, "But I can't leave Cecilia. What would she do?"

"Bring her along," they said. "The women help too, with the coffee and dinners, and the painting and cleaning up."

And Leo blinked back at them as if they were stupid and said, "But there is work enough for her at home."

So Knochenfeld was hammered and sawed into place that spring without the hand of Leo Krauss. He and Cecilia would ride by in the wagon now and then with the kids all loaded into the back and a baby under Cecilia's arm and they would sit at the end of the road and watch a while and sometimes they would have a lunch of what appeared to be hard-boiled eggs and pickled beets and bread, the older kids flinging rocks at birds with their slingshots until Cecilia waved them wearily into submission, and then they would just pack up and roll away as quiet as they had appeared, infuriating everyone, though they all bit their tongues because Mike Weiser, and Marian, too, had worked harder than anyone and donated a good deal of money besides, and, then again, Mike was a pretty good sort and no one wanted to make him feel bad, being now a relation of sorts to Leo (though no one would have said as much to his face).

————

There was a stretch of time, then, when no one saw them. Not even Ma Reis, busy as she was with the work at Knochenfeld. It seemed as though Leo and Cecilia had disappeared again. And people waved their hands and rolled their eyes and said, "Another baby."

The church was almost complete. The new bell hung gleaming in the tower, and everyone was so busy and preoccupied that no one thought much about Leo or Cecilia, not even her sister Marian, carefully embroidering the elaborate cloth that would grace the altar.

And then one Saturday, a day as windy as they'd seen that spring, the dust lifting up from the fields and sifting across the roads like water, Krausses turned up again. The crew at Knochenfeld had about decided to give up on the outside finishing, the wind so strong it was knocking them all around like sparrows, when they saw Leo's wagon coming down the road.

Someone said, "They must be bored out there, they picked a hell of a day for sightseeing," and someone else said, "Or else that Christly wind blew them this way," and everyone hurrying to finish what they had started and to pack up paint and clean brushes and store tools, the dust blowing into everything, their teeth even, and no one noticing that Leo did not stop the wagon at the end of the road to watch but instead pulled right into the yard, right up to the front steps of the church, with the dust from his wheels blowing over him, and no one even yet paying him much mind until he stood in the wagon and called out for Father, not even getting out, just standing and yelling for him like that over the wind and the hammers and Dionysius Eichert's screechy old adze saw that he insisted on using—though it drove everyone half crazy—because it had once belonged to his wife's uncle's stepbrother or someone back in the old country and it had been used to build the old cathedral at Culelia and had been reported to somehow have saved someone's—maybe the stepbrother's— life or something, God knows how, when he'd fallen from the roof, and so it had long been believed among the Eicherts to be somehow blessed. No one could hear a thing when that old saw was going and it drove Father half mad; he locked himself in the rectory with cotton stuffed in his ears and would not come out except now and then to stand scowling in the yard to see if it still looked all right, the church that is, or, troubled as he was by bad bowels, to hustle across to the outhouse by the shelterbelt.

So Leo stood there in his wagon with the wind howling and the saw screeching and the hammers knocking, and hollered for Father, and finally a few stopped what they were doing and said, "What? What is he saying? What does he want?"

It was only then that everyone noticed that, though the five children were all in the back of the wagon in their usual places, Cecilia did not sit beside Leo on the seat. Mike Weiser descended his ladder and walked over and looked in the back of the wagon where the kids sat around a long bundle wrapped head to toe in old sheets, swaddled up like a baby, and he said, "Oh, Jesus, Jesus."

FIVE

S omeone went to summon Father Rieger and he came
out onto the steps then with his black cassock snapping
around him in the wind, and everyone stood silenced,
watching, some of the women's hands up over their mouths,
until Leo hollered again from the wagon, and this time they
all understood: "If that graveyard's ready, I got a burial to
make."

The graveyard wasn't ready, though Father agreed later, after
much hushed negotiation, to consecrate it that afternoon. Some
said afterwards that Mike must have been involved again, since
Father wasn't the sort to bend the rules, not for anyone, and this
made twice he'd done so for Leo, the least likely recipient of
Father's—anyone's—grace.

When Marian had been taken home by two or three of the
other women, Mike, who stood gripping the edge of the wagon
box, finally managed, "Leo, when did this happen?" but Leo only
shook his head, as if he did not understand.

The oldest girl, Magdalen, who, though only a child of about
six herself, juggled a fussing infant on her knee, said, "Saturday
she couldn't get out of bed. For the washing. Then Sunday—"

The child stared blankly at Mike a moment and then dropped her face, though not in grief, it seemed, but in confusion.

"Sunday," Mike breathed. "Good God, Leo. Why didn't you send for someone?"

And Leo still standing there as if he did not understand what on earth Mike was talking about.

Ma Reis came out of the church basement, then, wiping paint from her hands onto her apron, with Art behind her. "What is it?" she said over the wind, looking around. "What is going on?"

Mike opened his mouth as if he would say something. Then he wiped a hand across his forehead and turned away, studying the horizon beyond the church, and Ma stepped forward, looked into the wagon.

"Oh, dear God," she said. Her hand up over her throat and Art holding her elbow.

Leo stood and waited, for once, without speaking, his suit jacket flapping loudly against his side.

Art and Ma Reis took the Krauss children home with them. Once they were gone, Mike said tightly to Leo, "Come now, bring her to my place. Marian will take care of her."

And Leo blinked and said, "But it's too late. She's dead."

Mike just nodded and took the reins from him, climbed up and said, "Marian will take care of her."

———

Cecilia Krauss was buried late the following afternoon in a wooden coffin Mike patched together with extra wood from Knochenfeld and this time Leo did not arrange for any photograph to be taken. He just stood around in the churchyard, in the wind, looking puzzled, pointing to the coffin whenever someone spoke to him and saying, "But that has to be good, not? That wood is holy." And the Krauss kids—all but Magdalen, who stood holding the baby—running around and shouting and tumbling, as if they did not comprehend, either, what had happened.

And what exactly had happened, no one ever did find out. There was some talk at first, mostly from Marian, and from Ma Reis, too, though Mike and Art must have done their best to dissuade them, about an investigation, but nothing ever came of it. What was there to prove? Cecilia was overworked, certainly. Maybe she was sick, too. Probably she was.

"And anyway," Mike said, "a man cannot be charged with working his wife to death. If he could, half the men around would be guilty." Which Ma had to admit was true.

No, there was nothing that could be blamed on Leo, not officially, and eventually even Marian gave up trying and was made to console herself with taking the three youngest of Leo's blue-eyed children to live with her and Mike and to raise them as their own, hoping something might still be done with and for them. Leo did nothing to stop it—what would he have done with little ones? Maybe he thought it was just as well. That left the two older children, Henry and Magdalen, who did not want to go and whom Marian would not take anyway, since, as she said, they were clearly already Krausses and beyond her help.

In the weeks following, the church at Knochenfeld was finished and Marian's cloth on the altar and the walls painted a pale blue that reminded not a few of the colour of a certain familiar dress, though that had not been the intention. The cemetery, too, was completed, enclosed by a low wrought-iron fence, now an officially consecrated cemetery, Cecilia Krauss the first to grace it; Leo, some said, the one who put her there.

SIX

It was no great surprise that Leo no longer came to church, and at first the barren pew where he and Cecilia used to sit with their children was such a distraction it was as if the eye of God himself peered down upon it. But, as with most things, Cecilia's absence eventually became so familiar that it was, with few exceptions, as if she had never been there. After all, hardly anyone had known her well. And so, in time, over that first long winter in the new church, most thought little about her, unless they happened to catch the blue-eyed gaze of one of the three small children who now sat scrubbed and dumbfounded between Mike and Marian.

Leo did not turn up again until the following spring. He appeared, but not back at church Sunday mornings, as might have been expected. Now he came to town on Saturday nights, riding in, not broken and bereaved as everyone expected him to be, but sitting straight upright on the wagon seat as he used to, no perceivable trace of sorrow on his bony face; it was as if he'd never been married at all. He would ride in Saturday nights and he would go to the social, or if there wasn't a social, to the bar (with, they could only presume, what was left of Cecilia's money), still wearing that godforsaken suit, usually three sheets to the wind already, but sitting there looking pleased with himself, and everyone turning the other way as he passed or casting him scornful looks, thinking of those kids alone back at the shack, but what could they do about it? And Leo just nodding the whole time, to the left and to the right, just like he used to do in church. No one realized—though they surely should have—that he was not coming to town just to drink.

One night close to Christmas, Leo, looking particularly smug, rolled through town and straight to the hall, where he went strutting in, the pockets of his suit, every single pocket, bulging. He crossed the dance floor and walked right up to Viola Hahn—a dark-eyed, plump little thing, known far and wide as a beauty, a real catch, half the young men around were mad for her—sitting at a table with some friends, all ruffled up with vanity, and Leo stood before her a moment. Then he reached into his pockets and pulled out handfuls of Japanese oranges, not just one or two, but handful after handful, and plopped them on the table in front of Viola and into her lap. Then he just stood there grinning, as if he'd offered her a pile of diamonds, while those oranges rolled all over the place and out onto the dance floor. Whatever else Leo thought Viola would do with those oranges, or with him for that matter, it was quite clear to everyone there that he hadn't thought she would laugh at him, which is what she did do, after plucking an orange from the table in disgust and tossing it into Leo's face. It thumped dully off his nose, and half the people there laughing right along with Viola, the younger ones anyway. The older ones just shook their heads and thought of Cecilia and thought of the children alone back at the shack and then they thought quickly of other matters in case they should begin to feel ashamed that they had not so much as been out to Leo's place even once to check on those children.

As for Leo, he stood there in front of Viola, looking surprised, hurt even, but only for a second, no one would have noticed it if they had not been watching him closely (which no one ever was, since they had already decided what they would see there). Then he looked around at everyone laughing, and he started laughing, too, and nodding, as if it were a joke he'd played, as if he'd meant to be funny, and everyone was reacting just the way he'd hoped they would. Just standing there nodding and laughing and everyone thinking, *He's so stupid, he doesn't even know he's being laughed at,* and this, since they were certain they knew when they were being laughed at, was what they found funniest of all.

But Leo did know. He stood there and laughed a minute and then he did a little dance and turned to walk away, pretending to slip on one of those oranges, pretending, though most thought he really had slipped and that just made them laugh harder. He pretended to slip on one of those oranges and then he walked right out the doors into that December night, reminding Mike Weiser, who was not laughing, of that night seven or eight years earlier. Some of the young people had picked up the oranges and were tossing them at the door after Leo. But Mike got up from his table and, taking a paper sack from behind the bar, he walked around quietly, between chairs and dancers and tables, collecting the oranges, dropping them into the sack, scraping up for the garbage the ones that had been smashed or stepped on. Then he tucked the sack under his chair.

On the way to church the following morning, Mike stopped at Krausses'. While Marian waited tight-lipped in the car, he knocked at the door and, without speaking, handed the paper sack to Magdalen, who stood in the doorway, rubbing her eyes against the winter light.

No one saw Leo for a long time. Not at church, not at the hall, not even at the bar. No one saw hide nor hair of him, that is what they said, except maybe Mike Weiser, but when anyone asked, he just shrugged and shook his head and said obliquely, "Oh, well, that's how it goes," and spoke, instead, of the weather.

———

The next time anyone saw Leo Krauss was the following spring, he just kept turning up that way, that's what people said, like a goddamned dandelion, you couldn't get rid of him. The next time they saw him he was heading through town. Mike Weiser was standing with some others outside the hardware and when Leo rolled by he called out, "But, Leo, where are you off to?" and Leo just lifted a hand and kept right on going, kicking up a trail of dust in his wake.

SEVEN

Eight years earlier, on that same airless day in August that Leo Krauss and his siblings had committed their father to the old cemetery at Johnsborough, their neighbourwoman, Helen Schoff, had stood in the doorway of her own farmhouse watching her husband, Stolanus, in the home field with the other men, as he moved in the heavy, rippled air with an attitude solemn, spare and unflagging, and her son there, too, stretched out under the shade of the wagon box, out of the evening sun. Usually he perched on top, with his bare feet plunged to the ankle in hot grain. She would have liked to sit there with him, their feet buried in that strange soft grain, soft like the Sand Hills or the way she imagined beaches made of the tiniest pebbles could be just at nightfall, warm and alive with the remembered energy of the sun. She would often stand and watch him as he sat sifting the grain through his hands, knowing that he was picking out mangled heads and torsos of grasshoppers, light as paper, to collect in his pockets for her to find when she was doing the washing, so that she would pretend to shriek and throw her hands up in the air and he would giggle and hide his face. He would sit there all day, were they to allow it, moving from his perch only to pet the draft horses that stood patiently drowsing in the heat, or when the thresher came with another load; then he would scramble away to the edge, being careful to keep out of the men's way as they stabbed and heaved with their shovels to disperse the incoming grain to the four corners of the box, knowing that any interference would mean the worst shame: he would be sent home. Usually, if she agreed, he would stay with the crew until dusk, flushed and giddy with the teasing that always came at coffee time.

"Stolanus, where's this one's shovel?"

"Look here now, his hands are not even cracked, you are too easy on him."

"You got a man here almost. He should work like the rest of us."

And he would sit with his mug of cold water, ducking his head and bouncing a little with the effort of not looking too pleased, heels thumping the sides of the wagon.

But today he did not sit and tease with the men; the heat had worn him out and now, in the evening light, he lay still and sprawled in the shade beneath the hot and gilded wood of the wagon box, eyes closed, as if he might already be sleeping. It was no wonder. The heat had burned them all out, radiating as it had between earth and sky in blistering ripples since dawn, the risen wind at noon whipping it up with dust from the field and the harvest until even breathing became a task too exhausting, the fine chaff sticking to wet skin, creeping beneath collars and cuffs. The price to pay for a bumper crop, the best they'd seen so far, though she and Stolanus had always somehow managed to do a little better than the farms around them.

Helen reached inside her dress and scratched beneath the damp straps of her underclothes, then straightened her skirt and examined again the basket on the porch, a late supper to take to the men in the field: cold chicken from last night's meal, leftover boiled potatoes dressed in onion and vinegar, bread and pickles, thick slices of cream kuchen. A fresh jug of water still cool from

the well. It was not a large meal, certainly. She could not bring
herself to cook, particularly meat, the sickness hanging with her
all day now, the mysterious, impossible weight of the new life in
her resting like a stone, heavy and yet precarious too, as if it could
topple her, again—a dangerous illusion, that weight, with its sug-
gestion of perfect solidity, a subtle, as-yet-formless permanence.
It would be easy to be lulled into false security, infallibility. She
had made that mistake before.

But this time would be different, that is what she told herself.
She would not work so hard. She would do only what needed to
be done, nothing extra. She and Stolanus had agreed, and to hell
with the tongues that would wag should they find her in the middle
of the afternoon stretched out in bed with dishes in the wash basin
and dirty clothes piled up in the corner and even the breakfast
table yet to be wiped. She would rest more. She would eat well, as
much as she could keep down. What else could she do?

"See the braucha," Stolanus had said, thinking more could be,
must be, done—other precautions, a tea maybe or some herbs,
he'd heard onions.

"What about onions?" she'd wanted to know.

But he wasn't certain, maybe it wasn't onions after all, but
garlic—anyway what did he know, he just thought maybe, surely,
the braucha would have something, prayers, an incantation, what
could it hurt?

"She has ways," he had said. "Maybe something she could give
you."

"What, some potion?" she had said, stubbornly. "String garlic
around my neck?"

Helen did not want to see the braucha, with her Bolshevik
charms and potions and prayers, in her ugly sod hut, it was
as bad as a cave, and her rotting teeth, that stink of garlic. All
that superstition and black magic. Brauching. It was obscene. For
God's sake, did they not have a doctor here? Did they not have a
priest? Brauchas, they were for the old country. Baba Yaga, that's

what Helen called her, though Stolanus did not like it, the same old argument.

"Have some respect, she's an elder."

"An elder witch, and a Russian, too."

"Yah, part Russian, but also part German. Her mother from Franzeld, too, just like your own."

"Nothing like my own. My mother was not Russian."

"So? And what of that?"

"What do you mean, so? How can you say it? They are all dogs. And murderers."

"And what about the Germans, eh? What about the *Lusitania*? Belgium? Verdun? We are not innocent, either. All this blood."

Always the same. And always she took it too far, she could not help herself.

"Yah," she would mutter, "like your father."

Personally, she'd had nothing against him, her father-in-law. Only that she didn't think much of his stance against the war. A deserter from the Russian army, Pius had slipped across the border into Rumania, cutting himself off from his parents and brothers and sisters, marrying and coming first to America, then to Canada with his young family, finding, God knows how, where others—Weisers and Hechs and Reises and countless neighbours from Kleinliebenthal, his former village in Russia—had settled. Stolanus did not like to think of his father as a coward, did not like to hear him called that. But that's just what he was, as far as Helen could tell. And because of it, because his father was a coward, Stolanus heard little about his family back in the old country, especially now that Old Pius was dead. Though that was just as well. Better to cut those ties. They did no good, just dragged you down. Things had grown worse back there, far worse, and what could they—she and Stolanus and the others who had come over—do about it? Sit around and feel sorry? Feel guilty that they prospered in the new country while back home everything crumbled? No. Hadn't she left her own family behind as well? Things were terrible there, yes, but what good to dwell on it, to look backward? And now, since the war, there were no more letters, and so it was easier still to forget.

Oh, some still sat around moaning about it, their beloved Russland, the villages there, Kleinliebenthal, Franzfeld, Mariantal, Josephstal. For her part, Helen was glad to be gone from there, was proud to be here. She was a German. A German Canadian. Some others, she often thought, would do well to follow her example, but they were always crying and moaning about the homeland. "Russia is not the homeland," she always said to Stolanus afterwards. "We are Germans, not? If they want to mourn, mourn for Baden, or Alsace. That is the homeland."

And now, worse shame, some were calling themselves Russian. That's what they put on their children's birth certificates. So the children born before the war were all German and the ones born after were all Russian. To protect them, the parents said, so they will not be hated here, will not be judged. Stupid. Her baby would be German, just like his brother. And she would not be ashamed. She would teach them to be proud, here in this new country with Russia and all its hardships and demons far behind them. She would not sit and cry with the rest of them about how good the old country was, how beautiful, how easy life there. If it was so easy, why had they left? She often wanted to say, *You don't like it here? So go back. They are killing Germans there, that's how good it is. They are lining us up and shooting us like dogs.* That is what she would have liked to say, but she did not.

Things were hard here, too. In some ways harder, but only in some. Here they had good machinery for the seeding and the harvest. In the old country they did it on foot, with hoes or scythes, breaking their backs in the sun. And now Stolanus was talking about a grain truck. If the crops got in without mishap, he had promised to buy a car, a real motorcar, as early as that fall. Yes, a good many things were better here. But the big thing was, they were free. And if Isabel Martin and Mae Smith and Iris Bell and those others looked down their noses and said the Germans should be deported if they weren't so good at cleaning houses, they were certainly no worse than the Russians. And anyway, no matter where you go there will always be someone to hate you. So, what of it? You work hard and soon you have more than those who mock you, and that is your reward. Here they would work hard and grow rich and fat. Already they were ahead of some others, the ones whose crops were never as bountiful.

And they would have more children, her and Stolanus. A big family. They would bury no more children, children not yet even children (except for little Katerina, who she would not think of, could not). No, the rest were not even babies, only blood.

This was her home now. She had soaked this earth with her blood. German blood.

But no more. She would be especially careful. The threshing crew would eat cold meals now and then if they must. She would not be a fool, like Rosalia Eichert, like Esther Hech, like Marian Weiser and Ma Reis, and the others, getting up before dawn just to be the first to hang out their washing Monday morning. And Ludmila Baumgarten, the worst of them, she was not fooling anyone, they all knew she hung it in the dark Sunday night, the Lord's Day, just to look as if she was first Monday morning. It was stupid. Helen would not compete with them. And she would not feel guilty about it, though she knew what they would say.

"Only one little one at home and she can't even bring a hot meal to the field?"

"Can't even bake a ham, boil some potatoes?"

"What does it take to boil potatoes?"

"That's nothing, I heard Stolanus sometimes does his own cooking."

"No. Not really."

"Yes, really, do you think I would lie about it?"

"Ach, for shame. If my husband . . . well."

"That's how it is, caught by a pretty face."

"Pretty? That skinny thing?"

"I wouldn't call her pretty."

"Well, better than some."

"I'd like to know who."

"Oh, enough already, she didn't mean you."

"I never said she meant me."

"Well, I didn't."

"Anyway, I wouldn't say pretty."

"Well, she must be something, not? She must have caught him somehow, not with her cooking, that's for sure."

And they would laugh, while the older women shook their heads and said, "In my day a woman worked. We were not so soft back then."

But she did not care what they said. Let them talk. If it wasn't the meals, they would find something else to wag their tongues at.

She looked again at the basket. It was a small meal, and that was enough. The men would not starve. They would not even be very hungry, would not eat much anyway, in this heat. The hired man— hired boy, she always said to herself, for they were all boys now, since the war—ate like a sparrow. So there was only the Schneider brothers to worry about. And they were bachelors so they would be happy with whatever they got. She added another loaf of bread and a jar of chokecherry jam to the basket, then stepped from the porch into the overwhelming evening, the final hard blast of heat that came before sunset, the hot, soft earth as she crossed the field, stubble scratching dryly at her ankles, the scorched hum of grasshoppers. One zinged up against her cheek with a sting, then another, catching in her hair, but she could not hit them away, her arms full of the basket and the water jug. She did not like them, but she was not afraid of them, either, in spite of what the women said about her, just because at a ball game once she had flipped one off her dress with a little jump, hardly a jump at all, and only because it had startled her. She had seen the smirks on the other women's faces. Well, what did she care what they thought, anyway?

As Helen neared the threshing crew, Stolanus saw her. He did not wave or even nod, just continued, bending with the shovel and heaving. They would not stop simply because supper had arrived. She would stand and wait with the food until they were finished loading; then, when they planted their shovels in the grain and climbed down from the wagon box, she would dish up their plates and fill the cups and pass them around. Then she would sit and watch while they crouched in the shade and ate silently, shovelling the food into their mouths in huge bites, but without haste, efficiently, not out of hunger but only necessity, not even tasting it, so what did it matter that it was not an elaborate meal? It was the women who cared, who made such a fuss. To impress each other, outdo each other. The men did not even notice what they ate.

She set the basket in the shade of the wagon, then went around to the front end and peeked at her son who lay sleeping there beneath the box, his face pink and swelled with the August sun, a dusting of earth over his eyelids and his lips, parted slightly in sleep, his cheeks smeared with dirt and sweat, his hair so blond with summer. He had her mother's colouring. Northern German. The rest of them were southerners, Alsatians, the dark ones, the gypsies. The ones who had emigrated to the Black Sea steppes. Then again to America, to Canada. Still moving, some of them. And this one now, where would he go?

Behind her someone killed the engine on the threshing machine. The men climbed down, swiping at their faces with hankies. She took the food out of the basket and handed the plates around, feeling, as she did so, that out here the food did not seem so much after all. How was it that being out in the fields seemed to diminish everything that way? It was like looking the wrong way through a magnifying glass. And that leftover chicken, would there be enough after all? She frowned meaningfully at Stolanus, hoping he would understand and not eat much himself so there would be enough for the others. But he seemed not to notice, either her look or the small portion on his plate. And so they crouched there in the shade alongside the wagon, all in a row, the hired boy, as always, a little apart from the others and hunched over his plate, his black hair cropped so close above a permanently serious face, not looking at anyone, not speaking unless someone spoke to him first. He was shy, homesick maybe. Helen often wondered about his family. Poor, obviously. Some farm misfortune, or some other tragedy. The father dead, maybe. The kids sent out to work before they could even wash behind their ears. She had dished his plate up last, saving him a little extra chicken, he was so thin. His shirt far too short in the sleeves. When she did the washing Monday, she must remember to add a little to the cuffs. She tried to catch his eye as she handed him his plate, but he just ducked his head and accepted it as he accepted wordlessly all the little things she did for him. It was not much, but it mattered, she thought, it must matter, to know someone cared about you. Sad, she always thought, he looked very sad. "Ach," Stolanus constantly said, "he's fine." But that was Stolanus.

When they were all dished up, she sat down in the shade and poured herself a cup of water.

"Did you hear?" Rochus Schneider was saying. "They will change the name in town."

"Yah," Stolanus said, "because Prussia changed to Triumph. Everything they do, we have to do, too."

"They took a council vote. Sent a letter to some bigshot and the bigshot said, all right, change it if you want to change it. They're holding a contest. To come up with a new name."

Helen had already heard about that, or overheard, at the store the other day. Town council wanted a name "less suggestive," which meant less German. She grimaced over her cup of water.

"Not only that," Rochus said, "but the street names, too. That's what council said."

"Good, give them something to do with their time."

"What do you think, Helen? What's a good name for the town?"

"It has a good name," she said.

"But if you had to choose."

"London," she said. "Then we can all wear top hats and drink tea from little china cups."

"Ach, Helen," Stolanus sighed.

But Isidore Schneider just laughed. "I'll take some of that good German coffee just so long as there's some of that kuchen there to go with it. And I'll call it whatever you want."

Helen poured everyone coffee and passed around the kuchen. After she put the coffeepot in the basket, she bent and reached a hand beneath the wagon, pressing her fingers against the boy's flushed cheek. But he did not stir.

"Worn out," Stolanus said quietly, from behind her. She nodded and rose and poured herself another cup of water.

"You should hear the names they've come up with," Isidore said. "They had them in the paper. Tipperary."

"Tipperary?"

"Lucky," Rochus put in.

"And then all the ones you might expect: Wheatley, Wheatown, Wheatland, Wheatplain, Wheatville, Wheatking."

"Wheat-in-the-arse."

"That's right," Rochus said. "Isn't that Scherler and Haegert and that bunch? I guess that's what you get when you have a town council of Protestants: Wheat-in-the-arse."

"Yah, that reminds me, did you hear one of the nuns up at the convent there broke her arm?" said Isidore. "Had to get it all wrapped up in a sling and everything. I guess she was walking down the street the other day and passed Squeaky Scherler and Ed Haegert coming out of Wing's and they said to her, 'Well, and what happened to you?' 'Oh,' the nun said, 'I fell in the bathtub.' 'Oh,' Ed said, 'that's too bad.' Then, after she walked away, he turned to Squeaky and said, 'What's a bathtub?' And Squeaky said, 'How should I know? I'm not Catholic.'"

"One of these days, you'll tell that joke in the wrong company," Rochus warned, glancing quickly at Lathias, who seemed not to be listening.

"Ach." Isidore waved his hand good-naturedly. "If they can't take a joke, they should stay home."

Rochus squinted up at the sun and said, "We should haul that load in, not? We got another round or two before dark."

"Yah," Stolanus said, rising.

(But not too eagerly, Helen thought, so as not to look as if he had been waiting for one of the men to suggest it, not wanting to rush anyone. That was his way. Helen didn't think much of it. If there was work to do, he should say so.)

"I'll go," Lathias said, setting his plate on the ground. "I'm finished."

"Yah," Stolanus said, "all right. I wouldn't say no to another coffee."

"That's right, let us old ones rest a while. Leave the young ones work."

Stolanus held his cup out toward Helen and she rose again with the pot and filled the men's cups.

"I don't know," Isidore said, loud enough for Lathias to hear. "Is that such a good idea? Can he even run the horses yet?"

The men laughed again, and Lathias smiled, just a little, and nodded and climbed up onto the wagon seat, clucking the horses into motion, sending the wheels creaking forward.

Helen whirled, coffee sloshing down the front of her dress. "No," she hollered, but the wagon was already moving.

EIGHT

Helen remembered this: there was blood on her hands. There was so much blood everywhere and she kept trying to wipe it away, to wipe it from her son's eyes, saying, "He can't see, he can't see," and wiping, wiping, so much of it, everywhere, and Stolanus yelling, "Get back, get back, for Christ's sake," as he lifted that little body in his big arms and ran to the house, stumbling across the soft, hot field, the boy's legs and arms bouncing with the motion, as though he struggled to get free.

And her just standing there in the field watching them go, feeling the sticky blood on her hands, opening and closing them, opening and closing, until Rochus Schneider (or maybe it was Isidore) took her by the arm and she stepped forward (didn't she? she thought she had) and then collapsed, as if there were no legs beneath her at all, and Rochus saying, "Come on, come on," and he ran, too, dragging her almost, through the field, and there was blood there, right there in the stubble and the dirt, and they ran over it, they followed his blood home.

———

For three days he lay as if dead. Then, at dawn of the third day, much to everyone's disbelief, the boy opened his unbandaged eye, looked Helen in the face and said, "I did," as clear as day. They would remark upon that later, they would speak of that—the clarity of that little meaningless phrase—over the dim light of supper tables, with a hushed and solemn air, as if there might at least have been some message for her, for Helen, a revelation or a prophecy or an accusation, something. They spoke of it in hushed tones, for it could just as easily have been one of their own, that is what they said to their children, "It could just as easily have been you," though they were not believed, never believed in matters of love or tragedy, and at every table mothers made silent counts of heads, just to be sure, and they thought of the boy and crossed themselves and felt relieved, yes, God help them, relieved for themselves and for their children. And they spoke of it again the following morning, in the café and the grocery and the hardware. They listed the ones taken, swallowed by wells and dugouts and sloughs, frozen to death just steps from their front doors, thrown or trampled by livestock, struck by wagons and trains, or, less dramatically, by rheumatic fever, measles, influenza. They spoke of it all through that day and during the weeks to come, when they learned the boy would live after all, when they learned how the accident had thickened his tongue, confused his brain, and through those weeks their compassion and relief somehow turned to righteousness and judgment, for wasn't it Helen, with only one little one, who refused to participate in any of the ladies' functions because, or so she said, she had too much work at home, wasn't it her? And they baked their bread and kuchen and buns to take to her, with lips pressed tight now in compassion, yes, for they were not cold-hearted, they would not wish ill upon anyone, certainly not, but wasn't it Helen who turned up her nose at them all? Yes. And now she would have a hard row to hoe. The boy would never be the same. Head injuries, they were the worst, better to be dead. Did they not all remember old Martin Schlesser who had been kicked by a horse and how he would walk around town all day with his hand not down the front of his trousers, but, worse still, tucked inside his open zipper, even at the supper table, even in church? It was terrible for the ladies and the children, but worse still for him. Yes, better to be dead. But, no, they would not think it. And what about the hired man—that halfbreed, wasn't he?—from God knows where, what did anybody really know about him after all? He was not still with them, surely, not with the boy marred that way, destroyed, for life, and him the cause of it? And what was it the boy had said when he'd finally awoke? *I did?* No, no, *I will,* I'm sure of it. And what was that supposed to mean? Some kind of threat? Head injuries, they were the worst, remember dirty old Martin Schlesser?

That is what they said, while the boy lay for days as if dead, while that August sun glared on undiminished, while the crops lay too long in the fields—and they spoke of this, too, the waste of it, though the Schneider brothers and Art Reis and some others had done what they could, and if no one else had come to help them, didn't they have their own crops to worry about? And if rain had come, and it had, wasn't that God's way of saying, *Let it be, for I mean it to be thus?*

That third morning, with the autumn rain falling heavily upon the felled crops beyond the window, the boy looked her straight in the eyes and said, though he could not have meant anything by it, was not even yet conscious, "I will." Then he closed his eyes and slept again.

And Helen still kneeling there by his bed saying, "What? What? What will you do?" Until Stolanus led her away, and down the darkened stairs, to rest.

By evening, she had miscarried.

———

Yes. Helen miscarried again, as if in the sparing of one life another must be sacrificed, as if they—her and Stolanus—could not be allowed too great an allotment of grace. Helen miscarried, her last, though she may or may not have known that at the time. When she woke that evening with terrible cramping in her abdomen and a taste of blood in her mouth she would not let Stolanus send for the braucha.

"What can she do?" she said. "If God wants all my children, what can anyone do?"

But God did not take all her children. The boy lived, though everything had changed for him, and for Helen and Stolanus, and for the hired man, too. For all of them. And everyone said, "That's how it goes sometimes." It wasn't, after all, so unusual. Too much work. Too many children. The cemeteries littered with the graves of the momentarily unwatched.

That first evening, before the doctor arrived to stitch him together, the braucha came and washed and dressed his wound and covered him in her ointments and mumbled her prayers over him and laid crosses and sacks of herbs at his feet, while Helen stood frowning in the corner, and she came back every day after until the boy spoke (though if the doctor was there, she waited downstairs in the kitchen until he left).

When the boy finally spoke, she nodded and said, in German, "He will," nodding still, "live."

Though when the doctor came later he said, "Sometimes this kind of thing happens. I don't expect you to understand. It happens. Sometimes the all-but-dead will get up and walk around, talk a little. So don't make too much of it. Don't raise your hopes, if you see what I'm saying. He is not out of the woods yet."

And Helen spent the rest of the evening reciting those words to herself, *Not out of the woods, he is not out of the woods,* until they began to take on a comic, mythical ring, as if it were from some fairy tale she'd once heard, and she began to laugh a little, to herself, after Stolanus had led her away from the boy. *Not out of the woods.* How funny. And she lay on the bed and laughed herself to sleep, dreaming briefly of the vast, black, treeless prairie.

———

"A blessing," Father Reiger said that following Sunday in church. "Let us give prayers of thanks on behalf of Stolanus and Helen, let us give thanks for the sparing of their son's life. God is good. Let us praise Him for this blessing." And they did.

That was before they saw the scars. The ones on the outside and, later, slowly, over time, the ones on the inside.

"Minor damage to the brain," the doctor said.

But minor damage was enough. And then, on top of it, the seizures. It seemed that was what marked him most of all, more than the scars on his face or his mangled skull or his thickened speech, that was what really rattled people. Maybe he had escaped death, some said, after his first seizure in the schoolyard at recess, he had escaped, but by whose intervention? Maybe blessing had nothing to do with it. *Vom Teufel besessen*—possession—that was what they had called it in the old country (blaming, as always, what they did not understand on God or the Devil).

So the boy was spared, to be tortured and laughed at, poor child, who could not help the scar healing badly over his eye, pulling it down at one corner so that it seemed he looked in two directions at once, who could not help his slow speech, could not help himself when a fit came on, and it was awful to see, it horrified everyone, and so they made a joke of it, of him, to hide their fear—death so close to the living—the children following their parents' lead. They were cruel to him during school when Sister Canisia was distracted, and after school much worse, such a long walk back to his farm. Sometimes Lathias, the hired hand, would be there waiting for him by the caraganas at the edge of the school steps, waiting to walk him home, and then they would fall back, only the meanest and oldest of the boys trailing them, throwing clumps of dirt and stones. But Lathias was not always able to be there.

Things worsened, until finally Helen pulled him out of school, kept him home except for Saturdays when he would go to town with Stolanus on errands and on Sundays when he would sit between Stolanus and Helen at the front of the church, and Lathias behind them, not beside them, for reasons of his own.

It was Helen who insisted they sit there in the front row where everyone could see, thinking all the time to herself, *To hell with you all, I will keep my son at home to protect him, but I am not ashamed, don't you ever think I am ashamed of him.* And he would sit there, small and pale and scared looking, or not scared, amazed maybe, the way he would roll his eyes around, looking at everybody and not looking at anybody, his face so skinny, as though it was just bone there and that awful scar and the whites of his eyes so big, like the eyes of horses in a lightning storm. And Helen and Stolanus sitting there straight as boards, staring ahead at the pulpit as if Father Rieger was so interesting they just couldn't tear their eyes from him; they sat like that every single Sunday without once turning until the recessional hymn had been sung and even then not stopping in the yard to talk a moment like everyone did, though Stolanus might have liked to. He would nod, sometimes, say hello, but never pause, and Helen already seated with the boy in the wagon, straight-backed and implacable as iron.

Soon those Sunday mornings in church were very nearly the boy's only outing. His Saturday visits to town almost nonexistent now since the day that little pink-cheeked Sylviana Lenz, who had been a grade behind the boy at school, claimed that he had touched her.

"Touched how?" her mother had asked.

But Sylviana could only shrug and say, "Just touched."

It had all come about one afternoon when Stolanus stopped with the boy at Stednick's Dry Goods to pick up a few things for Helen. He was at the front counter and the boy must have wandered around to the back of the shop where Sylviana stood wondering what to buy with the egg money her grandmother had given her as a special treat, on the occasion of her tenth birthday. She was standing at the back where all the sewing things were kept, fabric and buttons, and lovely shimmering rolls of ribbon (Stednick's always kept two colours of ribbon and Sylviana checked each time she was there, just to see if the colours had changed) and puzzling over whether to buy herself the dark, serviceable blue, which would go with both her good dresses and would not get dirty, or, less practically, the softest, palest pink she had ever seen, pink the way wild roses were at the Sand Hills in June (knowing in her heart it would be the pink she would choose, but deliberating over it just long enough that she could feel later she had made a wise and not simply an impulsive choice).

Just as she was running her fingertips over the roll of pink ribbon, imagining how it would look tied up in her hair on Sunday and how envious it would make her very best friend Clara Schmitt, who always got everything she wanted, the boy appeared at her elbow.

Poor Sylviana (who, if truth be known, was prone to nightmares, her brother Art whispering in her ear each night, *Hope you remembered to use the outhouse, hope you won't need to pee in the night, so dark out there, hope the Schoff boy won't get you*), poor Sylviana was so startled that she dropped the roll of ribbon and it unfurled across the floor and settled under a shelf of lye soap. So startled, so afraid, she just stood there.

The boy looked at her and looked at the ribbon and said, quite reasonably, "I will get it."

Which is just what he did, though when he had wound the ribbon back up on its cardboard spool and handed it to her, she could not, somehow, lift a hand to take it from him, and so she just stood there and the next thing she knew, she was crying, her grandmother there at her side, and old Mr. Stednick with her.

"What is it?" the shopkeeper said harshly. "What's going on?"

And both of them looking at the boy standing there dumbly with the pink spool of ribbon unravelling in his hands.

Then the boy's father was there too, saying, "What is it? What has happened?"

But the father was looking at her, at Sylviana, and not at all at his son, as if it were she who had done something, and that made her feel she should cry harder. Perhaps Sylviana should have spoken up then, should have told them just what had happened, but she could not, poor thing, she just could not speak for crying. Grandma Lenz, who felt so bad for her granddaughter, bought the entire spool of pink ribbon.

And so, not wanting her grandmother, who had spent all that money, to think that she had not earned the ribbon, did not deserve it (*Just think, Clara, the whole roll*), she told her mother later that the boy had touched her and then she went to bed with the spool of ribbon on the top of her night table where she could see it. But then, sometime during the night, she got up and tossed the ribbon into a drawer and slammed it shut. She did not sleep well, and when she rose the next morning Sylviana took the spool from the drawer and threw all that ribbon down the outhouse.

When her best friend Clara Schmitt said, "But, Sylviana, why? Why would you do such a thing?" she said that just the thought of that boy touching it made her skin crawl, made it the ugliest thing she had ever seen. That is what she said.

Years later, a lifetime later, when Sylviana told the story to her own grandchildren, she chuckled, and then frowned and shook her head, and said, "You know, I can't even think of his name, that awful boy. I don't think I ever knew it."

———

Of course there were those who were kinder, who were guilty only of making no effort to befriend him. Others, the cruellest ones, teased and bullied, even the girls, yanking out clumps of his hair in the schoolyard, throwing rocks, slipping prickly pears into his coat pockets so that his fingers bled, filling his lunch pail with dog shit. And worse. So Helen and Stolanus kept him home. Or, Helen did.

Stolanus said, "Ach, he'll be fine. It's just boys, not?"

And Helen said, "But you are stupid."

And so he stayed home. It must have been very lonely for him, there on the farm with only Stolanus and Helen locked in their private griefs, and Lathias his only companion, and Krausses of all people their nearest neighbours, though it was just Leo there then with the two older children, and no one ever saw any of them, it was as if the place were abandoned. At least, that is what the boy sometimes thought when he stood at the edge of the yard chewing sunflower seeds and looking toward the Krauss farm, eerily idle there against the hills. Only a mile or so distant, it might as well have been on the moon.

But Lathias was good to him, and when Helen would allow it, he would take him places, would take him riding down to the river, especially in winter if it was not too cold, for that was when Lathias had the most free time.

They would ride, those mild winter days, Lathias leading the way on his buckskin mare and the boy always following a little behind, mounted on a gentle old half-blind sorrel that had been with Schoffs longer than Lathias had. Across the frozen fields they rode and off that flat, predictable land into the sudden, striated, prehistoric river valley, astonishing in its random, canyonlike contrast from the geometrical perfection of the tableland above and around it. Often they would sit their horses a few moments on the Bull's Forehead above the old fording place, looking down into the river valley and across for miles in every direction: upriver toward the Forks, where the muddy Red Deer and the blue Saskatchewan flowed their separate though destined courses; across the valley to the bad-blood place where the traders' fort had stood and then the halfbreed village, nameless, its existence so brief it was almost as if it had never been; and downriver, beyond the brown, near-bald hump of Sturgeon Island, hardly an island at all, parting the waters on its ancient back, blindly nosing its way toward the rail town of Estuary (which in less than a decade would be a ghost town, victim of a whim of Canadian Pacific to build a branch line diverting grain flow south), and on, beyond the townsite to the ferry there mired eerily in half-ice. If they turned around to look behind them, upriver, along the lip of the valley and partially obscured by brush lay the old woman's place, the old braucha, the crumbling slant of sod house primordial, squat as a toad, and out-buildings almost indistinguishable from the cracking earth and the strangling, stunted bones of wolf willow and chokecherry and birch, leafless and bewildered, silvering in the thin and nocturnal-like light of late November. And beyond the old woman, Schneiders' and Weisers' and Eicherts' and others, hazed by distance. And the boy's home, too, and beyond that, sunk into a slight depression in the level earth and backed up to the edge of the Sand Hills like a cornered cat, the Krauss place.

Later in winter, when the ice was good, they would go out on the river with skates Lathias made by wrapping a length of number-nine wire around blocks of wood cut to match the size of their boot soles and secured with pieces of old leather, cumber-some but functional.

In the summer, if Lathias had the time and the water was low enough, they would fish, the boy wading in sometimes, or even swimming, though Lathias, who sat and smoked and watched him, would have preferred that he did not. Or, if the water was high enough, they would pull from the brush a raft they had made and pole slowly across the swirling, muddy water to the other side where the fort used to be, gone now but for the rotted remains of foundations where the buildings had once stood. They would find things, arrowheads, of course, and beads and flint and stone tools, which Lathias said were for cutting and pounding and scraping, and, once, the boy plucked from the mud a mini-ature buffalo carved from an unidentifiable pale wood. He had spent the remainder of the afternoon sitting on the muddy river-bank staring at the carving in the palm of his hand, turning and admiring it from every angle. He had taken it home, intending to drive a hole into it with a nail and run a string through to make a necklace, a gift either for Lathias or a charm to keep for himself, he had not yet decided which. But as soon as he put the nail to the charm, it split in two, and just as it did, his father came in. The boy saw him hesitate in the wide doorway, as if to go out again, but then he stepped toward him and said, too loudly, "So, what have you got there?"

The boy said, "Nothing," and slipped it all—charm, string and nail—into his pocket and stood staring dumbly at his father, the hammer still hanging from his hand.

Later, he tied the two halves together with the string, wound round and round, and he tucked it into his shirt pocket, then took it out again and, compelled by some faint notion of ritual and rightness, moved it to the other pocket, the one over his heart, and crossed himself, as he often did in moments of great solemnity, and said, "The Lord be with you," and, because no one else was there, he answered, "And also with you."

At night, he slipped it under his pillow and fell asleep dreaming of herds of buffalo crossing the unbroken prairie, and of the buffalo jumps Lathias had shown him and the piles of bones partially unearthed in coulees near the river by spring mudslides and which the boy now kept in an apple crate out behind the barn, along with the shed antlers of whitetail and mule deer he sometimes found in the brush around the Sand Hills.

He had other treasures, too, kept in a box beneath his bed—lead musket balls, teeth, the petrified bones of animals even Lathias did not recognize, arrowheads of all colours and sizes—things they found at the old fort and the trading post, things Lathias said had belonged to the surveyors and the traders: bent and rusting forks and spoons, cans of tinned vegetables and meats that Lathias split open with his hunting knife on a rock, a woman's high-heeled boot, impossibly small, with the lace still in it, buttons, shotgun cartridges, a single perfect silver coin.

Sometimes, when they had tired of digging around the old foundations and root cellars and in the mud of the cutbank that occasionally revealed buried treasures as the steady water washed the earth away, they would just sit on the bank and eat their dinner and Lathias would tell him stories, about the old days. The boy never seemed to tire of them, and Lathias did not mind the telling, it was a way of going home.

And so, when Lathias was not working, and sometimes even when he was, the boy was almost always with him. He followed Lathias around like a little lost puppy, that is what people, the kinder ones, said.

"Ach," they said, as they had once said of Leo and Cecilia Krauss, "even a crooked pot has got a lid, not?"

The others: "Tell me, what does a man his age want with a boy, and a boy like him? What does that halfbreed think he's doing?"

NINE

The boy loved him beyond sense and reason. He loved the horse-smell of his bunk in the loft cornered off and made private with close-stacked bales of straw, loved his worn leather boots and the hunting knife he kept tucked with some books and photographs and other things in a small chest by his bed and the wooden rosary nailed to the wall. Loved the mystery of him, too, the way he spoke, the German that was German but not quite the way everyone else spoke it, either, the way he ate salt and pepper instead of jam on his buttered bread, the things he knew about: the old fort, the Indians who had lived there for a time, the fur traders; how he knew that pile and circle of stones atop the Bull's Forehead was not just from farmers clearing their land, as his own father had said, knew that it should be respected and not touched. Yes, the boy loved all that mystery, maybe loved that most of all, loved that when anyone asked Lathias where he had come from, he just said, "South," and when they said, "Where, Eastend? Maple Creek? Havre?" he nodded vaguely and said, "Around about there." The boy loved walking with him at the river, fishing in the summer for the pickerel and pike they would gut and then string up in the

74

smokehouse until the strips were brown as leather; skating on the blue, treacherous ice in the winter; digging around where the old fort used to be. Most of all, the boy loved his stories, the old stories of bloodshed and ghosts, though they sometimes kept him lying awake at night, listening to the peal of coyotes and the rattling of bones across the darkened fields.

When there was not time for the river, they would sit in the long evenings behind the barn where Lathias, and on rare occasions Stolanus, would go in order to smoke without the silent weight of Helen's disapproval.

Lathias and the boy would crouch down there behind the sweet wild rose bushes in the evenings, and Lathias would pull a cigarette from his pocket and light it and sit for a while and smoke slowly, just staring out at the beginnings of a moon, ghostly in the still-light sky, and listening to the slow croak of crickets beneath the granaries and watching hawks swoop over the fields and, sometimes, a coyote loping in the distance, until the boy could stand it no longer and he prodded Lathias's boot with his own and said, "Come on. Tell it. Tell that one."

Lathias would say, "What one?"

And the boy would say, "You know. About that girl."

"No," he would say. "It makes you too sad."

"It doesn't," the boy would say, "it won't. Not this time."

And Lathias might resist a bit more, teasing the boy a little, and then, at last, he would tell it, just the way he always did, just as the boy knew he always would.

"All right," he would say, leaning back. "All right. It used to be," he would say, "that this whole area from north of the Forks down south to the Sand Hills and east along the river as far as Harrison's Landing was so dangerous hardly no one would come here. Before that, people were through here all the time. Different tribes. Sometimes they would fight, warring parties raided from the south. This was a place where people passed through. Always moving. Following the buffalo. But, then, when the fort was built, people started to stay longer and longer. Whites. Europeans. Americans. Frenchmen. Indians, too, because of the whites and the fur trade."

"And that's when everything changed," the boy said.

"That's right." Lathias flicked ashes away from his cigarette. "The trouble began one winter, and the first to die were four Iroquois working for the fur traders, killed by a band of Gros Ventre kicked out of the fort. Some Blackfoot found them and buried them and covered the shallow graves with stones, to keep the animals away. But the Gros Ventre dug them up again and cut off their hands and feet. Then, later that spring, more were killed. Ten Iroquois, two white men. All working for the fort. The Gros Ventre rode their horses around and around the stockade, singing and hooting and waving the bloody scalps of the killed men on long poles."

Lathias glanced at the boy, who always looked away at this point, out into the middle distance, as if better to see the image of the riders, or else not to see it at all.

"Soon," Lathias said, "the Blackfoot brought word there would be an attack on the fort. So, just as quick as the ice was out on the river, the traders packed up and left. Good thing, too. People had begun to think of this as a bad place."

"Not even the traders would come, then," the boy put in, "not even for furs, not even for money."

Lathias nodded. "Two years the fort stood empty while the Indians slowly tore it apart for wood. Eventually what was left of the place burned, no one knows how, or no one said, anyway. When the traders came back all they found was a charred place in the earth and so they started to build another fort, just down-stream of the Forks. By Christmas, they had no food and trade had come to a stop."

"And they couldn't even hunt, right?" the boy said. "Because of all the fighting?"

"Yes, they were afraid to leave. And so they sat inside their fort, starving, freezing, wondering why they'd come in the first place and how they could get out."

"But they were greedy, weren't they?"

"That's right. It was not enough for them that they get out with their lives, no, they wanted to sneak out with all their property, didn't want to leave nothing behind. They thought the Indians would kill them for their ammunition and their liquor. For tobacco."

"Would they have?"

"Maybe. I don't know. I wasn't there."

"Your grandmother was, though. Right?"

"Great-grandmother. She was just a child then, not much younger than you."

"They figured they were pretty smart," the boy said, "those traders."

"They did. So they thought and thought, how could they sneak all their things out of there? In the end, they came up with a big plan, how to get the Indians away from the fort. So they built this kite, in secret, a big white one, and on a night when there was no moon, they flew it, up from the fort, brought out all the little kids to see it. They made sure the Blackfoot kids especially were there. I guess it must have looked like a bird, or a ghost maybe. They let the kite be carried away by the wind so it looked like it had disappeared. None of the kids had seen anything like it. They were all excited, afraid. They ran to tell the adults."

The boy leaned forward, rubbing the heels of his palms together lightly in anticipation. They were coming to the good part.

"So," Lathias went on, "among the Blackfoot there was a medicine man and he had a daughter. She was the youngest of all his children, and his favourite. She was very beautiful, this girl, but she was not right."

"But born that way."

Always, the boy said the same thing, and always it twisted Lathias's gut.

"Yes," he said after a moment, "she was born that way. She was always around somewhere. And she was there that day the traders played their trick on the Blackfoot, she was there, standing in the yard of the fort with the other children, watching that great white bird, and when the bird disappeared, she began to cry. My great-grandmother tried to comfort her, and stroked her hair and wiped her tears and kissed her, but she cried and cried and then she ran out of the stockade, back to the Blackfoot camp.

"Word of the ghost bird spread quickly. The next morning the chiefs came to the traders' hall and the traders' interpreter showed them a paper with some marks on it and said, 'This is from the Master of Life. It says you are to go away from the river and stay many days. Otherwise you will meet with a big party of Assiniboine and Cree.'

"While they were talking, the kids played out in the yard. The medicine man's daughter was there, drawing pictures in the dust with sticks, when this peddler, a short man with a red beard—"

"Stinking of rum," the boy said.

"Stinking of rum, this red-bearded peddler came and watched her. She was not afraid of anyone, and so when the peddler gestured to where the kite had disappeared into the river valley and motioned for her to follow him, she nodded and the peddler took her by the hand, out of the yard, toward the river."

"What did he do to her?"

"No one ever knew. He must have taken her in a canoe downstream. That's where his body was found later, his throat slit with his own knife. The medicine man's daughter must have done it. But she did not come back to the fort and she did not come back to the Blackfoot camp."

"Why didn't she?"

Lathias shrugged, shook his head. "She hid back up a draw, in one of those hollows where the runoff washes out chunks of earth and rock in the spring. When she didn't come back, the men went out to search the hills. They searched all that day and all that night and they called and she must have heard them, but she didn't answer. Maybe she did not want them to find her."

Lathias leaned forward and rolled the long ash from his cigarette off against the sole of his boot.

"The sun rose and set and rose again. Still, the men could not find her. There was much discussion about what to do. But after three days, the chiefs decided it was best for the tribe that they move on as the Master of Life had commanded. 'My friend,' the chiefs said to the medicine man, 'the river takes many. Come with us. Do not bring bad fortune upon us.' But he would not go.

"Days passed, and nights, while the medicine man searched those hills along the river. The traders packed up and snuck out of the fort. The medicine man might have seen them, the traders, but he did not notice, or did not care. He cared only for his daughter. But she was a small girl and the prairies are huge, especially for a man searching for his child. She could have been anywhere. She could have drowned.

"When the medicine man found the peddler's body plucked and bloating in the brush, he dragged it back to the stockade and dumped it there in the dust of the yard and said, 'Here is your son. Where is my daughter?' But by then, it was just halfbreeds there. The traders were long gone. That is what they told him. 'They are gone. They tricked you all.' It was then that the medicine man knew his daughter was dead. He turned and walked out of the stockade for the last time, back to the abandoned Blackfoot camp. He prayed and worked his medicine on the Bull's Forehead, and brought stones and placed them all in a circle, praying for a vision, a sign. But there was nothing. On the third day he collapsed. He lay there for some time. Then he rose slowly, looking up at the sky, that morning sky red and yellow and fast with clouds—like it looks now, see, as if it is all moving. Three hawks screeched and circled a rocky outcrop. And the medicine man knew. His daughter was dead.

"He followed the hawks and brought her back and laid her on a mound of stones, her black hair shining in the sun. He stood over her and cursed the valley and the river and the land in every direction.

"When the Blackfoot returned and learned of the trickery, and of the medicine man's daughter, they knew this was a bad place, the land around the Forks, all the fighting and bloodshed and trickery and grief. It makes a man do crazy things, this place. Not a land to live on, but a land to pass through. They decided to leave, for good this time. But the medicine man would not go.

"After his people left, he gathered up his amulets and rattles and threw them far out into the river. Then he sat down beside his daughter."

Lathias stopped then, stubbed the butt of his cigarette into the dust.

"Winter came," he said. "And the wolves. That spring a small hunting party from the medicine man's tribe returned, looking for buffalo. There was no sign of him, or of his daughter, either. They searched for them both, coming down to the fort, but no one there knew anything. Soon they stopped searching. It would be only their bodies they would find. Maybe not even that. And they said, 'It is better. He was gone the way of bad spirits.'

"And soon they realized, too, that no buffalo came. The land was bad, the river, the circle of stones on the lip of the valley, the sky above and around it. And so they left.

"After that, there was no more trade here, not much. More traders, different traders, opened the fort again a few years later. Blackfoot were here, then. Blood, too. And others. Hundreds. Thousands. But everything had gone bad. The Indians would not trade. They were angry. They fought, with the white men and with the Assiniboine and Cree. With the Gros Ventre and Sioux who sometimes raided from across the medicine line. It was a bad time. They refused to bring fresh meat to the fort, and everyone inside was afraid to leave. The fort was abandoned in the spring, as soon as the ice was out. People came and went for a while, Indian, white. Nobody stayed long."

"Except the bone people," said the boy. "Your grandmother's people."

"Yes, they stayed, and some of these were killed, too. They built the old village that used to be there. Set up trading posts across and up from the Bull's Forehead, by the fording place. But there was no more buffalo. There was only bones, then. So they gathered up the bones, and they sold them. Then, when the bones were gone, they were poor, starving."

"And that is how it will always be," the boy whispered.

Lathias shrugged. "That is what my great-grandmother said. She said the land is cursed. That is what she told my grandmother, when she was a girl. Then, when my grandmother married my grandfather, a German from Russia with a bit of money in his pocket, her mother thought, *Things will be better now for them. They will have food. Their children will not starve.* And, for a while, it was good. Then drought, then influenza, then hail, then cutworms. And then my grandmother told my grandfather, 'We should leave.' But he just laughed. He did not want to go. He was from the old country. He was used to ghosts. They can't let go of them, they bring them with, across the ocean."

"So now," the boy said, anticipating him, "there are twice as many ghosts on this land."

Lathias nodded. "The ghosts born here, the ghosts brought over."

"But they did leave," the boy said. "In the end."

"Yes. If my grandmother knew I came back, she would say I was crazy."

He would always end the story the same way, every time. He would laugh a little humourless laugh and light another cigarette and sit staring at the gathering dark, and he would say, "Maybe I am, a little bit."

And the boy would sit and watch him.

"Is that true?" he would ask.

And Lathias would say, "Is what true?"

"Any of it."

And, after a long silence, Lathias would say what he always said: "Does it matter?"

THE HILLS

ONE

No one standing outside the hardware that Saturday morning, five weeks to the day since they'd seen Leo ride wordlessly out of town, could have said they were surprised to see his wagon roll back in. They were all—Mike Weiser and the Schneider brothers and Art Reis and Stolanus and Lathias and the boy and a few others—standing there listening to Joe Schuling tell how one of his heifers was struck by lightning, struck dead right where she stood, by Jesus, how he'd found her blackened and belly-up in the field, stinking like nothing he'd ever smelled before. And all of them listening, trying to decide was he pulling their legs or not, when somebody said, "Well, by God, look there."

For down the street came Leo in his wagon. He looked just as he had when he'd left, there was no perceptible change in either his appearance or demeanour; but on one side of him was seated a big, dark-haired, dough-faced woman of thirty or so, though it was hard to tell for sure, and on the other side a girl of maybe fifteen, though it was hard to tell that, too, with long, wild hair of the duskiest red any of them had ever seen, and all three of them sunburnt and dirty and grave-faced, rolling past as if there were not some dozen men standing there staring at them go.

Mike lifted a hand and might have called out a greeting but for the looks on all three faces and the way they stared straight ahead as if there was nothing and no one that could interest them on either side. Then, when the wagon had almost rolled past, the red-haired girl turned her eyes upon them and stared as if she knew those men for exactly what they were, and that gave every last one of them a strange kind of feeling.

(*Kind of like the willies,* they told their wives later—except for the Schneider brothers, who had only each other to tell—*but not quite like that either. Why don't you make some sense,* the wives said, *like what, then?* And the husbands shrugged and shook their heads and said, *I don't know.*)

After they'd disappeared down the road, Joe Schuling finally said, "Kee-rist Almighty."

And that was enough to break the strange half-spell they all seemed to be under, of disconcerted and dumbfounded amazement, and so to convince themselves that the girl had not given them the willies, they said, "You think that's a wife he's got there?" and "Which one?" and "With Leo, who knows."

At first, little was known of the two women (or the woman and the girl, depending on how you looked at it), who they were or where they'd come from. For the first few days, no one saw them. But things and people being as they are, it didn't take long for word to get around, about the fact that they were there at all and where they'd come from in the first place. Marian Weiser's people, Dunhauers, down in North Dakota, had written to Marian that Leo—though that is not what they called him in the letter, nor to each other, when he lurched his wagon into their yard and said, outrageously, "My wife is dead. Cecilia is. I need another."—had been to see them.

Marian's brother wrote: *He is lucky he is alive. If Otto had let me, I would have shot that sonofabitch right where he sat. Come home,*

Marian. Already two of your sisters dead up there. Who knows but that you could be next.

The brother did not, thanks to Otto, shoot Leo, but after chasing him out of their yard, the brother got on his horse with his shotgun and followed Leo down the road to make damn good and sure, as he said, that the bastard dog did not come back.

Leo was not unaware that the brother rode behind him, down the long dusty road lined thickly with brown-eyed susans just beginning to bloom, a shotgun slung over his shoulder. Another man might have cracked the reins to his mule and made a beeline north. But Leo drove on, in his shambling wagon that looked as if it would bust apart at each bump in the road, to the next farm, where he said, "My wife is dead. I need another."

And the brother behind him on his horse, calling out, "Yah, that's right, give him a wife if you want to send your daughter to an early grave. Better still, bring her out and I'll shoot her here, save this dog the trouble."

And so, everywhere he went, doors closed to him.

Until, as always seemed to happen for Leo, one finally opened.

"What do you want? What are you selling?" the man asked from the doorway before Leo's mule had planted its cracked hooves in the dust.

"My wife," Leo—exhausted, incoherent almost—began.

And the brother, who, though not tired, was growing bored and feeling that it soon must be suppertime, said, "I'll shoot her here."

The man in the yard frowned at them. "Have you been drinking? Get on with you."

"I need a wife," Leo said.

"He put the last one in her grave," said the brother. "Up in Canada. That is what they do with wives there."

"Canada, eh?" the man said.

"That's right."

The man narrowed his eyes a minute at Leo and then, ignoring the brother, said, "Come inside."

"All right," the brother said to the man, "don't come crying to me when she's dead." And, swinging his horse around, he rode off toward home. In spite of himself, and because he secretly disliked—though he knew only by reputation—the man whose yard he had just left, he thought, *Good riddance, then. At least he won't be our problem.*

———

Good fortune, indeed, had been smiling upon Leo that morning when he rode into the yard of Anton Brechert, a man who considered himself largely put-upon, who considered even the smallest of human trials a burden and the greatest of human trials an outrage and who was still burdened mightily by the child his eldest daughter had borne out of wedlock fifteen years earlier; a man who felt the burden of that shame—as he was wont to call it—just as keenly on the day Leo Krauss pulled into his yard as he had on the day the bastard child was born.

When Leo had said, *I need a wife,* Anton Brechert had eyed him carefully up and down and felt for the first time that here was someone who might just help ease his, Anton Brechert's, burden at least, if not his shame.

Leo climbed down from his wagon slowly, as though it required great effort, as though he were undecided whether he should do so. It would not do to appear too eager. He ducked into the house behind the man, folded himself into the chair offered at the kitchen table, and sat waiting.

Anton Brechert stood a moment, studying him, this unlikely suitor with his wrists thrusting from the frayed cuffs of his suit jacket, knees straining the faded grey fabric of his trousers, hands gripping his dirty cloth hat like a wheel. Maybe he was trouble, and then again, maybe he was not. Who was he, Anton Brechert, to judge? He looked again at Leo, his old suit, his lightless eyes. Impossible to guess his age. The whole effect was of something left too long in the sun. Leo sat hunched, crumpled almost, though from the length of his body and the size of the room or from simple humility, Anton Brechert could not tell. And from his clothing, from his pores, came a smell; not only the musky, human, identifiable smell of an unwashed body, but something else. Something sulphurous.

"I need a wife," Leo said at last, then turned his eyes to where a young woman stood over a pot at the stove, her fair hair curled up prettily in the steam. "I have land," Leo said. "My wife is dead. There are two children yet at home. They need a woman." Watching all the while the girl at the stove, plump and shining in the steam and the sunlight streaming in through the small window with the smell of fresh earth.

"Yah, sure," Anton Brechert agreed, sensibly, "a child needs a mother. And a father, too." Then he followed Leo's gaze to the girl at the stove. "No," he said, frowning, "she is not for you. She is the youngest. She will stay home and care for us."

He studied Leo a moment, as if deciding something, then jerked his thumb toward the corner behind the stove and said, "You take that one."

Leo looked to where a heavy woman with dark hair sat hunched over some mending. Though the room was narrow and cramped, he had not noticed her. The woman did not look up but continued the smooth motion of her needle.

Leo wondered if she was deaf. But what he said was, "How old is she?"

"Old?" Anton Brechert said, "What does old matter? You are young?"

"No," Leo admitted, "not that, not young."

"Well, then, what do you want with young? Young is nothing but trouble. You take this one. She is a good worker. She won't give you any trouble."

"What is going on here?" said an older woman, stepping from the doorway of an adjacent room. "What are you talking about?"

Snapping her eyes from Anton Brechert to Leo and back again.

"Nothing." Anton Brechert shrugged. "Just business."

"What business?"

Anton Brechert stared at her, then said, roughly, as if he were accusing the old woman of something, "This man needs a wife. He's a good man. He has a good home."

"And you plan to send Mary? Have you lost your mind? Do you even know him?"

"I know enough."

"What? What do you know?"

Anton Brechert turned to Leo. He sucked his teeth. "Are you Catholic?"

Leo glanced at the old woman in the doorway before nodding.

"There," Anton Brechert said to her, "what more is there to know?"

"Well, she can't go, and that's that."

"And why not? She should go, before there is more trouble."

"More trouble. My God, she's more than thirty."

"And what about the girl? She won't be any trouble? They are all the same. One as bad as the next. She should go. And the girl, too. She will be as bad as her mother—worse."

"The girl? My God. You've lost your mind."

"Pack your things," he said to the big woman in the corner.

She did not move, but kept sewing, placidly, untroubled, and Leo thought surely she must be deaf or an idiot.

"What," the old woman in the doorway said, "and you expect them to just go, without a marriage even?"

"Marriage," he sneered. "When has she ever cared about marriage?"

"But this is madness."

"Mary," he barked, and the woman in the corner raised her head, and her expression was mild and uncurious. "Get ready," Anton Brechert said. "Tell the girl to pack her things too, or she goes with nothing."

"You cannot send the girl," the old woman said. "I forbid it." Though there was nothing of conviction anymore in her voice, and the big woman, Mary, had already put aside her mending, and risen in heavy obedience.

"The girl goes too," said Anton Brechert.

And Leo, who had been looking from one to the other of the Brecherts, finally said, "What girl?"

She was brought into the kitchen to stand beside her mother. Leo, who had been sitting looking at his hat, slowly raised his eyes to the girl who was not really a girl (and not even a very clean girl at that), but a woman almost, or she seemed to be, it was hard to tell, and the longer he looked the harder it became. Her hair was pulled back severely from a dirty, freckled face and covered over with a dotted black kerchief, the pale face of a child, though the front of her dress, a loose dress of bleached sacking which might have been white were it to be washed, was stretched tight across breasts that seemed far too developed for a girl otherwise so thin and long-limbed. Her eyes, large and such a glittering reddish brown they looked almost reptilian, stared fiercely back at him without curiosity or shame either. Leo dropped his gaze to his hat again. He was not, at first, aware that everyone was looking at him, waiting, as if he should say something; the girl, her mother, the old folks, the pretty sister at the stove, even she had stopped what she was doing and just stood there, waiting, too, the ladle dripping onto the scrubbed floor.

"Mary," Anton Brechert finally commanded, "tell her to take down her hair."

Leo looked up then.

"What for?" snapped the old woman. "What does it matter?"

"Tell her."

Mary said something quietly to the girl. But the girl just stood there, paying attention to neither of them, looking only at Leo, viciously now, as if in confrontation or disgust.

The pretty sister at the stove spoke then, hesitantly. "Papa," she said. "Why?"

Anton Brechert nodded. "He will know," he said, pointing his chin at Leo.

"Do as he says." It was Mary again, the mother, speaking quietly, without looking at either the girl or the old man, but only at her feet.

The girl stood there so long Leo thought she would surely not obey. But, then, without taking her eyes from him, she raised a thin and filthy hand and slipped the kerchief off her head, shaking out brutally, perversely, a mass of hair so deeply red it did not look like human hair at all, but like the coat of some animal. It was not beautiful, that hair, but savage. Or the expression in her eyes made it so.

"You are crazy," hissed the old woman in the doorway. "You have lost your mind. Would that I had killed you when I had the chance."

The girl laughed then, a strange sound, more a bark than a laugh, perhaps at the old man, Anton Brechert, perhaps at the old woman who defended her. She might have been laughing at some private recollection or at nothing, for all that her expression gave away. The old woman shook her head and, turning slowly, left the room, followed shortly by the sound of a door shutting somewhere in the house. In the silence that came after, no one seemed to move, to know what to say or do, waiting, perhaps, for some sign from the girl herself.

Finally, the pretty sister at the stove, Anna, said softly, "Put on your kerchief, Lisbet. Go and see Mama."

The girl paused a moment before dropping the dark kerchief at the feet of her grandfather. Then she turned and walked out, exposing with each step the soiled bottoms of her feet, moving as easily as if she had just excused herself from the breakfast table. As if there had been no public or private humiliation. The old man made a noise in his throat, part fury, part disgust, the kerchief lying there between them until the pretty sister bent to retrieve it, saying, almost under her breath, "Why, Papa?" and Anton Brechert sucking his teeth and nodding again, said darkly, "No one can say I am a dishonest man. I want him to know what he is getting. There, you see how he looks away. He knows what I mean. He cannot even raise his eyes."

Leo glanced up at the old man, then down again.

"Whores," Anton Brechert breathed. "One made a whore, the other born one."

"Papa."

"Hold your tongue, Anna. And take care yourself. I would not be so easy a second time."

Anna, the pretty sister, blushed furiously and glanced once at where Mary still stood, waiting. But Mary would not look at her, and so Anna grabbed her ladle and stirred the steaming pot with studied intensity, her back turned stiffly toward them.

"Well?" the old man said. "Will you take her?" He did not say *them.*

There was a long moment, then, in which there was no sound, no movement, among them, but for the steaming of the pot and the bluebottles bumping their weightless bodies against the bright window glass.

"What is wrong with her?" Leo said finally. "With the girl."

"What do you mean, what's wrong with her?" Anton Brechert said, too quickly. "Didn't I just say? She's a whore begot of a whore. She bears the mark of her mother's sins upon her. What do you mean what is wrong?"

Leo did not know exactly what he had meant. Only that, looking at the girl, and looking at the others, he had felt that something was wrong. Not what the old man was saying. But something else. Something in the way those reddish eyes had looked right through him. Into him.

"But there is something . . ." he said again.

And Anna, turning suddenly at the stove, cried, "Oh, no,

nothing, only that she used to bite her tongue until it bled, only that she sees—"

"Anna!"

"—she knows things. She's just a child, Papa, you can't send her, don't—"

"Enough," said Anton Brechert, thumping his fist on the table so that the cups all jumped and clattered. "Enough talk." He breathed heavily, looking around at them all. Then he said, "Anna, make yourself useful—get some flour and potatoes, two sacks. A bag of sugar. Put it in the man's wagon." Then he turned to Leo. "Well?"

Feeling all those eyes upon him—the old man's as vicious as the girl's had been, daring him to decline, Anna's spilling with tears, Mary's veiled and placid—Leo was reminded of his own father, his mother, docile and beaten, the vicious intimacy of his brothers and sisters, his childhood in the cramped little shack.

"Well?" the old man said again. "Will you take them?"

And Leo rose, nodded, and went out to the wagon.

Two

When Leo arrived home with his new family, he found that the last of his old family had gone, the girl, Magdalen, to the convent run by the Ursuline sisters on the edge of town, of her own choosing, or so Mike and Marian told him, and the boy, Henry, to no one knew where (or if they did know, they did not say). And who could blame them? is what people said. The younger three were still with Weisers, and if they had any inkling or intuition or even outright recollection that Leo Krauss was their father, they certainly hid it well; they seemed to have forgotten they were Krausses at all, and so everyone else seemed to forget it, too. Marian even changed the children's names, whether legally or not no one knew, so that when they started school they were Weisers, and better off for it, as far as anyone knew or cared.

And so the last of Cecilia's children were gone. Leo stood in the doorway of the empty old shack and knew he would not have them there again.

Someone, possibly Marian, whether from charity or guilt, had tidied the place, swept and scrubbed the floors, wiped clean the crusted counters and opened the windows to the June air that seemed, like everything else, to sour and darken upon entering the Krauss shack. She had even dusted and righted above the kitchen table the old skewed photograph of Gus in his coffin. Leo stood there staring a moment, then he held open the screen door to let the two women inside.

"Well," he said, when they had stepped past him, "here it is, then."

———

Ma Reis walked over to Krausses' that first Saturday with some freshly baked cinnamon buns (the very quality of which she felt was enough to establish without delay to the newcomers her position as an irrefutable authority in the community) to welcome the two women, and, of course (Ma would see no reason to deny this), to find out a little more about them.

Ma told later how the yard was as bad as it always had been before Cecilia, perhaps worse, stinking of blood and chicken shit and all that garbage everywhere (though it looked to Ma as if one of them—the two women, surely not Leo—had attempted to rake it into indiscriminate piles which the June winds had made short work of redistributing), and Cecilia's flower tins blown around, too, caked with dirt and rust, the desiccated plants still hanging tenaciously in withered strands, and that impossible garden all gone to kocia weed and Russian thistle that had dried and regrown and dried again so that you could no longer tell there had ever been a garden, had you not known where to look for it, and the flowerbeds, too, that had once spilled with larkspur and bachelor's buttons and hollyhocks and sunflowers: all gone. Only a few bottles remained hanging in the branches of the cottonwood; most, whole or in shards, lay scattered across the dirt beneath the tree.

Ma stood in the yard at the foot of the unpainted porch, just looking around, taking it all in, thinking someone would come out to greet her since they must surely have seen her coming down that long, open road, how could they not? But no one came. She called out. Once, twice. Still, no one.

She said later, "I was never a one for superstition, but there was something about that house of Leo's that always gave me the shivers. And so I just stood there, hoping someone would come out, thinking I might have to climb those rotting stairs and knock after all, and thinking how foolish it was that I was afraid to do just that, kind of going back and forth with myself, and wondering, too, what on earth I should do if someone did answer and invite me in to sit and have coffee at that table with that picture of Old Krauss dead in his coffin hanging over us. And so I stood there and waited and crossed myself, I surely did, knowing someone might very well come to the door after all and invite me in and that I would have to swallow my disgust at all that filth and sit and drink my coffee and be pleasant."

But she needn't have worried, that's what she said later. Just as she was telling herself she was behaving like a schoolgirl, that she should get up there and knock, for heaven's sake, the screen door creaked open and a girl—the daughter, Ma assumed—stood staring down at her, she wouldn't say unfriendly, but not really pleasant either.

"Hello," Ma said, "you must be the new girl."

The girl tilted her head slightly in what Ma took to be a nod and they stared at each other some more.

Ma said later: "I don't know what got into me, but I stood there just as if I didn't have a brain in my head, just staring at that poor girl, Lord, what she must have thought of me."

What the girl must have thought of Ma, no one knew. What Ma thought of the girl was this: *Lord God Almighty, that is the skinniest, palest, strangest, most beautiful girl I've ever seen. But, Lord, so thin. The child must be near starving to death, and yet developed well beyond her years, God help her.*

When Ma described the girl to others, she said she had long limbs that made her appear taller than she was, and long thick hair a strange wild cinnamon colour that fell down around her shoulders, face freckled, eyes the same odd reddish brown as her hair. The girl's dress was askew at the hem about ankles so thin they looked as if they would snap should she take a step forward. Feet plunged into wear-beaten shoes heavy and brown and far too large. And so maybe because of the intensity of the girl's stare or maybe because Ma herself was nervous and uncomfortable or simply for lack of anything else to say, she blurted, "Oh, my dear, are you wearing Leo's shoes?"

Of course, she meant it to be helpful, meant to suggest that she might find her something more appropriate, but she realized later how stupid it was when the girl flushed up right from her dingy white collar to the roots of that cinnamon hair, so that she gave the odd impression of being all red and white, hot and scorching, as if something burned there.

Perhaps the girl would have replied then—Ma could see she had offended or at least embarrassed her—but, just at that moment, the mother appeared. Or, not quite appeared, for she did not join her daughter on the porch, but only peeked through the screen door at the girl's back, her body mostly hidden by the doorframe, as though she did not wish to be seen. She was a big woman, even by ample standards, with her apron tied up over a large belly and her face round and white and full as the moon.

And so that the woman could believe she was not seen, Ma just smiled at the daughter and set the baking firmly on the step and said, "Tell your mother Hady Reis stopped by. Everybody around here calls me Ma. I'm the next farm over that way, should she need anything. Tell her I said to come for coffee sometime."

And then she turned and left.

But she said later, "I could just feel them watching me walk away and, I swear, it was all I could do not to turn around and look back. Lord Almighty. But listen to me," she said, waving one of her big hands dismissively. "I sound as superstitious as that old goose-ass Ludmila Baumgarten."

Though there was no denying: it downright gave her the willies. It really did.

THREE

Even those who were not superstitious—like Ma—still were, if only a little. Ma Reis, too, would cross herself if she passed a cemetery after dark, though she did not believe, as some claimed, that if you looked into an open grave a loved one would be dead within the year. That was a bit much. But she was the first to agree that a red evening promised good weather, that a yellow streak at the horizon was the first sign of hail, and that if a pin was dangled by a thread over a pregnant woman's belly, it could foretell the sex of the child.

And there was, of course, *die Wetterregeln*: if January stays mild, spring and summer will bear fruit; if February is cold and dry, August will be hot to fry; a dry March, a wet April and a cool May bring much wheat and much hay; first love and the month of May seldom pass without frost away; June, more dry than wet, means good wine in every vat; on St. Gall's Day, in the barn the cow must stay; December with snow and chill promises grain on every hill; and, most important, people make the calendar, God makes the weather.

But *die Wetterregeln* was not superstition, as Ma was fond of pointing out, it was common sense.

Now, she didn't go in for all that old country nonsense; and the braucha, well, she could take her or leave her. Ma liked to say that though the braucha might know a thing or two it was buried under a pile of old country horseshit. Which always reminded Ma that when she'd developed a rather stubborn and irritating wart on her hand as a young girl, her grandmother had tied a thread around the wart three times and advised her that, on the next night of a full moon, she bury the thread in the manure pile and say three Hail Marys over it. She did and, much to her amazement, the wart was gone within the week.

And then, too, years later, after she and Art had come over, when her own youngest was sick with the colic and she was at her wits' end with his ceaseless wailing, the braucha had come at her mother-in-law's insistence and put some fresh cow manure (*very* fresh, as she recalled), a little peppermint oil and some sugar into a cloth and tied it up and gave it to the baby to suckle. Then, taking him behind the open kitchen door, the braucha had muttered something—verses or prayers—so softly that Ma could not hear and she was struck with a sudden unease that quickly became horror and, just as she was moving to snatch her son away, the child gasped, coughed a little and quieted. The braucha handed the infant back, rather roughly Ma had thought at the time, and collecting her sack of payment from the table, left without saying anything to Ma at all. The crying spells had never returned. So who was she to quibble with the nonsense faiths of others? Still, she preferred to keep her feet firmly planted in earthly things, as she said, even if sometimes her head and her heart wandered elsewhere.

And, of course, there was the case of Charles Hatfield. Hatfield, the rainmaker, who was only a man and like all other men, yet was something more, belonged somehow to the heavens, too, to that wondrous accumulation of swelling thunderheads on the horizon of a drought year, thunderheads bearing only inches of rain, it was true, but rain nevertheless. Four inches of rain. Four inches—

only enough to overfill a teacup—to make an ordinary man a worker of miracles. Ma remembered very well how all the talk that summer before last had been about Hatfield, the great rain-making wizard out of California, who had erected (for a hefty fee) a cauldron high up on the edge of Chappice Lake, eighty miles west near Medicine Hat, for the paid but nevertheless unenviable task of bringing rain. And, amazingly, he had. To the anxious, to the dry, to the dust-weary; that June, unexpectedly, unbelievably, he had. It rained; beautiful, soft, soaking showers. Even the Sand Hills greened and blossomed.

Then those who had hoped rejoiced, and those who had scorned said nothing, took the rain and were thankful anyway, for it fell over the land of the hopeful and the land of the scornful in equal measure.

Some said, "We should charge them, too," (meaning those who had not paid). "Where's their dollar? Maybe next time I won't pay neither, and take the rain just the same, how would that be?" But still they were thankful. All but Leo Krauss, who said, "I will take my rain from God or not at all. I will not reap what is sown by sorcery and black magic."

And so he had let his small fields grow green with weeds, green and useless with piety, though others said it was not piety but just laziness, and if anyone could make God an excuse for laziness and sloth, it would be Leo Krauss. So there was no harvest at Krausses' that year, not even of potatoes, and when they were hungry, his children, Henry and Magdalen, starved from eating last year's rancid lard straight from the tin, and their clothes could not bear any more mending, while all around them everything greened and prospered, all the women in new lacy hats and the boys with gleaming pocket knives and the girls in bright pretty dresses, as if they were flowers that had just bloomed, still, Leo told them, "You will not worship false idols," though they had not mentioned worship, they only wanted to eat.

After Hatfield, there had been no more rain and then no snow, not much to speak of, a thin crust that melted and refroze so often it no longer resembled snow but dirty ice, brownish, spare. Then it was spring again, dry, continuing on through the summer, into fall. Early the next spring, there was talk: would they hire him again? At Knochenfeld, after Mass, they said: "We should hire him ourselves maybe." And others argued, "What for, when they will do it in Medicine Hat or Swift Current or somewhere where there is more money and we get the rain for free?" But that was not right. It was stealing. "Stealing?" some asked. "Could you steal rain? Could you steal air to breathe?"

So they asked Father Rieger, and Father Rieger wiped at his nose with a parched hanky and said through his yellowed teeth (yellower still because of the hanky which the parish ladies took turns keeping whiter than white), "Pray. Pray for rain. Say ten Hail Marys. Say ten Our Fathers. Say an Act of Contrition. Pray."

So they prayed. They said ten Hail Marys. They said twenty Our Fathers. They said so many Acts of Contrition they ran out of things to be sorry for. And no rain came.

Then it was June, the hot, furrowed land dry and brown as the hand of God.

FOUR

Into that parched summer, as if the very foulness of the choked air summoned him, emerged Leo with his new wife and daughter: his daughter now—not by blood or affection, but by sheer misfortune—whom he dragged to church that first Sunday, dragged by her arm, though not roughly, it seemed, but dragged nevertheless, and Mary following behind like a patient cow, nothing written in her face, up the church steps and inside and to the pew where he had always sat, not bothering to genuflect as he usually did, and not to sit either, but just standing there, waiting, the girl beside him, not looking to the left or to the right, but just down at those awful brown shoes. It was then that some of the women noticed the dress she wore, it was familiar somehow. Why, it was Cecilia's old wedding dress, the one sewed by Marian, was it not? (Though, as Ma Reis pointed out later, the girl certainly was in need of a dress, and why not that one as well as any other? Should it go to waste?)

When Father Rieger came in, Leo stepped out into the aisle, still holding the girl by the arm, and said, without preamble, "She needs a baptism."

"For God's sake," Father Rieger hissed, "speak to me about it later."

"What for, when we can do it now, and then it is done?"

Father Rieger insisted that Leo sit down, that they could discuss it later, and, giving the altar boys waiting before him a little shove, continued on.

But Leo called after him, "Do not put off until tomorrow what can be done today, Father." Then he added, "That's just laziness, not?"

Father turned back to Leo in a fury, speechless, the girl between them, standing calmly in the aisle in Cecilia's wedding dress—who would have thought?—and those big ugly shoes, so skinny and lost-looking, and in spite of it all, pretty, too, beautiful even, strangely beautiful, everyone could see that, and maybe it was because of that, because she was beautiful, that they pitied her a little. And her mother, who was not beautiful, standing there with her rosary wrapped around her fist, hanging her head in humility or shame or hatred or piety, no one could tell which. They pitied her, too; they remembered Cecilia and they pitied both of them.

Mike Weiser stepped forward then (perhaps spurred by Marian's fumings) and asked Father, if it was not too much of an inconvenience, because the girl was new (as if Father didn't know), maybe they could make an exception and have it all done with.

Father said, "The Catholic Church makes no exceptions."

"I didn't ask for an exception," Leo put in. "Just a baptism."

Father turned and gave the altar boys another shove then, a bit harder this time, and they all three continued on, up to the altar, where Father proceeded to sprinkle—a little overzealously, some thought—the congregation with holy water. But Leo stood his ground there in the aisle with the girl beside him, and so finally Father said, "Take your seat, please," and when Leo still did not move, they both just stood there staring at each other across the pulpit while the congregation shuffled and exchanged loaded glances. The silence went on so long that Ludmila Baumgarten turned nervously on her piano bench and began to play "The Little Brown Church" ("Always looking for an opportunity to sing," Ma Reis said under her breath. "You'd think her ass was tied to that piano bench"), but no one was following her lead, and Father waved a hand at her peevishly, saying, "Ludmila, for God's sake," and then, to Leo, "I must ask you to leave." To which Leo said, "The sin will be on your head, then," and he led the two women down the aisle and out the door, Mike Weiser following after him.

"Leo," he said, on the church steps, "what is this?"

"She needs a baptism."

"All right," Mike said, puzzled. "But let me talk to Father. Let it wait. Maybe he will do it next Sunday. Sunday is soon enough, not?"

"But," Leo said, and he looked at the girl beside him as if surprised to find her there, attached to him by the arm, "what if something should happen to her? Then what? She will go to hell, not? If she is not baptized?"

Mike Weiser narrowed his eyes, frowning. "But, Leo," he said, cautiously, "what could happen? Father will baptize her next week maybe. What could happen before then? She will be fine." Though Mike was really thinking, *What is it to you, Leo?*

And Leo nodded a bit and studied the girl, as if trying to determine, just by looking, whether or not Mike was right, whether she would be fine.

"She'll be all right," Mike said again, "don't worry. You can look out for her, not?"

"How can I do that?"

"Well, why not?"

"She won't come in the house."

"What do you mean?"

Leo shrugged. "At first, she did, then she didn't."

"She must come in sometimes. Where does she sleep?"

"In the barn."

"The barn? But why?" Looking at the girl now, too.

Then Mary spoke up. "That is where she wants to sleep. It is up to her. She is a big girl."

Mike turned to the girl. "Is that true? You want to sleep in the barn?"

The girl just stared back at Mike, as if she had not heard.

"It's the woman," Mary said then, looking anxiously at Leo.

"What woman?"

"Enough of that," Leo said. "Don't talk so stupid."

"What woman?" Mike said again.

"The one who comes at night—"

"Hold your tongue," Leo warned.

Mary looked down at the floor and was silent.

"What is this, Leo?" Mike said.

"Ach," Leo said, "some nonsense. Never mind. Some excuse she has, for sleeping in the barn."

"Is there some reason?" Mike asked the girl.

The girl glanced over at Leo.

"You see?" Leo said. "I give them a good home, and they want the barn. For no good reason. It makes no sense."

Mike watched the girl a moment, but she only gazed off now, out into the distance, as if whatever they spoke of could have nothing to do with her.

"I guess if she wants to, she wants to," said Mike uncertainly. "What does it matter?"

"It matters that she has not been baptized."

"Yah, but why the hurry?"

"If something should happen."

"Nothing will happen."

"But if it does."

"What could happen?"

———

So the girl slept in the barn. Mike Weiser confirmed it. He took a ride out there that afternoon, just to check on them.

"I don't know why," he said afterwards. "I must have rocks in my head." He said, sure enough, the girl was sitting out in the barn, on some blankets she had spread over a mattress of straw in the corner. Mike said that when she saw him come in, she quickly hid something behind her back and wiped her mouth on her hand. She was barefoot, though she still wore the old wedding dress, and those big shoes lay kicked beside her pallet.

Mike pretended he hadn't seen anything, he said to her, "I'm sorry. I don't mean to trouble you, I just wanted to see if, well, if everything's all right."

But she just sat and stared at him and did not reply. Mike didn't know what else to say, felt a little foolish that he'd come at all. What business was it of his? So he nodded and tipped his hat to her and went out.

He said afterwards how he could smell chokecherry jam as soon as he walked into that barn, the whole place was rich and sweet with it, and her lips stained that deep bruised colour—she must have found some of Cecilia's old preserves.

"I'm glad she did," Mike said. "I don't know what they are living on out there, but it isn't food and it sure as hell isn't love. I feel sorry for her. For that girl, and for the mother, too."

That is what he said, but what he thought, what he admitted to no one, was this: *God help me, I stood there in that barn looking at her and I felt sorry and ashamed all at the same time because all I could think was how damned pretty she was in Cecilia's old wedding dress and how her lips would taste like chokecherry jam.*

———

Mike Weiser wasn't the only man around who felt ashamed of himself when he looked at her, at Elisabeth Brechert. There were prettier girls around, pleasanter girls, certainly cleaner girls. But there was just something about her, it was difficult to say what it was exactly, to admit it at all, even to themselves, something that made people—men for certain, maybe women, maybe even children—want to touch her, that cinnamon hair, or her lips, or that white, white skin, speckled over prettily like an egg. And, more than that, the way she seemed not to care. Not about that, not about anything. Other girls in the parish were jealous of her, of course, the way some can be when another girl bests them (especially one as lowly as she: a Krauss, for all intents and purposes), and that without even trying, the worst of insults. And the young men acted like she was nothing to them, acted as if she were beneath them, the way they do when they want something but don't want the other fellows to know they want it. They all thought about her, you could see it in their faces when they looked at her, or pretended not to look at her. They all sneered at her or laughed at her or downright ignored her, all the young people, in spite of that something she had. Maybe because of it.

FIVE

The very next day, Monday, Lathias sat mending some harness by the stables. Helen was out in the yard, too, taking wash down from the line, before the wind came up and dirtied everything all over again. Stolanus had gone to town, on some errand forgotten that morning, and Lathias was wondering if the boy had gone with him, having not seen him since lunch. But, just as Lathias was about to go look for him, the front door of the house opened and the boy peeked out, glanced to where Helen stood with her back toward him, and then bolted straight across the yard toward the root cellar, holding something balled up under his arm. After a minute or two, when the boy did not reappear, Lathias put the harness aside and crossed the yard after him.

The boy had left the cellar door wide open—too trusting and inartful himself to be successfully deceptive. Lathias was used to finding his own books lying open on his bunk or his hunting knife out of its sheath, photographs misplaced; but the boy would never harm anything, never steal, and so Lathias would put his things in order and say nothing.

The boy stood now in the root cellar, half in a shaft of sunlight that fell through the open door, quickly stuffing a flour sack with the last of the apples Helen had saved over from the previous autumn.

Lathias was puzzled but only momentarily. It had not been difficult to see in church the day before, how the boy looked at that new girl, Leo Krauss's girl; not with embarrassment or shock or indignation or disgust, but with a kind of reverence, as if it were an angel standing there in the aisle and not simply a girl (and not even a particularly tidy girl at that); and then, just that morning, the boy had been there with Lathias and Stolanus outside the hardware when Mike Weiser said, "I don't know what they're living on out there." So it did not take Lathias long to guess what the boy was up to.

"Old Blackie's gonna love you today," he said from the doorway.

The bag slipped from the boy's hand and apples spilled out around him.

"By God," Lathias said, "you know how to treat a horse right."

He bent and began gathering up the apples, and the boy knelt, too, dropping them back into the sack.

"It's not stealing," he said. "I'm not stealing them."

"Does your mother know?"

The boy looked past him, as if she might be there. "Will you tell her?" he said.

"No. But you keep feeding them horses like this they'll be too fat to work and then you'll have to answer for it."

The boy picked up a few more apples. After a while he said, "It's not for the horses."

"Oh," Lathias said. "Is that right?"

"It isn't any of your business anyhow. That's what I think."

"It isn't," Lathias said, handing him an apple. "But leave a little behind, not? Your mother's sure to notice if you clean her right out."

The boy knelt there, thinking about it, then he returned a few apples to the bin, not looking at Lathias where he crouched in the doorway watching him.

"There," the boy said, his face flushed up, and he stood, not quite looking at Lathias. "All right, then." Rubbing his palms against his thighs. "I'm going out for a while," he said.

"All right."

"I don't have to tell you where."

"You don't have to tell me nothing."

"All right."

"All right."

The boy scratched the back of his arm. He studied the apples in the sack. Finally, he said, "That girl in church there, you know who I mean?"

"I think I do."

"Did you think she was pretty?"

"Yes," Lathias said, "I think she was."

The boy nodded, thoughtfully. "How old would you say she was?"

Lathias shrugged. "Your age. A little older."

"How much older?"

"Couple years maybe."

The boy pursed his lips, nodded again.

"All right, then," he said, and lifted the sack.

"All right," Lathias said. "Don't be too long." Then he added, though he already knew the answer, "Your mother know you're going somewhere?"

The boy just stood blinking at him.

"All right," Lathias said. "All right. Go on."

Lathias watched him cut across the back pasture and straight for Krausses', through the scant brush along the Sand Hills. There would be less chance of meeting someone that way, though Lathias worried about this less than he had when the boy was younger. It was not the first time he had gone there alone—out to the Sand Hills—without telling anyone, though Helen would have been horrified to hear it; for her, nothing had changed. The boy understood this, too, and so he would often sneak away from the house, when Helen was preoccupied, as she often was now, lost deeper in herself each year, it seemed, or when she lay down for the long afternoon rests she had begun to take daily. Stolanus did not notice, or if he did, thought nothing of it. And so it was only Lathias who knew that the boy sometimes left the farm.

In earlier years, Lathias had followed him, just to see where he was going, to make sure he was safe. But the boy never went far. Only out to the Sand Hills and back. And, of course, it seemed that the boy must someday surely turn and discover him there. But he never did. And so Lathias would trail him to the Hills, watching as the boy poked around in the brush or sat in the shade of a chokecherry stand, eating berries.

Once, during those first years, he'd watched as the boy pulled something from his pocket and stared into his palm. Lathias watched as the boy kept angling his head to the left, then to the right, then back again. It wasn't until the boy ran a finger across the scar on his temple that Lathias realized it was a shard of mirror he held. Where he'd gotten it, Lathias could not imagine. Surely not from home, for Helen had long ago packed away the old mirror she'd kept in her bedroom, packed it away sometime after the accident. When Lathias realized it was a mirror the boy was staring into, he turned away, walked home, feeling sick. After that time, he never stayed long. When he was sure the boy was all right, he would go home.

Eventually, when he saw the boy leaving the yard Lathias let him go alone. But once, he said to him, "You know you can never go to the river without me."

And the boy said, "Why would I do that?"

And so Lathias did not worry. He was not a child any more. He needed to do some things on his own. Otherwise, how would he survive as a man? Lathias knew that he could not watch out for him forever. It would be impossible.

Of course, the boy knew early on that Lathias was following him. How could he not? He was not stupid. At first he thought it might be some game. Then he realized, no, it was the same as

Lathias waiting for him by the school steps all those years ago.

"I can't always be with you," Lathias had told him back then.

"I know that."

"And so you have to be careful."

"Of what?"

Lathias had stared at him. He just shrugged, shook his head. Then he said, "You know how deer lie quiet in the brush by the river, and you can't see them, you could just about walk right over them before you do?"

"Yes."

"Do you think you could do that, if you needed to?"

"Why?"

"Because," he said, feeling frustrated, caught in his own inability to speak frankly. He did not want to scare the boy. But, still, he did not want the boy to be treated badly, teased. To be hurt any more, by anyone. So he said, "They do that when they are scared. Do you understand?"

"Yes," the boy told him, sensing Lathias's frustration, "I understand. I see what you're saying."

But he did not see. What had deer to do with him? After that, he tried it once, under an old bent willow on the edge of the Hills. He lay there for a long time, barely daring to breathe, keeping still, still, waiting. He even nibbled at a few blades of dry grass. Scratched at one haunch with his hoof. Nibbled. Sighed. Waited. *Surely*, he thought, *surely, something will happen now.*

Nothing ever did.

———

Today the boy did not stop to sit on the warm sand and stare out at the fields, as he liked to do, but walked steadily, following the line of the Hills, toward the Krauss farm squatting there, impossibly almost out of sight among the scrub and dunes, as if the whole place were sinking, returning to the primordial dirt from which it had come and to which it belonged. When he got close enough to see the yard, he wondered what he should say to the girl anyway. He had not thought that far ahead. So he stopped walking and stood trying to think what to say. And as he stood there thinking, he almost turned back, decided that he would turn back, he must. That was when he saw her. She was seated away from the yard a bit, out on the trail that led from the farm to the main road, her back against a stone pile, her white dress pooled around her in the dirt. He stood watching her, admiring the way she seemed to be there so naturally, a pale flower—or not a flower, but a rock herself—then he flung his sack across his shoulder and walked on.

Maybe she heard him coming, maybe she did not, the boy could not tell. But she did not move to look up, even when his shadow fell across the dirt she was drawing in with her finger. He stood watching, then crouched down and put the sack at his feet. He both did and did not want her to turn toward him, notice him. He knew how he would look to her. So he kept his face turned away slightly, the way he always did. Waiting on her. But she said nothing, nor made any sign that she had noticed his presence at all.

"I like that," he finally said, not looking at it. "That's a nice picture you made."

She lifted her head then, and the boy glanced at her, out of the corner of his eye. The sun hit her full in the face. Up close, he was amazed at the strange cinnamon colour of her eyes, at the gold flecks floating there, all that beauty at once. He almost turned to face her, caught himself just in time, watched out of the corner of his eye again as she stared at the pattern of circles and lines and crosses she had drawn there. Of course, he knew it was not a picture, not a drawing, that was not what he meant. There was no deeper meaning; it was something to do. He understood that, had spent many an hour passing the time in similar ways. But he could not now say that, it would sound foolish, and before he could think what to say, she reached out and in one smooth motion wiped out the drawings with the palm of her hand.

He rubbed his own palms on the front of his trousers, thinking that perhaps he should go. But he did not. He watched her ignoring him, glaring out at the line of the horizon that rippled faintly in the heat. He lifted the bag a little, let it thump against his leg.

"I live over there," he said, motioning with his thumb. He waited. "We're neighbours."

He began to grow nervous. What more could he say? He thought of the apples in the sack at his side. Stupid. What had he been thinking?

"Well," he said, and stood as if to go.

"I saw you," she said. "In church."

"I saw you, too."

She nodded. The boy chewed his lip. Then he pointed at a pile of something she held in her lap, half covered in the folds of her skirt.

"What you got there?"

She unfolded the skirt, revealing a pile of glass shards—clear and coloured, blue, green and amber—and scooped some up into the palm of her hand, holding them up to him.

"What is it?" he said, touching the shards with the tip of his finger. He thought she might pull her hand away, but she did not. He picked up an amber one. "Where'd you get them?"

She waved vaguely with her hand toward the Krauss farm behind her.

"Looks like a point," he said, holding it up to the light. "I have one this colour."

"What's that?"

"What?"

"A point."

"What the Indians would use, for hunting. It's a piece of rock worked with a stone, so it's pointed, like so," he said, holding the shard of glass up, "for arrows."

"Oh," she said, unimpressed. "I used to find them. Back home."

"Did you keep them?"

"What for?"

The boy shrugged. "I have a boxful, under my bed. We find a lot, down at the river, down around the old fort."

"What fort?"

"Down at the river there. Used to be. They're gone now, mostly. But we find a lot of good stuff, me and Lathias."

"Lathias?"

"He lives with us. He's older. He takes me places. To the river. He found a hunting knife there once. Blade was rusty, but it was still good. He cleaned it up. Looks good as new. It's a good knife. I could show you sometime. And arrowheads. And I've got all kinds of skulls and bones. Teeth. Old rifle cartridges. Lead musket balls, even. Real lead. All kinds of things. I could show it to you."

"What for?"

"Just so you could see them."

"I mean, what do you keep that stuff for?"

He shrugged again. After a moment he said, "I guess I just like it." Then he added, "I don't like to think of it out there. Just left." He shrugged again, embarrassed.

She nodded and turned away, dragging her finger through the dust.

The boy watched her a bit. Then he said, "Where'd you get all that glass, anyway?"

She looked up at him sharply. "Back there," she said, tilting her head toward the Krauss farm. "It's everywhere, under that big tree, you know, by the house there?"

"No," the boy said, "I've never been there."

"There's bottles tied there, up in that tree, and jars, too, but I guess some of them smashed, all that glass, it's everywhere. I cut my foot," she said, pulling off her shoe. There was a vivid gash along her instep.

"You should clean that," the boy said, "with some alcohol. Looks infected. See where it's red there?" He reached toward her foot, then pulled his hand back. Stuck it in his pocket.

The girl stared at her foot, then slipped her shoe back on. She looked up at him, studied him so long that he began to grow uncomfortable and he turned his back to her, pretending to look out at the horizon.

"Where'd they come from," she said, "all those bottles?"

"I don't know," the boy said from across his shoulder. "I've never been there."

"It's right in front of the house there, you can't miss it."

"No, I mean I've never been there at all, to Krausses'."

"Oh." She frowned up at him. "That seems kind of funny," she said, after a while. "How come?"

The boy kicked his toe at the cracked dirt. "Just never have. So what?"

"Seems kind of funny, that's all. You living so close. Don't your folks get on with him neither?"

"Who?"

She jerked her head toward the farm again. "Him."

"Oh. No. I guess not. I guess they don't."

She nodded again, slowly, and tilted her head at him. "How come?"

The boy shrugged. "My parents don't like him much, I guess. Lathias, neither. Nobody does." After a moment, he added, "I don't know why. He seems all right to me."

"Well," she said, "he's not."

"Why?" he said, turning back toward her. "What does he do?"

"He doesn't do nothing," she snapped. "What did he ever do to your folks?"

"Nothing, I guess."

"That's right." She shook her head in annoyance, looked away. Then she said, "So, it's just because your folks don't like Leo? That's why you've never been there?"

"I guess."

"So it's not . . ." she said, and she lifted her hand and then dropped it, "it's not that there's something . . . kind of funny about the place?"

"Funny?"

She shook her head. "Just . . . strange?"

"Strange how?"

"Oh, nothing," she said irritably, and rattled the glass in her lap. "Never mind." An ant had crawled up on her ankle and she reached down and crushed it between her fingertips, rubbing them together until it was just a paste there, which she wiped on her dress. She studied her fingertips and then she said, "Was he married before, or did he have a sister or something?"

"Who?"

She flashed her eyes at him. "Leo."

"Oh. Yah," the boy said, "he was married." As if it could not be otherwise. "A family, too. Gone now." Though, of course, she would know that.

"And," the girl said, "his wife, was she . . . was something wrong with her?"

"How should I know?" the boy said, sounding irritable too now, though he did not mean to be.

"This is her dress," she said, "isn't it?"

"How should I know?" the boy snapped again.

After that, neither of them said anything for a while.

In the end, feeling sorry, he said, "What's your name, anyway?"

"Elisabeth. My grandfather used to call me Rusalka."

"That's a nice name." Though he did not specify which.

"No, it isn't."

He waited, but she did not ask his name.

She said, "I think it was her that put those bottles there."

"Who?"

But she just shook her head and said nothing more.

It was a moment before he realized she was staring at him, that he had forgotten himself and had turned fully toward her as they spoke, exposing the ugly, scarred side of his face. He quickly turned his face away, squinted his eyes at the horizon again, where a hawk circled lazily. But she just kept staring at him that way until she had stared so long that it was awkward for him to stay and awkward for him to go. And so he just stood there beside her, sweat forming uncomfortably between his shoulder blades.

Finally she said, "You talk kind of funny."

He wrinkled up his nose a minute. Was she making fun of him?

"Are you German?" she said.

"Yes," he said, surprised, "isn't everybody?" Of course, he knew that was not literally true, knew that it sounded stupid. He had only meant everyone around the parish. Even Lathias, who was only part, was still German. That was all he meant, but he could not now say it.

"Then why do you talk like that?" she said. "Sort of funny. Like your tongue is swelled up or something. Is something wrong with your tongue?"

"I should go," he said.

"Why?"

He looked over his shoulder. But Lathias was not there.

"Because," he said. "I just should."

"No. Why do you talk like that? What happened to you, that scar there?"

He scratched the back of his neck, almost lifted his hand to brush across his forehead, dropped it instead. Then stuck it back in his pocket.

"Did you get kicked by a horse or something?"

He shook his head.

"What, then?"

He squinted at the horizon. "It was a horse," he said, knowing he was lying but not knowing what else to say. Not wanting to speak the truth of it, maybe, not even to her. Especially to her. "A horse did it," he said. "A white horse." He shrugged.

"How old were you?"

"Four. Or five."

She stared at him. "Were you four," she said, "or were you five?"

"Four." Was he?

"Do you remember it?"

"I should go."

"If something like that happened to me," she said, "I would remember."

"I remember," he said.

He did not. He had been told what had happened, that he had been caught under the wheel of a wagon, that is what his mother had told him, without any more of the hows and wheres, just that, *caught under the wheel of a wagon.* Sometimes he said it to himself, over and over, like a chant, as if he might find sense or meaning in its repetition. Relishing the coarseness of it, the stupid horror. The banality. *Caught under the wheel of a wagon.* He knew that much, but he did not remember it himself, did not remember any of it, not the before, not the after. And maybe because he did not remember, maybe because to tell her anything, he must make up something, maybe because of that, he thought, *If I have to make some up, why not all? Why not kicked by a horse, why not thrown from a horse, why not struck by lightning? Why not?*

And so he said, "I remember. It was a horse. I was hiding. In the stable." Had he been? Now that he said it, it seemed true.

"Why?"

"It was a game. Just to see would anyone miss me."

"Did anyone?"

"No."

"No." She nodded. Then she said, "Not your mother?"

"I don't think so. I don't guess she did."

"I bet your father missed you. Fathers always miss their sons. If you are a daughter, they don't miss you, only if you are a son.

That's how it is." She pulled a blade of speargrass at her side and stuck the tender end into her mouth. "So what happened?"

"There was a horse," he said, feeling that, in fact, he had been there, that the horse had been there, huge and pale and shifting in the darkness. He could smell the sweet, hot, green smell of that horse, could hear it huffing into the cold air of the barn. "I was hiding there in its stall, it's warm there, in the winter, you know. If you put your hand up by the horse's nose it will snuff out steam and warm your hand. Kind of wet-warm, you know that feeling? And sweet, like hay when it's fresh cut. That's what I was doing. I heard my mother calling. It wasn't my father, it was my mother. I thought I heard someone coming. I peeked out under the rails and there was someone, I thought there was someone out there. I backed up, so they wouldn't see me."

"And then what?"

"And then I woke up. I was in bed. There was bandages all around here." He pointed in a circle around his head.

"And?"

"And . . . the . . . braucha was there."

"The braucha?"

"The healer—"

"I know what a braucha is. Didn't you have a doctor?"

"I don't know. I think so. I think later a doctor came. I think he gave me some medicine. It was brown. Brown medicine. In a brown bottle. It tasted—" he almost said *brown*, but stopped himself in time, knowing it was stupid. "Bad," he said.

"You remember all that?"

"Why wouldn't I?" He almost turned to look at her, but caught himself again.

She frowned at him. "Okay," she said then, something shifting in her tone—a softening, the boy thought. Was it? "All right," she said, and stirred with one finger the pile of shards in her lap.

She didn't believe him, he could see that much, and it annoyed him. Why shouldn't she believe him?

"That's a pretty bad scar anyway," she said, without looking up. "Is that why you talk like that?"

But he just stood there, wanting to leave now, but still, in spite of himself, not wanting to, either. Why couldn't they talk of something else?

"What are you going to do with all that glass?" he said.

She pursed her lips and sifted a palmful of shards through her fingers.

"Some of those look pretty sharp," he said. "You might cut yourself there."

"I might," she said, scooping up another handful. "But I doubt it. I never get hurt. Not that way."

"But," the boy said, "your foot."

"I never get hurt," she said again. And then, as if to prove her point, she closed a fist viciously around the shards.

"Don't," the boy said, but when she released the shards and turned her palm to face him, there was no mark there, she might as well have been gripping a fistful of dandelion clocks.

"See?" she said. Then, standing, she scooped up all the shards and flung them out to the brown summerfallow, and they both stood and watched them land in little, soft puffs of dust.

"I should go," the boy said, wondering what had changed, why she seemed somehow angry.

"Go," she said.

"I'll see you, I guess. On Sunday," he said.

"I guess."

"Are you getting baptized?"

"No. Why would I?"

"Why not?"

"Why do you talk like that?"

"I should go," he said.

"So go." Then she added, "What's in that sack, anyway?"

Six

L athias had wondered if it was a good idea, letting the boy go over there like that. Who knew how the girl would react to him? And though he'd seen Leo lurch past behind his old mule earlier that afternoon, he could return at any moment. Lathias kept one eye on the road, thinking he could ride over and get the boy if he saw Leo heading home. And, then, he did not know the mother, either. As the morning wore on, he periodically walked to the edge of the yard and looked out toward Krausses' until, around noon, he spied the boy coming back across the field, dragging the empty sack behind him. Then he busied himself with the chores, so as not to appear as if he had been waiting, as if he had been worrying.

When the boy walked up behind him, he said lightly, without turning, "Oh, so you're back. Well, and how were the horses? Blackie still favouring the front left? Might have a look at him later."

"She wants to come with us."

He turned and studied the boy. "Wants to come with us where?"

The boy looked down at the sack twisted in his hands, and then back up at Lathias.

"To the river," he said, and grinned.

———

All week Lathias tried to think of excuses, reasons, why she should not join them. All week he watched the skies, hoping for bad weather, a sudden storm. And all week he had been picturing the boy's face, just how he had looked, all lit up from inside, when he'd said, *She wants to come with us.*

They weighed upon him heavily, those words. He felt sick to his stomach at the prospect of it, of her. And that look on the boy's face, the pure joy. It alarmed Lathias—yes, he had to admit it—to see the boy so happy. Who knew what this girl was about? Already the boy put so much faith in her. Or, not faith, hope. She was all he talked about. And what could she want with the boy, anyway? That is what he wondered, hating himself for wondering it. But, he reasoned, she must be lonely too, it is just company she wants, alone there at Leo's place. And, then, they could not be so far apart in age. A year, two. Three maybe. The boy always seemed so much younger than he was. It was vaguely disturbing to Lathias to realize the boy was going on thirteen already. Almost a young man. And the girl was what, fifteen? Not sixteen yet, surely, though it was difficult to tell. So it made sense, didn't it? It was only natural. That is what he told himself. But still, he wondered, in spite of himself, knowing it was a judgment against the boy. He was not slow, not stupid, that was for sure, but he could seem that way if you didn't know him. The way he talked, his habit of ducking his head, looking askance at people, as if he could hide the scarred half of his face. But he was not stupid, no, far from it. Did the girl know that, could she know it?

Already, Lathias disliked her; or if not disliked, certainly distrusted. He had half a mind to walk over to Krausses' and see for himself what she was about. But it would be worse than inappropriate. Totally unwarranted. Absurd. And then, too, what if the boy found out he had done so?

That is how the week passed for Lathias, going back and forth with himself, trying to dissuade his head of what his gut was telling him.

And then it was Sunday morning and she was there in church, directly across the aisle from him. And he sat behind the boy and watched him turning to look at her every few moments, not even trying to hide his stare. And then Lathias felt he must look, too. He sat fighting it, rubbing furiously at the calluses on his palms, until at last he did look. And there she sat, face turned forward, bland and expressionless, all that red hair tucked into the collar of her dress, as if to hide it. She sat there beside Leo and did not turn to look at either of them, until, as Lathias walked back from Communion, she lifted her eyes once, so briefly he wondered later if she had really done it at all, and looked directly at him. And he said to himself, *Is it for the boy's sake that I am worried? Is it for his sake, or for my own?*

———

After breakfast, Stolanus leaned back in his chair and said, "And what will you two do today?"

"We're taking her to the river," the boy blurted. "To the fort there."

Helen raised her head sharply. "Who?"

"Neighbour girl," Lathias put in, casting a glance at the boy. "Krausses."

"Krausses?" Stolanus said.

"That one Leo brought back?" Helen said. "Do you know her name, even?"

Lathias looked at the boy.

"Rusalka," the boy said.

"Rusalka?" Helen frowned. "What? That's a witch, not? Rusalka?"

"Ach," Stolanus said, "that nonsense."

"I didn't say it wasn't nonsense. But what kind of name is that for a girl? What kind of people they must be. Rusalka."

"No," the boy said, alarmed at his mother's reaction. Would she not allow him to see her now? Rusalka. He had not known it was a witch. "No," he said. "I was just joking. Her name, it's Elisabeth."

"Well, which is it," she said, "Rusalka or Elisabeth?"

"Elisabeth," he said, looking to Lathias for help now.

Helen narrowed her eyes. "How do you know her name?"

"I told him," Lathias said, glancing again at the boy. "I heard. In town."

"And Rusalka, why did you say that, then? Where did you hear it even?"

"From me," Lathias said. "A story I was telling him."

Helen tsked, but gently. "I wish you wouldn't do that, those stories."

"Yes," he said, "you're right."

"They scare him—"

"Ach," Stolanus interrupted. "It's good for the boy. Put some hair on his chest."

"Elisabeth," the boy said. "It's Elisabeth. She's not seen the old fort. She's not even been down to the river."

"I don't like you boys down there, at the river," Helen said, as she always did, and Lathias allowed it, as he always did, though he was twenty almost, a man. "You stay away from the water. And that old fort. I don't like it. All those rusty nails, what if he should step on one? What if a building should collapse on them?"

"Ach, Helen," Stolanus said.

"There's no buildings any more," the boy said.

"Then how can you tell there was a fort?"

"There's some timbers still," Lathias said. "Foundations. And other things."

"Well." Helen frowned. "I hope you're not thinking of going over to Krausses' to get her."

"No."

Helen studied them.

"I don't know," she said. "I don't think it's a good idea."

"Sure," Stolanus said. "And why not? She's our neighbour. We see her in church. We know enough. She's not a stranger."

"She is a stranger."

"And so what? What does stranger matter?"

"I don't like the idea of them going over there, to Leo's."

"He's not going there. Didn't they just say that?"

"She said she would come here," Lathias said. "She said she would walk over."

"It's good for the boy," Stolanus continued, "get to know some other young people."

"Why? What is good about it?"

"We should wait for her outside," Lathias said to the boy.

"That's right," Stolanus agreed. "She might be too shy to come to the door. You know girls."

"Rusalka," Helen muttered after them, "I'd like to know what kind of a name that is, that's what I'd like to know. You ask her. If she shows up even."

And Lathias thought, *That's right, she might not come at all. Why would she?*

But when they stepped out of the dim kitchen with its perpetually closed curtains, out into the overwhelming spring sunshine, she was already there by the barn, waiting.

SEVEN

Hair of the devil, hair of the witch, that's what Lathias's mother had always told him.

"Don't you never touch a girl with red hair," she'd warned.

"I don't want to touch nobody," he'd said.

"Well, when you are touching nobody, make damned good and sure she doesn't have red hair. She will put a mark on you. That is how they do it. Tools of the devil. Whores they are. And wicked as a six-clawed cat. You make damned good and sure."

He'd just turned away and said, "I don't want to touch nobody."

That seemed like a lifetime ago now. He had no recollection of his mother's hair being other than grey; to him, she'd always seemed old. He'd asked her once, while she sat with her sewing in the evening, a time when she always seemed more peaceful, or as close as she ever came to it, not flying around as she did during the day from child to child, chore to chore, on the cusp of a rage, asked her, "What colour was your hair?"

And she'd stopped a minute and stared at him as if she had no idea what he could be talking about.

"Your hair," he said again, faltering under her black stare, "what colour was it?"

She frowned at him and pulled a long strand from the bun at her neck, turning it slowly in her fingers by the dim light of the kerosene lantern. In that light, it glowed prettily, more silver than grey. He longed to reach out and touch it with the tip of his finger, almost lifted a hand to do so.

But then she said, slowly, "Well. Would you look at that." And she sat staring at it a moment. Then she put her sewing aside and looked up at him, as if she might say something. But she didn't; she just stood and said, "It's late. You should be in bed," and disappeared into her own bedroom, pulling the burlap curtain shut behind her.

Lathias never did learn the colour of his mother's hair. Never would now. For all he knew she was long dead in her grave, ungrieved by him except indirectly, prematurely. She had died for him long ago, upon the moment of his leaving. That was how it was when you walked away from something, from a place, from people—no bouts of mourning, just a perpetual state of grief, beginning with your leaving, with your decision to leave. Grief, though it is you who have died, and not the ones you have left behind. They go on, without you. And what is life, anyway, but one long grieving? That is what his mother had once told him. Loss after loss after loss.

He looked across the yard to where the girl waited without seeming to wait, her long hair throwing sparks in the sunshine, and he thought, *But Mother would be turning over in her grave if she knew.* And then, startling himself, *Knew what?*

"Come on," the boy said, waving him over, and he realized he had been standing in the middle of the yard, staring, like a schoolboy.

She looked up as he approached, but he barely glanced at her.

"This is Lathias," the boy said to her, and Lathias nodded and she nodded and then, not knowing what else to do, Lathias stepped into the corral and began saddling the two horses, the boy's and his own. When he was finished, he led both mares into the yard where the boy stood beside Elisabeth, not speaking, just waiting, his hands jammed down into his pockets.

"What about Elisabeth?" the boy said to him, eyeing the two horses.

"What about her?"

"What will she ride?"

She stood with her arms folded across her chest, seeming not to listen, as if the conversation could not possibly have anything to do with her.

"You ride?" he said to Elisabeth.

"I can walk," she said.

Lathias handed the reins to the boy. "She can ride on with you," he said.

"I can walk," Elisabeth said. "It doesn't matter to me."

"Pretty far," Lathias said.

She shrugged.

Lathias put his boot into the stirrup and swung himself up. "Walk, then," he said pleasantly, and pressed his heels to the mare.

Before he was out of the yard, he glanced behind him, to where the boy sat in the saddle, reaching down to give Elisabeth a hand up, and her ignoring the hand and hoisting herself up by putting her foot in the boy's stirrup and gripping the cantle awkwardly with both hands. Lathias waited until they were caught up behind him and then they rode on that way, and Lathias thought, *All this open land stretching out on either side of us and we ride as if we are following a path through the woods.* And he thought, *This is going to be a long afternoon.*

"Why don't you ride up here?" he said over his shoulder.

"Where?" the boy asked.

"Up here," he said. "Beside me here."

"Why?"

"So we can talk."

"About what?"

"Nothing. Never mind."

And so they kept riding along that way, one after the other, through the blown pasture, the horses stepping steadily across the rolling hills, over barrel cactus and gopher holes, through great pale patches of speargrass rippling softly, toward the river, the minty smell of sagebrush all around them, and Lathias began to relax into the rhythm of the ride, as he always did. The sky and the wind and the hypnotic pull of the horse beneath him. So he was startled a little when the girl called up, "What are those?"

Lathias pulled back on the reins and turned.

"What?" the boy said.

"There," she said, pointing at the long line of grass mounds rising up from the prairie just to the west of them. "They look like graves."

"They are graves," the boy said.

"Whose?"

"Don't you know about them?" the boy said in baffled amazement. "*Die Pferdekenner*? The Horseman?"

"No," the girl said.

"Lathias can tell you," he said. "Can't you, Lathias?"

Lathias leaned on the pommel. "It's just an old story."

"It's not. It's true. Tell her. About the soldiers. And all the sugar."

"Oh," Lathias said, not wanting to tell the story, not wanting to tell her, but not really knowing why, either, "it's nothing."

"Please."

"You tell it. You know it as well as I do."

The boy sat staring at him, hurt by his tone.

Lathias sighed, glanced briefly at the girl, who sat waiting behind the boy, her hair blowing crazily about her head. He watched as she brushed it back from her face.

"It's nothing," he said. "Just, all this land here, this pasture, used to belong to this German. He had a lot of money. He was crazy about horses. Those are his horses, right there." He turned and clucked the mare into motion.

"No," the boy called. "That's not right. Tell the story. About how he loved them. About the soldiers. Lathias."

Lathias stopped, turned again. The girl was watching him, but he did not look at her. He could see from the corner of his eye how she gathered her wild hair and tucked it into the collar of her dress. He fiddled with the reins, looked out at the horizon. Finally, he draped the reins on the pommel and swung a leg over and sat sidesaddle. He pulled some tobacco from his shirt pocket and some papers and he rolled a cigarette against his leg and licked the paper shut and smoothed it and said, "Well. This old horseman, *die Pferdekenner* the oldtimers called him, or sometimes *die Pferdefreund*," he said, "he was crazy about horses. He hadn't ever married and he'd come over alone and he didn't have nothing in this world but his horses. They were beauties. Not the heavy farmhorses everyone uses, but long-necked, high-stepping, warm-blooded beauties. They were something to see. People claimed he would sometimes let one or two of them overnight in the house with him, but I don't think anyone ever knew that, it was just one of those things people say.

"Anyway, the war come along and the army sent soldiers around to all the farms, taking horses to use in the war. Sometimes they paid a little bit for them, mostly they just took them, but only from the Germans. That's how it was. Enemy aliens, that's what they called the Germans."

"And everyone tried to act like they were not German then," the boy put in, "right? If a child was born, they put 'Russian' on the birth certificate. Even some of the towns changed their names. Triumph used to be called Prussia."

"Right," Lathias said. "So the soldiers came to take horses, sometimes they took the only horses people had, but what could they do? They had to give them up. Well, someone got word to the Horseman that they were coming. I don't know if they thought maybe he could hide them or something, all those horses, God knows where, but they came to warn him. So this old horseman, he takes his shotgun—he wasn't supposed to have that any more either, they'd taken everyone else's, all the Germans', but somehow they must have missed that one—so the Horseman, he takes his shotgun and, while this neighbour's watching, he goes out to the pasture and he whistles all his horses over and he dumps a big sack of sugar right there in the field, real white sugar, God knows where he'd got so much. But he dumps out this sugar for the horses and then he ropes them all together. Then he sits down beside them and he waits and waits, and the neighbour's wondering what the hell he should do, whether the Horseman's gone a little crazy or what, and just then, they both see the military truck coming down the road, and the neighbour shouts to the Horseman, but he just sits there with the shotgun across his knees, calm as anything, just looking up at the sky and waiting. When the military men stop the car and get out and start walking toward him, he stands and raises the shotgun and the neighbour shouts and the military men shout and point their rifles and shout some more. But the Horseman has no intention of shooting them. He turns his shotgun upon his horses. After the first shot those horses go crazy, flailing their hooves and shrieking and pounding at each other, all knotted together with that rope and trying to run and the dead ones falling, and the Horseman just keeps right on shooting, reloading and shooting again, and again, shoots every last one, and then, before the military men can even think what to do, he puts the gun in his own mouth."

Lathias turned the cigarette between his fingertips. "When it was over, the military men just stood there, and the neighbour, too. I can't even imagine it. God, those beautiful horses. That poor bugger. How he must have loved those damned horses. That is the way it is, you know, when you don't have much."

"And the soldiers just left him," the boy added, after a moment, "they left him lying there in the field, didn't they, Lathias? Just left him there. Dead."

Lathias nodded. "They left him there, dead or dying. They were so disgusted. All those good horses, you know, the senseless killing, that is what they said. 'Leave it to a goddamned Kraut,' they said, 'a stupid Rooshian.' All that senseless killing, that is what they said; as if there could be sense in another kind. Then they just drove away, leaving the Horseman there in the field, one less German, the neighbour standing over him. He went away then, the neighbour did, and came back later with some others and buried the Horseman and his horses, too, right there where he'd shot them. Some people thought that was wrong, that he should have been buried proper. But he was never a religious man. It seemed right, to bury him out here with his horses. What would he have wanted in a churchyard?"

They sat quietly, then, the three of them, watching the wind feathering the long grasses on the mounds, their own horses shifting their hooves and pulling at the shorter buffalo grass beneath them, oblivious.

"They wouldn't have buried him in the cemetery anyway," Elisabeth said. "Would they?"

Lathias shook his head.

"Why?" the boy asked, looking from one to the other.

Lathias said, "He shot himself." And then they just sat some more, just staring at the graves.

"Which one is his?" Elisabeth asked. "The Horseman's?"

"I don't know," said Lathias. He pulled a packet of matches from his shirt pocket and lit the cigarette he'd been holding. "I never wondered."

"You used to cross yourself every time you passed here," the boy said. "Remember that? You told me you always would do that, when you first came here."

"Yes," he said, "I did."

"Why?" the girl said.

Lathias looked at her, at the hair pulled free from her collar and whipped up again by the wind, how she reached up and gathered it, as if it were flowers she plucked from the wild air.

"Because you were afraid?" the boy said. "For protection?"

"No," Lathias said.

"Why, then?"

"I don't know," he said. "It just seemed like the thing to do."

"But not any more," Elisabeth said.

"No," he said, and took a long pull at the cigarette. "Not any more."

She nodded, as if she knew what he was talking about, though he could not have explained it himself.

"Do you remember," the boy was saying, "how they said he took such good care of those horses? Remember?"

"Yes."

"And how he would brush them and talk to them and feed them carrots from his hand and oats in great china bowls—they were china, right, blue china, from the old country?—and how he loved them more than anything, those horses. Remember? Those were china bowls, right?"

"Yes."

The boy climbed down from his horse then and took the reins, stepped over to the graves and stood looking at them. The girl climbed down too, and stood beside him.

"But," the boy finally said, just as he always did, "he killed them."

"Yes," Lathias said. "He killed them."

"That's not killing," the girl said. She stood there in the wind, her skirt pressed tight against her legs.

"What is it, then?" the boy said.

"I don't know. But not killing. There wasn't any hate in it."

"It's still killing. Isn't it, Lathias?"

Lathias thought a moment, watching her.

"So," he said, "the war was not killing, because there was no hate in it, no hate between the soldiers?"

"No, that was killing. There was hate there."

"But they didn't even know each other."

"That's the easiest way to hate."

The boy was quiet, listening to them, just standing there in the wind, and Lathias noticed that he did not keep his face turned away from her any longer, whether by fault of memory or familiarity. He stood staring at the graves, and staring at her, and then he said, earnestly, just as he always did, "But he shot them."

And Lathias said, "Yes."

When they had stood there a long time, all three of them staring at the grass rippling smoothly across the graves like water, she sighed and said, "Well, that is a sad story, anyway. I am sorry for them all."

Lathias looked at her, at all that red hair flying out around her and thought, *No, she is not like others. It is not that she is kinder, or gentler, there is nothing of that. It's something else, something . . . older.*

The boy stood looking at her, too, his forehead all furrowed up, and then he said, as if she did not comprehend, "But, he shot himself." His voice rising a little.

"Yah," she said. "And? So, what of that?"

"It was the head. He shot himself in the head. Don't you understand?"

And she said, "Yes, I do."

"But that's not sad," he said, "it's . . . I don't know, it's horrible."

Elisabeth shrugged. "Yah, and sad, too."

The boy shook his head, threw his hands up in frustration. "But there was blood," he said, shouting almost, "there was blood everywhere." And he bent down and said, "Look, look here," pointing at some rusty lichen. "Blood," he said.

Lathias expected her to laugh, smirk even, the boy was acting such a fool. But she did not, only stood there watching him
through her blowing hair. Lathias could not figure out what had
gotten into the boy, or how to stop him, either, without embar-
rassing him further.

"Red," he went on, "from his blood."

When Elisabeth did not bend to look, did not seem to react at
all to what he was saying, the boy dropped the reins he had been
holding and said, "And that is not all. Sometimes at night you
can hear a hissing, a rattling—have you heard it? Some say that's
crickets or grasshoppers or even rattlesnakes. But it isn't. I'll tell
you. It's the Horseman trying to saddle his horses and ride right
up out of the earth. Isn't it, Lathias? Tell her. Lathias has heard
it. Haven't you, Lathias? And so have I."

It occurred to Lathias then that he was trying to scare her,
really scare her, and he thought, *What in God's name for?* At first
he thought maybe the boy was just trying to get her attention,
mimicking other boys he'd seen at school or after church, older
boys, who would tease the girls they liked until the girls would
grab their hands and squeal, *Stop it now, stop it. You're frightening
me.* But it was more than that, had become more.

Lathias watched Elisabeth as she stood listening, her bottom
lip sucked in so far it had turned white around the edges. She did
not seem the type to scare easily. But when the boy quit his foolish antics, quit running around, pointing out depressions in the
earth—"A horse lay here, and here, and just here, that is where
the Horseman lay bleeding, before the neighbours buried them
all. He's down there now, waiting to ride up some night, all of
them are waiting, isn't that right, Lathias?"—when he stopped
and stood panting, looking at her, waiting, she just released her
bottom lip and sighed.

"It's a sad story," she said again. Then she turned and stuck
her foot into the stirrup and pulled herself up by the pommel and
sat waiting for him.

Lathias glanced quickly at the boy's face—reddened with anger or hurt or embarrassment—and he tried to think what to say to him. But he could think of nothing. He was surprised at the boy, disappointed. And looking at him, it occurred to Lathias that the boy's anger, his hurt, his embarrassment even, was not because the girl had simply refused to react, had refused to be shaken by him, but because of something darker: he had been operating under the illusion that he had finally found someone lesser than him, had finally found someone weaker, a Krauss foundling. Lathias could not believe his own blindness and stupidity. He had thought the boy's reverence simply that of a boy for a pretty girl. But it was anything but simple. Not just her prettiness the boy revered, but her shame as well, what was pathetic in her, what was base, or more accurately, what others saw as base. That's what appealed to him, what drew him. Here, at last, was someone he could feel superior to, not so much to put her down, but to raise himself up. And, yet, when she did not shun him, did not turn away from him in disgust and horror, he was disappointed, and he thought to impress her some other way. But he could find no way. She was not easily impressed. She was not easily anything, it seemed. She just was. The boy could not have chosen a more impossible audience, could not have seen or predicted, in fact (and maybe because of her hardness, her remoteness), that she was so far above him, she was all but untouchable.

It was not so unusual, Lathias knew that, of course; everyone did it in one way or another, himself included, that defeating of the self, that old human folly; we are lonely, yet we need to be alone; we are afraid, yet we need to feel fear. Almost as if, in the absence of love or pain, in the absence not just of faith in God, but of God—Father, Son and Holy Ghost—for what is God without faith?—in the absence of all that, we look for other signs that we are not dead, that we are living, much as it can be said that we are.

And even though Lathias understood it, he could only sit in helpless amazement while the boy's face screwed up in humiliation, yes, and in rage, too; the repressed and unfathomable rage of the vulnerable, the castigated, the reviled. And because Lathias did not know what to do, what to say, he just stuck his cigarette into the corner of his mouth, swung his leg back over the saddle and lifted his reins from the pommel.

"Let's go," he said over his shoulder, but the boy just stood there.

"Aren't you coming?" Elisabeth said, and when the boy did not respond, she drew up the reins herself. "Come," she said.

But the boy sat down on a small boulder and turned his back to them.

Elisabeth watched him a bit, then she tapped the reins to the horse's neck and rode past him, and past Lathias.

Lathias waited.

"Come on," he said to the boy. "Ride on with me. Like old times."

Still he did not respond.

And Lathias thought, *He just needs some time,* and so he followed the girl toward the river, slowly, so that the boy could catch up when he was ready, thinking, as parents have uncomprehendingly thought of their children, lovers of their loves, those who wait of those who leave, universally and throughout the ages, *He has been foolish, and now maybe he knows it, he will just need some time.* Not realizing that time can magnify as well as diminish.

After they had ridden a bit, Lathias reined in and turned, but the boy was not there on the boulder. At first he thought, *So he has gone home, then,* and he looked back along their route from the farm but could see him nowhere. Lathias was just about to call out, though the wind would have made it pointless, when he did see him. He was stretched out in the long grass by the Horseman's graves, and he thought, with some irritation, *Well, and what is he up to now?*

When he saw that the boy's arms and legs jerked in the grass, Lathias's gut clenched. He yanked the startled mare around and dug his heels, sickened with the possibility that he might not get there in time, that the boy might swallow his own tongue. Sick with the knowledge that he had stood by and let the boy upset himself, had done nothing to calm him. That he had as much as walked away from him.

He leapt down before the mare had even stopped, and stumbled to him, sliding to his knees, and he took the boy's head in his hands.

"Hey," he said, "hey." Wanting the boy to focus on him.

But the fit had already passed. The boy lay motionless and spent, staring up at that impossible dome of sky at Lathias's back, mesmerized, as if he could see through it to all that lay beyond, unmoved by what he saw there, however horrifying or glorious.

Lathias held the boy's head and talked to him, the way he always would, not really saying anything, just talking, the way you might talk to an infant. "Shh, shh, there now, it's all right, there, there, all right now."

The boy did not say anything, just lay with his eyes closed now and his arm up over his face, to block the sun, Lathias thought, and he shifted his own body to further shade him. But then he could see the boy was crying a little, and so he stopped talking, too, and pretended that he had not seen the tears streaming out from beneath his arm, and he just sat and held him and watched the green, sweet grasses rippling across the Horseman's graves.

He sensed her behind him before he saw her, and that feeling of distrust, dislike, rose within him. What business had she there? He glanced over his shoulder, expecting that old familiar look of revulsion, or even fear, that the boy's fits seemed to inspire. But she just stood there beside the boy's horse, much as she had while the boy had been telling her about the Horseman, with the reins in her hand and that bottom lip sucked in, that lip the exact colour of wild roses. Lathias turned away.

Finally she said, "What's the matter with him?"

Lathias told her, briefly, grudgingly. She said nothing, only sat down in the grass, a little apart from them and facing slightly away, and Lathias had to respect her, in spite of himself, for that small courtesy. Surely she had seen the tears, too.

After a moment, she said, "You should stroke his hair," and Lathias asked her why, and she said, "That's what I'd want someone to do. If it were me."

The boy uncovered his eyes and looked over at her then, and Lathias was astonished to realize by the look on the boy's face that, though his tears were real, he had been pretending, had faked, the seizure. His cheeks were rosy and pink from the sun, not bloodless and deflated, the way they always were when he came to. And he had none of the drained exhaustion in his eyes. They were reddened and puffy with tears, but they were not hollow; they glittered brightly beneath lids half closed against the light of that veilless sky.

And for the first time since they'd known each other, Lathias felt angry with the boy. Angry and shocked and disgusted, yes, he had to admit it. He had never known the boy to deliberately deceive that way, had not even thought him capable of such pure and calculated dishonesty. Such manipulation.

Lathias opened his mouth to say something, to give some voice to his anger, but then, for the second time that morning, he shut it just as quickly. What could he say? So he helped the boy to sit up and then he turned his head away and pretended that he had not noticed the pretending. And thought to himself, *So we have begun to deceive each other. And her, too. We hardly know her and already we are tied to her in this deception, this deception because of and for her.*

And yet, even as he blamed her, even as he resented her presence, the way she had changed things between them, between him and the boy, in spite of all that, he liked her. Could not help himself, the way she sat there so unobtrusively, with her back to them. He liked her quietness, her seriousness, the way she frowned and considered before speaking. She was not like any other girl he had known. She seemed older, yes. Wiser and sadder. And he liked that, also, her sadness. Liked that most of all, not because it made her vulnerable, but just the opposite: somehow, her grief made her stronger. And there was something else, too; something he couldn't quite put his finger on.

"It wasn't hate," she said then, quietly.

Lathias did not answer at first. He sat looking out over the Horseman's graves, thinking about it. Finally he said, without turning to face her, "What was it?"

"It was love," she said. "Just love."

EIGHT

Father Rieger agreed to baptize the girl in a small private ceremony, not out of generosity or devotion or enthusiasm or duty even, but only to have the thing done and Leo out of his hair (knowing, as did everyone else, that were he, Father, to refuse the rite, Leo would not let it alone: the girl must be baptized, and soon). And like everyone else, Father had to wonder why, what exactly Leo was up to now.

"Ach," Mike said, "he's just concerned for the girl."

And everyone else, including Marian, exchanged looks which Mike chose to ignore.

"Anyway," he said, "that's his business, not? That's between him and God."

And someone said, out of the corner of his mouth, "I thought he *was* God."

And Mike chose to ignore this, also. "Let them have some privacy, anyway," he said, "if not for Leo, then for the girl and her mother." And he nodded, pleased with his words. "Live," he added, "and let live."

But privacy was not in Leo's plan. He insisted things be done right, as he said to an already irritable and impatient Father

Rieger one morning after Mass—while Mary and Elisabeth waited, a little apart from the others who chatted in the vestibule with one eye fixed on Leo and Father—insisted that nothing be left out, either because of, as he said, laziness (here Father flared up silently, excused himself and walked stiffly down the aisle to the confessional, entered and closed the door firmly behind him, leaving Leo sitting and staring after him, then emerged a moment later, crossed himself, and returned), or, said Leo here, because of miserliness either (to which Father could only excuse himself again, adjourn to the confessional and then return), after which Leo sat blinking at him and said, "That's not the outhouse, you know," at which point Father excused himself again, walked back down the aisle, through the vestibule, out the double doors, climbed into his wagon and disappeared down the road, leaving Leo to sit waiting, until the stained-glass windows began to turn shadowed, at which time he must have realized that Father had no intention of returning, and, feeling not a little put out, walked outside to find that Mary and Elisabeth had gone home without him. He climbed into his wagon and snapped the reins.

When he pulled into his yard, he found Mike Weiser waiting for him, sitting in the old cane chair on the porch.

"What are you doing here?" he said. "Where's Mary?" And he hollered for her across the yard.

"No," Mike said, "no, no, that's all right. We can talk out here. No need to trouble Mary." Though no one had come to the door when he'd knocked, anyway. "Father was to see me."

"Yah," Leo flared up, "and what does he mean leaving me sitting there? What kind of a shepherd is that, who leaves his flock?"

"Ach, Leo." Mike shook his head. "Father says he will baptize the girl. Saturday."

Leo blinked. "Sunday, not?"

"No," he said. "Saturday."

"And what kind of a baptism is on Saturday? It must be Sunday and that's that."

"But, Leo, a little privacy is not so bad. You know how people talk. And Mary so shy, and the girl . . ." He glanced toward the barn and lowered his voice. Though there was no sign of her, Mike knew somehow that she was there, listening from the shadows. "Well," he said, looking back up to where Leo still sat in the wagon. "Maybe it's better that way."

"What is better? Sunday is the Holy Day, the Lord's Day, and Sunday it will be."

Mike sighed. "After Mass, then." Though he knew it was no use, the man was stubborn as a post and, Mike was only now beginning to see, just as dumb. "Meet Father halfway at least."

"What halfway? Limbo?"

Leo slowly climbed down from his wagon and walked up his porch steps. Then, with one hand on the latch, he looked down at Mike and said, "We'll be there Sunday. At Mass. If he don't baptize the girl, I will."

And nodding, he entered the shack, letting the door slam shut behind him.

———

Sunday came, and with Mike and Marian Weiser standing by as godparents, and with Leo and Mary and Lathias and the boy and his parents and the rest of the congregation looking on, the girl bent her wild head over the font. Father, tight-lipped, dipped a bit of water (to which someone quipped, "Give him some soap while he's at it"), and the girl claimed Jesus Christ as her Saviour and was thereby officially baptized, as far as anyone present knew or cared, into the Catholic Church and the Kingdom of Heaven, without incident or upheaval, earthly or otherwise.

NINE

If Leo cared one way or another that Elisabeth spent every Sunday down at the river with them—with Lathias and the boy—he certainly gave no indication, at least not that any of them noticed, not at first anyway.

Each Sunday after church, the girl would walk over to Schoffs', cutting across the fields, past the row of granaries, skirting the edge of the yard, to the barn where Lathias and the boy waited with the horses, the boy toting the lard tin that held the lunch he had packed, enough for the three of them and a little extra for Elisabeth. They would mount the horses, Elisabeth riding behind the boy, and cross the yard toward the river. Helen was often at the window watching them go, though no one but Lathias seemed to notice her there. And Stolanus, in his heavy, pleasant, baffled way, lifting a thick hand at them from wherever he happened to be occupying himself in the yard, calling after them lightly, each time, "Yah, don't go too fast, but make home come quickly," which didn't quite make sense, as it was generally a farewell to departing visitors. But that was Stolanus, always just missing the mark; how he managed to prosper, no one really understood, and so they could only assume it must have been by the grace of God.

From Schoffs' they would ride, always single file—Lathias, then Elisabeth and the boy—across the Horseman's wind-rushed pasture, past the graves, off the plains and into the valley, another world. They took the raft across to the fort most days now. Elisabeth had begun to collect a few glass bottles there of green and amber and blue that she would wash in the river and tuck into the pockets of her dress, "For the cotton-wood tree."

Of the three of them, it was she now who found and kept the most things, who would continue to scour the fields around the fort and the cutbank long after Lathias and the boy had tired of it and waited for her crouched beside the raft, hoping she would notice their waiting, though she never did, or if she did, she did not care. She would search until her pockets were filled—some-times only with stones that had, for whatever reason, caught her fancy—and then she would take her collection to the river's edge and wash and then dry and polish them on her skirt, holding up to the sunlight the objects rescued from obliteration, every conceivable scrap a treasure. Once she found a ragged length of yellow sateen ribbon, quite wide, dirty and pale with age and fraying at the edges where the threads had come unwoven. But she took that down to the water, too, and scrubbed and scrubbed and wrung it out and smoothed it on a rock in the sun. When it was dry, she tied it up in her hair, and Lathias crouched there watching her, thinking that old rag was probably the prettiest thing she'd ever had in her life; or if it wasn't, she sure wore it like it was.

Sometimes they would not cross the river, but stay on the near bank beneath the Bull's Forehead, where the boy would paddle and float in the cool, murky water while Lathias sat and smoked and watched, and Elisabeth waded around the edge and hummed and sometimes talked to herself or repeated nonsense rhymes in the old tongue:

"A B C
Die Katze liegt im Schnee,
der Schnee geht weg,
die Katze liegt im Dreck,
Dreck geht weg,
Katze isch verreckt."

But she never entered the water past her shins. The boy would tease her sometimes, splash at her where she waded in the shallows, believing it was the water that she feared. But Lathias knew better. Elisabeth cared nothing for the slow, swirling, opaque river, or even for the venomous rattlesnakes that sometimes hunted mice and rabbits in the brush at the water's edge and which they could sometimes, in high summer, hear humming there; rather, she detested, even feared, in a disgusted, superior sort of way, the enormous, benign bullsnakes and for no other reason than that they had once come upon one with its jaws around the head and upper body of a young rabbit (though the boy, out of intentional blindness, insisted it must be a rat, or at the very least a gopher, and so Lathias let him believe it was so). All three of them had crouched there in the brush and watched while the snake inched its mouth, with impeccable, slow precision, down the rest of the animal until the entire rabbit had been consumed and the snake lay there in the sun, swollen and sluggish, unable to move even when Elisabeth jabbed a stick at it, and clicked her tongue in disgust. Lathias knew, too, that it was not the gross predation she disliked, the devouring of the prey, but rather the dumb and satiated defencelessness of the predator.

"If I had a hatchet," she'd said suddenly, "I'd hack that thing in two."

The boy had looked up at her in surprise, shock even, his eyes glazed with fascination and a mild horror.

"Why?" he said.

But Elisabeth ignored him.

"I'd chop its ugly head off," she said. "I'd shoot it," she said, "if I had a gun."

But she had only the stick, so she gave one vicious whack that curled the bloated snake in upon itself with surprising suddenness and made the boy jump—as if he were the one who had been struck—and then she ran off.

From then on, Lathias noticed, she spent most of her time in the water at the edge of the river, where she poked her long stick into the mud at random, as far out as she could reach (since, by her own admission, she could not swim), looking, she claimed, for the pits of quicksand that Lathias had told her peppered the river bottom beneath the Bull's Forehead on either side of the ford-ing place and at least as far east as the ferry-crossing at Estuary, probably even beyond.

Since the river was low, the boy sometimes suggested they wade across along the gravel bars visible just beneath the surface, but Lathias would forbid it, remembering his grandmother's sto-ries of those who had disappeared—an older cousin; a guide for the fur traders; a young officer from the detachment at Harrison's Landing—as if pulled by the devil himself into the dark river bot-tom when the water was low enough to tempt them across.

His grandmother had told him once about the two Mounties who had crossed there, right beneath the Bull's Forehead, right where they now sat, how the first made it across, but the second, the younger, who, for whatever reason, had not followed care-fully the footprints his companion had left in the mud, became trapped, struggled, the other Mountie trying to pull him out, try-ing, trying, until the mud was at the man's chin, in his mouth, and he begged his companion, *Shoot me.* And the other man had pulled his revolver, cocked it and aimed, and the other praying, begging, eyes squeezed shut, *For God's sake.* But in the end, the man could not pull the trigger, could only sit and watch as his friend went down, or maybe he did not watch, but sat with his eyes shut tight and only listened.

Lathias would look out at the shallow, dark water and he would think about the fabled bodies down there suspended upright in a watery darkness, airless and permanent and cold even in the heat of August, the river flowing endlessly above them and the long frozen winters there beneath the ice and he would feel cold, too, in spite of the heat that settled into the valley, and then he would rise and call his companions and they would return home, wondering at Lathias's silence. But most days, he would just sit and smoke and not think of those darker things. He would watch the boy swim, and watch the girl, too, but only out of the corner of his eye (her hair wild and the hem of her white dress wet with the river). He would not turn from the boy while he was in the water, not for an instant. (Though he did not say, *Not even for her.* Instead he told himself, *Especially not for her,* and he could let himself believe that was the truth.)

On those days, they would eat a slow lunch and then, while it was still half light, they would ride back up one of the draws, Elisabeth and the boy in the lead and Lathias following, watching the hem of her dress drying in the desiccated air, stiffened and brown with river water, her slim and dirty ankles against the horse's flanks, rising palely out of the ugly dark shoes like the stems of cattail reeds in winter; the horses lunging and picking their way across the barrel cactus and the prickly pears closing their brief yellow blooms to the coming dark, and up and out onto the prairie where the morning's wind had finally begun to settle, as it almost always did before sunset, as if its cycles, too, relied upon the rising and the setting of the sun, and all that great grassy land stretching before them, calmed and stilled, and even the Horseman's graves quietened now with the slow coming of evening.

TEN

By August, in those long, airless, languorous days before harvest, Lathias had more time to spend with them, with Elisabeth and the boy, and they would ride down to the river most afternoons, when chores were done and there was little to do until supper but sit and mend tack and smoke, watching through narrowed eyes the rippling crops ripening in the sun (though sometimes now Elisabeth came much sooner, came almost before breakfast was through, and sat wordlessly on the rails in the barn or the stables, fiddling with a thread on the cuff of her dress and watching, from beneath her hair, Lathias go quietly about the morning's work; sometimes she was already there waiting for him in the shadowed corners of the barn when he rolled the big doors open, though he would not admit that he looked for her there, would not admit that he could sense her before he even saw her, as if she were not a living, breathing being, but only the memory, the ghost, of one who had once been, one he had known; as if, even upon seeing, he did not see, but only remembered. They would not speak as he went about the chores, but just exist uncomfortably there together in a hot, disturbing mutual silence, the dust motes turning in the morning light and the slow scratchings and mutterings of the farm coming to life around them.

Once, as Lathias was scooping buckets of oats from the feed bin in the barn, she said, quite unexpectedly, "I heard something about you."

Lathias stopped and stood looking at her, the bucket half raised in the bin.

When he did not reply, she said—looking smug, he thought, but a little frightened, too, or watchful, as if she was not sure how he would react to what she would say, whether she should say it at all—"He told me. Leo did."

Lathias did not, as a rule, care much what Leo Krauss thought or said. But with her sitting there, leaning toward him, while the dust motes turned slow spirals in the air between, he wanted to know: *What, what did Leo tell you? About the accident? Is that what he said?* Feeling that old creeping horror and despair, that rush of guilt like the dark thundering of a hundred hooves. He almost did ask her, but something stopped him: the implication of her words, the intimacy. Not what she knew, but the fact of her knowing, the way it brought her into his life without bringing him into hers.

He straightened and wiped a hand across his mouth and looked at her, was about to speak, when she said, so quietly, "I'll tell you." Her eyes glittering with an emotion Lathias could not identify. "A halfbreed. That's what he said. A dirty good-for-nothing halfbreed."

Something in Lathias relaxed, then. Or not relaxed, but slowed, that pounding against the earth. Slowed, and sickened. It was not what he had thought. Not the accident at all. *Halfbreed. Dirty. Good-for-nothing.* The same old words he'd heard all his life, from his own mother even. Now from her. On her lips. And he thought, fiercely, *Her, too. Her. Everyone. Always.* Thinking, *What does it matter, anyway? What could it?* But he knew in his heart this, too, was a lie.

Elisabeth leaned forward on the rail. "Is it true?" she said.

And perhaps without meaning to, perhaps out of habit, he said, as he did with the boy, "Does it matter?"

Their voices so thick and quiet it was as if they had not spoken at all, only watched each other through the lazy turn of chaff, the moment drawing itself out until it seemed that one or the other of them surely must do something, must speak, though that was not possible, either.

When they heard the boy climbing heavily across the fence and down into the dirt of the corral outside the barn doors, Lathias turned quickly away and bent and dipped the bucket full and hoisted it up, and then the boy called, "Aren't you yet done?"

But Lathias did not reply, only stood with his bucket and watched as Elisabeth jumped down soundlessly from the rail upon which she sat and walked out of the barn doors, disappearing into a flare of light in the yard.

———

The remainder of that long dry summer passed in the mute intimacy of routine, the invariance of their days. The boy did not notice that something subtle had changed between them, or did not seem to notice. And to each other, Lathias and Elisabeth spoke little. She no longer waited for him there in the barn and he told himself that he did not notice her absence. Most afternoons they rode down to the river, the same way always, wordless, single file, as if they were strangers, and sometimes with fishing poles and buckets of bruised worms the boy had plucked from the manure pile. Their catches never amounted to much: a few muddy pickerel and pike, never the ancient, monstrous sturgeon which on rare occasions they glimpsed arching its dark spine from the water and which Lathias knew the boy secretly angled for (and secretly feared), though of course he never said as much. Most often they went to the same spot beneath the Bull's Forehead, where the banks were lined thickly with willow brush beneath which they could find some small shade, and privacy, too, on those occasions when others came to the river.

It was no real concern of theirs, those few who came to the river to fish or swim or picnic, as they were almost always farther downstream from the Bull's Forehead, down where the near bank of the river levelled into a broad sandbar and the willow brush gave way to a few big, parched cottonwoods drooping their dusty branches out over the brown water. Someone had hung a rope swing there, from one of the larger branches, many years ago—three decades almost, according to those who claimed to remember—but as far as anyone knew, no one used it, not since that first day it was strung up and Ollie Werner gave the inaugural jump to cheers and whistles, whooping as he sailed out over the water, blowing an exaggerated kiss to his pregnant young wife, who shook her head and frowned in mock displeasure and said, "Ach, but he's a child himself," before he plunged, grinning, beneath the murky surface and never reappeared. The last anyone ever saw of him, a briefly swirling brown eddy that uncoiled itself and flowed on, tranquil and inexorably to the east.

Since then the rope had hung lifeless, ghostly as a noose, though of course no one would take it down; would not tempt God and Fate.

For a few years afterwards the picnics stopped, from reasons of respect or superstition, no one was certain. But after the war, when the single tragedy of Ollie Werner had been put into grim perspective, people began to return again to the open, sandy spot on the river and Ollie Werner became little more than a folk tale, a rumour, *Had it happened even?* And by now well accustomed to the necessity of selective forgetting, everyone laughed and joked through the deafening hum of grasshoppers up the draw, and drank their rich, dark chokecherry wine (the air sweet with it, mingled with the musk of sagebrush and yarrow and wolf willow baking in the sun, until no one could tell any longer whether their heads buzzed pleasantly with the wine or with the hot perfumed air), and sat with their sleeves and their pantlegs rolled up and their summer dresses hiked past their knees in the shade of the cottonwoods shushing dryly and throwing beams of sunlight from their leaves like daggers, or floated and splashed about in the wide brown river, tepid as bathwater (the children taunting each other farther and farther out, to where the currents swirled crazily, *Be careful Ollie doesn't get you, he's down there, you know,* until an alert parent roared them onto the bank, where they sat shivering in the relentless sun, elbowing and jostling each other briskly and pretending disdain to hide their relief).

On picnic days, the boy often stood slightly downriver, staring shamelessly, and Lathias would try to distract, coax him away. Elisabeth, on the other hand, pretended she could neither see nor hear anything, anyone, though sometimes Lathias saw her flinch and glance up when the girls squealed and flapped and shrieked (not in alarm or distress but in giddy encouragement, the sound like the incomprehensible, moon-addled screechings of pheasant hens in autumn). But she was always quick to recover and carry on poking her stick into the mud, steadily, the hot flush of her cheeks beneath her blowing hair the only thing to betray her.

————

Then it was almost September, and the land had grown golden, crunched dryly beneath their boots, and the days were shorter and Lathias became busy with the late harvest, leaving the house before sunup, returning at dusk, or sometimes after, when he would wash hastily by that long sliver of light at the western horizon, rubbing his hands and face and neck under the pump in the yard, half asleep before he had even climbed the ladder to the loft, awake again before he was aware he had slept, dreaming what he saw during waking hours—the endless swaths, the hot golden rush of grain, the suffocating, impermeable bell of sky burned white—until one day simply bled into the next and the moon rose hugely each night, red and swollen with the dust of the fields and the days red also and everything so hot and dry that fires began to flare up at the Sand Hills, where the brush was thickest, but without any recognizable cause, it seemed, as if by their own volition, and the men would ride watch-parties out though they could hardly be spared from the fields. But they took their shifts, all of them except for Leo Krauss, though by now no one had any expectations of him, who lived on their periphery, out there on the edge of the Hills. Some even suspected Leo was the cause of the fires.

"Well, and what for? What sense is there in that?" some said.

"God, when has sense ever had anything to do with a Krauss?"

And others: "Ach, leave him alone already."

"That's right, it couldn't have been Leo. Striking a match, that's too much work."

But as no one had any proof either for or against him and even those who saw no reason to blame him could not deny that he was capable of anything, they were left to their speculations, and so the blame—or at the very least, the suspicion—fell upon Leo by default and natural inclination. The rest all took their watch shifts, even Lathias, in spite of his long unease with the Hills, his grandmother's stories of the dead who walked there and his own almost-belief that it was the place where the Horseman rode in those long dark hours when the rest of the land slept. But how could he refuse? What could he say, *I will not go out there after sunset, those hills are haunted, the place where the dead walk*? No, he took his shift, riding out after a day in the field, at dusk, going as close to the Hills as he dared, the hair on the back of his neck rippled up like hackles on a dog and his hands so tense on the reins, his mare yanked her head and laid her ears flat and stepped erratically in the gathering dark. And so he spoke softly to the horse, "Easy now, easy, it's nothing," not to calm her, but to calm himself, to hear a human voice, his voice, puny under that huge, bruised sky, starless and scorched; the briefly windless, Godless hills rising before him, all darkened and golden and somehow alive, too, eerie and alive, more than alive, in that way that only the dead can appear to be. His own voice dead, too, so that, after a moment of talking, he realized it was better, even, to be silent.

It was then, in the dusk and unease of his own silence, that he heard, felt, the rattling of the Horseman out on the plains at his back, the eerie clacking of bones, and he reined in the agitated mare and sat prickling in the saddle.

That was when he saw her, or rather, saw what he at first thought, hoped, was a deer, stepping from the leafless branches of a willow, ghostly and profound. The mare lifted her head and stamped. Of course, it was Elisabeth, could only be her. It was somehow no surprise either that she should be out there, after dark, alone in the Hills. It was no surprise at all. And he knew, too, that she had seen him, had, in fact, been watching him, had perhaps even heard him talking stupidly to his horse. Had, perhaps, laughed at him, at the fear in his voice. He saw her slip out from the willow and run through the darkness, toward Leo's place, and he stopped himself—ashamed that he had even thought it—from calling out to her.

ELEVEN

October came and Lathias had more time to spend with them again, with the boy and Elisabeth. On sunny afternoons they would still ride down to the river, the valley stretching out before them, the leaves mostly gone from the scrub and willow and cottonwoods, the gullies and draws deeper, colder, with the lengthened shadows, the quick coming of November; the long grasses beneath their boots blackened with night frosts, the silence broken only by the occasional calls of wild geese flying in eerie formation across the sky stretching impossibly blue above them. At home, the grain was in the bins, the vegetables from the garden stored and waiting in the root cellar, the jars of preserves arranged in precise rows, the animals slaughtered, bled, skinned and ground into richly spiced meats and hung to cure, and everything quietened. Even the fires out at the Sand Hills had stopped. Everyone said, "See, what did I say? It was too much work for him after all," and, "Yah, that's right, Leo needs a rest now, too," and Lathias listened, and nodded and said nothing.

———

All Hallows' Eve arrived at Schoffs' the way it always did: without furtive rides after midnight across dark fields to the neighbours' to release livestock from pens or hoist farm equipment onto the roofs of barns or, if someone was at home, to knock and rattle and howl until finally invited in and given coffee or more often a warm drink of whisky in the light of the kerosene lantern and some bread and sausage and apple kuchen and maybe a hand or two of cards at the kitchen table before riding home considerably warmed to find your own chickens squawking disconsolately from the roof of your house.

At Schoffs', there were no pranks played: neither by them, nor to them. Only Stolanus and Helen and Lathias and the boy sitting around the table after supper, when the evening chores were done, and Helen offering to roast apples but no one but the boy wanting any, and nothing to say until Stolanus boomed, as he always did, "Well, and I hope we have no tricksters tonight, eh? Who knows but we'll find the cow in the outhouse tomorrow."

And no one either answering or looking at him, and even Stolanus not believing it himself.

Lathias excused himself, as he always did, and wished them good night, and the boy sat watching him go.

———

Halfway across the yard, Lathias knew, without seeing, that she was there.

"What are you doing?" he said into the darkness, hoping he was not wrong, but then again, who would hear if he was?

"Nothing," came the answer from beside the barn, and then he could see her, that white dress filled and glowing with moonlight.

"You should have put a coat on," he said.

"Why?"

"I can see you from here."

"I wasn't hiding."

He stood in the middle of the yard, neither approaching her nor veering away toward the barn doors. After a while she stepped a bit closer. He could see, then, that she had something wrapped around her shoulders, a blanket or a shawl.

"Anyway," she said, "it's not cold."

"Cold enough," he said, but she made no reply. "What are you doing?" he said again.

"Playing pranks," she said. "Isn't that what everyone does?"

"Not on him," he said, meaning the boy. "Don't do anything to him."

"I didn't," she said. "I wasn't going to."

"Oh," he said. "On me, then."

"No," she said, "not on you either."

He shifted his feet in the dirt. From the henhouse came the comforting sounds of cooing. A horse sighed from the stable.

Lathias looked up to the one window in the loft, then down at the open barn door.

"You think I was up there," she said, "up in the barn."

Lathias said nothing.

"What would I even want up there?"

Her voice had a strange quality, tremulous, as if she were shivering. Lathias rubbed his own hands together in the cool air and waited.

"I don't care nothing about your things. Whatever you have up there. Which is nothing, probably."

Still, he waited.

"I wasn't out playing any prank on you," she said, softer.

"Who, then?"

"Who do you think?"

"I don't want to guess."

"Don't, then."

"Pranks," he said, "like those fires?" He had not thought he would say anything about that, had not planned to. He could almost feel her stiffen in the darkness.

"That wasn't me," she said coldly.

"Who was it, then?"

"How should I know?"

"I saw you," he said.

"I saw you, too. Does that mean you started the fires?"

"You know what I was doing out there."

"Maybe I was doing the same."

"And Leo? Where was he?"

As soon as he said it, he was sorry. He did not know why he'd said it, did not even know what he'd meant by it. But he knew immediately it was the wrong thing to say.

She was silent for so long, he thought she would not respond. Finally he saw her dress stir in the darkness, as if she had been leaning against something, or sitting, and now she had risen.

"You don't know nothing about that."

And she turned and walked away, disappearing gradually into the night, that white dress growing fainter and fainter across the prairie, as if it absorbed the darkness, and he did not call after her.

When he reached the loft, he lit the kerosene lantern there and sat, looking around to see what she had done, scanning the room, his few belongings, lifting the covers on his bed even, looking under the pillow, lifting the covers again. But there was nothing.

———

The following day, the first of November, All Saints', she did not turn up at the Schoff place. Lathias and the boy rode to the river alone and, by mid-afternoon of that day, as if by some divine ordination, some law of the dead, the weather turned suddenly cold and the sky greyed over in one long, bleak sheet and the wind rose out of the north and blasted dull aches into the backs of their skulls as they stood on the riverbank, their hands jammed into pockets or covering their ears, and checked the slow progress of the ice across the water.

———

She came back, of course, the following week, and acted as if All Hallows' Eve had never happened. They both did. And so their trips to the river continued, much the same as they always had, except that now they went with a purpose: the checking of the ice. A huge herd of antelope had started coming down, too, just upriver from them. Sometimes the boy would bring carrots and try to tempt them closer, but they just stood on the bank and eyed him stiffly, ready to bolt should he take a step forward. And so he stood waiting, barely allowing himself to breathe, believing that if he held still long enough, they would come to him.

"Don't bother," Elisabeth said. "They won't come."

"Why won't they?" the boy asked.

But she did not answer.

One afternoon, when the river had almost sheeted straight across, Elisabeth moved to step onto the ice and Lathias grabbed her by the arm and yanked her back, letting her go just as quickly.

"It's not ready yet," he said, turning away, sticking his hand back into his pocket.

"How do you know," she said, "if you don't step on it?"

"It hasn't been cold long enough yet."

"How do you know when it's been cold long enough?"

Lathias shrugged. "You just know."

Then, as if on cue, one of the antelope from the herd upriver put one hoof out, stepped back, then stepped out again, tentatively.

"Why's she going out there?" the boy said. "Chase her back."

"They want to cross," Lathias said.

"But she'll go through," he said. "It's not thick enough."

"No," Lathias said. "She'll go back."

He was right. The doe stood there a moment and then retreated, back up onto the bank, and the whole herd moved off again, upriver.

Elisabeth watched from beneath her blowing hair. She still wore her black kerchief from the summer and over this she had pulled an ugly grey knitted hat that looked as if it had been stitched together from old socks, but her hands were bare and red. She lifted them to her mouth and blew on them and then, as if it were the most natural thing to do next, she stepped out onto the ice and her foot went through and she was plunged into water up to her knee.

"What are you doing?" the boy cried. "You're lucky it wasn't deep there."

"I know where it's deep," she said irritably, pulling herself out. "Do you think I'm stupid?"

This time, Lathias did nothing to help her, and she hauled herself out and stood dripping onto the bank.

"You'll freeze," the boy said. "Let's go home."

"I'm not cold," she said, wringing water out of the hem of her dress.

But when Lathias and the boy turned to walk up the draw, she followed.

Finally, around the end of November, Lathias cut six blocks of wood, about three inches by eight, a little longer for himself, and wrapped each block around once with wire; then he ran a thin leather strap under the wire on the top side of each block and they all—Lathias and the boy and Elisabeth—carried these skates to the river and strapped them onto their shoes and boots. They spent the afternoon out on the ice, with Lathias like an old woman cautioning them back near the banks when one or the other strayed too far out to where the ice thinned and thinned and thinned until it became a narrow band of black, swirling water.

From then on, as long as the weather was good, they spent most afternoons at the river. It was the boy, and not Lathias, who first noticed that Elisabeth never had enough clothes to keep her warm, and who suggested they bring extra. Lathias doubted whether she would accept them, and it was the boy, again, who suggested they bring a sack of clothes for all of them to put on when they strapped on their skates, so as not to single out

Elisabeth. To Lathias's surprise, Elisabeth accepted the extra clothing, watching carefully to make certain that Lathias and the boy donned theirs as well (though the extra and unnecessary layers made movement, particularly for the boy, somewhat strained). Lathias knew very well that Elisabeth was not fooled, but that she had decided, for whatever reason, perhaps of sheer necessity, to participate in their mutual deception, though she was always careful to remove all the borrowed clothing before leaving the river, in spite of the boy's entreaties that she keep them.

Only later did he realize it had nothing to do with pride, and began to suspect other, less noble motives; began to suspect that, for whatever reason, toward whatever end, she wanted someone—either Leo or her mother—to see her suffer.

———

Around this time, around the end of November or a little later, Leo started coming to the river. Not all the way down into the valley, but just to the edge where the trail began its steep descent, where he could sit in his wagon and look down and see them— Lathias, the boy, Elisabeth—wordlessly gliding along on the ice that glittered harshly in the unbroken winter sunlight.

The first time Lathias noticed, he called to Elisabeth, "Look, there's Leo."

And she did look, but not directly, just out of the corner of her eye, as if she did not want Leo to know she'd seen him. Her lack of surprise made Lathias wonder if Leo had been there before, watching them. Elisabeth only glanced up calmly, and then she did a very odd thing, Lathias thought, very odd indeed. Though she was a good skater (rather the best of the three of them, those long arms and legs were all grace and lightness when she was on the ice, her red hair swirling out behind her), though she rarely so much as stumbled on that cracked and uneven and dirt-pocked surface, on this particular occasion, when Lathias said, *There's Leo,* and when she'd looked at him, Leo, sideways, she tripped, hard, and fell face forward, banging her chin brutally on the ice. She'd cut her lip, or bit it, and blood ran steadily down her chin onto the ice. The boy and Lathias skated over and helped her up, but she brushed them away, saying she was all right, she was fine, and never mind, never mind, and she did seem to be fine, but there was blood everywhere, so red against the icy blue of the frozen river and her pale skin, that the boy in particular was quite alarmed, teary-eyed almost, Lathias could see by the way he scrunched his face up and reached out tentatively to touch Elisabeth's sleeve. She wiped the blood away and said, "It's nothing," but Lathias saw her look up the valley, to see if Leo was still there. Lathias looked, too, and he wasn't, and he wondered if Leo had seen the fall. But when he turned back to Elisabeth, she had finished wiping the blood from her chin and was already skating away from them, as if nothing had happened.

Leo came back a few times; he never stayed long, and there was no repetition of the incident, or anything like it. Eventually, the boy noticed him too, but, oddly, never mentioned it to Elisabeth.

Once, though, Lathias watched as the boy lifted a hand tentatively in greeting, a casual gesture, easy enough to return, but Leo did nothing of the kind, just sat there in the wagon staring down at them. Either he had not seen the boy wave, or he had simply ignored him, out of spite, or history (for though Leo Krauss had little enough to do with Stolanus Schoff now, the bad blood between them, and between Pius and Gus, and before that, back across decades and an ocean, still seemed to run in a sour vein). Or perhaps it was simply the perverseness of a man completely unconcerned with rightness or propriety or plain old common neighbourliness and civility. After a moment, the boy dropped his hand, and Lathias looked quickly away, so that the boy would not know that he had seen.

Elisabeth, on the other hand, simply ignored Leo's presence completely. He might never have been there at all. And so, after the first two or three visits, Lathias and the boy did the same.

———

Around that time, too, Elisabeth happened to mention—as they rode toward the river, the breath of the horses pluming out into the cold—something about Leo's barn. Lathias pulled up his horse and turned to her in real shock.

"But," he said, "you don't mean you're still sleeping out there?"

Elisabeth blinked back at him. "Why not?"

Lathias stared a moment in annoyance, and she back at him, with the boy between them, looking from one to the other, until she said, "What are you waiting for? Let's go," and rode on.

Later, when they were alone on the riverbank, the boy said to Lathias, "Does she?"

"No," Lathias said. Then, "I don't know. I don't think so."

But, truly, he could not have said; it didn't seem possible, and yet, why wasn't it? With Leo, it seemed, anything was possible.

"But she must be freezing out there," the boy said. "How does she stay warm?"

Lathias shrugged vaguely. "The mule would be in there, too. And the cows, maybe. It might not be so bad."

But it did not make sense to him, either. And there was, for the first time, an idea forming, an unpleasant idea, but so obvious he wondered that it hadn't occurred to him before.

Elisabeth was already out on the ice and Lathias hurried with his skates and caught up to her, wondering should he ask or should he not.

Finally, he said, "Elisabeth, does Leo bother you?" Feeling his face flush up hotly from his collar.

She barely gave him a glance, said coolly, "Doesn't he bother everybody?"

And Lathias said, "That's not what I mean."

"I know what you mean." Flashing him a dark look before bending on the pretense of adjusting a skate. Angry now.

Lathias thought she would skate away from him then, he was sorry he'd brought it up at all, it was stupid of him, beyond stupid. But when she rose, she turned her bright eyes upon him, her nose running a little in the cold, and she said darkly, viciously, "So full of yourselves. All the same. You think that is the worst thing a man can do to a woman? The worst that can happen? There are things worse than that."

And then she did skate off, her feet cracking at the ice, her red hair fanning furiously behind her.

"Did you ask her?" the boy said, skating up beside him.

Lathias turned in surprise, both at the question and at the boy's presence at all; he had forgotten about him. He laid a hand on the boy's shoulder.

"What?" the boy said, seeing the expression on Lathias's face.

Lathias just shook his head and squinted out at the frozen river.

"Did you ask?" the boy said. "About the barn?"

"No. I didn't."

They both looked to where she skated downriver, a dark shadow against the blaze of ice, and Lathias, for some reason, felt compelled to give the boy's shoulder a little squeeze. The boy looked up at him, frowning a little, his face against the winter light.

"You should ask her," he said. "She shouldn't be sleeping out there."

"No." Lathias removed his hand from the boy's shoulder. "She shouldn't."

———

There are things worse than that. Far worse. Had she said that? Had she said *far*? Lathias turned it around in his mind all the rest of that week, in spite of himself, in spite of not wanting to imagine worse things, in spite of not being able to imagine worse things. Proving her right, as she must have known he would.

———

Around that time, also, during that first cold snap of winter, Elisabeth began to ask about the braucha. They had seen the old woman sometimes, more often in summer, ancient, working around her yard, her sprawling garden, or coming down to the river for water, lugging across her shoulders the branch, on which hung the two big wooden buckets that must have been terribly heavy when full.

The boy often said, "But we should go help her, she is so old."

Lathias had thought so, too, but he always said, "No, she doesn't want help."

"How do you know?" the boy would say.

He didn't, of course. But something about the old woman always stopped him from approaching her the way he might approach someone else; something about her kept people away, made everyone forget she was even there until a difficult labour or influenza or something else the doctors could not cure. Then they were all quick to pound on her door, no matter the hour, and summon her, without discussion of payment (most paid, of course, and generously, though it be in meat or flour or lard or coal; and if they did not, it was only because they could not, and this, too, was acceptable to the old woman), summon her into the dark hours of a prairie night, knowing they would not be refused. Sometimes Lathias thought it was not something about the old woman that kept people away but something about people that kept them from going to her. Something he felt in himself. Fear? Scorn? Partly those things, but not quite those, either. Something, rather, that made him think of the phrase *close to the bone*. And yet he couldn't have explained it.

When the boy was younger, before the accident, he'd had nightmares about her. This was when she had still come to church, draped from head to toe in thick, dusty black even on the hottest days of summer, walking in her slow, rolling gait the three miles there, sitting alone at the back of the church, walking the three miles home. When the new church was built at Knochenfeld, two miles farther each way, she stopped going. A witch, that is what the children called her, some of them, risking cuffs on the ears from their parents. But the braucha paid them no attention, only nodded if someone greeted her and went on her way.

There had been one time, though, when they—Stolanus and Helen and the boy and Lathias—had crossed paths with her at the door to the church, and, all of them pausing awkwardly to let her go ahead, the braucha had stopped also and looked up at Helen sharply and nodded and then quite unexpectedly laid a curled hand, a claw, upon the boy's head and muttered something, nodded again and walked on. So quick, it was as if it had not happened.

The boy, very young at the time, said, "Who was that woman?"

And Stolanus said quickly, lightly, "That is the Grandmother."

"My grandmother?" the boy said.

And Helen snapped, "Don't talk so silly, you know it is not."

The boy had begun to cry, then, perhaps because of Helen's sharpness, though none of them really knew the reason.

Helen reached down and wiped his tears and took him by the hand. Then, turning to Stolanus, she hissed, "What was that? What did she say?"

Stolanus shrugged. "Nothing. 'Good morning,' probably. What does it matter?"

And Helen said, "Don't be so stupid."

"Well, why not?" Stolanus said. "It was nothing. A blessing, maybe. I don't know."

And Helen rolled her eyes and stepped inside the church, the boy still sniffling at her side.

Lathias, who had been walking behind them, had heard what the old woman said, or thought he had: *Grace of God.* That's all. *Grace of God.* A simple blessing, as Stolanus had said.

That night, the boy had his first nightmare about her—or at least they all assumed it was her, the old woman he would speak of—and it was the first of many to come. Hot, babbling, sweaty, wide-eyed nightmares. And, then, when he lay senseless after the accident and Helen had finally agreed to send for the braucha, and the old woman had come and leaned over the boy smelling of earth and garlic in the dim swirled light of the kerosene lamp, and brushed dried herbs across his face and dangled her rosary there and daubed her saliva mixed with ashes on each of his eyelids, and muttered strange phrases and prayers beneath her breath, and closed her own eyes and said, in slow German, *Then I passed by and saw you kicking about in your blood. And as you lay there in your blood, I said to you, Live. I made you grow like a plant in the field. You grew up and were the most beautiful of jewels, your breast was formed and your hair grew, you who were naked and bare,* fingering her rosary over him, while Helen stood tight-lipped and pale in the corner, then Lathias had changed his own prayer from, *Please, God, let him live,* to *Please, God, don't let him wake now, not yet, not now.* And he had not, the boy, and it was only years after that it occurred to Lathias that the nightmares had gone away, or at least, the boy did not mention them and neither did Helen or Stolanus.

So one day as they sat at the river, staring up at her hut, Lathias had asked him, did he ever still dream of the braucha, and the boy said, "Why would I dream about her?" And Lathias said, "You used to," and the boy said, "Used to what?" So Lathias said, "Nothing," and he did not bring it up again.

But they would see her sometimes, when they were down at the river, carrying water or hoeing her garden or tending her chickens, and Elisabeth had asked once, that first summer, who she was and they had told her, and she had just nodded, yes, there had been a braucha in Dakota, too, and no more was said.

But this one mild Sunday early in December—Lathias was leaving the next morning with Stolanus for Maple Creek, to get supplies and treats for Christmas, oranges and peanuts and those hard bright candies the boy loved, and Lathias had it in mind that he should get something for Elisabeth, something from the boy, it would please him so and God knew she would likely not get anything at home, and so he was tossing it around in his head, wondering should he, shouldn't he (though he already knew what it would be: a hair ribbon, a yellow one)—they were sitting on the bank in the thin dusting of snow that had come the night before, sitting there unstrapping the skates from their boots, the pile of dry brush they had gathered for a fire between them. It was already near dusk, they had skated longer than usual, because of the mildness of the day, and now hurried to warm themselves at a fire before returning home. Elisabeth happened to look up, then, to see the old woman, the braucha, crossing the draw below her place, with a sack slung over her shoulder.

"Look," she said, pointing with her chin, "St. Nicholas."

Though neither the boy nor Lathias laughed.

"What's she got in there?" Elisabeth asked.

Lathias said, "Cow chips."

He didn't want to say any more about it, knowing that they— Elisabeth and Mary—burned chips for fuel, also. Hardly anybody else did, almost everyone could afford coal, and the odour from the chips was strong and unmistakable. Lathias could sometimes smell it on Elisabeth's clothes and in her hair, a terrible smell, though on her it was not terrible, but rather earthy; a good smell, like dirt.

So Lathias knelt before the brush pile and reached into his coat pocket for matches.

Elisabeth was still sitting there, staring up at the old woman.

"I wonder if she ever gets lonely," she said, "living like that."

Lathias struck the match and held it to the brush. It flamed up instantly, the dry twigs snapping and crackling. He tossed the match into the flames. "She keeps busy."

Elisabeth turned her gaze upon him then, and he realized how stupid, how thoughtless, he had sounded. And so to try to cover it, he said, "I don't think everyone who is alone is lonely."

"You're not alone," she said, annoyed.

Lathias felt himself flare up. "That's not what I said."

"It's what you meant."

And before Lathias could reply, the boy—who had, as he often did of late, lingered on the periphery of the increasing familiarity between Lathias and Elisabeth, who had sat looking back and forth between the two of them as they spoke to each other now instead of through him—said suddenly, loudly, "Anyway, she's a witch."

Elisabeth frowned. "Don't talk so silly. You sound like Leo."

The boy's face reddened. "She is a witch," he said. "What do you know about it?"

Elisabeth and Lathias both looked at him in surprise, and Lathias thought, *My God, he is jealous. Of course he is. It is like that day at the Horseman's graves. Him playing the fool, trying to shock her, scare her.* And so he put his hand on the boy's shoulder and said, simply, "It doesn't matter."

But the boy ignored him, shrugged his hand away and leaned toward Elisabeth, who was unstrapping the skates from her shoes. "She is a witch," he insisted.

And Elisabeth said, very casually and without looking up, "Oh, like Baba Yaga, you mean?"

The boy paused. "Who's Baba Yaga?"

Lathias picked up his skates. "It's getting dark." But the fire was blazing hotly now.

"You don't know about Baba Yaga?" Elisabeth said, looking up at the boy, eyes glittering. "You should. She used to live in Russia, but I heard she came to Canada."

The boy stared at her from behind the high collar of his coat. "Where to?" he said.

"Nobody knows for sure," she said. "Just that it was by a river somewhere. Up on the edge of a river valley, so that she could look out and see where all the young boys and girls are, to see if they are down in the valley anywhere. A good place to steal them. Nobody can hear them scream."

The boy moved closer to Elisabeth, his hands on his knees.

Fine, Lathias thought to himself, *good, you can both be stupid, then. Go ahead, scare yourselves.* And he sat down on a rock by the fire and pulled a cigarette from his coat pocket.

"You're making that up," the boy said. "Isn't she, Lathias?"

"No, I'm not. Look how he says nothing. He knows about Baba Yaga. He just doesn't want to scare you."

"Why would I be scared? Tell me. What about her?"

"No," she said, "I don't want to scare you either."

"Tell me already," he shouted, standing up, his face reddened, though neither from the cold nor the fire.

"All right," Lathias said quickly, firmly. "I'll tell you. Sit down. It's nothing. It's not a good story, but I'll tell you. Sit down." He shot a look at Elisabeth. Was she smirking?

The boy sat, and Elisabeth turned her back to the fire and rested her head on her knees so that they could not see her face, and this bothered Lathias.

"So," he said to the boy, "there used to be a poor farmer—this was back in the old country—and he had a wife who was very sick."

"What was wrong with her?" the boy asked.

"I don't know. Influenza. I think."

"Did she die?"

"Yes, she died. But before she did, she called her only daughter and gave her something wrapped in an apron and said, 'I will not be with you any more, but this will take care of you.'"

"The apron?"

"The thing wrapped in the apron."

"What was it?"

"Shh, listen, and I'll tell you. She said, 'This will take care of you.' And then she died. When the girl opened the apron she found a doll made out of corn husks. It was an ugly doll and the girl did not really like it, so she just stuck it in her pocket and did not play with it. Now the farmer, he had always hated the daughter."

"Why?"

"I don't know. It doesn't matter."

"He didn't have a reason," Elisabeth said.

"He must have."

"Do you want to hear this story or don't you?" Lathias said, flicking the red ash from his cigarette into the fire. The boy was quiet. "So," Lathias said, "the farmer, who had always hated the daughter, decided to get rid of her. He took her to the forest at dusk, and he walked with her until they came to a little wooden hut standing on chicken legs—"

"Chicken legs?"

"Chicken legs."

"And with a fence around it," Elisabeth put in, "made of human bones."

Lathias ignored her. "'Go,' the farmer told the daughter, 'knock at the door and see if you can borrow some lard for our supper.' The daughter said, 'But who lives there?' And the father said, 'Your auntie. She will give you some lard.' The daughter said, 'But I don't know her,' and the father said, 'Do you want to eat tonight or not?' And so the daughter opened the gate—"

"Made of human bones."

"—and the gate creaked, *Woe to those who pass.*"

"Whoa?" the boy said.

"Yes, woe. Unhappiness. Bad fortune."

"Oh."

"Then the daughter walked past some trees and past a sleeping dog and she knocked at the door. No answer. She knocked again. Still no answer. By now it was just about dark and so she turned to go back to her father, but he was gone, there were just dark woods stretching all around her.

"Then the door of the house creaked open and standing there was an old woman with legs as thin as bones and teeth made of filed iron and hair on the backs of her hands and eyes that were all white. 'Yes, my dear,' said the old woman, 'what is it you want?'

"The daughter was frightened, but she said, 'My father sent me to ask for a bit of lard for our supper.' And the old woman said, 'Who is your father?' The daughter told her and the old woman smiled a little and said, 'Come in, then, and serve me for your bit of lard.' So the girl went in."

"Why didn't she run away?" the boy said.

"I don't know," Lathias said. "Maybe she was hungry."

"I would have run away."

"She would have caught you," Elisabeth said.

Lathias raised his voice. "So she went in. Inside the house was dark, too, and there was a stink, like burnt feathers—"

"And rotting flesh," Elisabeth said.

"—and the girl put up her hand against the wall to find her way—"

"And the wall felt like cold skin."

"—'Light a fire,' the old woman said. And so the girl had to feel her way around in the dark—"

"And sometimes she would step with her bare feet on round soft things that felt like arms or legs and sometimes she would step on other things that felt like wet hair and all the time she could hear the old woman breathing, sometimes very close to her—"

"Finally," Lathias said, "she found the kindling and the matches and set a small fire going in the fireplace and it began to get light in the house. She was almost too afraid to turn around, afraid of what she would see now that it was light, but she did turn around and she was surprised to find ordinary walls and an ordinary floor and nothing lying around anywhere and only bunches of dried herbs nailed everywhere to the rafters."

"Just like the braucha's place," Elisabeth said.

"You've never been in there," the boy said.

"How do you know?"

"The girl should have been relieved that it all looked normal," Lathias went on, "but it made her even more frightened. Then she saw the old woman sitting quietly in a rocking chair in the corner staring at her—"

"With those white eyes."

"Well," Lathias said, "she set the girl to work, and after a while she got up from her chair and said she had to go out but that she expected all the work to be done by the time she got back and a big pot of water boiling."

"And you know what that was for," Elisabeth said.

"What?"

"To cook her in."

"Was it, Lathias?"

"I don't know. Probably. But by then the girl knew the old woman was Baba Yaga the witch. So she sat by the fire and cried and that is when she felt something poking into her leg and she reached into her pocket and found that ugly corn-husk doll and she remembered her mother and she cried harder and said, 'Oh, Mother, if you can hear me, please help.'"

Elisabeth shifted where she sat, but said nothing.

"Well," Lathias continued, "as soon as she said that, the ugly little doll sat up in the girl's hands and told her, You must run away. But if you do the trees will lash your eyes and the gate will scream and bang and call Baba Yaga and the dog will tear you to pieces. Then the doll pointed to a shelf and said, On that shelf is a ribbon, some oil and a piece of meat. When you get to the trees, tie the ribbon to a branch. When you get to the gate, oil the hinges. When you see the dog, throw him the meat. There is also a towel and a comb. Take them and put them in your pocket.

"So the girl did as she was told and ran out of the house into the dark. When she reached the trees she tied the ribbon to a branch and they were still. When she reached the gate, she oiled it and it was quiet. She threw the dog the meat and the dog let her pass. Then she ran into the woods.

"Soon Baba Yaga came home and saw that the girl was gone. She flew into a rage. She screamed at the trees, Did you not lash her eyes? And the trees said, We have served you so long and you have not tied our branches with even a thread; she gave us a ribbon. And she screamed at the gate, Did you not bar her way and call for me? And the gate said, I have served you so long and you have never poured even water on my old hinges; she gave me oil. And she screamed at the dog, Did you not tear her apart? And the dog said, I have served you all these years and you have never given me even a scrap of bread; she gave me meat. So Baba Yaga beat the dog, and beat the gate, and beat the trees. Then she flew after the girl."

"How did she know where to look?" the boy asked.

Elisabeth turned around then and looked straight at the boy, and her eyes glowed in the light of the fire. "She followed her smell."

"Soon," Lathias said, "the girl could hear Baba Yaga coming behind her and the doll said, Quick, throw down the comb behind you. So the girl threw down the comb and a great, thick forest leapt up. Then she heard Baba Yaga chewing through the trees with her iron teeth, so the girl ran on and when she could hear Baba Yaga coming again, the doll said, Throw down the towel behind you. The girl threw down the towel and a great river rose up just as Baba Yaga came through the trees and caught sight of her."

"And Baba Yaga smiled at her," Elisabeth put in, "and her teeth and her fingernails were all bloody."

"But when Baba Yaga saw the river," Lathias said, "she ground her teeth in rage and then she knelt down and drank the river dry and set after the girl again. When the girl heard her coming, she said, 'Oh, now what will I do? I have nothing left,' and the doll said, Throw me behind you.

"The girl did not want to do this, because the doll was the last thing her mother had given her. But Baba Yaga was coming fast, she could hear her—"

"What did she do?" the boy asked.

"Just at the last second," Lathias said, "she grabbed the doll and threw it behind her. A great mountain rose up. The doll was gone. But the girl was safe."

After he finished telling the story, Lathias tossed the stub of his cigarette into the embers of the fire. He stood and kicked the embers apart with his boot and scooped up dirt and threw it on top and stamped on it again and said, "All right. Let's go."

"But," the boy said, "then what?"

"Then nothing," Lathias said, "she was safe. Baba Yaga couldn't cross the mountain. Come on. Let's go."

"But," the boy said, still sitting and staring at where the fire had once been, "where would she go, that girl?"

Lathias shrugged. "Home, I guess."

"But," the boy said, "she'd be with her father. She wouldn't be safe at all."

"Come on," Lathias said, "it's dark."

"That's not how I heard the story," Elisabeth said suddenly, from where she sat. "It didn't end like that."

"How did it end?" the boy said.

"Come on," Lathias said, "let's go." And he stepped to the horses, unhobbling them in the dark, but neither the boy nor Elisabeth moved.

"Well," Elisabeth said, "in the story I heard, the girl doesn't escape from the witch at all. She sits by the fire and cries because her mother has died and her father has left her to the witch and so she takes the doll and throws her in the witch's fire."

"What happens to the girl?" the boy said.

"When the witch comes home, she kills her and eats her and sucks the bones clean and breaks the bones up into a little basket and sends it to the girl's father."

"And, then what?"

"And then he falls down dead with grief, I guess," Elisabeth said, and stood up. "How should I know?"

"All right," Lathias said, "I'm going home." And this time he pulled himself up into the saddle and the boy jumped up and took the reins of his own horse and climbed up and sat waiting for Elisabeth. But she still stood by the smoking spot in the earth, standing so still there in the dark.

"Aren't you coming?" the boy said.

"No," she said, "you go ahead. I'll walk."

"In the dark?" the boy said.

"Why not?"

Lathias had already begun riding up the draw. "Come on," he called.

So the boy rode a few yards, then stopped. "Lathias," he said.

And Lathias turned around and they both looked behind them. They could hardly see her there, could not see her face at all, just her dress beneath the dark coat.

Lathias said, "It's cold."

"Yah," the boy said, "come on."

"No," she said. "I think I'll go see Baba Yaga up there, that witch of yours. To say you've been telling stories about her."

"I didn't," the boy said, his voice cracking, "I didn't say nothing. It was Lathias."

"All right," Lathias said roughly. "Enough."

"I didn't," the boy began again, but then Elisabeth burst out laughing, and both Lathias and the boy realized they'd never heard her laugh before—it was a strange sound, as if it was not a laugh at all, but a holler. Then she came toward them and as she neared she made a big show of wiping her eyes and such, as if she was laughing so hard she was crying.

"Oh, forget it," she said. "I made that all up. I've never even heard of a Baba Yaga before."

Lathias had half a mind to leave her there, for her cruelty, but he knew the boy would never allow it. So instead, just before she pulled herself up into the saddle, he said quietly to him, "Never mind. She's just the braucha, just an old woman."

That is what he said. He did not tell the boy that he'd heard Elisabeth's version before, too. She hadn't made it up at all, she'd heard it from someone. He didn't tell the boy that—what was the point?—he just rode on through the dark prairie, the boy and Elisabeth behind him, toward the dim lights of home.

————

Soon Lathias began catching her in other little lies, too. Maybe she'd been telling them all along and he'd just never noticed. But it was as if now that he'd caught her in one, he was waiting for others, expecting them. And they came.

There was one morning, he remembered it so clearly, the morning she stood waiting in Helen and Stolanus's yard while he—Stolanus—cut a new block of wood for her to skate on. She'd said she'd lost the other, but Lathias doubted now whether even that was true, and anyway it didn't really matter. Lathias was sitting a few feet away, preparing the wire and leather strapping, and the boy was beside him, kicking his feet against the frozen dirt.

"Danke," Elisabeth said to Stolanus, when he handed her the new block.

Stolanus smiled and waved his hand. "Ach, nothing. Have a good time with your friends."

But when she did not walk away, but just stood there as if waiting for something, he added, in his clumsy, slightly inappropriate way, "That's a pretty yellow bow you've got." And he pointed to the ratty old ribbon sticking out from beneath her woollen hat.

Elisabeth raised her hand to touch it and said, "I found it on the road."

And Lathias and the boy looked at her and then at each other and the boy opened his mouth to speak but Lathias shook his head and so the boy just stood frowning at her a little. And Lathias thought, *Why?* If she had said that the ribbon had been a gift or was important for some other reason, that it had belonged to her grandmother, or that someone had sent it to her or, well, almost anything, he could have understood.

But not Elisabeth. Her lies, at least the ones about herself, were rarely inflating. If Lathias or the boy had seen her in town at the grocery, she would say she had been at the hardware. If she had found a blue bottle at the fort, she would say it had been a brown one. Lathias could not understand it. She traded the ordinary truth for an even more ordinary lie. And, more than not understanding, Lathias felt uneasy. It reminded him that she often did what he did not expect and for reasons he could not begin to comprehend. It reminded him that he did not know her at all.

And he didn't, of course. *Friends,* Stolanus had said to her. But Lathias was not a fool. He knew they were not that, the three of them, never that.

TWELVE

"**D**ecember, and still no goddamn snow."
"Christ, if it's this cold, we should at least have some snow, not?"

"Another drought year."

"Maybe time to get that Hatfield back again."

"Ach, those crops were not so bad even. They just wanted better."

"Greed, that's what that was."

"I said they never should have brought him. I said, don't fool around with that stuff."

"Yah, I remember you saying that."

"What stuff?"

"All that black magic stuff."

"Witchcraft."

"That's right."

"Ach, you sound like an old woman."

"As bad as Ludmila Baumgarten."

"Here, you better throw some salt over your shoulder."

"Better throw the whole shaker."

"Christ, no, he'll break a goddamn mirror."

"Yah, you go ahead and laugh, go ahead, but you just tell me, have we had any rain since? Snow?"

"Christ, don't blame Hatfield, we never had no rain before."

"Another goddamn drought year."

"Not so fast now, there's still time. It's barely just December."

"December, Christ, yah, that's what I mean. Damn near Christmas."

That is what the men said around the coffee shop. And so, rather than think of drought, they thought of Christmas.

They thought of Christmas there at the coffee shop where old Wing and his wife had strung garlands of silver and gold tinsel, they thought of Christmas at Stednick's Dry Goods with the bolts of red-and-green checked fabrics, and they thought of Christmas at the bank and the livery and the hardware. And the boy, too, running errands around town with Lathias, listened to the conversations and felt the bristling, the undercurrent of something good to come, and he thought of Christmas, remembered, or thought he remembered, a time when all their friends and family gathered on Christmas Eve, dressed in their best clothes, the girls in ribbons, the boys in stiff high-necked shirts, and a big supper all laid out and lots of singing, at least three renditions of "Silent Night," and an uncle with his accordion, and then, late into the evening, the moment all the children had been anticipating with excitement and dread, the clanking of chains and jingling of bells that meant the Kristkindl had come, and the children would cling together, or climb onto the laps of their parents while the Kristkindl, all veiled and dressed in a moulting robe of fur, taunted them, going from house to house, and swung a long willow switch and growled, *Have the children been good this year?* And if the parents answered that they hadn't, he might strike them with the switch, or cuff their ears (or worse, dangle them down the well by their feet like he had done with Little Tony Lintz last year until Big Tony Lintz said, *Hor auf. Das isch genug.*), and then finally, thankfully, the Kristkindl would lumber like a bear back out into the night, and on to the next house, and then the children could laugh about it a little, just a little, and chase each other and squeal Kristkindl! Kristkindl!—the older ones anyway, the younger ones or those who had been punished still clung tearily to their parents, and there would be more singing, and then they would all bundle into the cutter or the sleigh or the stone boat and ride across the darkened prairies to midnight Mass, where so many candles burned they stung their eyes and Father Rieger robed in purple (or was it gold?) held forth in his dreamlike and inexplicable Latin and they would all sing "Silent Night" for the umpteenth time, and when Father Rieger said, *Peace be with you,* they replied, *And also with you,* and it seemed possible, all that peace, and when they said, *We lift up our hearts to the Lord,* it felt as if they were lifted up, and when they prayed silently, peacefully, all their hopes united and swirled up with the guttering candles and incense and muffled coughs toward the dim blue vault of ceiling and beyond, up up, and their hearts, too, for it was Christmas, the eve of the birth of Christ, and peace was with them all, all was peace.

And then they would bundle themselves back into the winter night, under blankets and robes, and race their horses home at breathless speeds, bells singing, tired but too cold and excited to sleep, and those horses and those bells and those icy stars, uncounted and uncountable, and that sky so black it was as if the nocturnal river had opened above them, poured over them. And the fathers would carry children into houses where they would sleep, dreaming of candles and the smell of oranges and the clanking of Kristkindl chains out in the winter night. They would sleep and wake and sleep again and finally it would be morning, Christmas, the sun glinting red and yellow off the hard snow. And they would bundle up and go sledding in the Hills, or skate on the slough or the river, even the adults. They would throw snowballs and build forts and throw snowballs again, and when they were done, another meal, enormous, with roasted meats and potatoes with cream and pies and cakes and Christmas breads, and then, when they were finished, some more singing again and maybe a few hands of cards, by the warm light of kerosene lanterns, long into the winter night.

("Yah, but," the men around the coffee shop considered, thinking of the dirt blowing in drifts down the streets beyond Wing's pink scrubbed walls, of the hard, frozen fields, the near-barren, brown valley and the slushy black coursing of the river beneath the ice, giving voice to the boy's own thoughts, "if there is no snow, it will hardly feel like Christmas at all.")

Once, the boy was certain (it must have been, for he remembered it being so), Christmas had been celebrated that way for them, too (in spite—though the boy would not have known this—of the other women's dislike of Helen, because of their fondness for Stolanus, and because of Pius and the missus, too, who had always been well liked and respected). Yes, they had all gathered at Pius's home, the family homestead. The boy was not wrong. Lathias remembered it, too, from his first year with them.

Then, the accident. That first Christmas afterwards, some of Stolanus's family came, and the Schneider brothers, out of tradition and goodwill, out of the desire to support Stolanus, and Helen, too, yes, in spite of her ways, out of the need to say, *Everything's all right, you see, nothing has changed.* But it had changed. They all sat around uncomfortably, Helen staring out the window as she often did back then, her grim silence casting a pall over everything, and everyone pretending not to look at the boy, his ugly scars, and the fiddles and accordions sitting untouched in the corner and the food growing a skin on the table, until the Schneider brothers excused themselves, and everyone else counting the hours until it was time for church, and then, well before the appointed time, the others, too, trickled out. (*Better to sit freezing in the cutter,* they all said, *than freezing in that house,* and, *But she could make a little effort, at least, the boy is not dead, after all, she could try to make us welcome, not? It would not kill her.*)

And, other than the Schneider brothers' brief visits each Christmas Eve, they had been alone ever since.

In his heart, and in spite of his hazy memories of a warmer time, the boy knew this year would be no different, except that this year there was hardly any snow, what little there was the wind had taken and plowed into hard brown drifts that didn't look like snow at all. There would be no tobogganing. But they could skate on the river at least—him and Lathias and Elisabeth—all Christmas Day, if they wanted to. There was that.

THIRTEEN

Christmas came and went and the weather turned colder, thirty below with a wind that made it feel like fifty, and so Lathias and the boy did not see Elisabeth for a while, not even at church, for Leo, it seemed, had stopped attending, again, as was his whim, though no one knew whether it was the cold or something else keeping him away, and truth be known, no one much cared. No one but Lathias and the boy, and even Lathias thought it was just as well. Though he was no longer angry with her for the incident at the river, the way she had tried to scare the boy—what was the point in anger?—he mistrusted her more than he used to. Hadn't he good reason to? That is what he told himself. And so when the boy would speak of her, as he frequently did, Lathias would just shrug and nod or shake his head and say nothing, leaving the boy to stand there with a watchful, puzzled expression. And if he thought about her now and then, it was nothing, and the boy needn't know.

One Sunday after Mass the boy said to Lathias, "We should just ride over there maybe, just to check."

"No," he said, "don't worry. It's just the cold."

Though he had considered it, too, riding over, just to check.

But he never did. He told himself it was the weather that kept him from doing so.

————

Then it was February and Stolanus's cows began to calve. Lathias would ride out into the brutal cold, during the night and then again before dawn and all through the day, sometimes with the boy, if the wind had died down and if Helen allowed it. The only blessing the lack of snow which made riding easier, in spite of the cold. Nevertheless, they lost many. It was terrible. Lathias hated to come upon them that way, especially if the boy was with him. They would hear her before they saw her, the cow, bawling out across the cold plains. He could follow the sound at night and find her, standing there over her dead calf, bellowing, charging at him sometimes, or butting at him violently with her big head, as he packed the calf up over the saddle and took it away to the rock pit.

"Why do you have to take it away?" the boy, who had been sitting waiting on the horse, his face tucked inside his collar, his mittened hands jammed into his pockets, asked one afternoon, his lips stiff and white with cold.

Lathias wiped crystals from his nose. "If you don't, the mother will just keep standing there. Won't eat, won't drink. Pretty soon she'll be dead, too."

Lathias said it matter-of-factly, to ease the boy's concern, but the truth was he never got used to it, either. He hated it every goddamned time. But he did it anyway. He did not want Stolanus to have to do it. He'd get up extra early, just so that he could give the herd a once-over before Stolanus had even stirred, assure him that they had all been checked. And, Lathias knew, Stolanus allowed it.

During those first winters that Lathias was with them, they'd ridden out together. That February a couple years after the accident was bad, too, worse even, and then a two-day blizzard knocking them out the beginning of March. That first blizzard night they lost three in a row. When they came upon the third, with

the mother standing stupidly, bawling, the mucous hanging brutally from her near-frozen muzzle, licking the little dead calf and
swinging viciously at Stolanus every time he tried to get near her,
it was more than either of them could take, exhausted and nearly
dead themselves with the cold. Stolanus kept trying to pick the
thing up (it was freezing already, the calf, he'd had to yank at it
where the cooling hide had frozen into the snow), while Lathias
tried to distract the mother, but after a few minutes of fighting
with the cow that way, dodging and shouldering at her, Stolanus
just kind of lost control, bellowed senselessly back at her, the
spittle flying from his mouth, the snow blasting him in the face.
Lathias watched helplessly as Stolanus ran at the cow, throwing
himself into her side, once, twice, hollering, trying to get her to
move away, and when she just stood there looking at him stupidly,
baffled, swinging her big head, he started pounding at her with
his fists, in the face, the muzzle, hollering and swearing, kicking
her in the belly. Lathias thought he was crying, too, though he
couldn't have said for sure. When a man goes crazy like that, he
thought, you sure as hell don't look him in the face too closely.
You give him that at least, that little bit of dignity.

Eventually, Stolanus just kind of wore himself out, and the cow,
too, because when Lathias stepped toward her, she just stood
there, they both did—her and Stolanus—while he hoisted the stiff
body onto the back of his saddle. Neither he nor Stolanus spoke
of it afterwards, but Lathias swore to himself that he wouldn't let
Stolanus ride out after any more dead calves. There's some things,
he told himself, a man shouldn't have to do, and he had not suffered himself the kinds of loss that Stolanus had, and him still a
young man. No, he did not suffer losses, he caused them. Didn't
he? And so it was only right that he collect the dead. It was the
least he could do.

But this February was the worst spring as far as losses since
that one year. It would warm up for a day or two, but then
temperatures would drop right down and that crazy wind would

pick up and it was as if that were some kind of signal for those animals to start to calve. It always seemed to work that way. Lathias was dead tired from riding, and distracted, as he had been at harvest. He did not see Elisabeth, or even the boy, who kept to the house most days now unless he was riding out with Lathias. He was glad they were not going to the river without him, the boy and Elisabeth, not only because of the danger of the thawing and refreezing ice, but also because, God help him, he felt a little twinge of jealousy. Not of them together, but of his own absence. It was a subtle difference, but a difference nevertheless. And then, too, he did not trust Elisabeth. Not since that night at the river when she had tried to frighten the boy. And the boy was so naive. He trusted everybody, everything. She could say anything, and it would be possible for him to believe her. She could scare him, terrorize him, if she chose, and he would take it, would not even recognize that her terrorizing was intentional. The boy could never believe someone would cause injury, however slight, on purpose. Like a little dog that way, willing to be kicked again and again, just sticking his tail between his legs and coming back for more. If Helen had not pulled him out of school all those years ago, he would have stayed there to be kicked. It was as if he thought it would all turn around one day, that tomorrow wouldn't be the same as today.

Lathias often thought that if he could have changed something about the boy, it would have been that. He would have made him see the world for what it was: one long grieving. He would have made the boy see the world in all its misery and ugliness. At least, that's what he thought then. But he was jealous, by his own admission, and he did not know that jealousy can make you see things that aren't there, make you miss things that are.

FOURTEEN

March came in like a lamb: the brutal weather broke and temperatures hovered just below zero, the skies big and blue and blinding with a cold, clear light. Calving increased but came easier, and, though tired, Lathias promised the boy an afternoon of skating at the river Sunday, before the beginning of spring breakup.

Elisabeth began coming by the farm again that week, though not to see the boy, it would seem, but only to sit and watch Lathias work around the yard. The boy would sit there, too, of course, not realizing (or perhaps realizing quite clearly) that it was not him she had come to see. Sometimes she'd find Lathias in the barn before the boy was even awake and she would perch herself on the rails and lean her head against the post as she used to the previous summer and just sit there all morning if it wasn't too cold, and sometimes even when it was. They spoke only to or through the boy, and so if he was not there, they did not speak at all, but by the end of the week Lathias had begun to relax again into her presence, into the companionship that was not really companionship at all but could not be called anything else either.

One morning, he happened to look up at her, something he

rarely did, and because he looked at her so rarely, and because she was therefore not expecting his gaze, he caught on her face an expression that startled both of them: he wouldn't quite call it desperation, but something very near to it. She turned her face quickly away and he almost did the same, both of them surprised, embarrassed. He almost did, but he was struck by something else in that instant. As he stood there watching her through the morning light, he thought this: that he would like to kiss her, right there in the sweet, cool-smelling, unbreathed air of the barn, that he should kiss her, he must, and all those bits of light turning so bright and cold between them, and neither of them moving, it was as if it had already happened, and Lathias thought, *If it has already happened, then there is nothing to fear, and it must have, I remember her lips now, it must have happened a thousand times.*

But it had not, and it did not, for just as he took a step toward her—had he taken that step or had he just thought it?—Helen came in and stood there in the sunlight streaming through the barn door.

"Is he with you?"

Lathias almost said, "Who?" but caught himself in time. "No," he said.

"But he has been gone from the house almost an hour," Helen said, looking from Lathias to Elisabeth and back again. "Without even his breakfast."

"I haven't seen him," Lathias said, and they blinked at each other a moment, him and Helen, before following Elisabeth's pointed gaze toward the hatch that led into the loft. And Lathias thought, *Yes. Of course.* And he closed his eyes, squeezed them shut. That old creeping guilt and despair.

When he opened them, Elisabeth cast him a meaningful look, smiled a little, or smirked, for there was nothing of warmth in it, and nothing of desperation either, it was as if he had imagined it. And he thought, *So she knew, then. She knew all along. And she was waiting for something to happen. She wanted it to happen. Maybe because of and for him. Was that it?* He looked back at her, searching her face. But there was nothing. She hopped down from the rail and walked past Helen and out into the sunlight, gone.

————

That night he dreamed her. It was not the first time. But where previously she had existed only on the periphery of other dreams, now she came toward him through the dusky night air at the edge of the Hills where he had been out riding, checking for fires that he could not find though smoke was all around him, drifting up from the Hills, she walked straight toward him out of the branches of a dried willow like out of the fleshless ribs of some desiccated beast, she came toward him and then she stopped and stood staring at him, the hem of her dress stirring a little in the last of the evening wind. He walked the mare closer, almost said, *You startled me. I must be tired, my eyes are playing tricks. Sure was a hot one today. Out for a walk, are you? Nice night for it.* But he did not.

Instead, before it had even become a thought, he was down from the horse and before her, as if he had been there a thousand times, kneeling in the bruised air, her mouth scorched and unsurprised, kneeling in the hot soft sand.

————

Later, in the early light, in his loft bunk, he would remember this: her hair fanned out like flames against the earth and the dry deafening rasp of crickets or bones in the still, dark air and the baked smell of smoke and sagebrush; the way her eyes seemed to darken and recede until he could no longer look at her face; and then the one cold, irrational thought that had, dreaming, struck him: *Where is he?* He had said it out loud, suddenly, *Where is he? Who?* she had said, *Leo?* Though that was not who he had meant. *Good God,* pulling back, into the night, *Is he here? Is he with you?*

You're afraid, she said. *Is that it?* Sitting up in the sand and him kneeling there. Kneeling there, and he knew she was right. *Is he here?* he said, *Is he here?* And before she had even answered, he thought, *He must be home, then—he was home, he was sleeping.*

Is that it? she was saying. Standing up, and all that darkness stretching out. *Coward,* she said, *coward.* And then she was running, away from him, across the fields toward Leo's shack. And all at once he was no longer afraid, the fear in him drowned by another feeling just as strong, just as old. In that moment, it was as if he existed in a place without time and geography, a dream place, as if he hurtled through all that darkness, not bound by gravity, but telescoping, travelling rapidly toward something so specific and finite it was as if he were looking at his own life in dilation, all that had come before flashing briefly, insignificantly, as he hurtled irrevocably forward, or down.

And he believed in that moment that everything had changed, that nothing that had come before mattered, that nothing would ever be the same again. He almost called out to her, in spite of himself, hating himself for it, that weakness, almost called across the smoky, blackened plains of his half-dream, knowing she could not hear him, knowing she would not answer even if she could. But he did not call out. Instead, he yanked the startled mare around and rode, blindly, brutally, in the opposite direction, under the fierce hot stars, away from the Hills and her.

FIFTEEN

Sunday came. The boy was there beside him in the barn, the skates in a sack across his shoulder.

Lathias did not look up. "You go on ahead," he said. "I have work to do."

The boy just stood there, as if he did not understand.

"Go on ahead," he said again, pulling his saddle from where it hung by a peg just inside the doors.

The boy said, uncertainly, "You'll come later?"

Lathias turned away. "I have work to do."

"But," the boy said behind him, "it's Sunday. You said Sunday."

Lathias just lifted a hand and walked away across the yard, the saddle over his shoulder, out toward the home pasture where his mare grazed with the other horses on the first sparse blades of grass.

"I wasn't spying," the boy called after him, "if that's what you think."

But he just kept walking. *Spying.* What did it matter? So what if he had been watching them. It was nothing. The boy could not see into his head. Could not see into his soul. It was nothing. Nothing had happened.

THE RIVER

ONE

Maybe the boy heard them over the beating of his own heart, those two riders moving steadily along the snowless horizon. Or maybe he felt them, the distant drumming of hoofbeats across the earth. Maybe he even thought, *There, it comes, I have only just placed that cross and already it comes, without even praying yet.*

Whatever the reason, when the boy looked up and saw the two riders in the distance, hazed by the smoke blown over from the brush pile burning at Hausers', he jumped down from the rubbing stone and ran to catch up to Elisabeth, calling her name against the risen wind. The domed sky curved depthless above them, and around on every side, settling at the unfettered horizon like the stilled edge of a bell.

As he ran, the boy thought of the two sagebrush twigs he had left in the shape of a cross as an offering atop the stone as Lathias had once told him, though he was too angry to think of Lathias now, too hurt, and so he thought instead of those riders that came because of it, that cross, and of the girl before him, witchhaired, waiting with the familiar expression of strained tolerance with which she often regarded him.

"Elisabeth," he shouted, pointing. "Two riders."

"So?"

"So?" he said, coming up beside her. "Don't you know? If you see two riders, you make a wish. To get rid of something."

She started walking again.

"Like a wart," he said, following, "or a toothache, or, or anything. You say, 'Give the back rider my toothache, in the name of the Father, the Son, and the Holy Ghost.'"

She stopped then and looked at him sharply. "Who told you that?"

The boy shrugged.

"Lathias," she sneered. "You believe everything he tells you?"

"Not everything," he said, but thinking, *Why wouldn't I?* Thinking, *But he said Sunday. He promised.*

She seemed angry, too, and the boy wondered if Lathias had done something to her, also, though Elisabeth did not always need a reason, it seemed.

"And you think that works?" she said.

"I don't know. I never tried it."

"So try it, then."

The boy looked back at the riders. The horses were not moving swiftly, but already they were almost out of sight.

"I don't have a toothache," he said. "Or warts."

"Try something else, then."

"Like what?"

"There must be something you want to get rid of." She narrowed her eyes at him. "What about that scar?"

The boy felt his cheeks grow hot. He turned away from her.

"It doesn't work like that," he said. "It has to be something you *can* get rid of." Wondering, as he always did, why she sometimes said those things, as if she were mean. As if she were angry with him for some reason, though he could not think why. Maybe it was Lathias, then. Angry, too, that he had not come with them. Angry that they'd had to walk because his father would not allow him to take the horses without Lathias.

"Hmm," she said. "What about Leo? Would it work on him, then, do you think? Is he something you can get rid of?"

"You shouldn't wish for that. You shouldn't wish people gone. What if they die?"

"What if they do?"

"You shouldn't say that."

"All right, then, I won't say it." She looked down at her hands. "What about these freckles?"

"They're nice."

She tsked. "Well, *you* wish for something, then. I'd try that scar if I were you."

He looked back at the distant riders. They were almost gone. "Do the freckles," he said.

"I'll do it," she said, "to prove it doesn't work." She closed her eyes. "Give the—"

"No, you have to kneel."

She clucked her tongue again in annoyance.

"Hurry," he said, looking over his shoulder, "you have to be able to see the back rider."

She dropped to her knees in the high brown grass, grudgingly, her hair whipping in her face.

"Elisabeth," the boy said, and she opened her eyes. But he could only shake his head, ashamed, for the thought, whatever it was, was already gone. It happened that way sometimes, not with Lathias as much as with her; nothing, where he knew there had been something a moment ago; like a sound that wakes you in the night, the awareness of a sound without the recognition. So, to fill the space he said only, "Hurry."

She closed her eyes again and he closed his, too, folded his hands.

"Give the back rider my freckles, in the name of the Father, the Son, and the Holy Ghost."

The boy crossed himself, and they waited a moment, eyes shut, hands clasped, the wind rushing between them.

"Well?" she finally said.

He opened his eyes.

"Oh," he said. "No." Knowing she would be disappointed, in spite of what she said, in spite of her supposed disbelief. He was sorry, too; not because of the freckles, but simply because Lathias was wrong: it did not work. Another disappointment.

She rose and they stood there a moment, bodies rocking a little in the wind.

"Maybe," he said, "it only works with warts."

But she said nothing.

"Maybe," he said, "you have to believe it will work for it to work."

She cast him a dark glance.

"It was good that you tried," he said. "It was worth a try, not?"

But he did not really believe that, either. Not today. Nothing seemed good.

"Anyway," he said, "freckles aren't the worst thing."

"Yes," she said peevishly. "It could be worse."

He knew what she meant. She might as well have said, *Look at you.*

He knew her well enough by now to know that she was in one of those moods. Later she would feel sorry for it, maybe, and be kind to him, say kind things, or as kind as she ever got, anyway. And think that maybe he had forgotten whatever mean thing she had said. But he was not stupid. He bore her no grudges, he was always ready to forgive, to be friends again; was eager for it. But he was not stupid.

Elisabeth started walking again and he followed her, through the smoky air, across the Horseman's pasture, past the sighing and softly undulating horse graves, beyond the homesteads, toward the river. When they reached the Bull's Forehead, they stood a moment, facing the wind and the river—frozen still along its edges, but running in a low, narrow channel down the middle, fluid and dark as a bullsnake. The boy scanned the hills on the other side, swiped with light and dark striations, and thought, *It did not work. Why didn't it? What did we do wrong? It is me. It must be. It is Lathias. And it is her, too. It is my own skin. It is the weather, maybe, and the earth and that sky, the stars and the planets and the ways of God. It is everything.*

She sat down abruptly in the long grass.

"Spring breakup soon," he said. But she made no reply. "Don't you want to go down?"

"No."

He glanced across at her, then squatted down by one of the stones that made up the circle on the hill. Sighed. What the boy chose to think of as disappointment—their separate disappointments, separate but similar too—still lingered between them, making them uneasy with each other, ashamed of their own hopes.

The boy rubbed his palm on one of the stones. "I know a story," he said, tentatively. "About how these stones got here, this circle. It's a good story. A medicine man put them here. For his daughter. She died and he—"

She looked at him then. "Another one of Lathias's stories."

He squinted back at her.

"You do believe everything he tells you." she said.

He pulled at the grass around his boot, but he did not answer.

She made a dismissive sound and shook her head.

After that they sat for a time, without speaking. He pulled at the dry grass, breaking it between his fingertips, tossed it aside. Looked out into the valley.

"River's low," he said. But she made no reply.

He lifted the tin syrup pail he carried and rattled it a little by its handle. "Hungry?"

"No."

And so he lowered the pail and blinked out at the valley, soft now in the late afternoon light, the creeping haze of the distant fire.

"Wind's changed direction," he said. "There's smoke, from over Hausers'. Brush pile. They should know better, all this wind."

It was only what his mother had said at breakfast. But his heart wasn't in it. At the thought of Lathias he sunk again into the perplexing guilt and disappointment and heaviness he had felt since that morning. *I wasn't spying,* he'd said. But that was not true. He had been spying. And on top of it he'd lied to Lathias. But he did not like to think of that. It was better to think of Lathias's wrongs. And wasn't he a little bit happy at Lathias's absence? Just a little bit? But he did not like to think of that, either.

"Anyway," he said instead, "it's smoky, all right."

When she did not respond, he rattled the pail again. He was hungry. He would have liked to eat, but he set the pail behind him, and he thought, *If I cannot see it, then it is as if it is not there.*

"Me neither," he said, after a while, "I'm not hungry neither." And he rustled his feet in the long grass so she would not hear the churning of his outraged stomach over the wind. But he would not eat. Not when she was unhappy; with him. He couldn't. Anyway, there was nothing he could do about it, her annoyance. Wait for it to pass. He wished she would speak, though. She could do that at least, sitting there in the smoky wind, motionless but for that hair, writhing, and the flapping black wing of her coat.

But she would not, it seemed, and so they sat and stared out at the river again, or up at the sky or over to where the old braucha's place hunched next to them on the edge of the valley.

Finally, Elisabeth stood and started walking down the draw.

"Wait," he said, and he rose and caught up to her, wishing he could think of something to say.

When they reached the riverbank, she stopped and stared out irritably across the ice, arms folded in front of her.

"Why didn't he come?" she said.

The boy looked down. "I don't know."

After a minute, she said, "He doesn't like me much."

And the boy said nothing, wanting her to believe it was true. Wanting himself to believe it. She looked at him, waiting, and when he did not respond, she said, "You think a lot of him. Don't you."

"Yah," the boy said, "of course."

She stared at him for what seemed to the boy to be a long time.

"You ever wonder why he stuck around?" she said. "All these years?"

The boy shrugged. "Why wouldn't he?"

But she just kept on staring at him, a funny kind of look on her face, and this time he stared back. And she seemed so angry with that, with his staring, that for a moment he thought she might reach out and slap him. But she did not. They only stood there at the edge of the river, locked in a gaze that it seemed neither could, would, break. Then, as they stood there, an odd thing happened. The smoky wind calmed, almost settled, and white flakes began to drift down upon them, infinitesimal, thrown into sudden feathery relief against the dark hills and the black coursing of the river's spine.

The boy lifted his head.

"Look," he said suddenly, forgetting her anger. "It's snowing."

Elisabeth watched him. Then she too turned her face to the sky.

"It's snowing," he said again, his voice lighter still, wonder-filled, almost amazed, holding his palms up to the silvered air. "Look."

Elisabeth reached out and, dabbing a flake from his palm, placed it on her tongue.

"No," she said, flatly. "It's ash."

And stepped out onto the frozen river.

Two

Lathias stayed in town all that Sunday, looking in the windows of the closed shops and sitting in a back corner of Wing's nursing a cup of coffee so long that Wing finally said, "You order now?" and Lathias got up as if to pay for his coffee and leave but Wing waved him back into his seat and, disappearing into the kitchen, came back moments later with a plate of steaming food. Lathias tried to object, but Wing just smiled and nodded and waved at him to begin eating, and so Lathias, though he was not hungry, thanked him and ate.

All day, guilt had been gnawing away at him. Knowing the boy had taken it hard, goddamn it, why did he have to take every goddamned thing so goddamned hard? But it was done now. If he had been hurt, then so be it. He would have to be hurt sometimes, a little bit. Wouldn't he? Otherwise, that's not living. *Oh hell,* he thought. *Christ Almighty.* Rubbing his face in his hands, the smell of the food sickening him, but eating it anyway, he did not want to seem ungrateful. But sick, he felt sick. Sick at his stomach, sick at his heart. Things were changing, had changed. But he could make it up to the boy, would make it up to him.

They would do things without her, like they used to. Not the river, that was over, they could not go without her now. The boy would not want to. But he would take the boy somewhere (but, even so, thinking, *Where, for God's sake, where would I take him?*), if Helen and Stolanus would allow it (thinking, *Even if there were somewhere, they would never let him go, Helen wouldn't*), but letting himself get carried away anyway at the thought of going, not just for a day or two, but for good, to live somewhere else, it would be easy for him to find work and the boy could live with him, start over somewhere. But then he thought of the scars and the seizures that would be the same no matter where the boy went, and he lowered his fork and pushed his plate away.

The big windows by the door had darkened and Wing and his wife glanced at him now and then, wanting to go to their own supper, no doubt, and so he took his coat and slipped some coins beneath the edge of his plate. He deserved no one's generosity or goodwill or pity, not today, maybe not ever. Nodded in thanks as he left. Thinking, *But I cannot avoid her, not forever.* That was not possible either. Amazed, suddenly, at the finiteness of possibilities. Knowing he must see her, must talk to her, and settle, finally, this thing that was or was not between them.

————

When he rode into the yard, it was full dark. He put up the horse and walked to the house, seeing through the window Helen at the stove over a boiling pot and Stolanus staring at the set table looking bewildered, as he always did when he found himself alone with Helen.

When Lathias came in on a blast of spring air, Helen dropped the spoon she was using and Stolanus half rose from the table. Lathias looked from one to the other.

"What is it?" he said.

Helen stepped forward. "He's not with you?" she said.

Lathias felt something sink in him, a sudden lurching and

dropping of his heart. A pounding in his head. He glanced to Stolanus, waiting also.

"No," he said, "I have not seen him all day."

Helen made a small sound in her throat, turned away.

"Ach," Stolanus said, "he is fine. Probably out in the yard somewhere."

Helen said nothing, just stood staring into that pot of boiling water, as if she might divine something there, but Stolanus waved Lathias over to his seat at the table and said again, the heaviness in his voice betraying him, as it always did, "He's fine. Out running around. That's what boys do, not?" And winked at Lathias, to convince them both, to convince all three of them, and maybe he even meant it, or believed he did, which amounted to the same thing in the end.

Lathias sat down at the table and Helen said, without turning away from her pot, "After dark? You know as well as I."

And she was right. Lathias knew it, too. The boy would never stay out after dark, not by himself, probably not even with Elisabeth. But he was with her, or had been, of this Lathias was certain.

Stolanus shrugged. "Maybe he's growing up, then."

"But he's afraid of the dark. He wouldn't stay out."

"Good, then," Stolanus said, "maybe he will learn there is nothing to be afraid of. It's good for boys, a little adventure." But looking at Lathias all the time. "What do you say, Lathias?"

But Lathias just sat there with his eyes fixed on the table, thinking, thinking, and he could not look at her, knew as well as she did: something was wrong.

Stolanus went on, eyes glistening, like someone with a fever. "This one here, he's had adventure. How old when you left home, Lathias? Thirteen?"

"Twelve," Lathias told him.

"Twelve. There. You see?" But still looking at Lathias, as if he expected an answer from him. "Anyway," he said again when no one spoke, "it's good, some adventure."

"It's that Krauss girl," Helen said, "that's who he's with. Isn't it. Was he with her?"

"I don't know," Lathias said. But he did, of course he did. "I think so."

"You see?" Stolanus said. "Out with a friend. It's only just dark. Let him be. He'll be home soon enough."

Helen stared a moment, then lifted the pot of boiling potatoes and flipped them into the basin to drain, water splashing up her arms and to the floor. She dumped them into a bowl and set it sharply in the centre of the table. Then she went to stand by the window, staring out at the still-darkening plains.

Christ, that darkness. Some nights, you couldn't see a thing. And Lathias thought, *Who knows what's out there, who knows what could happen out there? Anything. Everything. Or, worse still, nothing. Not a goddamned thing.*

And so the three of them waited there, listening to the rattling of the lid on the pot of stew that simmered on the stove, the air full of its thick, rich smell. Helen at the window and Stolanus and Lathias at the table, Stolanus breathing heavily, the way he always did, as if it cost him such tremendous effort. And Lathias wondering what to do, sitting there smelling that stew, trying not to let his stomach growl, though he did not feel hungry. Yet his stomach smelled the stew and betrayed him. He did not want Helen to hear, so every time it growled he shifted in his chair so that the legs scraped a little on the floor, until both Helen and Stolanus stared at him.

But Helen was not stupid. "Go ahead," she said flatly. "Eat. There's no point waiting."

But there was only the bowl of potatoes steaming away between them. The stew still simmering on the stove, the loaf of bread uncut on the cupboard. And so the two of them just sat there, each wondering if the other would rise and get the meal, whether he should, knowing Helen would not. Finally, Stolanus pushed the bowl of potatoes toward Lathias. Lathias dished some up and then pushed the bowl back to Stolanus and he dished some up and then they sat staring at the potatoes on their plates instead of at the potatoes in the bowl.

Stolanus did not mean for either of them to eat, as Lathias very well knew. The passing of the bowl was just a gesture, of discomfort and placation. Well meant, but useless.

"Maybe the barn," Stolanus said, after a while. "Fell asleep maybe."

"I just put the horse up."

"Maybe you didn't see him."

Then, as if it had only just occurred to him, Stolanus rose from the table to go check, but Lathias stood first, nearly toppling the table in his hurry to do so.

"I'll go," he said.

And Stolanus blinked at him and then said, "Yah, sure. That's right. Go wake him. Good."

But he did not sit back down, just kept standing there, half bent, his big palms on the edge of the table, watching while Lathias took his coat from the hook by the door.

Helen still stood at the window and Lathias gave her a quick glance on his way out, but she did not look back at him. He heard Stolanus call as he stepped out the door, "Hurry him up, then. We don't want cold supper."

But he just pulled the door shut in that careful, quiet way, the way people do when there has been a death.

As soon as he was outside, Lathias regretted it, the way he had closed that door, wished he had let it slam shut, casually, carelessly. It would have been a small reassurance, as if to say, *There is no call for decorum, the quiet closing of doors, there has been no tragedy here.*

Halfway across the yard, he turned back to see Helen still standing by the window. He knew she would be there, just as he knew the boy was not in the barn. It seemed as if Helen could see him out there across the darkened yard, well beyond the pale fall of the kerosene lantern through the window, could see him looking back at her. He almost lifted a hand to wave, then caught himself.

He quickly slid the big barn doors open and the horses nick-
ered softly and he stepped inside to where it seemed less dark,
he thought, the way it did when you came in from the prairie at
night, as if just the presence of walls and a ceiling somehow eased
all that darkness, that vastness, or at least kept it at bay, as if the
moon itself had snuck in, seeking shelter. He wondered, briefly,
if Stolanus and Helen had spoken since he'd left, wondered if
they ever spoke, wondered if Stolanus still sat at the table the way
Helen stood at the window, together in their grief and their fear,
but separated by it, too. He tried to imagine Stolanus crossing the
floor to wrap his big arms around her, however stiffly, tried to
imagine them at the window together. But he could not.

He climbed to the loft quietly, without a lantern, calling softly,
feeling his way around in the darkness—he did not want to startle
the boy—then, taking a lantern from the hook on the wall and
lighting it. But there was nothing. And he was struck, again, by
the aloneness of his life. Of his and the boy's. No, they were not
friends, it was true. They were just together in their aloneness,
the way Helen and Stolanus were together in theirs. Together in
their unluckiness.

He climbed back down the ladder and looked below, too, in
the horses' stalls, and in the cribs and feed bins. Nothing.

And now he felt a slow cold creeping like water in his belly.
And he heard, or thought he heard, the distant pounding of
hooves across the prairie.

He took a halter from a nail on the wall and slipped it over
the mare's head, and she eyed him curiously and huffed that they
should be going out again so soon and at such an hour.

Before stepping from the barn, he blew out his lantern so that
Helen, please God, would not see him ride away.

THREE

Mary Krauss stood at the kitchen window, peering out across the darkening prairies, seeing only the reflection of her own moonish face, her breath steaming the thin, cold glass. From the same window that afternoon she had watched her daughter walk across the fields toward Schoffs', watched the familiar quirk in the girl's gait that she'd had, it seemed, since she first walked.

A curse, her own mother had said back then, watching Elisabeth toddle unsteadily across the floor. *She will carry a heavy load.* And had insisted they do the test. So she'd sat at the table with the baby in her lap while her mother and Anna placed a pencil, a small hammer and a spoon within the child's reach. They'd waited while Elisabeth studied the items, waited to see which she would reach for—would she be smart, would she be strong, would she make a good wife? Elisabeth turned and looked up at her with that pale, quiet, baleful gaze, then swept all the objects from the table with one small hand. And her mother had nodded gravely, predictably. *She will carry a heavy load. Who knows what she will end up?*

And sometimes when the child looked at her it was as if she was cursed with a sort of heaviness after all, a weariness; old before her time. And as she got older, indeed, the way Elisabeth walked did look as though she were carrying something, milk pails or water buckets or potatoes from the garden, an odd and almost imperceptible bracing of her shoulders, arms out a little from her body as if for balance, hardly noticeable, not noticeable to anyone who had not watched her closely, who was not, perhaps, expecting to see something there. And she thought of her mother, maybe dead now. And she thought of Anna and the others, and she wondered why Anna had not written. So her mother must be all right, then. Otherwise, someone would have sent word. And Father? He would live forever, surely (though, of course, she was wrong, could not have known that he would be dead the following summer, an artery severed in the field, and that he would die slowly, staring up into a sky burned white with heat, and that he would not be found until the next morning, by Anna, sent out by their mother, who lay dying herself in the back bedroom, of what ailment, no one knew, since Anton refused to summon the doctor, and that Anna would stand a few moments looking down at him and then return to the house to tell her mother he could not be found, and that the mother would not learn the truth until he was discovered some days later by a neighbour, but by then the coyotes had already been at him; and that the mother would die, too, soon after, and Anna would be left alone there, going a bit touched, some said in later years, until she was an old woman, and then she was dead, too).

Sometimes, in Mary's lowest moments, she allowed herself to think this: *from the frying pan into the fire.* Like her mother. The worst view of things always. But what could she do? Nothing. Keep Elisabeth out of Leo's way during his bad times, just as she had done with her father at all times. And in spite of it all, in spite of Leo, his wild swings between penitent and sinner, in spite of it, he had come to her rescue. Hadn't he? He had saved her, from that old suffocating life of doom and silence and domination. He had saved them both, her and Elisabeth. Elisabeth didn't yet understand. But she would. Someday. When she was older. Then, her daughter would thank her.

Mary took the last of the flour from the bin in the pantry, and the tin of lard, the eggs she had gathered that morning, not enough but she would make do, then looked out the window again. Dark, the moon rising there to the east, lightless too, it seemed.

Of course, she knew Elisabeth was following that hired man around, that halfbreed, as Leo called him. Maybe even thought she was in love with him, though that seemed unlikely, with Elisabeth. But one never knew. And if there was a baby, then what? What would the halfbreed do then? Marry her? No. Perhaps, if he thought he was in love, and even then, it was still not likely. Love. She had not been in love herself, had never said, *I love you*, had not heard it said back. Sometimes, it seemed to count for so little between a man and a woman, this love, she was surprised at all the fuss.

She looked out the window again. Nothing. She could not stand there all night, looking back at her own face, featureless in the dim glass. There was something eerie in it. Seeing herself there, but not herself, either. The ghost of herself, the night shining through her. It was as if she were already dead. It gave her a bad feeling, a strange sense of something gone very wrong. She turned back to the stove. Surely Elisabeth would be home soon. What did worrying help? Too much worrying was like too much love: it wore you out.

She cracked the eggs and beat them in the tin basin with a little salt, the yolks still pale with winter, sifted in flour, a bit of water dipped from the bucket in the corner, and began to knead, the dough for the *schnittnudeln* pleasantly warm between her fingers. When it was smooth, she sprinkled flour across the wiped counter, lumped the dough in the centre and began to roll it out, evenly, rubbing flour as she needed on the wooden rolling pin to keep the dough from sticking, working by the small glow of the stove. She could light a lamp, but then she would not be able to see so easily out the darkened window should she choose to look, and then again there was not much kerosene. So she worked on, steadily, in the almost dark of a dead woman's kitchen.

Cecilia. Whose wedding dress was worn now by her own daughter. Sometimes, it was as if she knew exactly what Elisabeth meant, understood, though she had never felt a hand on her own face while she slept as Elisabeth had claimed. Nevertheless, there was something. As if she could feel her there, the dead woman, when she was working, as if someone watched over her shoulder. The feeling was so strong that once she had said aloud, over some cucumbers she was pickling, "Am I doing this right?"

At first, she had felt ashamed at her error, was glad no one had been there to hear her, for she must have sounded crazed, speaking to the dead, cold air. Then, when she became used to that presence always at her shoulder, she befriended it. Began to think of it as a her. Cecilia. And she would speak to her sometimes when she was alone there. And she did not feel foolish about it, but, rather, comforted. As if there were now someone who understood, someone who sympathized. There was nothing crazy about it. People often spoke to the dead. In a way, it was like praying, though she would never admit to this, not to anyone, especially Leo, bordering as it did so near to sacrilege.

It was not the same for Elisabeth, of course, who complained that first week after they'd arrived of feeling a hand brush her face in the night. At first, Mary had worried, had suspected Leo, and so she had sat up all night, watching him sleep, only to hear the girl make the same complaint in the morning. There was nothing violent in it, or threatening, she said, just a hand against her face in the night, then gone. But it had disturbed Elisabeth, and so she made a bed for herself in the barn, and there she remained, in spite of entreaties (from her) and threats (from Leo) that she return to the house. How she managed out there in the winter, Mary could not imagine. But the child had always had a mind of her own and so she had told herself, *If she gets cold enough, she will come inside again.* But she never had.

Mary, on the other hand, was glad for Cecilia's company in that little shack with its constant smell of sulphur. When she'd first arrived, she'd scrubbed everything down, emptied out cupboards and drawers, searching out the source of that stench. She'd found nothing. Just dirt, mouse droppings, cobwebs. The desiccated bodies of houseflies so ancient they crumbled to dust at a touch. And after she'd scrubbed everything with scalding vinegar-water, then opened all the windows so air swept through the cramped rooms, she was dismayed to find the house still stinking. She'd become almost used to it now. It did not bother her so much. Tonight she hardly noticed it at all.

Mary filled the big cast-iron pot with water and set it on the stove and stood over it, the watched pot, wondering again at everyone's prolonged absence. It did not bode well. Where could they all be? Elisabeth. Leo. Tonight, even Cecilia had not come.

FOUR

There was a bit of a smoky moon, not much, not enough to cast any light, so when Lathias was well clear of the yard he stopped and lit the lantern again, thinking, *If I cannot see him, at least he will see me. They could be lost out there, trying to find their way home.* But he did not believe that either.

When he reached the Horseman's graves he crossed himself as he had used to, back when he had first come there, nearly the same age as the boy, though that seemed impossible, that he had ever been the age the boy was now, and he tried not to think of that, of his own youth, gone now, and of the Horseman lying down there, dead and decaying also, and that rattling sound on the wind (he tried not to listen for it) that meant he was saddling his fleshless horses to tear up through the earth, to what awful resurrection or apotheosis or vengeance he could not, would not, suppose.

The smoke of the distant dead fire at Hausers' swirled the light across the fields, murky and hypnotic, and so Lathias looked out into the night instead. For a moment, he considered blowing the lantern out, thinking how he must look lit up on that end-less, unrelenting prairie, knowing that he could not see whatever was out there, but whatever was out there could see him. But he thought of the boy instead, of the boy lost in all that darkness, and held the lantern higher and called out for him, though his voice seemed to carry no farther than the lantern's faltering light, and he rode on, the mare snorting into the night and stumbling, the smell of smoke and the river in her nostrils, and in his own, and the fear there, too, and the distant dry rattling of bones, and he rode and rode and rode and then the boy was right there, God help him, was he seeing things? Right there in front of him, his face white from the light, and of it, too, as if brought into being because of and for it. As if he had not existed outside of it, could not have. The boy stood there in the light from the lantern, groping, as if still moving, his hands battering against the light, fighting it almost, and Lathias swung down, gripped him by the shoulder.

"All right," he shouted, "all right." Shaking him. "Are you?"

But the boy could not answer, could see the light before him but could not speak, all those bones rattling on the wind, the Horseman behind him almost, his demon horses, but there was all that light—was it morning?—it was so bright and someone shaking him, hollering at him, the Horseman gripping his shoulder, and all those hooves pounding the frozen dirt all around him, and he struck and struck, fighting to free himself, and then he felt it, that sudden tingling in his arms and legs, sucking the light, running through him, something hot and dark, it was coming, blasting furiously through him, like a train, like the fast pounding of hooves, like the wrath of God, and he swung his hands against it, all that hot blackness. "No," he cried, "no."

And Lathias saw it, too, the way the boy's eyes rolled up in his head. He held him tightly, pressing the boy's arms against his sides, holding him there, shaking.

"Easy," he said, "easy. Hang on." But he could not stop it.

FIVE

They came steadily, down into the valley. By wagon, car and on horse. Someone had lit a bonfire and it threw a weird and whirling light upon the undulating hills, the eerie embers of ice and the mad, slow flow of the river glittering darkly before and because of it. Ranged along the bank, lanterns and torches moved with a slow and meticulous grace, as if carried by other than mortal hands. It was cold, and a light snow had begun to fall, the flakes so fine and spare, some thought at first that they were not snow but only the wish of snow, the belief that snow, even then, with a girl drowned in the river, could be.

Later, some would remember stopping, at that moment when the snow began to fall, and looking around, marvelling at the strangeness, the peculiar beauty. Of course, it all still seemed so impossible, a mistake. Had they not just seen her the other day, in town with her mother? Remember, standing outside Stednick's, looking at the window display while her mother sold eggs to Stednick or bartered or begged more credit, more fool she, and the girl just stood there peeling chunks of paint from the windowsill until Stednick had come out and shouted at her, really the man did not know how to speak without shouting, and the girl just stood there staring at him, looking as if she could not care about him or his paint or his windowsill one way or another, and could not care either that Stednick stood there shouting at her while people passed on the street, she was not even ashamed, remember, just the other day? But, no, that was weeks ago, at least. Was it? My God, how time flies. Even so, only weeks. And now she was drowned. Gone. She was, and now she wasn't. They shook their heads. Impossible, they said, impossible.

Though it was not only possible, but inevitable; oh, not in this way, perhaps, or at this particular time, but some day and some way and so why not this way as well as any other? And that boy, could his word even be trusted? Perhaps the girl was home already. Had anyone checked? But there was that hole in the ice, and the boy, draped in that blanket, sitting there in his father's wagon, alone and imperious, it seemed, as if he held some dark dominion over those lights and those hills and that river. Over that girl. Over life and death. It put one in mind of something, of someone else . . . why, Leo Krauss, for heaven's sake, he looks just like Leo Krauss sitting there. But no, how foolish. He was just a boy. Wasn't he? Still, he looked so unconcerned. What could he be thinking?

If only they knew. The boy was not thinking much, his brain slow, cold; he knew only that some time ago, when the snow began to fall, someone had come to the wagon and draped the blanket about his shoulders and squeezed his hand (had they? It seemed that they had, but perhaps he had only wished it). Since then he had sat alone, watchful and shivering, marvelling at the silence, at all those people—so many, where had they all come from?—and those lights and that river. Marvelling at the dumb beauty of it. He tried to imagine the sun, the river flowing into it, east and east, raising it up, golden and glorious.

But it was dark. The glittering fire, the ghostly lanterns, even these seemed to throw no warmth, only a cold and eerie light. His head was heavy, and his limbs, too. He closed his eyes and let his head drop, felt himself sink and drift, down, down, and all that cold, dark water.

"Show us again."

It was his father, beside the wagon, dusted in a ghost of snow. The boy blinked at him, then climbed down with the blanket clutched about him and stood a moment, his father waiting, and others, too, he could see them now, waiting for him, and so he led them to the river, stood there staring, trying to remember in all that darkness. When they had first come, he had walked the bank, looking for the spot, feeling more sure. But now it did not seem possible, was he even remembering it right? Had it even happened? Part of him believed she must be home by now—had anyone checked? But he did not say that. His father stood beside him, waiting. And the others. The boy looked at the river, he wanted to be sure. Though it did not matter. The futility of it all was remarkable to him. But he did not say that, either. He merely pointed with the corner of the blanket.

"You're sure?"

He nodded, but he was not, he was no longer sure of anything. He had a vague memory, as of a dream, of Elisabeth far out on the ice, irritable and taunting—why was she so angry with him?— while around them the hills darkened and the wind died and the faint, dry rattle of bones drifted down into the valley.

Do you hear that? she'd said, calling to him through the darkness.

Where are you?

Can you hear that?

I can't see you, where are you?

Die Pferdekenner.

Don't.

"You're sure?" his father asked again.

"Yah," someone said from behind him, "how can he be sure?"

"It's too dark," another added, "he wouldn't remember."

"Ach, leave the boy alone. Hasn't he had enough?"

"It's not the remembering that's the question."

That is how it went, the boy standing dizzy among them, and his mother, his mother had not come, she was back at the house, but his father, where was he? And, Lathias? Someone held a lantern up to his face and he blinked, blinded, squeezed his eyes together, as if he would cry, as if he could cry.

"Leave him alone," someone said. "We don't know what happened."

"Maybe he should talk, then. Maybe he should tell us."

"You're scaring him."

He squinted his eyes, rubbed them, tried to see past the green glare of light. The blanket slipped from his shoulders, but he did not bend to retrieve it.

"Try and be sure," his father said.

"I'm sure." But he was not.

"All right," his father said quietly, "go back to the wagon."

But the boy just stood there, thinking there was something more expected of him, what was it? Something more he could say.

"Where is Lathias?" he asked, though that was not it either.

"Gone," his father said, "to get the mother."

The boy stood there, waiting; for what, he did not know.

"Go on," his father said again, but not looking at him, and then he walked away with the others, lanterns swinging, leaving him alone there in a pool of darkness.

———

Just before dawn a few of the men went home and came back with chains and ropes and grappling hooks made from pieces of old plows. Everybody stood and watched as they cast and pulled, cast and pulled, moving painstakingly downstream from where the boy said she'd gone through. The snow had stopped falling and it was turning colder again. Some of the women had brought coffee and cold meat and buns for the men dredging the river, and when the ones who were watching caught the smell of that food and coffee they realized how cold they were and they stood around stamping their feet and smelling that food, and then they said, *But there is nothing more to do, I guess. No, there is nothing to be done here. There is help enough now,* and they stood around a minute more and then they went home to their breakfasts.

A few stayed throughout the early dawn, still casting, though there seemed little point. The Schneider brothers, Stolanus, Mike Weiser, Art Reis, some others. There was a group of boys who had been watching upriver a distance, quietly at first, with their collars turned up and their caps pulled low and their hands jammed into their pockets, exchanging a forbidden cigarette between them, but then, catching the excitement of a death, the smell of it, the way animals do, one of the boys—the one who had come with the cigarette (the one who, as an old man in St. Joseph's extended-care facility in Victoria, would tell the story of the dredging to the attendants as they helped him with his bath, always too cold, but he would confuse the details so that sometimes it was the boy who had drowned and not the girl, always finishing in tears, begging for the cigarette which he was no longer allowed to have)—slid out onto the ice at the edge, retreated, ran out again, sliding in his big boots. Soon he was followed by others, quietly, tentatively at first, taking turns, feeling the danger, and then crazily, and all at once, back and forth, with wild whoops and hollers, farther and farther out, toward where the ice was thinner and the water deeper. By mid-morning, even they were cold and hungry and disappointed at the lack of a body. They went home, too. And the girls who had been sitting huddled together in a wagon, shivering, not from the cold, but from the idea of a death, and one so close to them, or not close to them, but close to being them, Elisabeth—Brechert, was it?—out there in the river, she was out there somewhere beneath the ice—*Just imagine, it could just as easily have been you, Clara, or you, Lena, it could have been any one of us. Oh, awful, how can you say it?*—even they began to tire of talking about how well they had known the girl, that Brechert girl—was it Brechert?—began to tire of outdoing each other in tales of their kindnesses toward her, and began to tire mostly because the boys who they had been pretending not to watch no longer whooped and slid on the ice and cast glances in their direction, and so they went home, too. Soon the men packed up their chains and ropes and hooks with half-frozen hands and loaded their own wet, cold bodies into wagons driven only of necessity by their wives.

Soon everyone was gone but Stolanus, and still Lathias had not returned with the mother. The boy was in the wagon, awake now, but Stolanus just stood there on the bank by himself, awaiting the girl's mother, staring out at the river, wondering, maybe, just a little, just briefly, for the first time in his life, if his son really was capable of hurting someone, of hurting that girl.

SIX

The boy did not remember watching that sun rise mute and cold above the colourless horizon. Everyone had gone, only his father stood looking out at the river, his wretched hands stuck up into his coat sleeves, his clothing wet and slowly stiffening in the cold. The boy watched him, watched the snow that fell lightly again settle on his father's dark cap, on his shoulders, his body so still he appeared to have frozen there, too, in that steady, windless cold, and he thought, *Someday, when I am old, when he has gone to his grave, I will remember this, my father standing there at the river with the snow coming down on him. I will remember this.*

When Stolanus finally turned, the boy lifted a corner of the blanket in greeting. Then, when his father did not wave back, he let it drop, feeling foolish, and still with that sick feeling in the pit of his stomach. His father appeared to be staring right through him. He bit his lip to keep from crying. Then he heard it, too, and he turned, and looked up to where a wagon was descending slowly into the valley, ghostly through the snow. Was it Leo? But it was not. It was Lathias, and beside him, Mary, though he did not recognize her at first, she looked different somehow, and it occurred to the boy that he had never seen her that way before, out in the open. Always she seemed to be half hidden, peeking around the edges of things, doorways, Leo. As they neared, he realized how heavy the woman was, he had not known it before, she was wide and soft, broad across her chest and a round belly swelling out from beneath her coat, Leo's coat. She was a big woman, but also, she was young. He had not known. As she stepped down from the wagon and came toward him through the veil of snow, in the soft light of a March dawn, she seemed much younger than he had thought. There was something pretty in her face, beautiful even, the way her dark hair swept back squarely from her fore-head, the curve of her nose, her mouth parted slightly and puffing in the cold, coming toward him, it seemed to take an eternity, and Lathias behind her, and his father coming, too, quickly, from the river, they all moved toward him, through the snow, it made him dizzy, all that slow, swirling motion converging upon him, and he thought, *She will want to know what happened now. I will have to tell her.* Thinking, *There is nothing to tell. She was, and then she wasn't.* His head light, ballooning with the impossibility of it all.

When she reached the wagon she stopped and stared up at him, her breath coming in short puffs he could read on the air, her upper lip wet and glistening. She stared up at him, he thought she would speak, but she only reached for him, her big soft hands, reached up at him, as if they would wrench him from his seat. He heard his father call, was aware that he was running toward them, was aware that the woman's mouth was moving now.

"*Bitte*," she was saying, clutching him in her strong hands. "Please."

Then everything went black.

SEVEN

"She would not have hurt him."

It was his father. The boy lay in his upstairs bedroom, warm and tucked beneath the feather tick, fully clothed, he realized, and his mouth felt dry and hot as if he had a fever.

"Maybe not." His mother, her voice coming too, through the iron grate in his floor. Talking to his father. It seemed impossible. And he wondered if Lathias were there, too, sitting at the table in the kitchen beneath him. The boy did not move, did not breathe, for fear of missing something, a word between them, the beat of his own heart.

He flinched at the sound of a coffee cup set down on the table.

"Do you think she thinks . . . ?"

"No."

"Why not? Some do already. Will say it. Are saying it."

"Ach, Helen. I don't know. We should send him to Heinrichs, maybe."

"Heinrichs? Are you crazy? They don't even know him."

"Just for a little. Let it all blow over."

"It will never blow over."

"Then Battleford. We will send him to seminary."

"He is not even thirteen yet."

"But they would take him. If we told them—"

"No! What are you thinking?" Dropping her voice. "They will never take him then. They will think the same as everyone else, that he's—"

"What?"

There was a long silence. Then his father said, "They will have to know about it, the seizures."

"Yes, that. Of course that. But not about . . . oh, I can't even think it. That girl."

"Think what? That he—"

"No!" Lowering her voice again. "No, for God's sake, he never would."

"I thought that you—"

"No. Just that girl. Isn't that enough?"

"What does that mean? Isn't what enough?"

"Nothing."

Then they were silent again. Through the window, the boy could see Lathias cross and recross the yard in the early light, enter the barn.

"I should go," his father said, after a while.

"Go?"

"They will dredge again this morning. Farther downstream."

"What for? What good will that do?"

The boy heard his father rise, the floorboards creak beneath his weight.

"You're going, then?"

"I said I was."

"But he will be awake soon."

"And?"

"And you should be here."

"And if I am here and not there, how would it look?"

The boy heard the rustle of his father's coat, knew he would then pull on his boots, his hat, and last, his gloves, first the right, then the left, always the same order, every time.

"Lathias will be here. He'll wait here with you."

"You should be here. You're his father."

"How would it look?" After a minute he added, "You don't need to be afraid of him."

"Don't talk so stupid. I don't know why you would say that. Afraid."

"I shouldn't have. Forget about it. But we must do something, not? We must decide. You know what they think, some of them."

"If it had been another boy—"

"But it was not."

"Does Leo know?"

"I think if he had we might have heard from him by now. He was not there when Lathias went for Mary. She wanted to wait for him. If you can imagine."

"God help us, he will try to make something of it. Mark my words."

Another long silence and then the boy heard his father pull the door open.

"Tell him I'll be back soon."

And the door pulled shut and silence descended, a heavier silence, as if his mother were not there at all, as if the house were empty. The boy leaned back and pretended it was. Then, after a minute, he closed his eyes.

He woke to hard sunlight, blinding, someone in a chair by the window. He lurched up from the pillows, remembering.

"Good," Lathias said, "you're awake."

Only later that morning, after his mother had brought him food on a wooden tray and the three of them—his mother, the boy,

Lathias—had sat there wordlessly watching the food grow cold, until finally she carried the tray back down to the kitchen, and only Lathias stayed, staring bleakly from where he sat, though not at the boy, but only out the window, though there could be nothing to see out there, his face pale and drawn deeply with lines at the corners of his mouth, his eyes reddened and hollow as if he had not slept, the hard sun glinting fiercely off his cropped black hair, only then did the boy speak.

"Lathias?"

"Yes?"

"What do they think?"

EIGHT

When Leo rose from his pallet by the stove, the fire was out—if there had been one at all—and the room was cold, a plate of food on the counter, cold, too, and hardened. He called out, though he knew by instinct and memory that the house was empty, the way one who has once known grief or despair will know the ghost of that feeling ever after, though they may not put a name to it. And he could not remember if Mary had been there when he'd come home.

The water in the tin bucket had crusted over with ice and he broke the dipper free, cutting his knuckles against the shattered surface, and scooped out a ladleful, the chips of ice knocking against his teeth, sending an ache back deep into his skull. He drank two more dippers, wiped his mouth on the back of his sleeve, called again, though for no other reason than to hear the sound of a voice in all that early quiet. He looked out the window. The wagon was there in front of the barn. And the mule, too, standing dumb in the adjacent corral.

He drank one more dipperful of water, wiped his mouth. Then he buttoned his suit jacket across his chest and pulled his hat over his ears and left the shack, his hands fisted against the cold.

NINE

Wing's had opened for business as usual, of course, there was no reason it shouldn't, though word of the girl's drowning had already begun to spread through town.

Ed Kotschky, who had heard word from Mike Eichert, had come to enlist help for the second dredging of the river. The news silenced the men, as they sat with their heavy coats unbuttoned, hunched and squint-eyed over their coffees in the smoky, pink-walled café, with Wing's wife at the counter and Wing himself hovering between the cash register and the coffeepot, wiping ketchup bottles and emptying ashtrays, for, though the men had not known the girl well, or in some cases at all, she was a girl nevertheless, and one of their own, as far as that went.

When it had been quiet for a time, Ed, who'd taken a minute to have a coffee (what matter now to the girl?), though he still stood with hat and coat on, warming his bare hands around the cup, repeated, "So, if any of you can spare the time . . ."

The men coughed, wiped at noses with checked hankies, stared deeply into cups of coffee.

Finally, someone said, "What's the mother's name again?"

"She was a Schiller, not?"

"Fox Valley Schiller?"

"Dakota, I thought."

"Herb knows her, from the shop."

"What is it, Herb? What's the last name?"

"I thought Dunhauer."

"Never heard of Dunhauers."

"Dakota, like I said."

"No, no, you're thinking of Marian Weiser's people. Leo's first wife, Cecilia. She was a Dunhauer."

"That's right. This one's a Brechert."

"Dakota, too, not?"

"I wonder if her people will come."

"Hell of a trip, this time of year."

"And another snow yet coming, I'd bet on it."

"Well, she's got Leo."

"Christ, yah. That's a real comfort."

"That's her only girl, too. Or was."

"She lost her first husband?"

"Wasn't ever a first husband. That's what Ludmila said. Or what Marian told her. Whether it's true or not, I don't know."

"That explains a lot."

"Explains what she's doing with Leo, anyway."

"Well, there's one thing for sure, those that live by the sword, die by it."

There was a moment of perplexed silence, until someone said, "What the Christ is that supposed to mean?"

"Means Leo Krauss, that's what it means."

"You think he gives a rat's ass about it?"

"It's not him, it's her that suffers. It's the missus."

"Well, at least that girl won't suffer no more. That's something, I guess."

And they were quiet then and nobody spoke of Leo any more. They slurped at their coffees and smoked, heads down, coughing and snorting and swiping at noses.

Ed, who had finished his coffee, who had been going back and forth with himself about it, wondering should he, shouldn't he, but not able to restrain himself in the end (they would find out anyway, sooner or later), he finally said, "That Schoff boy was with her."

They all looked up from their cups.

"Stolanus's boy?"

Ed nodded.

"The one . . . ?"

"That's right."

"He went through, too?"

"No," Ed said, "no. They were down there together, but only the boy come back. Stolanus's hired man—"

"The halfbreed?"

"He's Indian?"

"I thought German."

"He's half. Half German, half Indian. Or something."

"Now that you say it, he does have that look."

"Hell of a worker, though."

"And loyal to that boy."

"Treats him like a brother."

"I'm surprised he stuck around, after."

"Loyal, like I say. Those halfbreeds are like that."

"What? They'd as soon shoot you as look at you."

"Halfbreed, hell, there's a few of us would as soon shoot you as look at you."

"Well, he's loyal anyway."

"Hard worker."

"Funny they kept him on, Helen and Stolanus."

"Wasn't even really his fault, what I heard."

"He was driving, wasn't he?"

"Anyway," Ed said, raising his voice a little, "it was him that found the boy. He was running back from the river, I guess, the boy was. It was dark. He had one of them, what do you say, those fits he has."

"The halfbreed?"

"No, the boy. Christ, listen, will you? The girl wasn't with him. The hired man found the boy coming back from the river and he, the boy, had one of those fits. When he come to, he said she'd fallen in the river, the Brechert girl."

"Fallen?"

"Through the ice."

"That's the boy was run over by the wagon."

"He just finished saying that."

"Boy's not right in the head."

"Miracle he lived."

"Ach, he's all right."

"Those head injuries. Remember Martin Schlesser?"

"Schlesser was all right."

"Say what you like, he gave me the creeps and so does that boy."

"Normal, they say. Except for the fits. Harmless."

"Harmless? You think so?"

"There's a girl out there might beg to differ with you."

And that made them think of the girl again. Wing came around with the coffeepot but they all shook their heads and Ed put his cup on the table and said, "Well, I guess it's time."

When only two or three of the men moved to join him, he said, "It's got nothing to do with Leo. Nor that boy, neither. Think of the mother. Think if it was one of your own out there."

And then he put his money on the counter and pulled on his gloves, nodding to Wing as he went out.

TEN

Someone, out of duty or consideration, notified the constable, fifteen miles away at Triumph, that there had been a supposed drowning, and Corporal McCready—William Lance McCready, Macky to his friends, formerly of Havre, Montana, formerly of Saskatoon, Saskatchewan, who had late in his police career accepted, that is what he said, accepted a lateral promotion and who liked to say over and over, sounding more each time like he was quoting himself, *This is a peaceful place. It holds no interest for the cowboys, and the immigrants hardly ever get to town,* and who looked upon the occasional accidental deaths and tragedies, though he would never admit it, not even to his wife, as a kind of personal attack upon him, and who deeply resented that, in the case of a drowning, it was his job to lead the dredging of the river—though in truth he never did a thing but come out and stand there a few minutes, well back from the edge of the river so as not to get his boots wet, frowning and scratching his nose—and to carry news of the tragedy to the families—who already knew, since they were the ones dredging the river—this Corporal McCready came down to the river that first morning and stood watching and smoking and scratching his nose while the men cast hooks out into the river and hauled them back in through the ice, he watched a while and then he returned to Triumph and later that day, after a good lunch, drove out to Helen and Stolanus's and talked to the boy briefly and, finally, went on record to say that the drowning death of one Elisabeth Brechert had been, in his opinion, purely accidental.

That was his opinion, both as a professional officer of the law and as a member of this fine and peaceful community. And when there were some who voiced a different opinion, he said again that he had made up his mind and he meant to stick by it. What others thought, well, that was their own goddamned business and entirely outside his jurisdiction.

ELEVEN

So it seemed she was dead, after all, in spite of the disbelief, the absence of a body. McCready had confirmed it and that seemed to settle the matter in everyone's minds, everyone's except maybe the mother's, Mary's. Or that is what they said, *Ach, the poor mother,* who spent every day now down at the river, yes, they had all seen her there, walking the banks, or just standing and staring, as if the girl might just somehow appear, as if she might be alive, after—Was it a week already? No, not a week, not that long—well, anyway, if you're looking for the mother, she won't be at home.

But no one was looking for her, not any more. They were, in fact, happy enough to avoid her, for what was there to say, what was there to do? And then, she had never really been a part of the parish, either, kept too much to herself. Oh, she was not like Helen Schoff, that is not what they meant, she did not put herself above them, but she did set herself apart, made little effort, come now, no effort at all, to get to know anyone, always sending that girl to the door when anyone came (and she wouldn't be able to do that any more, no), and never even so much as looking at anyone when they spoke to her, sometimes they wondered if she was deaf, perhaps she was.

And then, too, she was Leo's wife, that is what really kept people away from her, before the drowning and after the drowning, people who would otherwise have gone out of their way to bring food and companionship following a death, throughout the dark, long hours, days, weeks, each blurring numbly into the next. A few did try, coming in groups of two or three, but Mary was never home, or if she was she did not come to the door and Leo would not invite them in, would simply take their offerings of food and bless them in a cursory, belligerent way and let the door swing shut in their faces. What more could be expected of them? After a day or two, they said, *Well, and we are sorry for her, for the mother, but are we to be abused for our goodwill?*

Ma Reis herself had been over several times those first few days and always her welcome was the same. It was enough to make her want to knock Leo's head against the wall. Not once did she see Mary, though she suspected, on at least one occasion, that the woman was, in fact, at home and not at the river as Leo had insisted when Ma pressed him. She thought, *If I can't catch her at home, I will watch to see when she passes, and I will follow her.*

Ma Reis sat by her own kitchen window all one afternoon, waiting. When Mary passed on the road around about nightfall, Ma grabbed her coat. Art was angry with her for it, it was none of her jeezly business, why did she always have to stick her nose into other people's business? And Leo Krauss's business, of all people. Did she not remember all the trouble Pius Schoff'd had with the old one? Those Krausses, leave them alone, they are nothing but trouble, and anyway it was almost suppertime, and what about that? That is what he said.

And Ma said, "Ach, you men are all the same, nothing is worth any trouble unless it has a wheel attached to it, or a hoof."

"Yah," Art said, under his breath, "there's a mule that's given me many a year of trouble."

"If you didn't want to trouble with a mule," Ma said, "you shouldn't have married one."

"Yah," Art said again, "that mule didn't give me much choice, if I remember right, and what am I to do about supper?"

But Ma was already out the door and did not hear him.

It was dark when she got to Krausses', and no lights on in the house. Ma stood in the yard a minute, Cecilia's old bottle tree tinkling a little in the darkness. She wondered whether or not to knock. Perhaps Mary was asleep already. She would not want to wake her, the poor woman must be exhausted. Then—she didn't know how exactly, it was kind of like the shiver one gets when someone walks over their grave—she knew all at once that Mary was sitting there on the porch, right in the old chair that Leo had kept there ever since he used to sit and watch Cecilia working in the yard. So she stood there quietly, knowing the woman must have seen her approach, thinking Mary might speak.

When she didn't, Ma said, very gently, "Mary? Is that you?"

The chair legs creaked a little and Mary said, "Yah, what is it?"

Ma walked up to the porch steps, asked if she might sit a minute, and when Mary did not reply, settled herself on the top stair. She thought, *No use beating around the bush,* and so she said, flat out, "You have an awful lot on your shoulders, Mary. Is there anything I can do to help?"

Mary said, "What is on my shoulders?"

Ma did not know how to answer. Felt, in fact, a little irritated with the woman's response—was she an imbecile?—and so she said, bluntly, "Well, Mary, losing your daughter that way. That is more than enough in itself, not? And then it must be so hard here anyway . . ."—might as well come right out about it—"with Leo."

The porch chair creaked a bit more and finally Mary said, "Yah, that is what everyone thinks, not? That it is so hard for me. That Leo is so hard." She paused and shifted in her chair. "Tell me," Mary said, "what is so bad about Leo? What does everyone think is so bad?"

Ma was shocked. She had assumed, like everyone else, that things must be bad for Mary, with Leo. Assumed that Mary must know herself that things were bad. How could she not? And she remembered Cecilia, then, and how bad things had been for her and the children. But, no, had they? Come to think of it, things had not been so bad at all. They had prospered, had even seemed happy. But Cecilia was dead. And her children as good as scattered by the winds, her children that were no longer her children. And so what was it that was so bad about Leo? What was it that they all despised so? Ma sat for a while, wondering how to answer, trying to say exactly what it was about Leo, what was so unforgivable, what he'd done that was so awful. And in the end all she could think to say was, "Why, he's just Leo. Just the way he is. Isn't that awfully hard to live with? You can't be happy here."

And Mary sighed and shifted and said, "With my father we lived with nothing, here we live with something. Maybe it is not always a good something. But it is something, still. Who is to say which is worse? Leo is not the best maybe. But I am not the best either."

A breeze rattled the bottles in the cottonwood tree. Ma sat quietly again, smoothing her dress across her knees. Finally, she said, "I am sorry, Mary."

Mary just nodded a little, a slight movement in the darkness. Then she said, "Those bottles, there. You hear?"

"Yes," Ma said.

"They're pretty."

"Yes," Ma agreed. "They are."

"Did Leo put those bottles there?"

"No," Ma said. "That was his first wife, Cecilia."

Mary nodded. "Leo married her," she said.

"Yes," Ma said. "That's right."

Mary nodded again. Finally she said, "So Leo put those bottles there."

"No," Ma said, "Cecilia did."

"But Leo married Cecilia."

What? Ma thought. *Has she lost her mind?* "Yes," she said, a little impatiently. "He married her."

"And so it was Leo who put those bottles there."

Ma was about to object again. Then she closed her mouth, sat listening to the bottles tinkling across the darkened yard.

"She comes sometimes," Mary said. "Cecilia does."

Bah, Ma wanted to say, *nonsense.* But she did not.

"She would come sometimes to Elisabeth. She would touch her face, in the night. At first I thought, Leo. And so it was good, her out in the barn, away from him."

Away? Ma thought. *That gave him free licence.* But she did not say that. Instead she just said, "Oh, Mary."

"I know what you think," Mary said. "But Leo would not hurt her. Not like that."

"How do you know, Mary?"

"I just know."

And all the while the bottles tinkling away across the yard. Ma began to be sorry she had come at all. She was not often at a loss for words.

"Will you go away?" she asked.

"Why?" Mary said.

"Well," Ma said, "you wouldn't want to stay," and then she added, "now."

"Why not?"

Ma shook her head in frustration. "Mary," she said, "you can't be happy here."

"What's happy?" Mary said. "Are you happy?"

"Yes," Ma said, after a moment, "I am."

Then Mary fell silent and Ma felt bad that she had said that, felt terrible that she had admitted to her own happiness, the fullness of her life (for it was full, she was very fortunate, her children, who were not perfect either maybe, nor was she, nor was Art, who knew she was a mule and loved her anyway), but she was sorry she had said it to Mary, had waved her happiness like a flag in Mary's face, making her feel worse. And so she added, "Mostly, I am. Not always, but mostly."

She wished that she could see the expression on Mary's face, who sat in heavy silence.

Finally, Mary said, "How do you know?"

"How do I know what?"

Ma waited.

"How do you know that you are happy?" Mary said.

Ma said later that was the saddest thing she'd ever heard. She said it almost made her jump up and take that big, sad woman in her arms and rock her like she was a little girl. But she never found out whether or not she would have, because just then, out of the darkness and the prairie, came the sound of a wagon, and pretty soon they could see one emerging as if out of the road itself, out of the earth, and Ma thought, at first, *It is Art, he has come for me, wanting his supper, the old fool.*

But it was not Art Reis, it was Leo. He lurched his old wagon into the yard, just a few feet from where Mary and Ma sat, he could not see them, and so he hollered, "Mary, get some supper on," and he climbed slowly down and began to unhitch the mule, fumbling in the darkness. When no one replied, he called out again, "Mary." But tentatively, as if he knew he would be calling out to an empty house, or not knew, but feared. It was fear Ma heard in his voice, and she was surprised and ashamed for him, for Leo.

The two women waited while Leo led his mule to the corral. Then Mary rose and opened the screen door.

Ma said softly, "Mary."

"I got to get supper on," Mary said. And she stepped into the house and let the screen door fall shut quietly behind her.

Ma heard Leo coming from the barn, then, and she said she didn't know what got into her, it was not like her to be deceptive, that was for sure, she liked to be open about things, but she scooted up onto the far side of the porch and crouched there so Leo would not see her. She just did not want to face him.

He stepped heavily up and through the screen and shut the peeling wooden door behind him. At first she only crouched there in the cold, her coat wrapped tightly around her, listening to the scrapings and thumpings as Mary went about making supper, wanting to be sure Leo was not still at the screen door where he would see her leave.

But then some small light began to glow through the window, from the stove Mary had lit, Ma assumed, and she poked her head up, just barely, well back from the window so the light would not catch her face. There was Mary working heavily at the counter, and, there, there was Leo, so near she could have reached out and touched him had there been no window between them. He was sitting at the table, his forearms resting there, watching Mary go about the supper. And the silence there, oh, the silence. It was unbearable, Ma said.

Soon a pot of water was boiling on the stove and Mary took the dough she had cut into strips for the *schnittnudeln* and scattered it into the water. Ma was so busy watching Mary, wondering at the heaviness in the woman, that it was a moment before she looked to see what Leo was doing. In fact, he was looking out the window into the darkness. Looking right at her, it seemed, and Ma caught her breath, clutched at the window ledge to steady herself. But then Leo pulled his hanky from his pocket, wiped at his nose and put it back, and Ma said she could relax again.

Ma was just about to sneak down the stairs and out of the yard, when Leo rose suddenly from the table, his chair scraping brutally against the floor, and she heard him say, his voice distorted through the thin, cheap glass, "Come now, Mary. Kneel down with me and pray."

"But," Mary said, gesturing to the stove, "supper."

Leo raised his voice. "Come," he said. "And pray for your daughter's soul, as well as your own."

Ma told Art later that it was all she could do not to pound against the glass, she was outraged, furious, as she watched Mary leave the pot of boiling water there on the stove and go to the table and cross herself and kneel with Leo.

But the fury passed quickly, was replaced by a kind of sickened awe, that Leo was not putting on a show after all, that piety of his, if that's what it could be called, that he was the same in his own home. Ma said she felt awful, ashamed, yes, ashamed, wished she had never stayed, crouched there in the dark spying on them, watching them kneel in the light of the stove and that pot that had begun to boil over, hissing and splatting and smoking, yet neither of them moved. She said it was worse, seeing that, than anything else she could have imagined going on over there. Mary giving Leo what no one else, except Cecilia, had ever given him, not because she loved him, as perhaps Cecilia had, but because she felt it was owed to him. She said it was awful, and yet, she had been wrong, yes, she could admit it even as she crouched there, seeing how they knelt shoulder to shoulder, so close in that cramped little shack. Yes, she had been wrong: it was not just awful; there was something beautiful about it, too, and touching.

And so Ma crept off the porch and walked home in the darkness, a terrible, tender feeling in her heart, a burned smell filling the air.

TWELVE

The good people of Knochenfeld parish waited until the end of that week, not out of any hope, however dim, that the girl's body might be recovered, it was too late for that, but only out of respect for the mother, who still walked the frozen banks each day, the dark river coursing on and on beneath the ice, walked, but without rage or hope, as some thought she might, her arms hanging at her sides, seeking, others said, neither miracle nor enlightenment, but only proximity, and that, too, only illusion, the girl's body could be anywhere by now.

They waited, and then, when it seemed pointless to wait any longer, they went to speak to Mary, though Mary was, as always, at the river (who would disturb her there?), and so they asked Leo instead, and Leo said, "Do what you want, what is it to me?"

Then they waited some more until, on Saturday morning, the church bell was rung a full ten minutes (no one knew what made Father Rieger so generous in this mark of respect and condolence; usually, as Ma said, he acted as if ringing that bell might wear it out). They rang the bell a full ten minutes and it was a cold clear day and the sound of that bell was like angels calling across the snowy fields. Most went to the Mass, bumping in wagons and motorcars down the frozen roads, even those came who had not known the girl, even those who had felt an acute loathing toward Leo, for the death of a child is a particular tragedy existing outside the bounds of both amity and rancour. They came wordlessly, as was only right and proper, to pay their respects and to pray for the soul of the dead girl. They came, their breath puffing out in plumes, their bodies bundled darkly against the cold.

But Mary and Leo were not there. The front bench where Leo used to sit with Cecilia, and then with their children, and then with Mary and Elisabeth, was now empty. There was no one.

And across the aisle, where Schoffs used to sit—the old folks, Pius and the missus when they were yet alive—and then Stolanus and Helen and the boy and that hired man, too, who was as good as one of them, he had been with them so long, that pew stood empty also. It was impossible not to notice, impossible to keep one's mind only on the girl and the brief eulogy delivered by Mike Weiser, who had known little enough about her; impossible not to think of the ancient rift between the two families—Schoffs and Krausses—and how it seemed there was, had always been, something between them, some darker destiny waiting to be fulfilled, it was not over, anyone could see that, sitting there staring at those two empty pews

No, none of them attended the service, the long Mass for the dead, not Krausses, not Schoffs, not even the hired man, the halfbreed. Not even he had made an appearance, though he had been a friend of sorts to the girl, not? Hadn't they always been down poking around the river together, him and the girl and the retarded boy?

But Lathias would not have gone to the service, not even if Stolanus and Helen and the boy had gone. He went to the river instead, not down beneath the Bull's Forehead, where the girl had gone missing and where the mother would surely be (her, of all people, he did not want to see). Instead, he went upriver, nearer the fort, and he would have taken the boy with him had Stolanus and Helen allowed it.

But Stolanus had said, "And what will people think, then, if he is not at the church, and then not even at home, but at the river yet? How does it look for none of us to be there for the service? It is as if we are confessing to something." Lowering his voice, though the boy was up in his room with the door shut, as always now. Stolanus tried, God knows, reasoned, insisted even, that they go to the Mass. But Helen just cast him a cold glance and set her shoulders firmly.

And he was right, Stolanus was. Already there were some, a stupid few, who blamed the boy, not out of some sense of justice or grief—for they had hardly known the girl, not known her at all—but simply out of instinct, to have something concrete amid all the uncertainty, blame the most concrete instinct of all, harder even than hate; and for the intrigue of it, also, though they would not admit to something so base, but it was true nevertheless. The same who had always been disgusted by the boy, afraid of him, even. *First that girl,* they said, *then who's next?* Just a few, but it is always the ignorant who make themselves heard, as Ma Reis observed. *None of our children are safe,* they said. And, *Children? You mean our daughters. They never did find the body, God knows what else had been done to her.*

Someone had begun leaving dead animals nailed to the fence-post at the entrance to the Schoff farm. The first a rabbit, gutted stem to stern. Helen found it there and quickly tore it down before the boy could see. Then other things: a cat, though not one of theirs; a prairie chicken; a sparrow. All gutted and bleeding coldly. It rattled Helen, though she knew it was stupid. Not the deaths themselves, nor the shock of it, not even the violence itself, but only the implied threat. Stolanus said it was just pranks, some young people maybe, without thought or reason or even courage behind them, only the tongues of their parents.

"Ach, you know how they can get caught up," he said, "listening to their parents talk, the parents sometimes stupider than the children."

But Helen took a darker view; she insisted it be reported to the police.

So Stolanus drove over with Lathias one morning to Triumph and they sat in McCready's cramped waiting area looking down at their dirty boots while Mrs. Ivy McCready cast them disdainful glances from where she sat at a little table sucking on a raspberry drop and typing a letter to her old girlfriend in Saskatoon. *You should just see now,* she had begun, when her husband opened the door to his office and nodded the two men in.

McCready sat and listened to Stolanus a while and then he said, in the tone he always used when talking to the immigrants, "You let me know if anything worse turns up, do you understand, if it gets worse. Do you get what I'm saying? Then you let me know."

When Stolanus and Lathias arrived home, Helen said, "And? What did he say?"

And Stolanus replied, without looking at her, "Nothing." Then he shut the door to the bedroom behind him.

———

So the boy was no longer allowed to leave the house. Helen was certain he would be harmed somehow, though Stolanus and Lathias did not agree. Whoever was leaving the animals was doing it out of sheer ignorance. There had been a couple other things: gopher heads tossed on the doorstep; the bowels of some unidentified animal. Lathias suspected Leo, though it was hard to say; would he really make the effort? But it was, without a doubt, an act that recalled Leo's father, old Gus; that vengefulness without sense, or without even clear reason.

And though he could not have explained why, Lathias was not really worried about Leo. Did not think much about him at all. He was worried about the boy. He had not been himself since the drowning, which, given the circumstances, was only natural, one could scarcely expect anything else. None of them had. He himself had not wept for her—why would he?—but only felt as if he walked around in a kind of fog, going through the motions of his life without really being in it, feeling strangely distanced from everyone, everything, from his own thoughts, his own body even. He did not want to think of her. It was better that he think of the boy.

But it seemed, when he sat in the boy's room, watching him stare out the window as if he were absent, too, to be more than shock, more than grief; the boy had become secretive and suspicious and fearful in a way he had never been before. He didn't seem to mind being kept at home, and he seemed to have no desire now to leave his cramped, sour bedroom, where before he had been eager to get out, go places.

And so, Lathias knew that what he had once wished to change about the boy appeared to have been changed after all: he had retreated, had hardened. And Lathias was sorry for it. And then he wished that it had not been changed after all, that his wish had not come to be, the way it often goes with wishes.

———

One afternoon, Lathias thought, *Has anyone talked to him even, really talked to him, about what happened?* It seemed they had not spoken in weeks, though it could not have been so long. He had not been up to the boy's room since the day after the dredging of the river, when they had sat together in a cold and bewildered silence, until the boy had said, "Lathias?" and Lathias said, "Yes," and the boy said, "Did they . . . ?" and Lathias said, "No. There was nothing."

Since then, they all—him and Stolanus and Helen—tiptoed around him, ignoring him, almost, as if they believed he had done something to her. *He must think we all believe it*, Lathias thought.

So he went up to the boy's bedroom, listened, and then knocked. When no one answered, he opened the door and looked in. The air was hot and stagnant and the boy lay sprawled in fitful sleep across his bed, the hair at his forehead and temples damp.

Lathias entered and closed the door behind him, then stood, wondering if he should wake the boy. Finally, he reached out and touched his hand gently to the boy's shoulder and the boy started up and blinked at him, as if he could not decide whether Lathias really stood there or whether it was still a dream, or who Lathias even was.

"Hey," Lathias said gently.

The boy settled back then, still watching Lathias with the veiled look he had assumed since the drowning, and it occurred to Lathias that perhaps the look was not distrust at all, or at least, not distrust the way he had thought—that someone might hurt him, might do something to him—but rather, simply fear that Lathias might disappear, too, that anyone could.

Lathias pulled the chair out a bit from the corner and settled into it, perching his hat on his knee. They sat a while in silence, until the boy pulled the covers up over his chest.

Lathias said, "Are you cold? You must be cold," and he pointed to the boy's wet hair.

The boy reached up. "So?"

"So, nothing. I just thought you might be cold."

"Well, I'm not."

Then they sat together, the boy watching Lathias, and Lathias pretending not to watch the boy.

After a while, Helen came up the stairs and into the room and stood there awkwardly and then, as if deciding something, crossed the room and put her hand against the boy's forehead, awkward, too.

"You are hot," she said, then pulled back the covers. "Wet," she said, in surprise, "soaked through."

Lathias sat and pretended to look out the window, wanting to leave, but unable to, not when Helen had just come in.

She tried to touch the boy's forehead again but he turned his head away. She hesitated, then went to the dresser and pulled out a dry nightshirt.

"Put this on," she said quietly. "I will dry your bedding by the stove. Come down and eat and I will dry your things." She paused again, her eyes flickering to Lathias and away. And then she disappeared down the stairs.

When she was gone, Lathias said, "She is worried about you."

But the boy did not reply, or even acknowledge that he had heard, just sat there twisting the damp bedclothes, and then he said, "It's because you are here."

"What's because I'm here?"

"She never touches me," he said, "when we're alone."

Lathias just looked out the window, not knowing what to say because he knew it was true. He sighed. He did not feel like talking to the boy about it after all, about Elisabeth. So he got up and flapped his gloves against his leg and stood there stupidly, his hat in his hand, and said, "Well." He said, "I guess I should get back to it."

The boy sat looking up at him.

"I guess you know I was dreaming," he said.

Lathias shook his head. "Why would I know that?"

"Don't ask me to tell you about it."

"I didn't."

"Because I can't."

Lathias, in spite of himself, said, "Why can't you?"

"I just can't. So don't ask."

"All right, I won't."

The boy squeezed his eyes up, like he was going to cry.

Lathias sighed and sat down again. He rubbed his hand across his mouth. After a minute he said, "You had a dream about her, about Elisabeth?"

But the boy just sat with his face all scrunched up.

"That's not real," Lathias said. "That's just a dream." Knowing it was stupid, but what else could he say? "Just try and forget it.

It's nothing." Thinking, *God help me, I don't want to hear about it, I don't want to talk about any of it.* "Maybe you could talk to Father Rieger," he said, though he knew that was absurd. Why would the boy want to? Talk to Father Rieger, of all people. As if that were even possible. But who else to send him to?

"What for?" the boy said.

"Just . . . if something is bothering you, I don't know, but maybe, just confession, just to make you feel better."

The boy stared a moment. "You think I did something?"

And Lathias thought, *Do I? Is that what I think?* "No," he said, "of course not."

And then it came to Lathias, all at once, so clear, he should have known all along.

He leaned forward, elbows on his knees, looked the boy straight in the eyes. "Do *you* think you did something?"

The boy just sat there, the bedclothes twisting and twisting.

"Do you remember," Lathias said, pulling his chair closer, "do you remember what happened? Before you blacked out?"

"I told you already."

"You told your father. I was down at the river." He did not say, *looking for her.* "Tell me now."

"She was on the ice," he said. The boy looked down at the bedclothes in his hands.

"And then what?"

"And then she wasn't."

That sick, heavy feeling seeped back into the pit of Lathias's stomach.

"Where were you?" he said. "When she—"

He took a deep breath, unable to finish, though there was no reason he shouldn't. What's done was done. What did saying it matter? But it did.

"I was up the draw. I was going home."

"Without her?"

"She was angry," he said. "We argued."

"About what?"

The boy's eyes flicked up at him, briefly, then back down to the twist of bedclothes.

"About you," he said.

Lathias looked out the window then, watching Stolanus by the barn where he fiddled with some machinery or a bit of harness, anything to keep him out of the house.

He sat staring that way so long that the boy finally said, "Don't you want to know why?"

When Lathias did not answer, he said again, "Don't you want to know why we were arguing about you?"

Lathias looked at him, steadily. "No," he said. Feeling a creeping rage now in his belly, thinking, *I cannot do things different. I cannot go back. Not now. So don't put me there, don't you put me there.*

But the boy screwed up his face again, as if he would cry, and Lathias said sharply, "It doesn't matter anyway. Never mind about that now."

The boy sucked his breath in, to stop the tears, said, "It does matter."

Lathias shook his head. "No," he said again, "it doesn't."

"She called you a liar." He said it quickly, and his eyes flashed and welled up again.

Lathias nodded. Then he shrugged and said, "I've been called worse things."

What could it matter? She was dead somewhere in the river. What did it matter now what she had said or felt, about him, about anyone? And he said, "Just because someone calls you a liar, doesn't make you one. Only you can do that."

"But she shouldn't have said it."

"So you were angry with her."

"I didn't want her to talk like that any more, about you. I didn't want her to say that."

"To say I was a liar."

"She was so . . . strange. It was dark. I wanted to go home."

The boy started to cry then. Lathias turned his hat in his hands, slowly. Ran his finger along the brim.

"What did she say I lied about?" In spite of himself, hating himself for it.

"Everything," he choked.

"Like what?"

"I can't tell you," he said, "I can't tell you."

He waited until the boy settled down a bit, and he said, "So you were not angry with her, then?"

The boy looked up in surprise. "Why do you keep saying that?"

Lathias looked out the window, turned the hat slowly in his hands.

"It was dark," the boy said. "And she was being so funny. That way she gets, as if she is angry with you even though you haven't done anything."

"So you started walking home. And she was on the ice. Why was she on the ice?"

"That's what I'm trying to say. She was angry. She said if I left her there—"

"What?"

"She said—"

And he started to cry again.

"What did she say?"

It came out then, all in a choked rush, so that it was difficult for Lathias to decipher what the boy was saying.

"She said she would probably die. That's what she said, that she would die, and I told her that was stupid and she said she would freeze to death and then it would be—"

"What?"

He stopped crying, suddenly, as if amazed at the words on his own tongue, the terrible weight of them. As if hearing them himself for the first time.

"It would be my fault."

Lathias bit at his lip, that old resentment rising again, though what could it matter, now? What matter resentment or mistrust or outrage? Elisabeth dead in the river. He turned his hat slowly, looking down at it. "Then what?" he said.

And the boy spoke, still in that slow amazement, as if it were the dream he was relating now, or as if time had slowed down, stilled, and run backwards. It made Lathias wonder if he was not confusing the two, the reality and the dream, or if he even remembered that night now at all as it had really been, and could anyone anyway? Was it even possible?

"I started up the draw," the boy said.

"And?"

"And she hollered at me. She was standing on the ice."

"Yes?"

"So I told her to come on, then, I would wait for her. But she just stood there. It was dark. I could hardly even see her. I was scared, a little, but I wasn't angry. I just wanted to go home. I called her. She just stood there. So I started walking. She was acting so funny, I just wanted to go home. So I started walking and I thought she would come, then, that she would follow me."

And then the boy stopped and stared down at the blankets and Lathias said, softly, "And then?"

The boy looked at him, his eyes large and feverish.

"I stopped," he said. "I turned around. I didn't want to go home without her. I was scared. It was dark. So I turned around."

"And?"

"She was gone."

Lathias swallowed, shook his head.

"What do you mean? Did you hear the ice crack or did she call out or what?"

"She was just gone. And I thought—"

"What did you think?"

"I thought . . . I thought the Horseman, and so I ran."

Lathias leaned back in his chair, looked out the window again, at Stolanus tinkering the hours away at the barn. *Gone,* he thought. *Just gone.*

After a minute, he said, "Is that what you told McCready?"

The boy shook his head, wiped his nose on the back of his hand. "McCready never asked me that."

And Lathias said, "What do you mean? What did he ask you?"

"McCready wanted to know did I push her in the river."

"That's it? That's all he asked?"

The boy flushed up, spoke so softly Lathias had to lean forward to hear him. "He asked if she was my girlfriend. He asked was I in love with her. He asked did we—"

"All right," Lathias said. "Never mind." He took a deep breath, looked out the window again. He sat like that a long time. The window frosted up from his breath, but he did not lift a hand to rub it clean.

Finally, the boy said, softly, "Do you want to know what I answered?"

Lathias shook his head. "That is a question you don't need to answer for nobody."

"She," he said, "she . . ."

Lathias looked up sharply. "Don't," he said.

"Before she went out on the ice, she said—"

"You don't need to tell me that."

"I want to tell you."

Lathias stood up. "I don't want to know." And he took his hat and his gloves and left.

THIRTEEN

All that week following the Funeral Mass the boy stayed up in his room, sorting through his boxes of junk in a troubled, abstracted way. Lathias worked around the farm with furious determination, mending fence mostly and doing other odd jobs that came with the milder weather, and, when there was nothing left to do, in the lengthening evenings, he mucked out already immaculate stalls and swept the barn again, while Stolanus smoked and watched him from the doorway, saying, "What, are you expecting company?" as always unaware of the biting implication of his words. And when the slatboard floors could not reasonably bear more sweeping, he picked up a curry comb and tucked himself into one of the stalls, and Stolanus would step his cigarette out against the ground and drop the butt into his shirt pocket and say, "Supper soon," and wait for Lathias to reply. But Lathias would say nothing, only watch Stolanus cross the yard, and then, when he had washed at the pump and gone inside, Lathias would do the same, turning up at the table to eat hastily and disappear again, out to the barn, leaving Helen and Stolanus to their own company.

The boy up there in his room seemed not to care, either about Lathias's absence or about the distance between them. At least that is what Lathias told himself. Thinking, *He can see it too now, what I am. She told him. She must have, about the accident. Told him it was me. And now this. Now her. And if I had been there, it would not have happened. It happened because of me. Again.* And he would stop brushing at the mare and lean his forehead up against her hot flank. Thinking, *Because of me.* Thinking, *I know what it is. I know what I should do.* But not able to do that, either.

And so that is how things went, those days. Lathias worked like a man crazed. Stolanus wasted time around the yard. Helen slept or stood staring out the kitchen window, out across the crusted fields, an untouched cup of coffee in her hand and the house a shambles around her, dirty, the scraps of the last meal still littering the stove and the table.

No one saw Leo, or heard anything about him at all, and that was just as well as far as everyone was concerned. And it seemed that everything had settled into that long, numb, dull period of baffled grief that follows a death.

———

Ash Wednesday brought new troubles. Stolanus and Lathias were out in the barn when the sound of a wagon approaching startled them both.

"Schoff," they heard someone holler from the yard, "bring your kid out here. Schoff!"

Stolanus and Lathias exchanged glances.

"Good God," Stolanus said. "Leo."

Stolanus and Lathias walked out of the barn together. Leo was standing in the wagon, looking around, and Mary was sitting beside him, her face tucked into her big black shawl.

"Leo," Stolanus said, carefully, "what can I do for you?"

Leo turned and stared at them, trying for that old look of superiority and disdain, but clearly more than three sheets to the wind, swaying and unsteady on his legs.

"You bring that boy of yours out here," he said. "I want to talk to him."

"He is sleeping," Stolanus said. "What is it?"

"What do you think?" he said, and he jerked his thumb at Mary who sat staring at her lap.

The sight of Mary brought that sick feeling back to Lathias again, doubly hard, brought the reality of it all back, and he stood there hoping she would not uncover her face and look at him. It would have been more than he could stand. He ducked his head and kicked at the crust of dirt beneath his boots.

"She wants to know what happened," Leo said.

Stolanus said, "He already told what happened."

"Not to me, he didn't. Not to her, neither." Leo swayed a little, muttered something. Then, "Tell him," he said to Mary. "Go on."

Stolanus took a few steps forward, said to Mary gently, "I— forgive me—I should have said sooner, I didn't know how, I'm sorry." He glanced at Lathias. "I am sorry," he said. "About your girl. My boy is, too. But there is nothing to tell that hasn't already been said."

But Mary did not move, made no acknowledgment that she had even heard.

"Are you bringing him down here or not?" Leo said.

"He already told what happened," Stolanus repeated.

And Leo sucked his teeth and nodded and said, "We'll just have to see about that."

Lathias was about to say something too, wanted to say something, not to Leo, but to Mary; he had wanted to say he had known them both, that the boy was not capable of hurting the girl, that he had loved her, yes, he would even have told that, would have betrayed that about him. But just as he was about to speak, he noticed that Mary had moved, had lifted her face from her shawl and was looking up toward the house, and so Lathias looked up too, and saw that the boy was there, standing at the window, looking out, his face so pale there behind the glass.

But the strange thing, the thing that caught Lathias, was that the boy looked somehow different. Lathias could not at first decide what it was, and then it struck him: *Why, he looks normal. It's the scar. The scar is gone.*

He stood marvelling at the boy, whole and unscathed and as he had once been. And it seemed, in that second, that the miraculous was possible, that a miracle had occurred before his eyes; or at the very least, that all that had come before had been a dream; that the boy was whole and unharmed, that there had never been an accident, that he had never caused one, that Elisabeth was not dead in the river, and that he had not caused that, either. Lathias's heart leaped up into his throat, he almost cried out from relief and joy and amazement.

Then the boy shifted in the window and Lathias realized it had been only a trick of the light reflecting on the glass or the way the glass itself warped at the place where the boy's face had been. There had been no miracle. The scar was still there. Elisabeth was still drowned in the river. And her mother still sat there in the yard, looking up at the boy, he down at her.

It was a moment before he realized Leo had spoken to him.

"What, are you deaf?" Leo was saying.

Lathias glanced at Stolanus, waiting also, then back to Leo.

"Can't you hear?" Leo said. He jerked his thumb toward Mary. "She wants to know what you were up to."

Lathias looked at Mary, but she had only dropped her gaze back to her lap.

"What, he can't speak neither? She wants to know what you were up to with her girl."

Stolanus spoke then. "Just young people, Leo, out having fun together."

"That's not what I saw," Leo said. "I saw it different."

Lathias stared back at him, his skin gone cold, though he did not know what Leo could be talking about.

"It was you," Leo said, and nodded. "Don't think I don't know. All along. It was you."

And then the crack of the reins and Leo and the wagon and Mary lurched away across the snowy yard, and Lathias watched them go and Mary did not look back. He watched them go and go, and when he tired of watching them, he looked back up to the window and watched as the boy stepped away, and then he was gone, too. And like everything else during the past few days, Lathias wondered what had been real and what imagined.

That is the way of it, he thought, *that is how my life has always been. Not watching things come, but watching them go.*

———

All that night he lay wide-eyed in his bunk, the certainty of his leaving settling over him like a dead weight. And he thought, *If I had gone when I should have, all those years ago, this would not have happened. If I had never come at all . . .*

But he had been over that so often it no longer held any real interest, or even any depth either, the way a word—the name of a loved one—can lose all meaning, all association, with enough repetition, can detach from the thing itself, not a name, but only a word, arbitrary, meaningless. The name of his own mother, like the colour of her hair, a thing he would never know, since it had been used by no one. Sometimes, he would run through all the names he could think of, trying them one after the other against what he could remember of her. Settling upon none. No, there were some things that could not be named.

Which always made him think of Helen and how when the boy lay dying, all those years ago—or so they all had thought—lay dying in his bedroom upstairs and Lathias lay in his own bunk in the loft, lay there in a hot agony of guilt and grief, just a boy himself and unable to face any of them, Helen had come to him.

She didn't have to, she owed him nothing, he would have understood if she had wanted him gone that very night, but she had not, she had come to him in the loft and he had turned his face away, ashamed of his tears, and she had put her hand on his forehead and it had been so warm and gentle. When she began to speak, it was so quiet, Lathias had to hold his breath to hear. "It's funny," she had said, "the things you remember." And then she had sat a while longer, and Lathias had wondered if she expected something from him then, an apology, but he could not, he would not have been able to speak to save his own life in that moment. And so he just lay there, his head turned away from her. Finally she said, "I was thinking tonight about the old folks, how they used to believe the dead could see. My mother believed it. When my grandmother died, I was eight, nine maybe. They laid her out at home, like they always did. She was in the big bedroom off the kitchen. Most people used the parlour for that, but we did not have one. I knew she was in there, and I knew she was dead. I remember my mother coming to me the morning of the funeral and saying, 'Go on in to Grandmother now. She'll want to see you before she's buried.' That's what she said. 'She'll want to see you.'"

She paused and Lathias wondered if she had finished, but he did not want to turn to look at her and so he just lay there, her hand on his head still now with remembering.

"When I went in," she said, "Grandmother was stretched out on the bed, as if she was sleeping, only she was on top of the covers and wearing her good church dress and her long grey braids were wound up on the sides of her head in a funny way I don't ever remember her wearing them. I had feared her eyes would be open. I was relieved when they weren't. I stood there in the doorway feeling relieved, but then I got scared all over again because I was afraid she would open her eyes, to see me, you know, one last time, like my mother said. I stood there praying that she wouldn't. And so I shut my eyes. I stood there with my eyes shut so that I wouldn't see if she opened hers. Then, when I figured I'd stayed in there long enough to suit my mother, and for my grandmother to have a good long look, I backed out and into the kitchen where everyone was standing around drinking coffee and I did not open my eyes until I'd pulled the bedroom door shut.

"My mother said to me, 'Did you say goodbye to Grandmother?' and I said, 'Yes, I did.' And she said, 'Did you stand where she could have a good look at you?' And I said, 'Yes, I did.' And my mother started to cry then, and tell me I was a good girl, that I'd made Grandmother real happy, and I just stood there nodding with a terrible feeling in my heart."

It seemed as though Helen would sigh, it seemed the moment for it. But she did not. She just sat there unmoving, and she said, "I've never been able to name that feeling, to say just what it was. I knew only that it was terrible." Then, she did sigh. "It's funny," she said. "The things you remember."

And they sat that way for what seemed like a long time, just sitting together, Helen's hand still on Lathias's head, and his face turned to the wall. And Lathias thought, *But you should be with him, why are you not sitting with him?*—even as he knew the answer. And there was no blame there between them, and he was young enough to believe there never would be.

Finally, he turned to look up at her. She was staring at the rosary over his bed, and he wondered if she was praying or if she was just staring off vacantly, just thinking, and that it might not have been a rosary at all that she looked at, but even just a nail in the wall, a length of rope, a cobweb, wondered if it wouldn't have made any difference. And he knew then it was true, there was nothing of religion or faith or hope even in her expression, and, before he could stop himself, he raised a hand and touched her hair, and they sat that way and then she took his hand, he thought she would move it away from her, but she did not, she just held it and pressed it to her hair, her cheek, and then lowered it, down to rest against the small swell of her belly, and she held it there. She would not have needed to, he would never have moved it away. He had watched her often, wondering what it would be like to put his hand to her belly, to feel the life there. He had thought there would be movement, that he would be able to feel the child, but there was nothing, just her dress against his skin and the rise and fall of her belly as she breathed in and out and in and out.

She had turned to look down at him then and she had wanted him to feel it, too, a movement there, he could tell by the way she sat so still, the way she looked at him so deeply, and then he did feel something, a quick ripple under the skin, and he pulled his hand away and she took it and put it back and they sat that way and then she leaned over and she kissed him, and he realized that he'd known all along she would. She kissed him on his lips, gently, and he realized he had never been kissed before, not by anyone. And then he was weeping again and so was she, her tears in his mouth. She raised her head, and stood and walked away again, disappeared down the ladder and out into the night.

Later, much later, he came to the house because the lanterns still gleamed there though it was much too late for a light, and he stood in the hot August night outside the kitchen door, not finding himself able to enter after all, stood there until Stolanus came outside, for what reason he never did learn, and discovered him there and looked at him as if he did not recognize him, just for a second, and they stood there together, strangers, the sound of crickets all around them in the darkness. Then Stolanus opened the door and stood waiting for him and Lathias went in and before he could even see the boy he learned that Helen lay in a pool of her own blood, the life he'd felt under the palm of his hand already gone, dead before it had lived. And he stood there in the kitchen, not knowing what to do with himself, and Stolanus opened the door to their bedroom to go in and he caught sight of her lying there, Helen, and she saw him, too, their eyes meeting, briefly, and then the door closed and there was nothing for him to do but go upstairs to the boy. And so he did, and sat by his bed all through the night, looking anywhere but at his face.

And the boy had lived but the infant had not, and Helen had never once looked at him, at Lathias, with anything but kindness in her eyes, though the kindness slowly grew distant and remote, as if it were a fondness she no longer felt, but only remembered. As if he, too, had died.

———

Just before dawn, he rose from the bed where he had lain, awake and fully clothed, and smoothed the blankets and took his saddle-bags from a nail in the wall and stuffed in his shirts and socks and underwear, his Sunday pants, a comb, his spare leather gloves and some few woollens. He lifted the lid on the chest and bent to gather his things, but in the early dark, it was as if the chest were empty, it yawned blackly before him, and so he only closed the lid and straightened, made the sign of the cross in the direction he knew the rosary hung, and descended the ladder, his saddlebags slung across his shoulder.

The mare was asleep and he laid a hand against her neck and spoke softly and she huffed and shifted her hooves against the floorboards, and he spoke again, and poured a tin of oats into the basin before her which she snuffed and pushed at unenthusi-astically while he pulled his blanket and saddle from where they hung across the rails and settled them over her, pulling up the cinches and buckling the saddlebags and strapping his winter coat in a roll behind the cantle, he led her out of the barn and away from the house. Only when he was well clear of the yard did he pull himself up and into the saddle and ride.

If he could get as far as the river, that is what he told himself. *If I can get to the river, without looking back, I will go.* And then, *If I can get to the river without hearing a coyote call, I will go.* And, *If I can get to the river without the horse stumbling, I will go.* And that is how he rode, through the predawn cold, the horse steady and sure beneath him. When he reached the Horseman's graves, he stopped a moment, made the sign of the cross, as he used to, and rode on, past them, toward the braucha's, the buildings just visible now against the barely lightening sky, and the river valley beyond.

When he got as far as the Bull's Forehead and the lip of the river valley he stopped again and looked back at the farms spread out there beneath a vast, bluing sky, the way the land just seemed to go on and on, right up into the horizon, as if the way things were here was the way things were everywhere, no mountains or oceans, no foothills or deserts or lakes, no forests, just unending prairie, for ever and ever. As if he could ride the rest of his life and never get out of it. As if he could ride the rest of his life and never get it out of him.

He put his heels to his horse and descended, down into the valley, west.

————

He rode for three days and on the third he stopped at a town for food at the Chinese café. When he had finished eating, he sat and stared out the window, waiting for the men to come in for coffee, and when they did, he sat a few minutes more and finally he stood up and he cleared his throat and he said, "Any work around here?"

The men looked up from their coffees.

"Ain't nothing but work around here," one of them said.

"Who're your people, son?"

"Schoff," he said. Weren't they? As much as anyone else. "Stolanus and Helen Schoff."

"Schoff. Never heard of them."

"Where's home for you?"

"East."

"What, Kindersley? Swift Current?"

"Round about there."

"They run out of work?"

"They all have money over there, that's what I heard."

"He's looking for a wife, maybe."

"Talk to Wally, here, he's looking to get rid of his."

Lathias stood quietly, waiting while the men chuckled and teased each other, thinking, *Things don't change much. Things don't hardly change at all, when you think of it. I could just keep riding and riding and things wouldn't never change much at all.*

"A wife is what you don't need."

"That's right, you're only young once. You have to enjoy yourself, not?"

"Just so long as you're not enjoying yourself with his wife."

Lathias stood waiting.

"Here, hold on once," one of the men said. "Wechter," he called to one of the men at a table in the back corner, "this young fella's looking for work. He promises to keep clear of your daughters. And your wife, too."

"Yah," someone said, "but will they keep clear of him?"

"What's the name?" someone called.

"Schoff. From—where'd you say you're from again?"

"Schoff? Never heard of them."

"You need to see Wechter, here. He's got all the money."

"And the daughters too, not?"

"Yah, six girls, he should be able to find one he likes."

"Not if Wechter has anything to say about it."

A tall man in a denim coat, with blue eyes that crinkled deeply at the corners, turned in his seat and looked Lathias up and down.

"What's this?" he said gruffly. "Hired man, eh?"

Lathias took off his hat, nodded. "Yes, sir," he said. "That's right. Hired man."

The big man studied him a moment more, then he held out his hand.

Lathias took it.

———

Stolanus looked to Lathias's empty seat, and then to Helen. She
ignored him, setting a bowl of gravy onto the table. She pulled
her chair in with a screech and passed Stolanus the platter of roast
pork. When he did not immediately serve himself, she forked two
big slices onto his plate and said, as if there were some connection, "He has already eaten."

"Lathias?"

Helen glanced up sharply.

"Oh," Stolanus said. "Of course. How is he?"

"The same."

She passed the potatoes, and then the gravy and the bread,
only serving herself after Stolanus had been served, filling her
plate enormously, as she always did, and then pretending to eat,
moving things around from one side of the plate to the other.

Stolanus cut his meat into pieces and then laid down his knife
and his fork.

"But," he said, "will we not wait for Lathias?"

Helen made motions of chewing, swallowing. "No," she said.
"Why should we?"

Stolanus frowned, turned his attention back to his plate.

After a few moments, he lifted his head again, watched her.
"Where is Lathias?" he said.

"You think I sit at the window all day to watch where he goes?"
She placed a small bite between her lips.

"Has he been in today?"

"No," she said. "I haven't seen him."

"I thought he had gone to town on errands for you."

"Bread?" she said, lifting the board toward him, though he
already held a piece in his hand. When he did not reply, she
lowered the bread to the table and said, "I haven't seen him, I tell
you. Check the loft. Maybe he is not well."

"His horse is gone."

"Well, then, I guess he's gone out."

"Without saying? All day like that?"

"Well, he is not a *child*," she said, emphasizing the word. Then she added, "He can do what he wants."

"Did I say he couldn't?" Stolanus frowned, looked out the window. "It's funny, though."

"Yes, isn't it, ha ha."

"That's not what I meant."

"I know what you meant."

"What are you talking about?" It was the boy. He stood at the top of the stairs, looking down at them, ghostly.

Helen half rose from her chair.

"Well," Stolanus boomed, "and look what the cat dragged in."

"Will you come down?" Helen said, still in her odd position, half in and half out of her chair, palms against the edge of the table.

He blinked down at them. "Where is Lathias?" he said.

"Ach, who knows," Stolanus said jovially, winking at the boy. "Spring fever, maybe."

The boy did not move, or change his expression.

"Town," Helen said, flicking her eyes toward Stolanus. "I sent him to town on errands." Then, when the boy did not respond, she repeated, "Will you come down?" And she pulled his chair out a bit from the table.

"No," he said, and turned and disappeared back up the stairs, as if he had never been there at all.

———

After Lathias had fed and watered his mare and turned her out to what he presumed was the home pasture, he walked to the neat, white house, his small bundle tucked beneath his arm. He paused on the doorstep, listening to the chatter and clattering of dishes that came through the open window. Before he had lifted a hand to knock, the door was pulled open and a little girl stood looking up at him.

"Who are you?" she said in German.

"English, Milly, English," a woman's voice called above the noise from inside. "Who is it?"

"Who knows?" the little girl called back in German. "He cannot speak, I think."

"Oh, Millie," came the voice, and the door was pulled farther ajar and a woman's face appeared there. "Yes?" she said.

But the little girl who still stood looking up at him was right: he could not speak. He only took the hat from his head, and lifted his bundle a little.

But the woman slapped a hand to her forehead. "Ach, but I would forget my head today. We're in the middle of Easter baking," she said, and wiped her hands on her apron, as if to prove it. "You're the new man."

When she said this, the noise from the kitchen behind her came to a sudden stop and the little girl pulled at her mother's skirt and giggled.

"He's handsome," she called into the kitchen behind her. "I win."

And the mother slapped her gently away.

"I spoke English," the little girl said indignantly.

"Get on, now, Millie," the woman said, waving the girl away. "That's enough, I think." And then to Lathias, "Forgive me." She stepped back a little and eyed him up and down and sighed before opening the door wide and saying, "Well, come in, for heaven's sake, and let's get some food into you before the wind blows you away."

FOURTEEN

Holy Thursday came without celebration or notice either by Krausses—Mary and Leo—or by Schoffs—Helen and Stolanus and the boy—who kept to themselves now more than ever, the hired man gone too now, that's what they'd heard, and Helen and Stolanus always with one eye cast over their shoulders, and who could blame them, everyone said, so much tragedy in that family, things always seemed to go wrong for them; but that was the way sometimes, wasn't it? The Lord giveth and the Lord taketh away. Well, they had their money for comfort, anyway. And what about this weather? If there was more snow coming, it should come then, and not wait for July. This crazy country. It is too much. It is enough to drive anyone mad.

On Good Friday, the sky cleared and the sun blazed with a warmth unusual for so early in the season. Water dripped tentatively and by noon trickled in steady streams from rooftops, down eavestroughs into oak barrels and through culverts, filling ditches as if they were canals, down, down, flooding creeks and sloughs and dugouts, and down farther still, toward the valley, as if called by the river itself, running coldly into draws with a high, giddy sound; the world was melting, the earth softening and coming slowly to life, all that Good Friday and throughout the night, the thaw continuing on into Holy Saturday, water and water and water, the ground beneath galoshes thickened with it, the good, rich smell of gumbo mud everywhere, and all across the parish, people shed hats and jackets and sour woollens to feel the sun against their skin, and the children shouted and jostled each other as they collected eggs from henhouses and carried them carefully inside to boil and then lower gently with a teaspoon to prevent cracks, still steaming, into mugs of dye and vinegar and cold water, all afternoon, dozens and dozens of eggs, checking every few seconds the shade of green or yellow or pink or lavender, then rolling them around to dry on sheets of newspaper so they could be rubbed with a little oil for shine and arranged in bowls and baskets and eaten—whenever one pleased, imagine that—with a little salt, the pretty pieces of coloured shell scattered outside doorsteps for good luck, out in the sunshine and mud, ah, take a good, deep breath, and everywhere one looked the air was bright and mild and filled with the improbably green smell of spring under a big, ballooning blue sky.

The weather was so mild and the thaw so hard and fast and the spring so sudden that everyone felt a bit addled, as if drunk on it all, as if pure sunshine coursed through their veins; the young men, in particular, all of them crazed and restless with spring, racing their horses wildly in the muck and wrestling and talking big, to the girls and to each other, making vast, impossible plans.

And that is how it came to be on Sunday morning, Easter Sunday, that Ronnie Rausch and Foxy Limbach rode optimistically down to the river in the pre-dawn light to see if the ice was yet out and could they get a raft in to do some spring fishing before church at nine. So there they were, standing at the edge of the river, studying the ice, or what was left of it, and rubbing their hands together, not from eagerness but only to warm them (for, though the sun would have power once it was up, the air was not yet nearly so warm as they'd hoped), and Foxy, who though small was actually the older of the two, being nearly seventeen, said, "Christ, it's too damn cold, let's come back after Mass."

"Sure," Ronnie said, "and the fish all sleeping by then, we won't catch nothing."

"Naw, that's only in lakes. In rivers it don't matter."

"Fish don't sleep in rivers?"

"Oh, they sleep all right. They're just not on any real schedule. On account of the water's always moving."

Ronnie nodded, as if that made sense, and looked around him. He spat over his shoulder, then gestured up to the eastern horizon, up the valley beyond the braucha's place, and was about to say something about the sunrise, maybe, or the fact that time was wasting, or to remark even upon the beauty of the dawn, though that is doubtful, when he stopped and hung his jaw and stood staring.

Foxy, who had been blowing on his hands, saw Ronnie's face, and laughed a little, said, "What in hell's wrong with you?"

Ronnie didn't say anything, so Foxy followed his gaze up the draw, toward the braucha's place crouched and silent in the dim grey light. But he could see nothing out of the ordinary.

"What?" he said.

Ronnie shook his head. "You didn't see that?"

"What?"

"A girl."

"A girl what?"

"A girl girl."

"Yah, yah," Foxy said, "I saw a girl, sure. There's girls running around all over this valley." He shook his head. "You been without a girlfriend so long you started imagining them."

"I sure as hell didn't."

"Probably a coyote."

"If that was a coyote, it was a hell of a pretty one." Then he added, "Call me crazy, but I'll be damned if—"

"What?"

"Nothing. Just, well, it looked a lot like, I'll be damned if that didn't look just like that dead girl."

"What dead girl?"

"That Krauss girl. Or Brechert, or whatever."

Foxy just stared at him. "That's not even funny," he said.

"I'm not trying to be funny."

"Good," Foxy said, "'cause you're not."

They both stood there a minute, puffing into the grey light, and finally Foxy said, "So, are we gonna fish, or what?"

Ronnie kind of hunched up his shoulders and scratched his chin and finally said, in an irritable, distracted way, "I don't feel like fishing," and then, before Foxy could say anything more, he pulled himself up on his horse and rode off, leaving Foxy standing there calling after him.

Ronnie rode straight home and, not even bothering to put up the horse, walked into the kitchen where his parents were just rising, his father drawing his suspenders up over his shoulders.

"What," his father said, "you give up already?"

"Did you expect them to swim up and jump in your pocket?" said his mother. Then she leaned her head up the stairwell and hollered, "Come on, up there. Church."

His father winked at him. "We'll go down later," he said, "after Mass. I'll show you how to catch a fish."

"What," the mother said, "on Easter Sunday?"

"Was Christ not a fisherman?"

"He was a carpenter, you *dummkopf*."

"But a fisherman, too."

"Not on Easter Sunday, he wasn't."

"Yah, and how do you know? They couldn't find him. Maybe he was fishing."

"What, Ronald, are you still standing there? You look like you filled your pants. What's the matter with you?"

"I saw her," Ronnie blurted out. "I saw that girl."

"What girl?" his mother said, pouring boiled water over the coffee.

"That drowned girl."

His father and mother both stopped and looked at each other.

"*Gott im Himmel,*" his mother breathed. She set down the pot and crossed herself.

"Where," his father said, sitting down, "in the brush?"

"No," Ronnie said, "not in the brush. Not in the river." He shook his head as if to clear it.

"Here, have some coffee. Sit down. Give him a minute, already. Can't you see he's upset? Look how his hands shake."

Ronnie sat, took the cup of coffee, set it down without drinking. "It was her."

"Yah, all right, then. Where was she?"

He looked from his father to his mother and back again. "At the braucha's."

"What?"

Ronnie added, "Alive."

"Ach." His mother swatted her hand through the air. "He's been drinking. Smell his breath."

"I haven't. I saw her. Running from the shed to the house. It was her. That hair. It was blowing all out behind her. Clear as day."

"He has been drinking," his mother said.

"Have you been drinking, son?"

"No!"

"And you saw the Krauss girl?"

"Yes!"

"Do you want people to think you are crazy?" his mother said.

Ronnie did not want people to think he was crazy; he almost thought he was a little crazy himself. He looked at his father.

"It was her," he said again.

"Think now," said his father. "Maybe your eyes were playing tricks on you."

Ronnie shook his head, rubbed his hands through his hair. Maybe he had been seeing things. It all seemed so distant now, fuzzy, like a dream.

"I don't know. It looked like her. I think it did. God."

"Wasn't Foxy with you?"

"Yes," he said, "but he wasn't looking . . ."

"Yah, all right, enough of this," said his mother. "I'll make you some breakfast."

His father raised his head in astonishment. "Breakfast?" he said. "Before Communion? On Easter Sunday yet?"

"The boy needs to eat. He is seeing things."

"And if I see things, will I get breakfast too? Look, out the window, *der Osterhase.*"

"Ach, you old fool. Easter bunnies, yet."

Ronnie sat there staring at the table, then at the eggs and sausage his mother set before him.

"Eat," she said, "so you don't talk so stupid. I'm going to dress."

And so he ate a little, his father sitting across the table with his black coffee, watching him. Finally, he put his fork down and just stared at the plate.

"Maybe, Ronnie," his father said after a while, "you should not go talking about this to others. Maybe it was nothing. You don't want to make something out of nothing."

"Are you still talking about it?" his mother hollered from the bedroom where she was pinning her Easter hat just so. "Enough already."

His father glanced over his shoulder, then dropped his voice. "If you're not going to eat that, pass it over. No sense going to waste, not?"

Ronnie passed his plate over.

"And maybe keep it to yourself," his father said, between quick bites. "Maybe that's best."

Though Ronnie was not sure whether he referred to the breakfast or to the girl. And so he sat there and stared into his cup of coffee, beginning to doubt what he had seen, wilfully perhaps, trying to come up with some other explanation. But when it was time to leave for church and he had still not come up with anything, he did what most do when faced with the inexplicable, the mysterious, the inconceivable: he told himself it could not possibly have happened, that he must, somehow, have been mistaken.

————

Later that morning, Ronnie sat beside his mother, watching as Ludmila Baumgarten straightened the silk flowers on her new Easter hat and moved from the piano bench to the lectern to give the reading.

Ludmila cleared her throat, touched the hat once more. "'Now upon the first day of the week,'" she read, "'very early in the morning, they came unto the sepulchre, bringing the spice which they had prepared and certain others with them. And they found the stone rolled away from the sepulchre. And they entered in, and found not the body of the Lord Jesus. And it came to pass, as they were much perplexed thereabout, behold, two men stood by them in shining garments. And as they were afraid, and bowed down their faces to the earth, they said unto them, Why seek ye the living among the dead?'"

Here, Ronnie looked at his mother, who pointedly fixed her gaze forward, frowning a little.

"'He is not here,'" Ludmila read, raising her voice for effect, just as she had practised, "'but is risen.'" She lifted her hand, pausing near her hat. "'Remember how he spake unto you when he was yet in Galilee, Saying, The Son of man must be delivered into the hands of sinful men, and be crucified, and the third day rise again.

And they remembered his words, And returned from the sepulchre, and told all these things unto the eleven, and to all the rest.'"

Ludmila bowed her head a moment over the text, then said, "Praise be to the Lord, Jesus Christ," and made the sign of the cross and descended from the lectern.

And Ronnie answered, along with his mother and father and the rest of the congregation, making the sign of the cross, "Praise be to the Lord."

When Father returned to the lectern, he looked out over them a moment. Then he began, "Luke reminds us not only of the power of the Lord, to lift from the dead His only begotten son, but also he reminds us of our own journeys. Like the women who journeyed to the tomb, we are all on our own slow walks toward death. Each step we take is another step closer to our own tombs. And the question we must ask ourselves is this: 'Is it the tomb I seek or life everlasting, a dwelling-place in the peace of the Lord?' The women came seeking death, at that tomb, but what they found was a sign, of life everlasting, and they went forth, to spread the good news. But these women, they were not believed. Another old wives' tale, that is what was said. And in the same way, there are those among us who reject what Christ has offered us, life everlasting. Life everlasting! Because they do not want to believe."

Ronnie shifted on the pew beside his mother and coughed and felt too warm, and his mother frowned over at him, but he could not sit still, the air was too close—why would someone not open a window?—and so he rose, and saying, "Excuse me, pardon, excuse me, please," he squeezed down to the end of the pew and into the aisle and toward the door, while Father Rieger frowned down at him, saying, "And so on this Easter Sunday morning, we must all ask ourselves"—his voice following Ronnie out the door and into the bright morning— "'Is it life everlasting which I seek, or only the tomb eternal?'"

The following day, Easter Monday, at around four in the morning, Penny Rausch, young Erv Rausch's wife (Erv being second cousin to Ronnie on the fathers' sides), went into labour, her first, and Erv, still in his underpants, ran out the door and hitched up the wagon in a frenzy, Penny's mother calling from the doorway: "For God's sake don't kill yourself, you idiot, this baby has got a while yet." Then, rousing her youngest son—Penny's brother—from his bed, the mother said, "But go with that horse's ass to see he even gets to the braucha's," and the younger brother making it to the wagon just in time to climb in as Erv lashed the horses and rode like hellfire out into the pre-dawn prairie.

But Erv Rausch was not a man known for his composure and good judgment at the best of times, and the panic and bleariness of the hour and the occasion had robbed him of whatever sense he might have had, so that when he reached the braucha's and leapt down from the wagon before the horses had even stopped moving, and the younger brother grabbing the reins and calling after him, though Erv was already running across the yard, slipping in the mud as he went, hollering for the braucha, and without even a pause, flung the door open to find crouched like a startled harpy on a pallet by the stove a girl with long wild hair, he, in fact, thought he had the wrong house. He was just about to turn in his confusion and run back to his wagon and drive God knows where, when the old braucha's voice came from a corner of the hut, "What is it? What do you want?"

Erv, who stood looking from the girl to the old woman emerging from the darkness, said, "My wife, the baby," and ran back to the wagon, where he sat tapping his foot there beside his young brother-in-law until the old braucha came out and climbed into the wagon, and he cracked the reins once more, the braucha clutching the edge of the seat to keep from being tossed out into the mud, heedless of the girl who stood watching from the doorway behind them.

Around noon, a healthy baby boy was born, Ervine Junior, and a neighbour who had stopped by on his way to town offered the old braucha a ride home to save Erv the trouble. Erv pressed some coins into the old woman's palm, saying, "Yah, yah, thank you, good," still dazed with the morning's events and, in his near delirium and the celebration that followed, thinking no more of the braucha or the girl until the following morning, Tuesday, when he sat thick-headed and bleary over his coffee in Wing's.

The men were teasing him, as they usually did (for though, as the men were fond of saying, Erv was a couple tines short on the plow, and he had an unparalleled reputation as a bullshitter and became aggressive and sometimes violent when drinking, he was also a hard worker and quick to help out a neighbour and that counted for a lot among them). So they were having a few laughs at his expense, and one of the men said, "I hear you gave the old braucha a shock," and another one said, "Maybe next time you'll remember your pants," and they all laughed, and Erv, wincing from the loudness of the laughter in his thumping brain, said, "The old woman, nothing. It was that girl that had the shock. Now that one jumped." Looking around in anticipation of the men's laughter. But the men only exchanged a look and said, "What girl?"

Erv said, "That girl at the braucha's. She jumped all right. God knows what she thought. But was I supposed to sit in the wagon and wait? Even old women need a fire lit under them, not?"

And someone said, "There's a girl living at the braucha's?"

"Who was she?"

And Erv thought a minute and then he said, "I don't know. It was dark, but the stove was going and she had a bed there in front of it, on the floor. I didn't get a good look at her. She had long hair, all messed up and hanging in her face. She kind of looked like a witch. Or something."

So the men sat there, trying to figure out who the old woman might have out there, if anyone.

"She's got no family around here no more, does she, the old woman?"

"Never had much to begin with."

"Just that one son who lived."

"Wasn't the husband dead already when they got here?"

"It was just her and the son. Strange bugger."

"But he's been gone for years."

"Maybe it's a granddaughter or something, come back."

Erv was starting to feel he was part of something important, and that was a position he was not used to, everyone taking what he said so seriously. And so he leaned forward and said, "I'll tell you something else, too. She"—-here he lowered his voice—"she was stark naked (it was a lie, of course, but what of that? How were they to know?)—stark naked," he said again, "as the day she was born. If you get my drift."

This did not have the effect upon the men that Erv had hoped.

"Maybe it was one of them Rescher kids."

"Rescher?"

"Remember Reschers, used to have all that land over there—left in that drought year."

"Which drought year?"

"Didn't she kind of take up with Reschers?"

"That's right, I remember that, too."

"Might be one of them Reschers come back."

"What the hell for?"

"How do I know? I'm just saying maybe it's a Rescher."

"How old did you say she was?"

Erv shrugged. "She wasn't a little girl, but she didn't look that old neither. And she had—" Here he paused, then cupped his hands at his chest and raised his eyebrows suggestively.

"Christ, Erv, don't you know what they're called yet?"

"I thought he had a kid now."

"Awful bashful for a married man."

"He only knows them on the cows—isn't that right, Erv?"

Ronnie Rausch, who had been sitting there quietly, shooting

funny looks back and forth with his father across the table, finally, Ronnie, seeing that the conversation was taking a different direction, piped up: "I've seen her, too, that girl."

But the father quickly said, "Ach, don't listen to this one, he sees a coyote and falls in love."

Erv said, "Did she have long hair?"

And Ronnie said, "Yes, she did. She had long hair. Red hair."

Someone said, "Must have been a fox, then."

The men laughed and Ronnie, known as a bit of a hothead anyway, he got all flushed in the face and stood up, sloshing coffee out across the table, and said, "That was no coyote and no fox. I know exactly who it was."

"Who?" Erv said, "Who was it?"

And the father said, "Sit down already, Ronald, and shut up now before your mouth gets you into trouble."

But Ronnie was not listening. He looked once around the table and then he said, "It was that Brechert girl that drowned in the river."

The men stopped chuckling then and exchanged glances across the table, and Ronnie's father said, "But for God's sake, Ronnie, use your head once," and then to the men, "You know how it is, these youngsters. Remember when Tony Beier thought he saw a grizzly out in the Sand Hills there, attacking a heifer? He swore up and down, and hauled a bunch of men out there with rifles."

"And he said how the grizzly had been hunched over the animal, beating at it and roaring?"

"Turned out it was Eichert's bull he'd put out to stud."

"Shot the damn thing before anyone could stop him."

"Or what about that Cross girl," Ronnie's father added, "when she said someone grabbed her leg when she was swimming?" He laughed a little, nervously.

"Yah, she wished someone had."

A few of the men nodded and someone said, "They are not thinking with their heads, those young ones."

"Tony Beier still shits his pants every time a bull looks at him sideways."

A few of them chuckled again, but Erv said to Ronnie, "Come to think of it, she did look like that Brechert girl. Skinny."

"Enough," Ronnie's father snapped, "enough, all this stupid talk. The girl is dead."

An uncomfortable silence fell over the table. Finally, one of the men said, "Does anyone know that for sure?"

"Ach, you're crazy."

"Probably one of them Rescher kids."

"Anyway, what business of ours?"

"Yah, and these two *dummkopfs* here, are we to believe what they say yet? I'd just as soon listen to Ludmila Baumgarten."

"Rausch, you need to get your boy a woman already."

"Rausch barely got one himself."

"Is that it, Ronnie? Are you looking from between your legs?"

"Just make sure you look up and not down."

"Ach, leave him alone."

"That's right, Ronnie. Never mind these old noodle-steppers. They haven't looked up in a long time."

While Ronnie sat frowning into his cup of coffee.

———

That night after supper Ronnie Rausch saddled up his horse and rode over to Erv Rausch's with a bottle of his father's whisky in his coat pocket. It didn't take much convincing for Erv to agree (*What, and will you let them all laugh at you that way? Treating you like a boy, not even a man?*), and so sometime that evening the two of them were hunkered down, shivering, behind the braucha's shelterbelt, passing the bottle between them.

"You really think it's that drowned girl?" Erv said, after a while.

"Hell, I don't know."

"Sure looked like her. Now you mention it."

"Sure did."

"Doesn't make much sense, though."

"Sure doesn't."

They sat and drank a while in the gathering twilight. An owl hooted from the far edge of the shelterbelt.

"Hey, Ronnie."

"What?"

"You believe in ghosts?"

"No."

"No, me neither." Erv shifted his position against a rotting stump. "I heard some stories, though."

Ronnie reached for the bottle. "Like what?"

"Well." Erv shifted again. "You know about the Horseman? The bones rattling and all?"

"Yah. I heard that."

Erv started. "You heard that? Tonight?"

"What?"

"You heard bones rattling?"

"No. Christ. I heard the story before. Sit down. What do you think? What did you even say that for?"

Erv eased back again. "I thought you meant—"

"I know what you thought. Quit talking about it already. Christ."

They each took a swig from the bottle.

"Probably wouldn't hear those bones anyway, down in the ground there."

"Shut up already."

Erv shifted again.

"What's the matter with you?" Ronnie said. "Sit still for once."

"I need to piss."

"So, go piss."

"Where?"

"How the hell should I know? Over there somewhere."

Erv looked over there, into the darkening row of caraganas. The owl hooted.

"I can wait," he said.

———

Just around dusk they saw her.

"Hey," Erv said, dropping the empty bottle in the dirt.

Ronnie grabbed him. "Shut up. She'll hear us."

"Well, and so what?"

"Christ, you're drunk. Keep your voice down."

Watching as she crossed from the hut to the chicken coop with a basket.

"She doesn't look dead."

"What's that supposed to mean?"

"Ghosts don't walk like that."

"I thought you didn't believe in ghosts."

"I don't."

They crouched there, watching as she unlatched the coop door and stepped inside.

"Was that her?"

"It was her all right."

"The Krauss girl?"

"I said so, didn't I?"

"Come on, then," Erv said, rising unsteadily.

"Come on, what? That's her, isn't it? What more do you want?"

"Proof," said Erv, and he lurched out from the shelterbelt and half ran, half stumbled across the yard to the chicken coop, Ronnie behind him, catching at his sleeve as he crashed through the door in an explosion of hens, a girl standing there in the darkness, alert but unstartled, feathers settling in her hair like ashes.

———

Ronnie claimed later—much later, after all was said and done and he was worried about clearing his own name (though, to his credit, he did not intend to lie about the facts but told it all just as he remembered it, as best he could remember it)—he claimed he kept pulling at Erv, worried the braucha would come any minute, wanting to get home, but Erv, he said Erv just kind of went a little crazy, saying stupid, senseless things to the girl, barring her way out of the coop when she moved to go past them. When she ducked to go under Erv's outstretched arms, that was when Erv tried to grab her, saying, "Come on, now, how about a little kiss, then," and the girl's dress tore—Erv said to Ronnie later that he hadn't meant to do that, said he hadn't even wanted to kiss her—why would he?—he had a wife, didn't he?—just wanted to get a look at her face, make sure it was really her, it was so dark in there after all. But Ronnie told it differently. He said Erv was pretty rough and all those hens flapping around and feathers everywhere and just a bit of violet dusklight from the doorway. Ronnie said it was hard to tell in the dark and confusion but he thought the girl was not really trying to fight Erv off, just turning her face away, letting him grab at her, and she did not cry out for help, she did not make a sound, or he thought she hadn't, all those hens flapping and squawking. When Ronnie finally caught Erv by the shoulder to pull him away, Erv turned and took a swing at him, and Ronnie said maybe they would have fought each other then, he was mad, too, mad that Erv had taken it all too far, had dragged him into something he wanted no part of, knowing it was his own fault, anyway, that he was the one who had begun it, who had brought Erv in the first place, and so it fell on him, Ronnie, the responsibility for the girl, and that was what really bothered him. So he had Erv by the jacket collar and was about to slam him up against the wall, when suddenly, the braucha appeared in the doorway with a shotgun, fired it straight up into the night sky (others reported later having heard that shot but not thinking much of it at the time, why would they?) and said something to them in Russian. They could not understand what she said, but the shotgun was pretty clear and so they staggered through the dark to the shelterbelt where they'd tethered their horses and Erv, the first there, went to untie his but then he stopped and held his hands up to his face, clenching and unclenching them in the dark, and he said, "What the Christ?" and then looked at Ronnie, his face all pale in the moonlight. "Are you bleeding?" he said. Ronnie wiped at his mouth and nose and said, "No, why?" and Erv said, "Blood, my hands, look at all this blood," and he stuck his hands right up in Ronnie's face and Ronnie said later that even in the dark you could see how they glistened. Erv felt all over his own chest, then. "She shot me," he said, "she shot me." And Ronnie saying, "Get a hold of yourself," feeling Erv's chest too. "You're not shot," he said, and Erv growing hysterical, "Where's it coming from? Christ Almighty," and wiping his hands on his clothes, lifting his hands again. "You're just cut somewhere," Ronnie said, "shut up already, it's nothing." But Erv wiping, wiping, "Jesus, they cursed me, goddamn it, they put a curse on me," and then picking up a rock and hurling it through the darkness toward the old woman's shack, hollering, "You goddamned, you crazy goddamned—" and Ronnie taking a swing at him then, to shut him up, but missing and falling in the mud at Erv's feet and then that overpowering stench of urine, and him saying, "Christ Almighty, what's that smell, what is that, good God, Christ, Erv, did you piss yourself?" and Erv kicking at him then, in the dark, and yelling, "You shut your goddamned mouth, shut it, you goddamned—" and then, before Ronnie could stop him, Erv loosed the rope that tethered both horses and threw himself onto his own, still hollering so loud it spooked Ronnie's horse, too, that went thundering off after Erv into the night, leaving Ronnie to walk home, covered in mud, drunk but sobering up awful goddamned fast; left him to walk all that way across the black prairie, all that long way, the braucha and the dead girl somewhere behind him in the darkness.

———

By the time Ronnie got home, he was stone-cold sober and mad as hell, stewing and fuming about how Erv had treated him and the dead girl both (*I might not know much,* he planned to tell Erv, *but I know you don't treat a girl that way, dead or not*), and then taken off with his horse to boot. His horse, for Chrissakes. And a dead girl come alive, Jesus, and all that blood, too. He wondered if perhaps Erv had really hurt the girl somehow, that it was her blood. Christ, it was all such a blur. He was spooked, all right. And worried, too, that he would be blamed, should the dead girl or the braucha decide to report them. But, then, what the hell was she doing there anyhow? And how come she wasn't dead?

When he got home, he washed and changed his clothes and then sat at the kitchen table and stared bleakly out the dark window all night, waiting for his father to rise for chores.

When his father finally walked into the kitchen, yawning, suspenders dangling, he saw Ronnie there at the table and said, "Oh, Christ Almighty, now what?"

"Shh," Ronnie said, frowning toward the door of the bedroom where his mother, with any luck, still slept. He gestured for his father to take a seat and when he had, Ronnie told his story, trying to sound as clear as he could, given the circumstances.

His father listened and nodded and when Ronnie was finished, he said, "How much did you drink, son?"

"I was drinking," Ronnie said, "but I wasn't so far gone I wouldn't know that girl if I saw her. It was her, all right. That Brechert girl. It was dark, but I saw her, close up. It couldn't have been nobody else."

"It doesn't make sense."

"I didn't say there was sense in it. But I know what I saw."

"And?" his father said. "What do you want to do?"

"I don't know." Ronnie lifted his own palms, stared into them. "There was all this blood. It must have been from her."

"Maybe we should go see Erv."

"No," Ronnie said. "I don't want nothing to do with him. I shouldn't ever have took him over there. He's crazy."

"Yah, and what if he tells someone?"

"He won't say nothing."

"How do you know?"

"Trust me," he said. "But the girl. What if she goes to the constable?"

"What, the dead girl?"

"What if Erv hurt her? What if she reports it?"

"The dead girl? You're worried that the dead girl is going to go to the constable? You see what I'm getting at here, son?"

Ronnie shook his head in frustration. "It was her, and she wasn't dead. No more dead than you or me."

———

So Ronnie and his father drove to Triumph that morning to see McCready, before somebody else did. McCready listened and picked his teeth and rubbed a smudge from the tip of his boot while his wife pretended not to listen from beyond the open door. When Ronnie finished speaking, McCready sat looking at him as if he might be waiting for him to leave.

When Ronnie didn't leave, McCready said, "Let me get this straight, make sure I've got all the facts here. There's a dead girl living at that old Rooshian's place, and she, what, she attacked you or something? Is that what you're telling me?"

Ronnie glanced through the doorway at McCready's wife. "Not that, no."

"Well, what, then?"

"It's—" Ronnie looked to his father and his father dropped his eyes down to his boots. "I think she might be hurt, maybe," he said to McCready. "Or . . . I think she might have got hurt."

McCready stared a moment. "I thought she was dead."

And Ronnie said, "Yes, yes. We all did. But, well . . ." He

shrugged. What else was he to say?

"Well, what?"

"She's there. She's at the braucha's."

"Not dead."

"I don't . . ."—Ronnie looked out the doorway again to where McCready's wife sat, openly staring now—"know."

"Maybe there's a language problem here. Is that it? Maybe we aren't understanding each other."

"No," Ronnie said, "you got it right."

McCready sucked his teeth. "What is it you want from me?"

When Ronnie did not answer, McCready said, "How old are you?"

"Sixteen. Almost."

"Uh-huh. So you and this Rescher—"

"Rausch."

"You were up to some funny business and now you want to have some fun with me, too, is that it?"

"No."

"You think the law is funny, maybe."

"No."

"Well, I'll tell you something, I didn't haul my wife out to this dusthole for a goddamned laugh. You people have given me enough trouble this winter. Some kid's dead in the river, some other kid pushed her maybe, somebody else is out to get the kid who done the pushing, oh, she's not dead after all, maybe just hurt. Christ. You think you can have some fun with me? Is that what you think? Well, you come on, then. I'll show you how fun I can be. We're gonna take a little ride out there and, I'll tell you here and now, that girl better goddamned well be dead. Do you understand what I'm saying? You get my drift here?"

————

When Ronnie Rausch and Constable McCready pulled into the braucha's yard, with Ronnie's father following at a good distance in the wagon, they both sat a minute staring through the specked windshield, and McCready said, "That her?"

"Yes, sir," Ronnie said, through his tightened throat, "I think so."

But not moving to get out of the car, either one of them, just sitting there looking (as if she, perhaps, could not see them) to where she sat on a little bench by the door, right there in the spring sun, basking, like a cat, with her bare white feet in the greening crabgrass and her hair all brushed out and shining, just sitting there, unmoved, expressionless, as if she had been waiting for them, or waiting for someone, as if she had known they would come. She looked so clean and white it made Ronnie wonder if all that commotion the previous night had even happened, if there had been any roughness, any blood, at all. And it made Ronnie feel downright odd to see her sitting there like that, as if she couldn't possibly be anywhere else.

McCready cranked the door handle, heaved himself up and out of the car. Ronnie got out, too, but did not follow McCready toward the house. He stood, instead, waiting beside the car, wondering whether the girl would recognize him, and, in some strange way, half hoping she would.

"Morning," McCready said, hitching up his pants. "Spring's finally here I guess not a moment too soon, do you mind if I ask your name?"

The girl squinted up at him calmly, almost pleasantly, but made no reply.

McCready turned to Ronnie. "Doesn't she speak English or is she a halfwit or what?"

The door to the hut opened then and the old braucha stepped out, her eyes squinted up so tightly against the light they were all but closed. She wiped at her mouth with a corner of her apron, then spoke to McCready in Russian, which only further annoyed him. He turned to Ronnie for translation, but Ronnie could not speak Russian either. Ronnie stepped forward, though, and, eyes on the girl, spoke to the old woman in German, telling her the constable wanted to have a word. But the old woman— out of spite or perverseness—only answered again in Russian.

So the four of them stood there, and McCready stamping his foot in the mud like a bull, and firing out questions that no one could or would answer and Ronnie staring at that girl, and finally he took a few steps toward her, the girl, and said, tentatively, in German, "But you are Elisabeth Brechert, not?"

"What's that?" McCready said. "What did you say to her?"

The girl stared back at Ronnie a moment and Ronnie thought that perhaps she would not answer him, either, and maybe she was deaf or dumb or something, or maybe she was a ghost after all, my God, he wanted to reach out a hand to touch her, see if she was real.

But finally she replied, in German, "I guess you know who I am or why did you come looking for me last night?"

He lifted his hands helplessly. "I just . . . wanted to see—"

"Well," she said, "here I am, then."

"Yes," he said, feeling hot, ashamed, pinned there by her stare.

But she said nothing more, just rose and went into the shack and shut the door behind her.

McCready said, "What's she doing? Is she coming back out?"

"No," Ronnie said. "I don't think so."

"Did she tell you her name?"

"No," Ronnie said. "But that's her. That's Elisabeth Brechert."

McCready stood a minute more, the old braucha peering back at him from beneath her black babushka, and he flung his cigarette into the mud.

The braucha walked over and picked it up and crushed it in her palm and said, in German this time, "You have no authority here."

McCready said, "What's that? What did she say?"

"You have no business here," she said again, in German. "You always come when the trouble is over. Get out of here, now. Leave the girl alone." And then she added something in Russian and nodded at him and made the sign of the cross.

"What the hell was that?" McCready said.

Ronnie shook his head. "She is blessing you, maybe."

"Blessing, my ass. I don't need to speak Russian to see that." McCready cussed under his breath again. "You're sure, then?" he said to Ronnie. "That was the dead girl?"

"Yes, that was her," Ronnie said.

"Well, then, get in the car," McCready ordered. "You can damn well explain this to her folks. If they want her, they can come get her. Get in the goddamned car."

And so Ronnie did, he got in the goddamned car and they roared out of the braucha's yard, leaving the old woman standing there watching them go.

Ronnie turned and looked back through the rear window.

"What's she doing?" McCready said, glancing at the mirror. "Is she still there?"

Ronnie said, "Yes."

"What's she doing?"

"She's just standing there."

"Christ," McCready said, digging another cigarette and matches out of his shirt pocket. He stuck the cigarette in his mouth and struck the match against his denim pants, inhaled deeply. "What is she," he said, spitting loose tobacco from his lip out the open window, "a witch or something?"

Ronnie sat thinking a moment and then he said, "No. She's Catholic."

And McCready barked, "A Catholic witch, well, now I've heard it all."

Ronnie turned forward in his seat just in time to see his father in the wagon.

"Where are you going now?" his father yelled as they roared past him.

But McCready did not slow and so Ronnie could only lift his hand in a helpless wave.

———

When they lurched into Krausses' yard, McCready said, "You do the talking. Seems no one wants to understand a goddamned word I say. Tell them what happened. Or, no, Christ, who knows what the hell happened, just tell them to go see the old woman. Tell them she's got their girl."

McCready slammed on the brakes and the car slid a little in the mud and he heaved himself once more and stood leaning against the hood, smoking.

Ronnie climbed out, too, looked down the road, trying to calculate how long it would take his father to get there.

"What're you waiting for," McCready said, "the Second Coming?"

So Ronnie rubbed his hands against his thighs and then walked up the stairs. He stood a minute before knocking on the unpainted door.

Leo answered so quickly it made Ronnie wonder how long he'd been waiting there on the other side. Ronnie took a step back.

Leo glared out into the sunlight peevishly, as if he could not believe this outrage called spring.

"What is it?" Leo finally said.

Before Ronnie could answer, McCready called, "Is that the father?"

"No," Ronnie called back, eyeing Leo nervously, "not really."

"Ask where the mother is."

Ronnie asked.

"What for?" Leo said. "What business of yours?"

McCready reddened. "Tell him," he ordered.

"Well," Leo demanded "what is it? What do you want?"

Ronnie stood there between them, not looking at either of them, but only down at his muddy boots, there on Krausses' porch, a house he'd once thrown stones at, when he was younger, when it was just Leo there and he'd heard he was dead, thrown stones to try to rouse the dead man before they—him and his friends— raced back home in the darkness, hearts thudding against their throats. Yes, he thought about Leo and he thought about Old Krauss, Old Gus, Leo's father, and he thought about all the stories he'd heard over the years about Krausses, and he thought about that girl, the dead girl, thought of her white feet, her hands, that girl drowned beneath the ice of the river, he thought and he thought, and then he turned to McCready and said slowly, "You can do what you want, but I'm not telling him nothing."

Then he walked down the steps and past McCready and, when he was halfway down the road, he could not say exactly why, only that it felt like the thing to do, he pulled his hands from his pockets and ran like hell, he ran and ran and ran under that big unsheltering sky, his boots slipping in the mud of the road and McCready standing there hollering after him.

McCready watched him run and then he turned grudgingly to the man frowning darkly from the porch steps and he said, "Ah, to hell with it," and slammed into his car and roared out onto the road and past Ronnie, yelling, "When you're all dead in the river, don't come crying to me."

After McCready had gone, Ronnie slowed, walked, looked back to see Leo in the distance, sitting smoking calmly on the porch.

Leo lifted his hand in a belligerent wave, so much disdain in such a simple movement.

So McCready had not told him, then. And Ronnie said, "Be damned if I'll be the one to do it. I'll be goddamned."

When he saw his father's wagon approaching, infinitesimal on the horizon, he ran again.

FIFTEEN

The truth was, through all those days and weeks following the drowning, no one really had thought much about Leo. Everyone supposed he had holed up in that shack by himself while Mary walked the river, just as he had in the months before his marriage to Cecilia and after her death.

He still turned up at church most Sundays, but he was alone now (no one could figure how Mary got out of going with him). He came in by himself, just as he used to in the old days, usually a few minutes late, but he did not now look to the left or to the right, but walked with a distracted air straight to his seat in the front, and sat through Mass, fidgeting and tapping his fingers and shifting his feet, and going through the motions, and then, during the recessional hymn, he would suddenly rise and walk out, before Father had even left the pulpit.

He's in a hell of a hurry to get home to an empty house, not? That is what people said of him. For it was not long before some were wondering, yet again, what exactly Leo was up to. It would have seemed that by then, after all that had happened, people would have learned to leave him alone. But there was just something about Leo. No matter how much they might have hated him, or were disgusted by him, no matter how angry he made a person, they were still curious, too. And, more than that, they had begun to feel—though they never would have admitted as much to each other, perhaps not even to themselves—they had begun to feel kind of sorry for him, too. It was a feeling that increased as Leo aged, and though he was not yet an old man, not even middle-aged, he looked much older. Since the girl's drowning, his skin and hair had greyed and dulled and his dark eyes had receded even farther into his skull; he was missing a few teeth now, whether by rot or accident, and at times he would slump into a defeated kind of slouch. No one would say humble; rather, it was as if his body was emptying of everything that had been holding it up and, hollowed, was folding in slowly upon itself. Leo had crossed into the realm of the aged; and where they had all formerly scorned and despised him, now they pitied him. But it was a pity without compassion, and so everyone still kept their distance, as they always had.

People would ask Mike Weiser about him from time to time and Mike would say sharply, "But what business is it of mine? It's no more mine than yours." Which was true. Cecilia lay under the crabgrass and orange sandflowers in the cemetery at Knochenfeld. And Cecilia's children, the ones whom Mike and Marian had taken, seemed to have no recollection of Leo as their father. Only sometimes, when they eyed him in church, they got a kind of funny, uncomfortable feeling in their stomachs, and a strange, creeping sense of familiarity, as if Leo were a bad dream they'd once had (and the eldest of the three was secretly convinced that between Leo and the Kristkindl, who made the rounds at Christmas, tormenting children, there was some definite connection).

So, what business of Mike's, indeed? Was he Leo's keeper? But they kept on asking and he kept on answering until he got so tired of it he figured if he could give them all an answer they might finally leave him alone about it. So one afternoon Mike took a drive out to Krausses', whether from grudging obligation or genuine concern, Mike would not have liked to say for certain.

This was not long after Easter, just a month or two after the drowning of Elisabeth Brechert. So Mike thought to use for an excuse—not that he needed an excuse, but with Leo one never knew—that he had come to pay his condolences. He toted along with him a pan of creamed chicken and some fresh baking from Marian, who had said, in answer to Mike's look of surprise, "Make sure you put it into Mary's hands. I'd see that sonofabitch starve before I would drop him a filthy crumb. If he eats of it, all I can say is I hope he chokes. You make sure and give it to her."

When Mike pulled into the yard, it was so eerily still, he thought at first there was no one home. Even the few remaining bottles and jars hung motionless from the branches of Cecilia's old cottonwood tree. Mike climbed out of the car and looked around, hearing a meadowlark call from somewhere beyond the granaries, once, twice. He had just reached out to open the car door, when he saw Leo's old mule emerge from behind the barn where she grazed fruitlessly in the dirt. So he dropped his hand and sighed and walked up onto the porch. He tried to peer through the screen door into the dark kitchen, but he could see nothing. He raised his fist and knocked. Waited. At first he heard nothing and he thought that perhaps no one was home after all, but then some rustlings came from inside and also a kind of a strange sound, almost like a squawk, as if Leo had some animal living in there, and, in truth, Mike would not have put it past him. He waited, but no one came and so he banged again and then opened the screen door a little and called hello.

He said later that he should have known better, that he should have just climbed right back into his car and gone home. He did know better, of course, but he had come all that way, and he was there now (and he was curious, too, he had to admit it). So he called out again and then he stepped into the shack, dark as always—in spite of the brightness of the day—with the dirty yellowed sacking pulled across all the windows, and he stood there, blinking into the dim, sulphurous room.

"Just a minute, just wait." It was Leo, his voice coming muffled from behind the closed door of the far room.

So Mike stood looking around the filthy room, barren almost, but for the kitchen table and two chairs, the dirty pots stacked up in the basin, and the old black-and-white photograph of Gus in his coffin. He stepped closer to it, looked at all the faces there, as if there might be some clue, though to what, he could not say. To what? But there seemed to be something there, in the twist of Old Krauss's mouth, the twist in all their mouths. The hardness there, the mystery. What was it?

A thump came from the far side of the room, and he turned away from the photograph. He listened, more thumping and then some rustling, a heavy scraping against the floor, as if Leo were moving furniture, and then Leo pulled open the door and stepped into the kitchen, looking glint-eyed and rattled. Mike thought how odd it was to see Leo like that, nothing ever seemed to make him nervous. So, maybe because of Leo's uncharacteristic nervousness, maybe because that picture of Old Krauss dead and the kids there all around him had given him an uneasy feeling, maybe just because he was finally tired of it all, tired of Leo, Mike felt a deep regret at having walked into Leo's business yet again, walked into God knows what, whatever Leo was up to now, and not even wanting to know either, not even wanting to wonder, just wanting to get the hell out now that he'd gotten in. They stood there like that a minute, with the dim room between them and neither knowing what to say, until finally Mike spoke.

"So, Leo, how are things?" he said edgily.

"It's good, things are good."

Mike cleared his throat, shifted his boots against the creaking floor. He said, "In spite of everything, I guess?"

Leo just kind of frowned at him, as if he had no idea what

Mike was talking about. Then a light seemed to go on for him and he said quickly, "Yah, yah, in spite of that, sure."

Mike nodded. He began to clear his throat, realized he'd just done it. "And Mary," he said instead, "how is she?"

Leo wiped a hand across his forehead, as if he was sweating. "She's good, yah. Good."

Then, while they stood there, that strange, muffled squawk came from the other room and Mike glanced past Leo's shoulder and Leo said quickly, "Well, good to see you, then. Goodbye."

Mike stared at him, tried to pretend he hadn't heard anything. "All right," he said, "give my condolences to Mary."

"Yah, yah," Leo said, practically herding him out. "Goodbye."

Mike opened the screen door, feeling terribly uneasy but curious again, too, God help him, and relieved, yes, that too, relieved just to be stepping back out of that dark, suffocating house—how did anyone live in there?—stepping back into daylight and air and life, away from whatever it was that Leo was up to, whatever he was trying to hide, but that couldn't possibly be any of his—any of Mike's—business anyhow.

So he stepped out onto the porch and down the stairs, letting the screen door bang shut behind him, and he climbed into his car and breathed deeply, glancing once more toward Cecilia's cottonwood, the sunlight glinting against the still bottles now giving the illusion of motion; and he looked toward the barn, too, and he looked around at all that slow ruin and decay, and he thought of Cecilia and of the girl and he felt a heaviness in his heart. He sighed and went to start the car and that was when he noticed the pan of creamed chicken and the buns still sitting there on the seat beside him, wrapped up neatly by Marian in a clean, white tea towel. So he sat there another minute thinking he should just go home, forget about all of it. But Marian had insisted he take the food to Mary. Another man might have dumped it in the ditch and washed the pans and returned them to Marian and said nothing more of the matter. But Mike was an honest man. He always kept his word. That's what folks said about him. He knew it himself. And when folks said a thing like that about you, well, you had an obligation to live up to it.

So he sighed again and he climbed back out of the car and took the warm pan and the buns and walked back up the steps and stood on the porch and lifted his hand to knock, and just then that muffled squawk came again, and it occurred to Mike—he could not believe he had not thought of it sooner—that it was Mary, that perhaps she was sick, and Leo not sending for the braucha or anyone to help, it would be like him. The same as it had been all those years ago with Cecilia. It outraged Mike, the very thought of it. So he swung the door open and stuck his head inside.

And there stood Leo, his back to the door, working busily over something on the kitchen table.

Mike said later that he just stepped inside, it was as if he was somehow compelled to, as if he could not stop himself, and it was as if time itself slammed that screen door shut on both of them and Leo turned and then they stood there facing each other and for some reason that Mike could not later explain, he thought of Cecilia, how he used to guide her small hands in the night, over his own face and over Marian's, he thought of that, and when he thought it, everything suddenly became clear to Mike, so clear that he was amazed that he had not realized it sooner.

He breathed then, "Jesus Christ, Leo, oh, Christ Almighty."

And he walked over, across the dark kitchen and past Leo and uncovered the thing that Leo was hiding and he stood there looking, and he said again, "Jesus Christ Almighty, Leo. Where did you get this baby?"

SIXTEEN

It was a long moment before either Leo or Mike said anything else or even moved, and that baby squirming there on the table between the two of them.

Finally Mike said again, "Leo. Where did you get this baby?"

As if on cue, the little thing screwed up its red face and began to howl, and Leo looked at Mike, as if he, Mike, should do something.

"Leo," he repeated, raising his voice, wanting to reach out and shake the man, feeling like a fool, saying the same thing over and over, "where did you get this baby?"

Leo seemed to come around then, and he scowled at Mike, as if he could not believe the stupidity, and said, "Well, and where do you think? It's mine."

The baby was screaming, and Mike shouted, "Mary had a baby? When did she have a baby?" And the baby screaming, screaming, and Leo not moving to calm it and so Mike yelled, "For God's sake, do something."

Leo said, "What?"

So Mike set the food he was holding down on the table and

picked the baby up and juggled it a bit and yelled, "Did you feed it anything? Is it hungry?"

"Well, and how should I know? Did it say it was hungry?"

And Mike yelled, "Feed it something."

"What?" Leo said again.

"For God's sake, Leo," Mike hollered. Jiggling that baby around, wondering what the hell to do. Then he remembered the creamed chicken. He picked up a dirty spoon from the table and wiped it on his shirt and spooned some of the rich cream into the baby's mouth. The baby stopped howling for a second, then choked and spat and screamed with renewed vigour, its face turning an alarming shade of red. And Leo just standing and watching as if, really, it were none of his business after all.

"Where's Mary?" Mike shouted.

"What, am I supposed to follow her around all day, to know where she goes?"

It's a damned good thing I'm holding this baby, Mike thought. *It's a damned good thing.* But knowing in his heart he did not have it in him.

"You don't know where she is?"

"She's not here, what more is there to know?"

And while they were going back and forth that way, the baby settled down and pretty soon its face calmed and its eyes glazed and it closed them and slept in Mike's arms and Mike looked down at the little pink thing and then he calmed a little, too, and he said, "But for God's sake, Leo. When did she have a baby?"

Leo shrugged and said, "Not long, three weeks, maybe, less, more—how should I know?"

Mike gritted his teeth, said again, "But nobody even knew. Did the braucha come? Did she see it? Or Father Rieger? Has it been baptized?"

Leo frowned and shook his head. "No, that's not for me, that church. I'm through with them."

"But you still come to church yourself."

"Yah, well, a man has to go somewhere, not?"

Mike shook his head in amazement. "But," he said, "you will have the baby baptized."

"No, he baptized Mary's girl and look what happened."

Mike blinked, uncomprehending. "What?" he said.

"Not a month later, drowned in the river."

"Leo, Father baptizes lots of people."

"Yah, so? And don't they die too?"

Mike just stood there, not knowing what to say. And so he looked down at the baby and said what everyone says: "Boy, or girl?"

And Leo said, "Girl. Cecilia."

Mike just stared at him. Finally, he said slowly, "Mary named this baby Cecilia?"

"No," Leo said. "I did."

"You named Mary's baby Cecilia?"

"Yah, and why not? It's my baby too."

Mike figured there was nothing more to be said to Leo, figured, at long last, that he had been wrong about him, all those years ago at the St. Valentine's dance when he'd thought maybe Leo had a heart beneath those bones after all. Figured, in the end, that Leo wasn't worth his time, so stupid and arrogant. Wasn't worth anyone's time or pity, either. He figured there was nothing more that could be said to, or done for, Leo, and so he just carried the sleeping baby into the other room and settled it into the apple crate there with some blankets and then he stood looking down at it a minute and feeling awful sorry for the poor little thing who did not know its own blood.

When he returned to the kitchen, he said, "That baby will want to eat when it wakes, Leo. I hope Mary will be back soon."

But Leo, he just waved his hand through the air and said, "Ach, Mary."

So Mike crossed to the door and opened it and said, in spite of himself, "If she needs help, anything, she knows where to find us."

And he went to close the door softly behind him so as not to wake that baby, thinking, *But God help that little thing, who did not ask to be born at all, who might yet live to regret that it had been.* But then he stopped, with one foot on the porch, because something had occurred to him, something he hadn't thought to ask. He leaned back through the doorway and said, "But, Leo, I don't understand. Why were you hiding it from me?"

And Leo just stood there in his dark kitchen, with his long arms hanging at his sides and that photograph of Old Krauss in his coffin pinned crookedly to the wall at his back. He stood there, and then he shrugged and said, kind of quiet, "All the others," and he looked out the window, squinted a little. Then he turned to Mike, shrugged again and said, "This one"—and he raised his hands in a helpless gesture—"I wanted to keep."

————

News of the baby travelled fast, as bad news always does. Almost everyone seemed to know that Leo and Mary had a baby and that the baby must have been born sometime in the days following the death of Mary's daughter, Elisabeth (though how that was even possible, they could not imagine), and that Leo had named that baby Cecilia after his dead first wife and that Mary seemed to want nothing to do with the child, whether because of the name or the father or grief, no one ever did find out, and that Leo, for whatever reason, perhaps even of necessity—though that, necessity, had never meant much to him in the past—perhaps of necessity, had assumed care of the infant.

But what, really, could be done about it? Mary had abandoned this child for her other child lost in the river. She still spent much of each day haunting the valley, anyone driving along the trails that ran past the river could see her sitting heavily on one of the rocks there. People had quickly become accustomed to her presence, and so they hardly noticed her, and it was only when an outsider came to town and asked about the strange woman alone at the river that they remembered.

Far more outrageous was the idea of Leo alone out at the Krauss shack with that baby; and rightly so, to give that some thought, since for her—the baby—something might still be done.

And since the news of the baby, it was easier than ever to be angered by Leo. Now that the secret was out, Leo had begun toting that baby to church with him, though he came now only occasionally, with the little thing all bundled up in scraps of cloth and burlap and tucked into an old apple crate. God only knew, everyone speculated, what he had done with it before, left it there at the house, they supposed, with Mary or without her. (And, though Leo brought the baby to church, he did not have it baptized and this was generally understood to be a crime against the infant and, more important, as Ludmila Baumgarten was fond of pointing out, a further outrage upon the community. They believed, too, that, as with all of Leo's actions, it had been intentional, and wondered if perhaps Father Rieger might intervene, on the child's behalf, but when Ludmila and some of the other women went to see him, Father Rieger only blew his nose and directed them to Psalm 127, quoting, "'Lo, children are a heritage of the Lord. The fruit of the womb,'"—here he blushed and looked away and finished quickly—"'is his reward.'" Then he placed his fingertips together and bowed his head. Though the women waited, it seemed Father had nothing more to say, and so, after an uncomfortable silence, Ludmila said, "Bless you, Father," and led the women out.)

So it seemed there was nothing to be done. And it was felt generally that Leo took great delight in flaunting the child in all their faces. He took that baby to church when he wanted to go to church and he took that baby to town when he wanted to go to town, and though it angered everyone, yes, they were angered at the very thought of Leo caring for an infant—who wouldn't be?—it also seemed unfathomable—but who could deny it?—that

Leo was as devoted a father as had ever been seen. Certainly (and this is what really rankled), a more devoted father than most, perhaps even all, of the other men around. Wives began to look at their own husbands and wonder why they could not, at least in this regard, have been a little more like Leo Krauss. And the husbands, if they had known what the wives were thinking, that they, the husbands, were being compared to Leo Krauss—the same Leo Krauss who had come not so many years previous to drink their liquor and ogle their daughters, their sisters—if they had known they were being compared to this Leo Krauss and coming up short, found wanting in the slightest respect, they would have had yet another and more immediate reason to hate him.

But no one could deny that Leo seemed devoted to the child, to little Cecilia. And more than that, he'd stopped drinking. Now when he came to town, he parked his old wagon in front of Wing's instead of the hotel bar. He went in every morning for coffee and a piece of raisin pie, always toting that baby along in her crate, as if it were a puppy he kept in there. And he sat at a table by himself, a little apart from the other men, and ate his pie and drank his sweetened coffee (*Six teaspoons of sugar, I kid you not, in one cup, where is the sense in that?*) and jiggled the crate with the toe of his boot, and, with God as their witness, they had never seen a more content baby in their lives—God only knew what he was giving it—but it let out a little squawk and Leo jiggled the crate with his toe—you could not call it rocking, there was nothing of comfort in it—and that baby settled right down and lay staring up at Leo with those dark Krauss eyes. And so Leo sat and drank and jiggled and chewed and did not listen to the men talking while the men pretended not to care that he was not listening, until finally, he was no longer not listening, and they no longer cared.

And that was how Leo found out about Elisabeth.

It was inevitable, of course. It was nothing short of a miracle that it had all stayed a secret so long, and a testament, too, to that lingering fear, or if not fear, at least caution, that the community had regarding Krausses. If Ronnie Rausch had not been so afraid to meddle in Leo's business, he might have been more inclined to tell what had happened that night at the braucha's (Erv, on the other hand, had other reasons for keeping quiet, that had little to do with Leo).

So this was a Saturday morning. Leo was sitting in Wing's, as usual, just finishing his pie. Now, typically, he would drink his coffee and eat his pie and then get up and make a hasty exit (while it was still busy enough that Wing might not notice, or so Leo thought) and not pay a red cent, leaving Wing to take the loss. At first the others did nothing, thinking that if Wing wanted to say something he would say something—what was it for them to interfere?—though it seemed odd to think that Wing would say something to Leo when even they themselves would not. Then they started to feel bad for Wing, so timid and fretful (*As bad as a woman,* that is what some of them said), and so one or the other of the men would pay Leo's share, usually the same men, Mike Weiser, Art Reis, the Schneider brothers. Some didn't care, wanted nothing to do with Leo, but, as Art Reis pointed out, this wasn't helping out Leo, who would eat the pie and drink the coffee regardless, it was helping out Wing and right was right, not?

But there Leo was this one Saturday morning, sitting alone at his table, stirring sugar into his coffee, his pie before him and the crate settled at his boots. The other men were still having a hard time getting used to the idea of Leo—of any man, but especially of Leo Krauss—sitting there among them with a baby, and now and then one or the other of them would shoot an uneasy glance at the crate to see was that baby all right in there, or maybe just to convince themselves that, by God, there really was a baby in there after all, when in walked Ronnie Rausch with his father.

"Well," one of the men said, "look what the cat dragged in."

"You two must be working awful hard out there. Haven't seen hide nor hair of you."

"Thought maybe you packed up and moved to Medicine Hat with the rest of the rich farmers."

"No, no." Ronnie's father waved his hand, a little nervously, as the two of them pulled up chairs and sat. "We just don't have money to throw away like you." He shot a quick look at his son.

"Don't listen to him," one of the men said, "he's sitting on a bundle."

"Is that right, Ronnie," said another, "does he stuff his mattress with it?"

Ronnie looked up from his boots. "What?"

"What's the matter with him?" someone said, nodding at Ronnie. "Looks pale."

"What, have you been sick?"

"Must be in love."

"Love, nothing, he looks like he's seen a ghost."

"What, another one?"

"Oh, yah, Christ, I forgot about that. Is that what's wrong?"

"Must be, he can't even talk no more."

"What ghost?"

"He's the one saw that dead girl. Up at the braucha's."

"Yah, I heard about that. Whatever happened there, Rausch?"

But Ronnie stood abruptly. "I'll be out in the wagon," he said, shortly, though the men hardly noticed him leave. His father still sat, twisting his hands in his lap.

"What about this dead girl?" someone asked. "I never heard about that."

"Yah, up at the braucha's there, him and Erv Rausch, not?"

"Ach, those two *dummkopfs*," Ronnie's father said dismissively, rubbing his palms on his pantlegs, "out passing the bottle around—"

"And they said they saw that dead girl there," someone put in, "that Brechert girl, that one Leo brought back—"

As soon as it had been said, they all suddenly became aware again of Leo, sitting over in his corner, who had just placed a

chunk of pie in his mouth. It was as if someone had slammed a
door, everyone sitting there, looking at Leo, but not looking at
him either, or even at each other, and trying to think of something
to say. Surely something must be said. But they could think of
nothing.

And then, while they sat growing slowly warm inside their
spring coats, no one either moving or lifting their cups for fear
of making a sound (and Ronnie's father pale now, too, and
wanting to go cuff his son on the ear for stupidity, though
Ronnie had said nothing, but just for beginning it all in the first
place), then Leo lowered his fork and pried off another chunk of
pie and raised it to his mouth and chewed slowly and swallowed
and pried another and lifted and chewed and swallowed, just as
if nothing had happened, eating steadily, taking a sip of coffee
now and again, and the rest of the men sitting and clearing their
throats and looking funny at each other and not knowing what
the hell to do, wishing someone would say something, but not
one of them willing to be the one to break the silence. So they
just waited like that while Leo finished his pie, scraped up the
crumbs and ate them, drained the last of the coffee from his
cup, wiped his mouth on his sleeve, picked up the box with the
baby in it, and walked out the door, just as he would have done
on any other day. And the men still sitting there, until someone
said, in a hushed voice, as if Leo were still with them, "Did he
hear, even?"

Rochus Schneider, who'd gone to the window to watch Leo go,
said, "He heard all right."

For there was Leo's wagon, rolling off into the distance, not
down the road that led to his farm, but cutting east, straight for
the braucha's.

Ronnie stepped back inside then, and stood looking at the men.

"Well, Ronnie," said Ronnie's father, "and are you happy now,
you and your big mouth?"

"Ach, don't get mad at him, he didn't say nothing."

"What's the big deal?" one of the men said. "The old woman will run Leo off. Be good for him. Teach him a lesson."

Ronnie said, "He's going to the braucha's? Leo is?"

"Shut up, now," said the father, "haven't you said enough?"

But Ronnie ignored him. "No," he said. "Listen. You can laugh all you want, you can say what you want about me, but . . . someone should go out there."

"Where? The braucha's?"

"What for?"

Ronnie rubbed a hand across the back of his neck, looked at his father. But his father was studying the floor. And so Ronnie said, "Just . . . there might be trouble."

The men looked at Ronnie's father.

Ronnie's father sighed and raised his head and wiped a hand across his face and nodded. "Yah," he said. And nodded again. "There might be trouble."

"Well," Art Reis said slowly. "It wouldn't hurt to take a ride out there, then."

And they all looked at Mike Weiser.

———

There was some discussion about who should go. In the end, it was Mike Weiser, who, in spite of his objections, was considered to be a relative of sorts; Ronnie Rausch; Ronnie's father, by his own insistence; and Art Reis, known for his level head.

The conversation as they drove along in Mike Weiser's car revolved mainly (since Ronnie's father had forbidden Ronnie to speak, and each time Ronnie raised his head, delivered him a sharp kick at the shin) around Krausses and the reputation they had built for themselves, until finally Mike said, "Ach, but what have they ever really done? Isn't it all just talk? They only hurt themselves, not?"

But no one seemed to agree and so by the time they were nearing the braucha's, Mike was starting to feel sorry for and defensive of Leo all over again, though he couldn't have said exactly why, only that no one could be all bad, not even Leo Krauss, and he said as much.

"Well, sure," Ronnie's father said, "you're related, it's different."

Art agreed. "Family's family."

To which Mike said, "The next man who says I'm related to Leo Krauss is getting a swift kick in the ass and I'll say no more about it."

After which the men rode along in silence, Mike staring peevishly ahead through the windshield and the men thinking to themselves that Mike was getting awful touchy these days, but maybe a man got that way where family was concerned.

Finally, Art said to Ronnie, "So, what is all this about that drowned girl anyway?"

And Ronnie's father kicked him before he had even opened his mouth, and so Ronnie just glared out the window on the other side of the car and said, "I'm not saying nothing. You just wait and see. Just see for yourselves. Then you can laugh all you want."

To which Ronnie's father said, "Nobody's laughing, you *dummkopf,* shut your mouth."

After that, nobody said anything.

When the car rolled to a stop beside Leo's wagon, they sat a moment, marvelling at the silence of the place. They had been expecting a scene, or at least Ronnie had, he was the only one certain that Leo would, in fact, find Elisabeth there, apparently alive and well. The others merely wanted to avert trouble between Leo and the old braucha, who did not deserve to have to deal with him. But the span of yard was silent, just the wind stirring in the tall grasses.

Art said, "Now what the hell is going on here?"

And he moved to get out of the car, but just as he was doing so, the door to the old woman's shack flew open and Leo stepped from the darkness, with the crate containing the baby under one arm, and the other hand gripping the girl they had all believed to be dead.

They just sat in the car, staring stupidly.

All except Ronnie, who said, "Who's the *dummkopf* now? Now who's laughing?"

Leo stood a moment in the doorway, frowning at the men. He had the dead girl by the hair, it seemed, though he did not appear to be hurting her. They both looked so calm.

Following Mike Weiser's lead, the men climbed out from the car.

Leo said, as if someone could have answered for him, as if he were the only one of them still in the dark, "What is this? What is going on here?"

But the men could not speak, not even to say, *You know as much as I, Leo. It's a mystery to me, too.* They were thinking, all of them, even Ronnie, his amazement renewed at having the girl before him again, *But this is impossible, she is dead. We dragged the river until our arms ached with the cold, we held a Mass, lit candles for her soul, prayed, for her and for the mother too, the church bell rang her to rest.* They had imagined her dead, out there in the river, everyone had. How could they help it? There had been no body.

"What is this?" Leo repeated, and shook the girl a little by her hair.

That seemed to snap the men out of whatever spell of shock and disbelief they had been under, and Mike stepped forward.

"Leo—" he began, but he was looking at the girl.

The old braucha appeared in the doorway then and spoke in Russian.

"What is it?" Art said, to no one in particular. "What is she saying?"

But no one knew and so they all just stood and watched while Leo took the girl, leading her by that wild red hair, not roughly, but very calmly and firmly, to his wagon. She did not seem to be struggling against him, either, just walking along beside him, her bleached dress swaying a little, her bare feet in the dirt.

Before any of the men could think what to do, Leo and Elisabeth were up in the wagon and jolting away down the road, Elisabeth keeping one hand behind her on the seat to steady herself, resurrected.

The men just stood there watching them go. It was some time before anyone said anything. Art Reis broke the silence.

"I'll be goddamned," he said.

The braucha spoke to them then, in rapid German, or mostly German, clutching at Mike's sleeve as she spoke. Then she nodded and went back into her shack, shutting the door firmly behind her.

"What did she say?" Ronnie asked.

Mike looked from one to the other. "She said: 'Look out for that one. That one is slippery.'"

The men stood around in the yard, frowning at each other. Art said, "Leo, or the girl?"

And Ronnie's father said, "'Look out for,' meaning take care of? Or, be careful of?"

Mike just shook his head.

———

There was nothing left but to drive back to town.

Ronnie said, "I told you she was there."

And they all said, "That's right, you did. She was there all right."

Then, after a minute, someone said, "Was she?"

To which the men could only raise their eyebrows and shake their heads.

"Christ," Ronnie's father said, "we should have touched her, see if she was real."

And then Ronnie said, "Erv." He had kept it quiet so long, he could no longer stand it. "Erv," he said, and this time his father did not stop him. "Erv touched her."

And he told, then, of the night in the chickenshed, the dark and the feathers and the blood on Erv's hands.

"You were drinking," Mike said.

"I'm not drinking now," Ronnie said. "And I just saw a dead girl walk out of the braucha's shack."

And the men could not really argue.

"So," Art Reis said, slowly, "she didn't go through the ice?"

"I guess not," Mike said. "I guess she mustn't have."

"She went through all right," said Ronnie.

"Why do you say that?"

"I don't know. Just, that night at the braucha's. She was strange before. But something's different now. She went through. Or something happened to her."

The men were quiet. They had thought so, too, that something was especially odd about her. But then, what was not strange about it all, the whole situation? They sighed, frowned out the windows.

Finally, Art said, "But what is she doing at the braucha's?"

They drove on in troubled silence.

When they stopped in front of Wing's, Ronnie said, "You laughed at me before, all of you did, and you can laugh at me again. But there was blood on Erv's hands that night. There's something about that girl. She's no ghost, I guess, you can laugh all you want, but there's something about her. You wait and see."

And, because there was really nothing to say about that, they went home, wondering the same thing, in spite of themselves: had she been raised from the dead, or had she never actually drowned? They tried to make some sense of it, though there was no sense to be found, and when they arrived home, they told their wives. The wives—Ma Reis and Erna Rausch and Marian Weiser—all said pretty much the same thing, which amounted to: *What, and have you lost your mind?* No, they told their wives, they had not lost their minds, had not even had a drink, and they'd seen her there, that Brechert girl, Leo's girl, she was alive, they'd seen her with their own eyes. And they each went on to explain, in remarkably similar versions, what exactly had happened, what had been seen, what had been said. And when the wives still shook their heads and waved them away and said, *Ach, don't bother me, go back and find your drinking friends,* the husbands said, *Leo Krauss was there and the braucha was there and that girl was there, too. She was barefoot and her hair was all hanging down and she was wearing that white dress, it was so thin that you could see . . .*

And then the wives did believe them and they sat at their kitchen tables over coffee and thought a while and then they said to their husbands, *So she is not dead after all.* And the men said, *No, I don't think so. But, Christ Almighty, I don't know.* And the wives said, *Don't be stupid, of course she is not dead. She ran away. From Leo's. And us all the fools for it, and her poor mother, besides. Good God. She ran away. And you let Leo Krauss drag her back.*

In defence of themselves, the husbands said, *But he did not drag her exactly, there was nothing violent about it.*

And the wives said, *I thought he had her by the hair.*

The men admitted this was true.

It was that girl, they said, *how can it be violent when she goes along with it that way?*

And the women said, *Oh, but you are stupid.* They said, *Tomorrow I will pay a visit to Mary. I will go and see for myself.*

SEVENTEEN

The next afternoon, Ma Reis drove over in the wagon to Rausches' and collected Ronnie's mother, Erna, who brought her two youngest children, and from there over to Weisers' and picked up Marian, Mike standing in the doorway, his arms at his sides, watching them go.

Marian eyed the Rausch children in the back of the wagon and said to Erna, "Well, and is that such a good idea?"

Erna shrugged. "I couldn't leave them alone. Not with that crazy new bull of Roy's not even penned, and Ronnie and Roy God knows where."

Ma Reis said, "I'd put that bull in the icehouse if I were you, Erna. I'd make sausage out of him. That's what I would do."

"You go ahead and do it, then," Erna said. "It won't break my heart."

"Art would just as soon see me in the icehouse," Ma said. "You should hear how he goes on about that thing. A bull yet, imagine that."

"These men and their bulls," Erna said, "always comparing."

The women laughed a little. Then they were quiet, and Marian said, "Well. What do you think of all this, anyway?"

Ma said, "Ach, those old fools," meaning the husbands.

"I don't know," Marian said. "It doesn't sound right, but where there's smoke there's fire."

"Well," Ma said, "we'll know soon enough. Tell you the truth, I wouldn't be surprised by anything, those Krausses. God knows what goes on there. What went on. It makes you wonder, what did that girl have to suffer there, with Leo?"

"All right, now, let's not forget," Marian said, and inclined her head meaningfully toward the children again.

Erna narrowed her eyes at them shrewdly, then turned back around. "Ach, they don't hear nothing, those two. Ears like their father."

The two children, a boy and a girl, listened from where they sat in the wagon box but could not decipher, in spite of their efforts, what the women were talking about or where they were going, either. It would be impossible to ask. And, then again, they did not really care. What could it matter to them? The girl, especially, did not care where they were going, only that they were going somewhere at all, anywhere. But years later, decades, when she was grown with grown children of her own, she would tell them, "I remember that day like it was yesterday. Ma Reis was driving, not Mom—Grandma, I mean—or Marian Weiser. I know that because we were flying along at a pretty good clip the way Ma always drove—you know she died many years later, in a car accident, she was an old woman then, I never heard the details, but I remember thinking, *Well, she must have been the one driving*—anyway, it was Ma Reis that day, and Uncle Dale and I had to grab on to the sides and to each other to keep from being tossed out onto the road.

"We had no real idea what was going on, only that it involved the drowned girl we had heard about and Krausses (I hoped that was not where we were going), and that it was somehow terribly important, though Uncle Dale seemed not to care much at all and I remember this bothered me, his not caring. And so I tried to make him care. I said to him, quietly so the women would not hear, 'They say that dead girl is alive. That one that drowned in the river. She was *dead* and now she's alive.' Uncle Dale would just hitch up his shoulders and say, 'So, she's alive, what is it to me?' and that would just make me try harder, until Grandma turned around and said, 'Lizzie, what are you talking about back there?' And then I was quiet.

"I was trying to scare Uncle Dale because I felt scared myself. But Uncle Dale would not scare and in trying to scare him I only succeeded in making myself more afraid. I did not want to see Leo Krauss, of whom I was terrified, a lot of us were, he was so strange and so awful, but worse than that, I did not want to see the dead girl, oh, she was always odd-looking anyway, and I imagined her climbing out of the river with her long wet hair all down over her face that way and coming toward me. It scared the daylights out of me.

"When we pulled into Krausses' yard, Grandma forbid us to budge from the wagon, to so much as put one finger outside of it (as if I would have). She handed us each a scotch mint from a paper sack she always kept in her purse for just such occasions, and reminded us of the lickin's we would get should we leave our seats, and then she followed Marian Weiser and Ma Reis up to the house. We sat and watched and sucked our scotch mints while the women stood on the stoop and knocked and called out.

"I was crying a little bit then and I sucked my mint harder to stop the tears which I knew would have made Grandma furious, they always did. I was certain that any minute the dead girl would come out that door and send them all—Grandma and Ma Reis and Marian Weiser—shrieking back to us (and part of me looked forward to that, a little bit, to see the adults afraid for a change, especially these adults, who never seemed afraid of anything). That's what a silly imagination I had. Oh, I could really scare myself back then. There was always so much talk of ghosts and spirits and the devil, everyone so superstitious. I don't think it was healthy. It sure wasn't for me, anyway. Uncle Dale, well.

"When the door of Krausses' shack finally opened, the three women all took a step back, all at once. I remember how funny it looked and I would have laughed if I hadn't been so afraid. And I leaned back in the wagon, too, as if those few inches could make a difference, could keep the dead girl from me.

"But it was not the dead girl who stood there in the doorway. It was Leo Krauss. Uncle Dale and I could not hear what they said to each other, Leo and the women. Leo did not seem angry, as I had thought he would be, but only aloof and annoyed, as he always did. He waved them all away and slammed the door in their faces.

"Ma Reis straightened her hat and marched down the steps and across the yard. I remember little puffs of dust came up from beneath her shoes, like smoke. Grandma and Marian followed and they all disappeared inside the big dark barn door, and then we were alone there in the yard.

"Uncle Dale and I waited a long time for them to come back out. Uncle Dale said to me, 'Is your candy gone?' It was, but I said no and made sucking motions so that he would believe it wasn't. Then we sat like that some more. I remember there was a meadowlark sounding from one of the rails by the barn. There wasn't much of a wind and so we just sat there listening to that meadowlark and picking bits of wood off the wagon box, with Uncle Dale looking at me sideways and me pretending to give that candy that I did not have a good suck every now and then.

"Finally, Uncle Dale stood and looked around the yard, and I said, 'Sit down once, do you want to get a lickin'?' And he started climbing out of the wagon. I tried to stop him, but you know Uncle Dale. Sometimes things don't change very much at all, do they?

"So I sat and watched him sneak across the yard and thought with some small satisfaction about the lickin' he would get when Grandma caught him. I did not want to go with him, but I did not want to stay there alone, either. Leo Krauss was there in the house, maybe watching me from behind one of those dark windows, and then somewhere, too, was a dead girl come back to life. And, thinking of it that way, a lickin' didn't seem so bad after all, and so I climbed down and ran after Uncle Dale. He had gone around the back of the barn, trying to peek in through the chinks in the boards. I stood so close he kept elbowing me back. 'What do you see?' I kept asking. 'Nothing,' he said, 'I don't see nothing.' We went all around the barn that way, just looking for a place to peek, or Uncle Dale was looking and I was just trying to stay close to him, glancing over my shoulder every now and then. Oh, it was awful. I tried to convince Uncle Dale to come back to the wagon with me. I even said I would give him the rest of my scotch mint, and he said, 'Do you think I'm stupid? You don't have any scotch mint.' And I said yes I did. And he said show him then. And I said I'd show him in the wagon, and that was when someone grabbed us by the backs of our coats. I screamed something terrible, and Uncle Dale did, too, though he denied it later. Oh, how we shrieked. Grandma must have thought we'd been killed. I closed my eyes and screamed and screamed and when I finally opened them and turned to look and I saw that it was Leo Krauss, I screamed some more. It didn't seem to bother Leo one bit, all that screaming. He just hauled us by our coats around to the front of the barn where Grandma and the other ladies had run out looking for us.

"Leo kind of dangled me and Uncle Dale in front of the women and then tossed us toward Grandma and said, 'Your kids can't mind their business either.'

"I wasn't screaming any more, but I was crying pretty hard and Uncle Dale had a death grip on Grandma's leg. I looked up at Grandma then to see how mad was she at us. But when I saw her face, it stopped my tears. Of course, I thought it was because of us, because of Uncle Dale and me, but then I saw the other women and their faces were all twisted up too, with an emotion I couldn't then name, and I thought, *But that's not because of us. It couldn't be.*

"Grandma said to Leo, 'You cannot keep her in there like that. After all that girl has been through.' And Leo said, 'Keep her? I don't keep her nowhere. That is where she wants to be. Ask her yourself.' And Ma Reis said, 'McCready will hear about this.' He was the constable at Triumph back then. The one that drowned in the river a few years later when the boat he was fishing in, or drinking in, more likely, tipped over. So Leo said, 'What does McCready care?'

"And while they're going back and forth that way, Uncle Dale tugs at my sleeve and points to the barn. I looked behind us then, for the first time, through the big barn door. And there was Elisabeth Brechert, the dead girl, sitting on a straw pallet in a corner.

"Of course, she did not look as I had imagined her, not ghostly, not deathly, but somehow seeing her that way, alive after we had all thought her dead, was more terrifying than anything I could have imagined. She was so utterly human. Only human. And that was the most awful realization of all. She was not dead. But one day she would be, that's what bothered me then. She would die, and so would I. So would we all. And so it was as if we were already dead, a little bit, anyway.

"I didn't understand it then, I don't even really understand it now. But I think it was the first time in my life that I realized just how complicated things are. One thing about getting older, you realize there aren't any answers. All those mysteries you spend your life trying to figure out. Well, they're mysteries for a reason, aren't they? Some of them, anyway. You could drive yourself crazy trying to figure it all out."

———

The children crouched there by the women, staring in at Elisabeth. And she stared out at them, as if they were nothing, as if they did not matter. And they didn't, Ma Reis knew. That was the thing. They didn't matter, not one iota. It reminded her of the way Leo Krauss looked at people. As if they were there, but not there. As if he was always looking through you to someone else.

"Well," Ma Reis said to Leo. "And what does Mary think of this?"

And Leo said, "What should she think? She should be happy that God has brought her back to us. Resurrected her."

Ma Reis made that noise she always made when she was disgusted by something but was too angry to speak. "Resurrected," she said. "Come now, Leo, you can't really believe that."

"She was dead," he said flatly, "and now she is alive."

Ma Reis said, "She was never dead, Leo. She was trying to get away. From you."

But Leo just stood there and stared at them blandly, as if it could not matter what they said. As if he was bored by them.

Ma said, "And the blood? What about that?"

And Leo said, "You tell me."

Ma Reis said, "No. It's McCready who will hear it."

And Leo just stood there staring, sucking his teeth.

So the women loaded the two children into the wagon box and climbed up onto the bench seat and left Leo, heading straight for Triumph and McCready's office. They rode along in silence for a while until Marian said, "And do you believe that, then, what she said?"

Erna shook her head and shrugged. They both looked to Ma, who stared steadily ahead down the reins. When she did not speak, Marian said, "Seems so impossible."

"It's possible," Ma said. "There isn't much in this world that isn't, when you think of it."

"But, still, it's so—"

"She fell in the river, she climbed back out. There's nothing so marvellous in that."

"But that boy, he would have seen her."

"He wouldn't have seen nothing. He said himself it was already dark. He was halfway up the draw."

"What I want to know is why she stayed at the braucha's so long."

"Wouldn't you? Did you see that place? Worse now than it ever was."

"And, then, Leo."

"Drunk again."

"Do you think he hurt her?"

"There was blood on her hands, or on her wrists."

"He must have done it."

"Then why not show someone, why not show us?"

"She's afraid. You could see it in her face."

Ma said, "She's afraid all right. But not of Leo. Of that I'm sure."

"How do you know?"

"Because I told her to come with us. I told her to come home with me. I said I would take her back to the braucha's if she wanted."

"And what did she say?"

"She said no. She said she didn't want to go nowhere."

"Now, what does that mean?"

"It must at least mean she's not afraid to be there with Leo."

"Or she's too afraid to leave."

"No," Ma said. "It's not Leo at all. It's herself she's afraid of."

Erna and Marian raised their eyebrows and exchanged glances across Ma's shoulder which Ma pretended not to notice.

"Well," Marian sighed, "we'll see what McCready has to say."

When they arrived at McCready's, the women had to knock several times before McCready's wife came to the door. She told them McCready was not in, and Ma said, "But that's his car right there."

McCready's wife flushed and said, angrily, "And what is that to me? I told you he's not here. If it's his car you want, well, there it is." And then she closed the door.

The women did not look at each other, but just stood a moment, and then Marian said, "Well, that's it, I guess."

"We'll send the men over," Erna said. "They'll take care of it."

Ma said nothing. Just turned and led the women back to the wagon.

Erna said, "You should have told about the blood, maybe."

Marian shot her a quick look and they were all quiet.

Then Erna turned, as if suddenly remembering her children in the back of the wagon. She stared at them hard a minute and then she handed them the sack of scotch mints from her purse.

When she had turned back around, the girl, who had taken the bag, threw it out onto the road. The boy was horrified. "What did you do that for?" he hissed.

But she could not have told him. She did not know herself. There was just something about that day—about that whole situation, the dead girl and Leo and Mary and Ma Reis and that boy, too, that retarded boy, she couldn't even think what his name was—there was something about all of it that gave her a terrible feeling in the pit of her stomach, a sense that everything had gone wrong.

———

The women felt it too, Erna Rausch and Marian Weiser and Ma Reis, and some of the others around the parish, that sense of things gone wrong, that perhaps there was worse even to come. And, of course, it was all complicated by everyone's feelings about Leo, his history. Though they would not have admitted it, never have admitted it, they were all a little afraid of him, even Ma Reis. And the men, too. Not afraid of what he would or could do to them, but afraid of what he was and what he wasn't. Maybe a person has to know someone like Leo Krauss, Ma Reis thought, before they can really understand that. It had something to do with his complete disregard for living by the same codes and standards everyone else did, and they held themselves and each other—even Ma Reis had to admit—to some pretty hard standards. But Leo, he couldn't have cared less. And that bothered them. They were a little afraid of him, sure. And even more, they were afraid of the girl, Elisabeth Brechert.

But they went over nevertheless, to Krausses', the men did, perhaps at the insistence of their wives, perhaps out of their own curiosity and disbelief. Art Reis and Mike Eichert and Ronnie's father. The two smaller Rausch children were already in bed when their father returned home later that evening, though only the boy was asleep; the girl lay staring into the dark, thinking of Leo Krauss and Elisabeth Brechert, and digging her fingernails into her palms to keep herself from falling asleep.

Ronnie and his mother sat at the kitchen table, drinking coffee. When Ronnie's father stepped through the door, they lifted their heads in unison, and Erna said, "Well?"

Ronnie's father sighed and pulled off his coat.

Ronnie and his mother exchanged a look. "Well?" she said again. "What happened?"

Ronnie's father rubbed a palm across his face and came to the table and sat, and Erna rose and poured him out a coffee and sat too, and they waited.

"Ach," he finally said. "All this trouble. How is it our business, even?"

"Did you see her?" Ronnie said.

He nodded. "Yah, I saw her."

"And the blood?" Erna said.

"Yah. The blood."

"And?" she said. "Is she cut, or what is it?"

"How should I know? What would you have me do, wash the blood off to have a look? She would not even let us look closely."

Erna clucked her tongue in annoyance. "So," she said, "is he putting blood on her, maybe? Is that what he's doing? Some kind of punishment?"

Ronnie said, "Why would he do that?"

"Does he need reasons?" Erna said. "Has he ever?"

Ronnie's father shrugged. "I don't know what can be done.

The girl is not hurt. The blood, well, I don't know. She wants to stay in the barn, that's what she said. He feeds her, or Mary does. McCready doesn't care. If anything's to be done it's up to the mother, it's up to Mary. It's their business, not ours."

But Erna was not yet willing to concede. "Maybe Father Rieger could go."

"No," Ronnie's father said, "he will not. He has already said he has had enough of Leo, that he will have him excommunicated."

"Excommunicated? Was Leo even baptized in the first place?"

"Who knows?" Ronnie's father said, already tiring of the problem. "Come on, time for bed."

He rose from the table, and then Ronnie did.

"Good night, Ronnie."

Ronnie did not reply, just climbed the stairs to his room and closed the door.

But Erna would not be deterred. "What about the braucha? Has anyone talked to her?"

"Put out the lantern."

"Someone should talk to the braucha."

"Ach, leave well enough alone."

"But that girl . . ."

"What about her?"

"Just . . . the way she is." Following her husband into the bedroom. "She's . . . I don't know how to say."

"Don't say, then. Come to bed. She was always strange, that one."

"This is different."

"Don't see things where there is nothing. Don't make a bad situation worse with imagining."

Erna nodded, vaguely, climbed under the covers beside her husband and sighed. Then, turning suddenly, she said, "I know."

"What?"

"I know what it is, what she makes me think of now."

"What?" he said, already feeling sleep settle over him.

"*Die laufenden toten Gestalten.*"

"Don't talk so stupid," he mumbled.

And pulling the covers tighter about him, he soon fell into the deep sleep of the untroubled.

But Erna lay awake, staring up into the darkness, thinking, *Tomorrow I must go see Ma Reis, and Marian, too. They will know what I mean. That blankness about the girl, as if she was there, but wasn't there, either.* She edged a little closer to her husband, who grunted in his sleep. Thinking, *That is what she is, that girl, and Leo, too, and Mary, my God, all of them, all those Krausses, I see it now,* Die laufenden toten Gestalten. *The walking dead.*

EIGHTEEN

Miraculously, word had not reached Schoffs'—of the girl's so-called resurrection—and they might not have heard at all, they so rarely saw anyone now, hardly left the farm, the boy himself never even left his room any more, that's what they'd heard, hardly spoke at all (and some still saw this as a confession of his guilt in the matter, though that had pretty much blown over, as most things did, given enough time).

Ma Reis, who, of anyone, would have been the one to go to them, was reluctant, knowing very well the state of things over there since the girl's drowning. And now the hired man gone, too, or so Art had claimed. She sat mulling it over, wondering exactly how it should be said, the best way to go about it. But Ma mulled a little too long. It was Ludmila Baumgarten herself who came by after Mass the Sunday following the girl's resurrection.

"Good God," Stolanus said, watching from the window as she hoisted herself down from her wagon. "And what is this about now?"

"Must be something"—Helen paused dryly—"important."

Stolanus moved to open the door.

"What are you doing?"

"Letting her in."

"And what for? I have nothing to say to her."

"You have nothing to say to anyone," he said, and opened the door.

Ludmila ballooned into the kitchen.

"Here, sit," Stolanus said. "Helen, is there coffee?"

Helen folded her arms across her chest.

Stolanus took the coffee and poured out another cup. Ludmila, seated now at the table, watched all the while, her hands pressed together to keep them from betraying her excitement.

"Thought I might see you in church this morning," she said.

"I don't know why you would think that," Helen remarked. "You never saw us there before."

Ludmila raised her eyebrows. "But maybe you've heard already," she said, addressing her coffee, so jittery she scarcely dared to raise the cup. "Maybe your hired man might have heard," she said, nodding pleasantly at Helen, "in town or something."

Helen and Stolanus exchanged quick looks. Helen turned away, busying herself at the sink.

"Heard what?" Stolanus said, though he did not especially care, either. Talk, talk, talk, what did it all matter?

"Everyone else seems to know," Ludmila went on, "but then that sort of news travels fast. I'm surprised you haven't heard nothing. And every Catholic from here to Fox Valley in church this morning—except you, of course—and a few Lutherans to boot. Everybody thought she'd be there, that they all would. I kind of thought so too. I was amazed they weren't."

"Who?" Stolanus said, growing annoyed. "What's this all about?"

"Leo especially," she went on. "You know how funny he is about church. I thought for sure, but then you never can tell, I guess." She lifted her coffee cup, propping her elbows on the table to steady herself. "But maybe I shouldn't have come after all. I don't want to be responsible for upsetting anyone. You know what they say, Kill the messenger—"

"What is it, Ludmila," Stolanus interrupted, "that you came for?"

"Well," Ludmila said. "I hardly know how to say it"—she lowered her coffee cup, looked from Stolanus to Helen and back again, then leaned forward and spoke, dropping her voice—"Elisabeth Brechert, she's alive."

———

After Ludmila had gone, they sat together in the kitchen, the pot of coffee growing cold between them.

"But this is good, not?" Stolanus said. "We must tell him."

"What," Helen said, in a low voice, "and upset him further?"

"But that makes no sense. He is upset because he thought the girl was dead—"

"Keep your voice down. She is dead. As far as he is concerned."

Stolanus lowered his voice too, and leaned forward across the kitchen table. "This is insane. He must know. Can't you see how he suffers?"

"Can't I see? Can't you? That is all I see."

"So let's tell him, for God's sake."

"Shh. No. He will not be told and that is that."

"Be sensible. He will find out one way or another. Eventually. And then what? Better to hear it from us."

"Not if we send him away."

"What? Now you want to send him?"

"With Lathias gone . . ."

"I can't believe I'm hearing this."

"If we have to."

"Where, to Battleford?"

"If the girl is alive . . . tomorrow, even. You can take him, first thing."

"We can send him if you like. But it will take time. We can't just drop him there."

"Why not?"

"It doesn't work that way. We need to write to them. Make an application. Or something."

"If he were to just turn up there, they would not send him away."

"God, you must be crazy, you want to abandon him there?"

"That's not abandoning."

"We can take him but we must do it right. And we must tell him about the girl. He should know."

"Never."

NINETEEN

The boy knew, certainly, that something had changed. Knew that his mother and father talked to each other more now than they ever had, in hushed, urgent voices that he could not decipher floating up the stairs to his room. Though he hardly tried. What could their conversations matter to him? And Lathias? He had not seen Lathias since that day Leo Krauss had come in the wagon and stood shouting in the yard. About him, he imagined, though he could not hear that, either. And he supposed Lathias had gone on a trip to Maple Creek for his father. Usually, he would come to say goodbye, if he were not already with Lathias, helping him to load the wagon, making sure he had food for the trip. But not now. Now he was alone.

Only, sometimes, his mother would come to the top of the stairs and stand looking at him, her hand on the doorframe, as if she might say something. But she would not. She would just nod and turn and disappear back down the stairs, speaking only when she brought his meals. "Won't you come down?" she would say. But he could see she did not want him to; his tray already in hand. And so he would shake his head and she would slide the tray onto the bedside table with a quick motion that made the boy think of that sick dog they'd had penned by the barn a couple years back, how Lathias showed him to shove the food beneath the rail with a stick and step back quickly, in case the dog should snap. The dog was rabid, it turned out, snarling and frothing and snapping at invisible enemies. One night after supper, after he had already gone to bed for the night, when he was almost asleep, he heard a shot crack the dusk, and he climbed from his bed and went to the window and saw Lathias there with the shotgun, standing over the dog, just standing there, as if he thought maybe the dog was not really dead after all. The boy watched a moment and then he climbed back into his bed. He was not sad, not about the dog. He was only sorry because he knew Lathias did not like to kill a thing. And that dog used to follow Lathias everywhere, helping him keep the herd together when they moved pastures, or cutting calves from their mothers at branding time, keeping coyotes away from the chickenshed, deer and antelope out of the garden. But the dog he had been was not the dog he was after the rabies. And now he was dead. Lathias had killed him. And he wondered why his father had not been the one to do it. He pulled the blankets tighter around himself and said a Hail Mary for the dog. And as he fell asleep, he promised himself, *I will not have a dog. Not when I'm older. Not never.*

It occurred to him now that no one had ever said anything about that dog, once it was gone. It had troubled him at the time, and it troubled him now. The empty pen, the dog dish gone, and everyone walking around like there had never been a dog there at all. He had climbed into the pen the morning after the dog had been shot, just to look around, to see if anyone would say anything. But Lathias passed him on the way to the barn and, later, his father, and neither of them even glanced in his direction. It was as if he was gone, too.

That silence. That was what bothered him. Lathias no better than his mother and father, really. And all those stories he told, it was as if he were just filling the silence. He never talked about real things, about things that mattered. Just stories. Lies, Elisabeth had said.

She had been different. Elisabeth had talked. He did not like to think of her, tried to stop himself, but she forced herself in, nevertheless. Just as she always had. And she had talked to him. About the accident, even. A thing no one else would. And about Lathias. Of course, Lathias.

"You really are stupid," she had said to him that night from the frozen river.

And he had hunched himself down, stabbing at the ice with a stick.

"You believe everything he tells you," she sneered.

"Why wouldn't I?"

"Because he's a liar," she said, "that's why."

And he looked up at her then, and he said, "Don't say that."

And she laughed a little and stepped out onto the ice even further and he watched her and he said nothing.

"You really don't know why he stayed, all these years?"

"He's my friend."

"I wouldn't want a friend like that." She kept stepping farther and farther out. "You really don't even know," she said, and shook her head. "Guilt," she said.

And he thought, *Through my fault, my fault, my most grievous fault.*

"It can make a person do funny things. Love, too." Stepping once more. "And they don't even know why. Don't know the real reasons. Love, they say. Hate. As if it was so easy to tell them apart."

The boy stood up. Elisabeth was a good distance out on the ice, out near where it began to thin and darken.

"Friend. You think he loves you?" she said. "Is that what you think it is?"

And the boy dropped his stick, and told her he was going home.

"Go, then," she said, in an ugly way. "And ask Lathias what

happened in the field that day. When you had that accident. Did you ever ask him if he was there that day?"

"I'm going home," the boy said, and he turned and walked up the draw and she called after him.

"Who was driving?" she called. "Ask him that."

But he just kept walking and that was when she hollered all those things about dying, about her dying there, freezing to death, how it would be his fault, and about the Horseman coming for him, all those horses, the air around him darkening, as if the horses roused the night from the earth.

"Can you hear it?" she yelled. "Can you hear them now?"

And he ran, then, scrambled up the draw, in the dark, his feet slipping against the loose banks of shale, his hands catching against barrel cactus and prickly pear, and not caring, not until he was almost to the top, and he turned around, to give her one last chance, panic growing in his chest. But she was gone. And he called out, once, twice. And then he thought she was playing a trick on him, maybe, that she was hiding and would scare him, and he did not want that, for her to scare him, and those horses, he could hear them now, rattling and rattling, and so he ran, he ran, past the Horseman's graves, and the earth thundered there beneath him.

The next thing he remembered he was at home, and Lathias there beside him. And he had learned Elisabeth was missing and they had asked him questions that he could not answer. And then they had gone to the river. And he'd seen the hole there in the ice.

In time, he had realized Elisabeth was right. About everything. Hate and guilt and love. Fear. They were all one. He felt them all. They sickened him, all those feelings. And Lathias, how he had looked at him afterwards. As if he felt them, too. And he had thought, *She was right, then. About Lathias. She knew.*

He had thought about it a long time, about Lathias and the accident. And he could not hate Lathias for it. But he could not love him any more, either, not because of the accident, but because Elisabeth was right, he had lied. And he had looked at Lathias and he had seen it all there in his eyes: love and hate and fear and guilt. It was all there.

And Elisabeth was dead, and he had thought, *What could it matter, anyway? What could any of it matter?*

TWENTY

Ronnie Rausch slept little. Always the same dream, always the river and the ice and the girl pulling herself out of it, coming for him across the darkened plains. During waking hours, the only thing he could think of: her. It was enough to drive someone mad. How long, he wondered, was this to go on? He had done nothing to her. Had tried to help her, even. In a way. It was Erv. Erv had been the one, Erv who had come upon him suddenly behind the barn last Wednesday, shouldering him up against the planks before Ronnie'd even known what hit him, too shocked to fight back, Erv's face above him, spittle flying, "You keep your goddamned mouth shut. You shut it. I didn't touch her. I didn't do a goddamned thing," and Ronnie, thrusting him off into the dirt, "I didn't say nothing," and then adding, "But I should have. Pants-pisser," and Erv coming at him again, and rolling around in the dirt until they wore themselves out, just as they had as children, shoving each other away and kneeling there, panting, wiping their mouths against their sleeves and spitting in the dirt, until Erv hauled himself up and said, "You just make goddamned sure," and Ronnie saying nothing, seeing the fear there in Erv's face now and letting it go, they were cousins after all, letting him disappear around the side of the barn and home to his wife and child (the child who would be dead of rheumatic fever before the year was out, a tragedy from which Erv would never really recover, in spite of the children that followed). Yes, Ronnie thought, Erv had been the one who grabbed the girl, the blood was on his hands, and so why should he be the one to suffer? And was she dead or alive or what was she, for Chrissakes? What was she?

And so, in spite of himself, one morning (after a long night in which he'd lain awake after dreaming, or imagining, that he'd felt the drowned girl climb under the blanket beside him in the dark, her naked body pressed against him, still icy wet from the river), he saddled his horse and rode across the fields to Krausses'.

Leo met him at the gate, as if he had been waiting for him, watching. When Ronnie saw him there, he almost turned and rode home again. But he could not. He must see the girl. Must speak to her.

"What do you want?" Leo said.

Ronnie sat his horse a moment, thinking. He wanted to talk to the girl, or to see her at least. Didn't he? Is that what he wanted?

"You get on home," Leo said. "There's nothing for you here. It's none of your business what goes on here. Get on home now."

But he could not; he could not speak, and he could not go. He sat there, his horse huffing and shifting her weight beneath him.

"You think I don't know what you want?" Leo snarled. "Dirty buggers. I know what you all want."

She appeared then, in the shadows of the barn doors, leaning up against them, barefoot, her toes curled over the edge of the floor, arms folded across her chest. Ronnie saw her standing there. *Just like a girl,* he thought, *like an ordinary girl.*

"You think I don't know?" Leo said.

But Ronnie just sat there, looking from Leo to the girl and back again, the horse shifting under him, and the earth shifting also. And still he could not speak, he could not call out to her, could not say, *It was Erv. I wouldn't, I never would.*

"You get on out of here," Leo said. "Keep away, hear? If I get my shotgun, you'll know all right. Goddamned buggers. Don't you think she didn't tell me what you did. Dirty sonsabitches. She told me. God will strike you down, you dirty—you get on out of here."

And, breaking off a dried stalk of thistle from beside the fence-post, he whipped it at Ronnie's horse, who tossed her head and stepped sideways in the dirt.

"Get on," Leo said. "You've done enough. Get on."

Leo raised the thistle again and hollered, and the horse neighed and flung back her head, kicked up her front hooves. Ronnie reined her in a tight circle, the sky spinning in a blue whirl over him.

"I just," Ronnie said, "I wanted to see—"

"You saw, now get on."

"But," Ronnie said, "just for a minute. Could I talk to her? Please. I'll—" He thought a moment, desperate. "I'll pay," he said.

Leo raised the thistle higher, and then stopped. He did not strike. No. He stood there, arm raised, and something dawned on him, so clear it was as if the voice of God Himself spoke. Slowly he lowered the thistle, and stepped forward, but without heat now.

"Get on," he said absently, mindless of the hooves and the dust and the crazy blue spin of the earth. But the boy, alarmed at Leo's sudden deflation, the dark gleam in his eyes, was already riding away. Leo swatted his hand through the air. "Get on."

TWENTY-ONE

Mary saw it all. From where she stood at the kitchen window, she saw the young man come and she saw Leo chase him away.

Good, she thought. It was just as well. Better that he leave Elisabeth alone, all of them, those boys. There was trouble enough without them. Trouble enough between Leo and Elisabeth, with Elisabeth alone. And who would have thought it, all this trouble, all this grief after the grieving should have ended, after the miraculous had occurred, her daughter was alive; she had died and been grieved over and now she was alive. And she, Mary, should be overjoyed, should be down on her knees thanking God, or so Leo would have it. She should be thankful, grateful. She was not worthy of such grace.

But she was not grateful, God help her. She felt only disorientation, a weird extension of her grief; grief that was not quite grief, either. Her daughter was alive, saved by the braucha, apparently, and by the grace of God. But she had lived down there with the braucha—how long?—as though she were dead, had let her own mother continue to believe she was dead (and she must have seen her down there, Elisabeth must have, must have seen her down there at the river every day in the cold, she must have seen her from the braucha's place), and now she was alive, and Mary looked like a fool: what kind of a daughter lets her mother grieve unnecessarily, no, *makes* her grieve unnecessarily, forces her to? What was wrong with the girl?

Oh, Mary knew well enough that between the two of them there had never been what you would call intimacy, affection even, but only a mutual awareness of the other's troubles. At least, that is what she had always thought.

Now, in the cold light of grief, she could see Elisabeth had never shown any consideration, not even as a child. Cold, her own mother had said of her. A monster, her father had said, a walking abomination. But then, growing up in that frigid household, even her own mother careful about displays of affection, yes, Mary could admit to herself now that she had not been a loving parent, and maybe that was what lay at the heart of the girl's coldness.

Elisabeth was her daughter after all, flesh of her flesh, blood of her blood. Even more: Mary felt consumed by her, now more than ever, as if nothing of herself was not for Elisabeth; consumed by her death, consumed by her resurrection, and always this devouring, as if Elisabeth had eaten of her flesh, drunk of her blood—and she had, she had: Mary remembered well the pain of nursing her, that little mouth against her breast, it was awful, as if she were being eaten alive, and she had pried the little vicious mouth away and her nipples were split and bleeding and in the baby's mouth there was milk and blood, and she had gone in tears to her mother and her mother had said, "Ach, Mary, but that is normal. That is how it is to be a mother. You should have thought of that sooner."

But it was not normal. Her nipples bled and bled, and soaked the front of her dress, and still the baby fed and fed and fed, as if she would never be full, and when she did not feed she wailed, and Mary wondered if there was milk coming or only blood, wondered if the baby were feeding on her blood and that maybe she was starving, maybe they would both die because of it, and she wept from the pain and the worry as she sat nursing the baby, endlessly it seemed, until Anna, dear Anna, could no longer stand to watch and she snuck warm cow's milk in a cloth teat when their mother was not watching and they fed the baby in secret and so Mary's nipples scabbed over and healed and her mother was never the wiser. Even now, Mary could still remember that pain in her breasts, that awful slow devouring.

The night she learned that Elisabeth had drowned in the river, she felt it again, that pain in her breasts, and she thought, *I am bleeding,* and she slipped her hand inside the front of her dress, just to see, though, of course, there was nothing.

And then the girl had come back—no, had been brought back—to her, to Mary, but would just as soon have left her mother there by the river, left her to throw herself into that icy water, too, as she had so often been tempted as she stood there watching the river flow by, east and east and east. Elisabeth would have left her, and what would she have cared? It was nothing to Elisabeth. But Leo had dragged her back. And now she would not speak, had not said a word since she'd returned, not as far as Mary knew, wanted nothing, only sat and stared at her hands whenever Mary went out to see her, to sit with her. Maybe Elisabeth hated her, that was possible, for bringing her here, for bringing her into the world at all.

Yes, better that they all stay away. And the halfbreed, too, from Schoffs', and that retarded boy. The one who had . . . but, what? Hurt her somehow? Or even . . . ? But she could not think it. In spite of what people had said. She could not think it of him, and more, even if the boy had intended to hurt her somehow, had wanted to, he could not have; she knew better of Elisabeth.

Mary walked to the crate and looked down at the child there, lying in listless sleep.

It was sick, the baby, the way it lay there, its little face all flushed up and hot. She stood looking down at it. But it was quiet now, had barely stirred all that morning. She would tell Leo to take it to the braucha. Something must be done. She did not feel affection for it, but she did not want to see anything happen to it, either. No, she would not want to see it suffer. She was not heartless. She was not a monster. She was its mother, after all.

TWENTY-TWO

Father Rieger was hearing confession. There were maybe a dozen or so people in the pews, sitting and waiting to confess or kneeling to do penance, when Leo banged through the doors. The way some told it later, Leo stepped into the church that day glittering with a dark light, looking for all the world like the devil himself. They all talked about it afterwards, at the café and the hardware and the grocery, stopped in the road, around kitchen tables and crouched in front of barns. Ma Reis was there, too, with Art, and when Leo banged into the church, Ma made as if to get up and confront him, but Art took her hand firmly and eyed her from beneath his brows and Ma settled back on the pew, frowning, watching it all, how Leo waited outside the confessional, tapping his feet and drumming his fingers against the back of a pew. Ma said later: "Father had Ida Rhenisch in there. But you know old Ida, everybody tries to get in to confess before she does, you know how she can go on, I don't know what all she has to say in there, but her life must be a hell of a lot more interesting than it looks, or else she's confessing for everybody else, which is more likely. So Leo stood there, waiting and waiting and waiting, and finally he banged on the confessional door and said, 'What, are you taking a shit in there?' I swear to God. And everything went real quiet, like maybe they—Ida and Father—thought it was the voice of God, and so Leo banged again and said, 'Enough of that nonsense now, you come on with me, I want to show you something in my barn out there, something better than anything that old noodle-stepper can tell you,' and when no one answered, he rattled the doorknob and said, 'Come on out, I know you're in there,' as if Father was hiding on him, and God knows maybe he was, but then Leo said into the confessional, 'Or maybe you two are in love?' and a few people laughed then and I don't know if Father heard the laughing or what, but anyway that door flew open and Father came blasting out with his black robes flying, like a bat from a belfry, that's just how he looked, and Ida Rhenisch poked her head out, and Father shrieking and flapping away at Leo, who just stood there as always as if he were the sensible, patient one, which only made Father angrier. He just stood there and when Father had pretty much burned all his fuel, Leo said, 'Well, and are you coming or not?' And Father said he sure as hell was not. That's what he said.

"So Leo stood there looking at him a minute and then he said, a little quieter, but still loud enough that everyone could hear so that it appeared that Father and Leo were in cahoots somehow, he said, 'It's worth the trip, Father. They could make you a bishop for that. Pope, maybe.' And Father said, 'What, for God's sake?' and Leo smiled a dark little smile and said, 'A miracle.'"

TWENTY-THREE

There had already been, of course, talk of a miracle, at least among the Ludmila Baumgarten circle. They were all crazy for it, that bunch, all the talk about miracles (Ma Reis said obliquely, "Yah, because they'll need one themselves, not?" and everyone knew exactly what she meant). They had all heard—had they not?—of the Virgin appearing at Lourdes? Of course they had. And didn't the Bible itself tell, too, of countless miracles? Had not Lot's wife been turned to a pillar of salt and Aaron's rod to a serpent? Had not the ten plagues—the blood and frogs and lice and flies and murrain and boils and hail and locusts and darkness and death—been delivered unto Egypt? Had not the Red Sea divided and the waters of Marrah sweetened? Had not the walls of Jericho fallen down? Had not the sun and moon been stayed in their orbs? Had not Jeroboam's hand withered? Had not Elijah been fed by ravens, and had he not been carried up to heaven in a chariot of fire? Had not a hundred men been fed with twenty loaves? Had not the Syrian army been smitten and then cured of blindness? Had not Daniel been saved in the lion's den and Jonah in the belly of the whale? Had not the lepers been healed and the water made wine? Had not others been raised? Oh, not just Jesus, that went without saying, and not even Lazarus, but what about the others? What about the Shunammite's son and the widow's son at Nain, what about Jairus's daughter? Yes, certainly, it was not without precedent, this raising from the dead.

But, that was only in the Bible, resurrection. That did not happen in real life, among them. Oh, and what about Lourdes, then? But that was not a resurrection, it was an apparition, a visitation, the Virgin Mother. But a miracle, nevertheless. Yes, a miracle, certainly, but perhaps it all should not be taken just the way it says in the Bible, as if it had really happened, perhaps it should not all be taken just that way. And how should it be taken, then? Well, with a grain of salt, like everything else.

And then again, the girl had not been raised from the dead at all, this Elisabeth Brechert, for no one had seen her dead. Though some may have said it—*die laufenden toten Gestalten*—they did not mean it literally, but only suggestively, descriptively (though there were always those who chose to take a darker view, a more scandalous and outrageous view, as if she really were the walking dead, but thankfully they were in the minority). Of course, the phrase did imply something darker, too, that brush she'd had with death, that taint, of the touched and of the untouchable.

(But the girl was not dead, of course. No. Whether by fate or accident or divine intervention, she was not dead, had not drowned. She had gone through the ice, as the boy had said, and into that cold nocturnal river and had even been carried, dragged, along under the ice a few yards, down as far as the bend in the river, where the current slowed and then picked up again and the ice was all out, and there she had, by fate or accident or divine intervention, surfaced in that frigid water and managed to fight her way to the muddy bank, or else the river spat her out there— and this is where, too, by fate or accident or divine intervention, the old woman later found her, or so it was supposed since no one ever did learn for certain and it was all pieced together in the usual way, as history always is, by hearsay and supposition and outright imagination—and that is where she lay, wet, freezing, too cold even to call out, and, even if she could, who in that vast empty prairie would have heard her anyway, that being the real question, and, in the end, the only one worth asking: who in the eternal silence of those infinite spaces could have heard?)

TWENTY-FOUR

After Father had closed the rectory door in Leo's face, he drove straight home, cracking his old mule needlessly across the back, it could not possibly go faster. He had a plan, and he would do it with Father, or without him.

He put the mule in the corral and then stopped at the door to the barn, hesitating. But before he could decide, Mary came out of the house, the screen door clattering shut behind her. She carried the baby.

"She is sick," Mary called. "Something is wrong."

Leo crossed the yard.

"Give her to me," he said, taking the infant.

"She is sick," Mary said again. "A fever. She is weak."

"No," Leo said, "she is fine."

"She needs the braucha," Mary said.

"She needs nothing. I will care for her. Worry about your own daughter."

Mary did not say, *She is my daughter, too.* She just stood and watched Leo frown down at the baby lying listlessly in his arms, only the slightest flicker of a movement beneath the blue eyelids.

Leo felt the infant's hot forehead. "See," he said, "nothing. She is fine."

Mary shrugged. "It is on your shoulders," she said, but without passion, without interest. "If something happens. Then you will be the one to answer for it—in this life and in the next one, too."

And she went back into the house, letting the screen door slam shut behind her.

Leo sat on the porch, little Cecilia resting limply in his arms. That red flush in the child's cheeks, and her lips, so dry and hot. The braucha. What could it hurt? If she would even see him after all that business about the girl. But what right had she anyway to keep the girl there? He should have called the law on her. He had not. She owed him, when you thought about it. He said a quick prayer over the infant and carried her to the wagon.

————

The braucha did not answer. Leo knocked again, then walked away from the hut and looked around the yard. The hens pecked placidly by the coop and the wind stirred in the tall grasses. He called out. Waited. Finally, he went back to the hut and banged on the door again and then opened it.

"Old woman," he said, "are you in here?" His voice sounding small even to himself in the vast darkness of that tiny hut.

He stepped down onto the dirt floor. The heavy burlap sacking was all pulled shut over the windows and he stepped to one and pulled it open and sunlight came dimly through and he opened another and then he turned, and was about to call out, though the dimensions of the hut were so small there could have been no need to, but he would have called out anyway, *Old woman,* because he was Leo Krauss, and he would have kept on calling out if he had not been silenced, yes, even he, Leo Krauss, silenced by what he saw there, before him and all around: on every inch of every whitewashed wall, a face, a hundred faces, five hundred, drawn there with charcoal from the fire, face after face after face, men and women, old and young, and when Leo had stared at those hundreds of faces long enough, individual faces began to emerge, there were the Schneider brothers, yes, he was sure of it, and old Arlen and Rita Gebler, Art and Ma Reis, no one could mistake her, Father Rieger at his pulpit, Wing and his wife, Ludmila Baumgarten, her husband Eddie, Roy and Esther Hech, Sister Benedicta and the others, he did not know their names, Mike Weiser, Marian, too, Brunhauers, Stolanus Schoff, his wife, the retarded son, the Fitz boys, Kaspar and Remigius, Viola Hahn, he could not mistake her either, the Eichert girls; face after face; all of the living, and the dead, too: Lucius Haag, Eugenia Weiser, Pius Schoff and the missus, Balzar and Ottilia Hech, Heironimus Schmitt, his wife Anna, Leonhart and Ida Rescher, and all the old folks, many Leo could not even recognize, or who looked vaguely familiar, disturbingly so, though he could not have named them, faces he had seen once or twice, faces he had never seen at all, faces from the old country, maybe, face after face after face, and there, my God, his own father, Old Gustav, and his mother, oh, he stepped forward, his mother there, her gentle, long-suffering face—is that how she had looked, after all?—and there, there was Cecilia, with that old distant look in her eyes, as if she were seeing already into eternity, good Cecilia, and over there the children, he stepped closer still, Magdalen and Henry, and the others—was that them?—my God, he would not have recognized them, his own children, he reached up to touch their faces and his fingertips came away blackened, he rubbed the charcoal dust between his fingers, yes, it was them, he pressed a fist to his eyes and then opened them again, yes, they were all there, everyone, all those now dead to him, a cemetery of faces, memorialized there by the old woman, drawn as if on a tombstone, as if that little cramped room was heaven, the place where the dead walked, they were all there, the old woman had put them there, but where was he? Leo looked again, face after face after face, until they all began to look like the same face, but not his, nowhere his, there were his siblings even, but he was nowhere among them. But he must be, he must be, for what reason would the old woman have left him out, why would she? Why? Nothing? There was nothing of him at all? He looked some more, but no, he was not there, and not little Cecilia, either. Nothing. Why would she leave them out? And the baby, what had she done, to be left out this way? It made no sense. Why would she do it? He said it out loud, a slow, creeping panic overtaking him. "Why?"

But the answer to that he would not, now, ever learn, for as he worked his way to the back of the hut, seeking his own face, his eyes found another, pale, as if she too had been drawn there, the old woman stretched on her pallet, cold, her eyes open in an eternal stare.

———

Margarehta Stehr, née Nikolei, formerly of Culelia, Dobruja, third daughter of Piotr and Anna Nikolei, deceased, widow of Joseph Stehr, deceased, mother of Peter Stehr, whereabouts unknown, mother of others dead or never born, friend of no one and companion to none, or so, at least, it had seemed; this Margarehta Stehr, this Russian, who had suffered what sorrows and had suffered also what joys (for *Alles isch in einem Sack,* it was all in the same sack, it all came from the heart, not?) no one knew, this old woman, the braucha, witch, faith healer, was buried with a full Catholic Mass the following morning at ten o'clock, a Thursday, buried in the cemetery at Knochenfeld, and the sky did not darken and lower, clouds did not gather blackly on the horizon and condense, torrential rains did not fall; lightning did not rend the sky, nor was it punctured by hail the size of a man's fist; spring snow did not blast forth in a blizzard the worst in recent memory; rivers and streams did not still and flow backwards, nor even slow in their eternal monotonous pace; the earth did not groan and split open; no funnel clouds whirled sickeningly, ripping barns and houses and cattle skyward in a terrifying apotheosis; no, there was not even so much as a crazed wind to tear hotly at the grasses and the dirt like the outraged breath of God.

One who once was, was no more; committed, returned to an earth of dust and ashes that welcomed her no more than it did any other, did not fold its arms about her, was only hacked open because of and for her and then closed over her, and it was done.

The earth should have stopped in its orbit, the sun and moon extinguished in a tandem cold death and the stars after her, plummeted to earth like outcast angels in unabating grief. But it was only a day in May like any other, a Thursday: mild, not unusually windy, the sky blue and clear and pocked with giddy sparrows who winged on, oblivious, troubled neither by the living nor the dead.

TWENTY-FIVE

"We should have gone."

"Gone where?"

"To the funeral."

"What for? What was she to us?"

"She was one of us, not? One of the community? And of the parish, too?"

"She was a Russian."

"She was an old woman. She helped many."

"But a Russian just the same."

"We should have gone."

"No. Better to stay at home. Let the Russians bury the Russians."

———

The old woman had not, technically, been deserving of a full Mass, having not attended church since the move to Knochenfeld some years previous. It was too long for her to walk, that is what everyone said. But, Father Rieger wanted to know, why did she not get a ride with someone? A woman of her stature, a woman of her importance in the community (though he himself did not condone her doings, they rang too much of paganism, of old country peasantry and ignorance and heathenism, it would not do), surely someone would have offered her a ride. And so it was her choice to stop attending Mass.

(He could not have known that no one ever did, no one had ever thought, through all that time, to even offer to drive her to church and home again, not out of ill will but only out of thoughtlessness, an understandable and therefore forgivable sin of omission.)

But Father had given her a full Mass anyway, fearing public outcry. Now he saw he needn't have; there had hardly been anyone there, Art and Ma Reis, the Schneider brothers, all the ones you might expect. But the church was only half full, not even. And so the bishop would not learn of it, that he had given a full Mass where a full Mass was not deserved. Or would he? Surely no one would say anything to him. Would they? He made a mental note to speak to Ludmila Baumgarten at his earliest opportunity. There was no reason she should not have a solo now and then, was there? No reason Mass could not be lengthened slightly to accommodate it. No reason at all.

TWENTY-SIX

The night after the braucha was buried, little Cecilia's condition worsened. She began to stir in her sleep and the flushed red look of her cheeks faded and paled and then paled some more and she opened her eyes and they glittered darkly in the dim light of the kitchen.

"There," Leo said to Mary. "You see? What did I tell you? She is better."

Mary crossed the kitchen slowly, wiping her hands on her apron, and bent over the child.

"She is dying," she said.

Leo sat a moment, blinking at her, as if he had not heard. He went to stand, then sat down again. His face darkened and he made a sound in his throat that was not unlike a growl. He stood again. Mary took a step back.

"What have you done?" he hissed, grabbing Mary by the hair. "What did you do?"

"Nothing," Mary gasped. "I did—she needs help. A doctor. She is dying. Leo."

Leo shoved her before him, toward the door, not loosing his grip, wrenching her by the arm, the hair. She was crying now, struggling, as they tripped and wrestled. Behind them the baby began to cry, too, weakly.

"You never wanted her," he said. "Now you want her gone. And me, too."

"Leo, no, Leo, listen, no, no."

"Get out of here." Shoving her toward the door. "Get out now, get out, all of you, whores, whores, you get out."

The screen door coming off its remaining hinge as they slammed through it, out into the spring night, and the girl there in the yard looking up at them.

"Elisabeth," Mary cried.

But Leo paid her no notice, hollering and shoving Mary down the stairs where she fell in the dirt, and the baby in the house behind them, crying, crying, and Leo down the stairs after Mary, yelling, "It's you. You did it. Tell me what you did, you tell me what you did," and, "No, Leo, nothing, nothing, listen, I never would, she is sick," and, "Whore, Jezebel," swinging at her now, her arms up to stop him, back and forth, and the heaving breaths and the struggle, and neither one even noticing that the baby had stopped crying, that the house had fallen silent behind them.

Leo was on his knees in the dirt, bleeding from the nose, and Mary crawling away from him, when the silence came upon them. They stopped and held their breaths, and then they noticed the girl was gone, too, Elisabeth.

Leo lunged for the stairs, tripping, staggering through the doorway, and Mary coming slowly behind him, gasping, into the kitchen, and stopped, the fire burned out of them both by the sight before them.

For there sat Elisabeth, in a kitchen chair beneath the picture of Gus in his coffin, and the baby on her lap, a smear of ashes in the shape of a cross on her little forehead and Elisabeth making the sign of the cross over her, saying,

"Jesus Christ walked over the land,

Carrying three roses in his hand;
One did sting, the other seared,
The third one disappeared.
In the name of the Father, Son and Holy Ghost."

She made the sign of the cross twice more and, without look-ing up at them, asked for water, lukewarm, with a bit of sugar mixed in, and a teaspoon, though neither Leo nor Mary moved from where they stood in the doorway.

"Give her to me," Leo finally said, but without conviction.

"I see it now," Elisabeth said mildly, and nodded her head without looking up, so they could barely hear her. "You touch this child," she said, "and I will kill you. I will do it."

Leo opened his mouth, flapped it shut.

Elisabeth looked up at him then, and in the same easy voice said, "She showed me, the braucha did. I see it now. I see you, Leo Krauss. I know who you are. And I see that man up there"—she nodded pleasantly at the picture of Gus over the table—"and I know who he is, too. And I have watched you, fighting your own blood. And I can tell you this: you won't ever get it out of you. And it's in her, too." She looked at the infant in her lap. "She is sick with your blood. And with my blood, too. My mother's blood. Bad blood, on both sides. She is dying from it. But I will get it out of her, and I'll kill anybody who tries to stop me."

And then she ran her hands over the child, from the crown of her head, down over her arms and her torso and her legs, and she whispered over her,

"I call you out, dark blood,
I call you out, Satan's blood.
Blood of sinners, I call you out.
Go in the wind,
In the name of the Father, Son and Holy Ghost."

Leo stood in the doorway. He did not speak and he did not move, but only stood listening and there was a sound in his ears like the flowing of a river, and he stood in the dark and he listened to it. And he was amazed at the sound, amazed at the calm in the girl's voice, in her hands, and he thought of Cecilia and he thought of the children he'd had with her, gone to the winds, and he thought of the blood running in their veins, too. And he knew the girl was right. He took a step forward and then another, Elisabeth watching him all the while.

"Please," he said, or thought he had, because Elisabeth nodded and turned her head away from him then.

Mary had gone for the sugar water, and she brought it in a little cup with the teaspoon and Elisabeth fed it to the baby, drop by drop, and sat there with her while Mary pulled up a chair and then Leo did, too, a little apart from the women, his hands on his knees, eyes glittering, and they both sat watching Elisabeth and the baby, and the night came in through the broken screen door, and the moonlight, too—the walls were blue with it, and the floor, their faces even—and the breeze stirred softly through it, and with it the smell of dirt and new grass and the sound of crickets and the faint tinkling of bottles from the old cottonwood, and Mary watched and Leo watched, bright and feverish, as Elisabeth prayed and fed the child, who did not know its own blood, and prayed again, hour after hour, all of them together there beneath that picture of Gus in his coffin, through the long hours until dawn.

PILGRIMAGE

ONE

They came. By horseback, wagon and car, they came down dirt roads, across newly seeded fields, before Mass had even begun, yes—from Knochenfeld and Johnsborough and St. Michael's—for word had reached them, they had heard the drowned girl was alive, yes, of course, they knew that, *die laufenden toten Gestalten* (that alone was enough to make them all want to see her), but that was not what drew them that particular Sunday, it was more than that: she had healed a dying infant, that little one of Leo Krauss's. (Little Cecilia, wasn't that it, after his dead wife? What, Mary was dead? No, no, not that one, the first one, Cecilia. Yes, she had healed the child, who would not otherwise have lived, or so they'd heard, healed with her own hands. It was nothing short of a miracle, that is what they had heard. But where had they heard it? Why everyone knew. But how did everyone know? Well, did it matter, there was a saint among them, a worker of miracles, did it matter where they had heard it? There was the baby, little Cecilia, but they heard there were others, also, the blind, the lame, the deaf, she had healed them all. But that could not be, they knew of no one who was blind or lame or deaf. Well, no, of course not, she had healed them, hadn't she?

But before they had been healed . . . ? Well, they were not from here, obviously. Where, then? Ach, how should I know, probably Triumph, they are all blind and deaf over there, anyway, are you coming or not? Yes, I'll come, then, just to see, I don't believe it myself, but I wouldn't mind seeing. Oh, you'll see, all right.)

Only on Sundays, that is what Leo had told them all. Only on Sundays. Father Rieger stood on the church steps, watching them all come and watching them all go, back down the road, toward Krausses'. Then he turned on his heel and went inside, locking the rectory door behind him.

———

Mike Weiser and Marian sat in their car at Knochenfeld, watching the last wagon roll away.

"My God," Mike said, "I never would have thought it."

Marian turned to him in astonishment.

"Don't tell me you believe it, too," she said, "all this nonsense."

"No," Mike said. "I never would have believed it would all come to this. It just doesn't seem to end, one thing after another."

"That's Leo Krauss. I told you. Many a year ago, I told you. And you never wanted to believe me. Always wanted to see the good. But it's always trouble with him, nothing but trouble."

"Yes." Mike sighed and nodded. "And you were right."

He started the motor and clunked the car into gear, pulling out onto the road behind the others.

"Now where are you going?" Marian said.

Mike just stared over the top of the steering wheel.

"Good God," Marian said. "But you never learn."

"No," Mike said. "I guess not. I guess I don't."

———

When they neared the Krauss place, they could see Leo there at the gate, a shotgun slung absurdly across his shoulder, as he stopped with an upraised palm each wagon and car and horse.

Sometimes the people handed him something which he stuffed into the right-hand pocket of his suit jacket. More often they turned around and headed back down the road, passing Mike and Marian as they went. Mike pulled the car to a stop at the end of the line.

"And just how long do you plan to have us sit here?" Marian said.

But Mike did not answer. He only sat watching as people turned back and rode past them.

Finally, Mike leaned out the car window and called to an old man and woman he did not recognize who were just passing in their buggy. "What is going on?" Mike said. "Why are you leaving?"

"It is too much for us," the old man said, reining up. "The wife here has had bad pains in her stomach, but it is just too much."

"I don't understand."

"Why, we can't pay what he's asking. We have just a small farm, south of the Sand Hills there. We're not made of money." He looked over at the old woman, placed his cramped hand over hers. "I am sorry for it. But there's nothing we can do."

And the old woman smiled a little and squeezed the old man's hand.

Then he chucked his mule into motion and they rolled off down the road.

"Well," Marian said, "and there you go. Charging money to see that girl. He cannot sink any lower."

"Wait a little," Mike said, though tightly now, "we will talk to Leo himself. We don't know the whole story yet."

Marian made a little snort. "Yah, he is taking the money for the girl and her mother. He will build them a new house, maybe. Or buy that girl a dress that fits. Or some shoes, even, or maybe a little food. Satan, that is who he is. Everyone knows it but you. You think because he lost a wife and you lost a wife that you have something in common, or that you should be sorry for him. Is that it? Is that what all this has been about?"

Mike snapped a look at her, and Marian knew she had gone too far, knew she should not have mentioned Eugenia, the dead wife (her own sister, and so she had a right to speak of her, had she not?). But she had gone too far.

"Wait a little," Mike repeated, "we will talk to Leo."

Marian snorted again and looked out the window, but said nothing more.

They reached the gate at last. Leo came toward the car, the shotgun thumping his side with each step.

"Good God," Marian breathed. "Is he alive, even?"

For Leo looked worse than they had ever seen him. He had lost weight, though he could hardly afford to, and his eyes had receded even farther into his head and they were bloodshot and sore-looking, as if he had not slept in weeks. His hair, hanging untidily over his forehead, had fully greyed and it matched perfectly the tone of his skin and the dusty, faded old black of his suit so that he gave the impression of being all one dull colour, except for the eyes which burned darkly there.

"Leo," Mike greeted him, solemnly, "it's been a long time since we've seen you."

"And did I put something in your way," Leo drawled, "that you could not see me?"

"We haven't been around much visiting," Mike said, "that's all, with the seeding and that. Busy, you know how it is this time of year."

Leo coughed and spat in the dirt, wiped his mouth on his sleeve, but said nothing.

Mike shifted in his seat. "We'd heard you had some troubles, Leo," he said carefully. "With the baby. How is she?"

Leo seemed to sink a little, at the mention of Cecilia, to soften. "She won't give her back," he said pathetically, as if he were a child. He stepped unsteadily toward them, eyes burning, and Marian clutched Mike's arm, in spite of herself.

"He's drunk," she hissed.

"What's that, Leo?" Mike said. "Who won't?"

Leo stared at them, then rubbed a hand across his face. He pulled a small bottle of clear liquid from his trouser pocket, unscrewed the cap and drank from it, wiped his mouth again on his sleeve. He took a long time replacing the cap and putting the bottle back in his pocket, swaying a little on his feet. Marian squeezed Mike's arm meaningfully, but Mike did not look at her. Leo put a hand out as if to steady himself.

"God," Marian breathed, "is it turpentine?"

Leo looked up at them, squinting, as if he could not place them.

"He's going to fall," Marian whispered, and Mike put his hand on the door handle, as if to get out.

But Leo did not fall. He just stood staring, and when he finally spoke, it was the old Leo again, or a glimmer of him at least.

"Is it the baby you are wondering about," he said slowly, "or is it the girl?"

"Well, both," Mike said. What was the point in lying? "I wouldn't mind seeing her, if she's around."

Leo nodded, grimaced or smiled, they could not tell.

"That's right," he said. "Everybody wants to. Do you think I'm a fool?"

When Mike realized Leo was waiting for an answer, he said, "No, Leo. I never said you were."

Leo nodded again, as if he had just made a point. Then he said, "Anybody wants to see the girl, has to pay. It's only fair." Leo coughed again, viciously, and spat. "If I let you in for free," he said, "then I have to let everyone in."

He gestured behind the car, where others waited.

Marian started to speak but Mike shot her a look. "How much?" he said to Leo.

"How much have you got?"

Mike hesitated, dug his wallet from his pocket, pulled out some bills and handed them out the window.

Leo fingered them without looking. "Not enough," he said.

"Not enough? Good God, Leo. How much are you charging?"

"You pay double. Once to see the baby. Once to see the girl."

Mike opened his mouth, snapped it shut. He pulled some more bills from his wallet.

"What are you doing?" Marian said under her breath. "I've never seen you so stupid."

Mike handed the money out the window and Leo took it.

"How long will it take?" he said, gesturing to the people who had gone in ahead of him.

Leo shrugged, but said nothing.

After a minute, Mike said, "Leo, if you don't mind my asking, why that gun?"

"And why not?" Leo raised his voice. "What is it to you? None of your business whether a man protects himself. A man needs protection, not?"

Mike cast a glance at Marian.

"But, Leo," Mike said again, "isn't that dangerous? Are you . . . do you know guns?"

Leo stared at Mike a moment, swaying, blinked his burning eyes. He said, "It's not loaded. Do you think I'm stupid? You think I don't know better than to walk around with a loaded gun?"

And then he grinned blackly, and waved them on.

———

"Aren't you coming with?" Mike said.

They had parked outside the barn and he had taken his hat and moved to get out of the car, and he noticed that Marian just sat there with her arms folded across her chest.

"No," Marian said, "you go."

Mike glanced at the dark barn, hesitated. "Are you sure?" he said.

"I saw her in there once already," Marian said. "I don't need to see her again. I know what Leo has done."

"It might be better," he said, "if there's a woman. She might talk, then."

"If you want to see so bad," Marian said, waving her hand in disgust, "then go see."

Mike did not want to go see. He would rather have started his car and driven back home with his wife, back to his house with the stained-glass windows, back to a quiet afternoon and a good supper of baked ham and boiled potatoes and creamed corn. He did not want to see, but see he must. He had some responsibility in all this, did he not? Was it not because of him that Cecilia had come, and therefore because of him that she had died? Was it not because of him also, then, that Leo had sought out and found another wife and brought her and brought this girl, too? Was it not because of him, then, that there was yet another Krauss infant in this world? By God, he could not walk away from it all now, no matter what he thought of Leo. And so he took his hat and climbed out of the car and slammed the door and stood there a minute in the dust, and then, finally, he went inside.

———

When he returned, not five minutes later, he got quietly into the car and started the engine and backed out of the yard and past Leo, who watched them go without acknowledgment, and onto the road and turned for home.

Marian, who had been watching him warily out of the corner of her eye, said, "And? Did you see the girl?"

"I saw her."

"And did she say anything?"

Mike did not reply.

"Did she talk to you?" Marian asked again.

"Yah," Mike said. "She talked."

"Well, and what did she say?"

"She didn't say anything at first. You know how she is. Then I told her the braucha was dead."

"Didn't she know?"

"No," Mike said. "But she didn't really seem surprised, either."

"Well, no, the old woman must have been at least a hundred. Nothing very surprising in that. What did she say?"

"Christ, I don't know." Mike rubbed his eyes. "She talked about circles, or, something. God, she sounded as crazy as Leo. She said, 'That is how it goes, then. She was right about that. Everything goes in a circle.' She said, 'Wait, it will come around again.' And I said, 'What will?' And she said, 'Everything.'"

"What does that mean?"

"That's what I say. I have no idea."

"And is she what Leo says, a saint?"

Mike shook his head. "No. Christ. She's just a girl. Just a child. She might be a saint, having to live with Leo, but there is nothing miraculous about her, if that's what you mean. The braucha taught her some things, she said, the old ways, the old brauching. But that is all."

"But . . . healing that baby?"

Mike shrugged. "Luck, maybe. Maybe she would have gotten better anyhow. Who knows. I wasn't there. I didn't see what she did. The brauching works a little bit, I think. Sometimes. There's some sense in it. And so maybe that's all it was."

"And the blood, what about that?"

Mike turned to look at her. "They are cut."

"Leo is cutting her wrists?"

"Someone is."

"Well, if not Leo, who, then?"

"Christ, I don't know. I don't even want to know."

After a moment, Marian said, "But that night at the braucha's, with Ronnie and Erv Rausch. There was blood, even then."

"That's right," he said. "There was. Even then. Even before she was back with Leo."

Marian looked out the window.

"But . . ." she said, after a while, "why would she do that?"

"God, how should I know? Why does anybody do anything? Attention, maybe?" Mike shook his head. "I think, in the end, that there isn't really anything very special about her at all. Maybe that's it. She knows it. She's just a girl, just like any other girl, a little unhappier than most. But just a girl all the same."

"Well, I don't think that's true. She was never that," Marian objected, "she was never just a girl."

Mike sighed. "But that's the thing," he said, "I think she was. I think that's all she ever was."

Two

Father had sat all that Sunday morning in the rectory, a red shaft of light from the robes of St. James the Greater in the window-glass—his attribute, as always, a pilgrim's staff and drinking bottle—fallen brightly across the Bible before him. It was a little game he liked to play, matching the colour to the passage. Green for most of Genesis; brown for Job and Leviticus and a good deal of Exodus; yellow for Psalms and Corinthians; orange for Judith; blue for Proverbs; purple for Ephesians and the Song of Solomon; red for a surprisingly large portion of the book, including all of Deuteronomy and Revelations. Of course, it made it difficult to read, that coloured light. He had been gradually edging the book to the right, as the sun came more fully around to that side of the church, but the red light had followed him and now the window blazed with the full force of the midday sun. He could see he would have to move elsewhere. Instead, he closed the Bible. He had been reading Judges again, the story of the Levite's concubine. It had always troubled him. He could not make sense of it. But still, he felt drawn there; as often happened when something was troubling him, he sought not solace, but insight, in the Word of God. He had read it twice over, how the

Levite's concubine had run away, and how he had gone with his servant to her father's house to bring her home again, how they lodged on the return journey with an old man. He read it again, but there was nothing, no guidance there, no enlightenment. He scanned down the page to the passages that troubled him most. He read silently, moving his lips, "While they were making merry, and refreshing their bodies with meat and drink, after the labour of the journey, the men of that city, sons of Belial, came and beset the old man's house, and began to knock at the door, calling to the master of the house, and saying: Bring forth the man that came into thy house, that we may abuse him. And the old man went out to them, and said: Do not so, my brethren, do not so wickedly: because this man is come into my lodging, and cease I pray you from this folly."

And further on, the most troublesome passage, "I have a maiden daughter, and this man hath a concubine, I will bring them out to you, and you may humble them, and satisfy your lust: only, I beseech you, commit not this crime against nature on the man. They would not be satisfied with his words; which the man seeing, brought out his concubine to them, and abandoned her to their wickedness: and when they had abused her all the night, they let her go in the morning. But the woman, at the dawning of the day, came to the door of the house, where her lord lodged, and there fell down. And in the morning the man arose, and opened the door, that he might end the journey he had begun: and behold his concubine lay before the door with her hands spread on the threshold." Father Rieger shifted the book out of the coloured beam of light. "He thinking she was taking her rest, said to her, Arise, and let us be going."

Father Rieger closed the book. He did not need to read further, of how the man put the dead woman across his donkey and returned home with her. How, once there, he took a sword and divided the dead body of the concubine into twelve parts and sent the pieces into all the borders of Israel.

Father Rieger sat a moment, staring at the pages. Then he pushed the book from him, rose and took his hat from the hook on the wall. He locked the rectory door and then the main church door, something he did not usually do, and then walked down the road toward Krausses'. He did not bother with a horse or wagon, he knew he would not walk long.

He waved at the first wagon that approached and it pulled over. Father climbed up and settled himself onto the bench seat next to the driver, a young bachelor man Father recognized from the town parish, though he knew him not by name.

"Krausses'?" he asked, and when the driver nodded, Father said, "Drive on."

Soon they joined the scattered procession of wagons and cars and horses and, after a long and uncomfortable wait in which neither of them spoke, they pulled into Leo's yard.

The driver, the bachelor, wrote later, many years later, in contribution—along with three poems about wheatfields—to a community history book (and, though the poems about wheatfields were printed, Sister Bernadine, the editor, insisted the rest be omitted and the history book committee quite agreed):

Father's face, this was Father Rieger, then, and not Father Huff who had that affair with Mildred Brunhauer, his face was all screwed up like he'd eaten a sour pickle. Leo was three sheets to the wind by the looks of things. He come over with a shotgun God knows why. It must of made Father nervous. Sure as hell didn't make me feel none too good. I'd heard folks were coming by the hundreds, all day, but by the time we got there it was late and there was no one. Just Leo. He said to Father, "Thought you might have brought your girlfriend with you." That was Ida Rhenisch. I was worried Father might go at Leo the way I'd heard he had at confession a few days earlier, for something Leo had said about the girlfriend, Ida. But he didn't say nothing. He sat there looking sour. Leo said to Father, "That's two dollars." Father said, "You can't be serious, that's an outrage." Leo said, "Two dollars, and a bargain at that price." Father said, "I won't stand for it." Leo said, "You can sit, then, but you sure as hell aren't going in." Neither was I, at that jeezly price. Rob a crippled man blind, them Krausses. I went to turn the wagon around, but Father said, "Stop." He reached into his cassock and pulled out some bills and handed them down. Leo took them. He waved us in. I don't know if Father payed for us both or what. I never asked. When we got to the barn we climbed down. Leo said, "Come on, then." He took us in to where the girl sat holding the baby in a corner stable. That was Mary's baby. Mary was Leo's second wife. Leo told the girl to hold up her wrists. She wouldn't do it. She wouldn't even speak. We could see there was blood there, anyway. It was on her wrists. Leo told us how the baby had been brought back from the brink of death. That is what he said. He said the brink of death. He said to the girl, "Show them what you did." She wouldn't. She just sat there staring at him. Like she wished he was dead. So he showed us himself how she ran her hands over the child and how she put ashes on its forehead. He told us what she had said, a chant or a prayer or something. I can't remember exactly. Leo said to Father that the girl had been resurrected. That is what he said. Resurrected from the frozen river. In case we had forgot, which we had not. He said, "Well, Father, what do you make of that, now?" Father just ignored Leo. He asked the girl her name. She told him. He asked her where was she from. She told him. He asked how old was she. She told him. He asked her mother's name. She told him. So on and so on, until Leo said, is that all he could think to ask her? And Father said, no, he wanted to ask her about the blood, and Leo said, "It's blood, what more do you want to know, do you want to know its mother's name, too?" Father said, "How much does she

bleed?" Leo said, "Does it matter how much? Is she more of
a saint if she bleeds more?" Father went to the girl. He took
her wrist. He wiped it with a hanky. Then he took the other
one and wiped it, too. He looked at them a while. He said to
Leo, "Do you take me for a fool? This girl's wrists have been
cut." "What do you mean?" Leo said. "You know exactly
what I mean," Father said. "Look here," he said. He held up
one of her wrists and there was a long cut there, right across
her wrist. Not deep, but enough to bleed. "She looks like
she's been hacked at with a dull knife," Father said. He threw
the hanky at Leo's feet. It was bloody. "I knew you were
stupid," Father said, "but I never would have expected this,
not even from you. Have you no shame?" Leo got all worked
up then, too. He waved the shotgun. He said, "I never laid
a goddamned hand on that girl, I never have, you ask her, I
never touched her." He said to the girl, "Tell them, you tell
them." The girl did not say nothing. Father said to Leo, "You,
Satan, you will pay for this one day. You will pay for all of it.
You mark my words." He left and I followed him out. None
too soon for me. Leo chased after us into the yard. He said,
"You make her give me that baby, then, if you won't make her
a saint, then you get that baby back." Father ignored him, in
spite of the gun, which I was having a hard time forgetting
myself. It was Leo Krauss, you know. I climbed up on the
wagon seat with Father. We drove away. Leo hollered after
us, "Goddamn you, goddamn you." I did not look back. I
don't know if Father went to the constable over in Triumph
or not, it was McCready back then, useless as tits on a boar,
but he might have gone to him. I don't know. I was thankful
to be getting out of there without a bullet in my ass. Crazy
Leo Krauss. It was no wonder. Them Krausses were never
nothing but a sack of shit in skin. But that's how it happened.
And you can print it just the way I wrote it, Sister Bernadine,
though I know you will cross out all the cuss words.

THREE

Ron Wechter's crop was mostly in before Lathias even arrived and so when that was finished, Ron walked him over to the machine shop and put him to work on a stubborn thresher they would need come harvest. Lathias looked at the thresher and said, "I don't know threshers too good." And Ron Wechter slapped him on the shoulder and said, "Well, you got 'til August to get acquainted." And he laughed at the look on Lathias's face and said, "Don't worry. I won't keep you too long from the horses. I was young, too, once." And he walked off, leaving Lathias alone at the shop with only the cats for company. Now and then he would hear one or the other of Ron's daughters out in the yard, clucking at the chickens or calling to each other or bickering until they would see him there at the shop and then they would fall silent. And Lathias thought, *My God, was it me, then? Was that my fault, too?*

Sometimes the youngest girl, Millie, would come and stand in the doorway, leaning up against the frame and sucking noisily on a red stalk of rhubarb, her bare feet in the dust, and Lathias would not be able to look at her, for all that she reminded him of, and soon she would disappear, too, and he would be alone until Millie returned midday to summon him for lunch.

Once, after standing and watching him a long while, she had said, "Where are you from anyway?"

He had glanced up at her briefly. "East," he said.

"Hmm," she said shortly. "Seems like maybe you don't want to say."

"That's right," he said, without looking up. "I don't."

"Seems a little suspicious, if you ask me."

"I didn't," he said, and began banging needlessly at the thresher with the hammer, the shop filling with the hard clanging of metal against metal. Be damned if he could figure out what he was supposed to do with the thing. After a moment, he ceased clanging and dropped the hammer to the dirt and sighed. The girl still stood in the doorway.

"You know what you're doing there?" she asked.

"Not really."

"Didn't think so," she said, and sucked on the rhubarb. "I bet you can ride pretty good, though, can't you?"

"I can ride all right."

"And I bet you can make a bow and arrow, too."

He looked up at her. She was gazing at him shrewdly.

"Why would you say that?"

"Millie!" her mother called from across the yard.

And so she just smiled and flashed her eyes at him and said, "Oops. I almost forgot. Dinner," and skipped off toward the house.

———

Meals were always the same. After Lathias washed his hands and forearms and face at the pump, he removed his hat and ran his wet fingers through his hair and went to the house and sat at the table while the girls bustled around the kitchen, speechless, and only Millie eyeing him from across the table, swinging her bare feet.

Finally, the mother would say, "Oh, for heaven's sake, girls, sit down and eat once. He won't bite." And Millie would bark out a laugh, delighted. "Go ahead, go on and eat," the mother would say to him. "No need to wait for these gooses. Honestly. You'd think they'd never seen a man before."

And one of them would say, "Mother," quietly, and they would sit and smooth their skirts and pass platters and bowls, and cut and chew and drink with their eyes on their plates, and the mother would sit looking at them, baffled, and begin talking of the weather or the seeding or the plans for the following day, and Lathias nodding and eating, thankful when the meal was through and the girls rose to clear the dishes and pack up the food they would deliver to their father in the field.

"Well, Millie," the mother said one day as they were finishing up, "and how was it at Esther's? Has Ruth got her garden in yet?"

Millie shrugged and wiped her plate clean with a piece of bread and ate it and reached for another. "She took me and Esther to town," she said. "We got a licorice."

"And? What did you learn in town?" the mother said.

"Nothing," Millie said, buttering her bread thickly.

"You might as well stay home, then."

"There's no licorice at home," Millie said, and grinned at her mother, and one of the older girls said, "Millie," and then, remembering Lathias, turned her eyes back to her plate and blushed.

"Oh," Millie said, brightening. "I almost forgot. We were at the grocery, and we had to wait forever and ever for Esther's mother to get all her things, that's why she bought us the licorice, so that we wouldn't stand around bothering her, that's what Esther's mother said, and so we were sitting there on the window ledge so Esther wouldn't get her dress dirty"—she rolled her eyes, shook her head—"you know how her mother is, I would die if I had to live in that house. So we're just eating our licorice. I was trying to make mine last but Esther just gobbled hers like she always does, it's no wonder she's so fat—"

"Millie."

"—and then wants some of mine which is not fair even if her mother did buy it, like she said. I don't think that's one bit fair, do you?" Millie asked the table in general. She did not wait for an answer. "So we were sitting there eating and Mr. Willis, he's always so miserable and watching to make sure we don't touch anything, he told Esther's mother—and he said I should be sure and tell you, and talked so loud and slow he must think I'm retarded—"

"Millie."

"—and said he was closing the store early so he could take his wife, you know how she suffers from the gout, that is what he said but if you ask me it's just meanness that's her problem, so he could take her to see a healer. Well, that made me laugh. You can't heal ugliness."

"Millie!"

"Anyway," she continued, "Mr. Willis said to tell you"—here she raised her voice and spoke very slowly—"Not. To. Bring. The. Eggs. To. Morr. Ow. Be. Cause—"

"That will do, Millie."

"—he won't be there and neither will his ug—"

"Honestly," the mother said, setting her cup down sharply, and shooting a look at Millie.

"Anyway," Millie said, stuffing the rest of her bread into her mouth. "That's what he said."

"I heard about that," one of the older daughters said, tentatively, glancing quickly to Lathias and back to her plate again. "About that girl. That healer. A saint, that's what I heard."

"Oh, Martha told you that," said one of the others. "I wouldn't believe a word she says."

"Martha is so full of sh—" Millie began, and her mother fired her a fierce look, and so she finished quickly, "her eyes are brown."

"Martha does tell tales," put in another girl.

"No," said the first girl. "It wasn't Martha. I overheard Father

Hintz. When I was cleaning the church. And, Mother, I don't see why I should always be the one—" And, then, remembering Lathias, she bowed her head and cut furiously at her meat.

"Well," said the other girl, "I heard from Martha. About that girl. I thought it was just one of her stories, but do you know what they're saying? About that girl?"

"What, dear?"

"She was raised from the dead."

All the girls stopped eating and lifted their heads.

"Oh, good," said Millie, "so there is hope for Mrs. Willis after all."

"Oh, silliness," the mother said, ignoring Millie.

"No," the girl said, "it's true. *Die laufenden toten Gestalten.* That's what they say. She was dead, that's what Martha said. Drowned in the river, fell through the ice while everybody stood there watching and no one could do a thing. She was gone. When they found her body, they took her home and laid her out and held prayers and a vigil and everything and then at the funeral she just sat up, that's what Martha said. She just sat up and started talking. Resurrected, that's what everyone said. And now she can heal. She lays on hands—"

"And they will make her a saint," put in the other girl. "That's what Father said."

"Oh, pshaw," the mother said. "I wish you girls would use your heads sometime. Do you believe everything you hear? What do you say, Lathias? Are they not silly?"

But Lathias had lowered his knife and fork and sat staring at the girl who had been speaking, so hard that she became nervous and put her elbow in her plate, rattling it against the table and tossing food, causing Millie to laugh again.

"Do you," Lathias said to the girl, "do you know the name?"

The mother cried, "Don't tell me you believe it, too. I never would have thought."

"Please," he said, "did you hear that girl's name?"

"Why, yes," the girl said, blushing furiously. "It's the same as Mother's. Elisabeth."

———

It could not be. That is what he told himself. All that afternoon, alone in the shop, he replayed the conversation, trying to make some sense of it.

"Why, don't tell me you know the girl?" the mother had said.

But Lathias had only wiped his mouth and thanked her for the meal and excused himself abruptly, leaving them all sitting and watching him go. And when the little girl, Millie, had strolled over afterwards, the mother had come to the door of the house and called her back.

"But why can't I?" he'd heard Millie say, out in the yard, and then the mother speaking in a hushed voice, and the little girl said, "He is not. You don't know a thing about him."

And then the girl was ushered inside and the kitchen door shut firmly behind them.

Surely, the rumour could not be true. Gossip, it was. And what a fool he would be to beg time off to ride back and check. A fool here, and a fool there. It made no sense. And then there was the boy to think of, too, who by now must know he was gone. And if he should just turn up again? No, he could not do it, could not do that to the boy. He'd already done enough.

But if it was true? If she was alive?

And back and forth that way with himself, as always, when it came to her, unable to make a decision. But there was no her, he reminded himself. Was there? No. She was dead. She must be dead. She had to be.

FOUR

"What is it?"

"I have good news and bad news, son."

"What is the bad news?"

"Why the bad news?"

"I won't enjoy the good news anyway, if I know there's bad coming behind."

"Why don't you take the good news first?"

"What is the good news?"

"But listen—are you listening?—don't tell your mother I told you. Don't let on."

"What is it?"

"You won't tell her?"

"No."

"All right, then. It's . . . I don't know even how to say. That Krauss girl, or Brechert or whatever, your friend there . . ."

"Elisabeth."

"Elisabeth. She is alive. Did you hear me? The braucha, she rescued her or something, or found her, down at the river. Are you listening?"

"When?"

"That same night, the night she fell in."

"Did she fall in?"

"Well, yes, I guess she did. I think so. Isn't that what you said?"

"But we looked for her . . ."

"Yes, I guess she was already gone. She was already with the braucha by the time we all got there."

"Alive? All this time?"

"Shh. Yes."

"Did you see her?"

"No."

"Then how do you know?"

"Others have seen her."

"All this time? At the braucha's?"

"Yes. The braucha kept her there, at her place. Maybe she was sick, from the river. It was cold that night, she must have . . . I don't know. But she was with the braucha there. I know it must be a shock. But it is a good shock, not? She is alive. That is good news. I thought you would be happy. This whole time, she was alive."

"Is she at the braucha's now?"

"No, she is at home. At Leo's."

"Oh."

"I thought you would be happy."

"Can I go see her?"

"No. Not yet. Wait a little. Give it some time."

"Why?"

"Well, Leo. He can be funny. This is all such a shock. Give it time."

"Lathias will take me. I said, Lathias will take me. What is it?"

"Well."

"What?"

"Lathias."

"What about him?"

"He's not here."

"Where is he?"

"Gone."

FIVE

All that evening, after he talked to the boy, Stolanus sat
out behind the barn, smoking and worrying at a stalk of
grass until it was shredded to nothing and his fingertips
stained faintly green. Perhaps Helen was right, perhaps he never
should have done it. That look on the boy's face. He had thought
he would be happy. But he was not. Any fool could see that.
There was nothing of happiness in him any more. What good to
pretend? And so maybe Helen had been right, after all. He should
never have been told. They should have packed him up and taken
him to Battleford. He would be better off there, not? Away from
this place? This place that had taken from him, that had taken
from them all.

But, no, he thought, no, it was not right to lie to him. He
was suffering, because of the girl. Wasn't he? And if they could
ease his suffering? Hadn't he suffered enough? By God, hadn't
they all? And wasn't he sick to death of pretending things were
all right? That things would get better? Christ, why was it up to
him always to see the good, while Helen allowed herself to sink?
Well, if she wanted to sink, so be it. But he would not sink with
her. And he would not let the boy sink, either. His son. His son,

for Chrissakes. And he dug his heel in the dirt and returned to his thoughts of the previous night. He had lain awake thinking of all that had happened in the past few weeks, of the girl and then Lathias and all of it, and good God when was it all to stop? All this trouble. And when he could not sleep, he had gone outside and sat there on the stoop staring out at the night, no answers there, either. But as he sat looking out at the night and the Krauss place in the distance, the faintest glow of a light there, an idea had come to him, slowly at first and then all at once, so clear. A way to fix things. He could see then, how it was all falling into place. How it was a second chance, for the boy, for all of them. Helen would never have it, would be furious. And so it would have to be done without her. And wasn't it his right? Was he not the man? And if a man could not make a decision about his family, about his own son, what kind of a man was he at all? And he thought of his own father, Old Pius, who would never have allowed things to go so far. Would have made the hard choice, if it needed to be made. Hadn't he always? Isn't that what he had always taught? Everything happens for a reason, doesn't it? And where had his faith gone? That old faith, the faith that his father and mother had, the faith they needed to do what they had done, to leave everything behind and come to this country. That faith that things would get better. Where had it come from, that faith? Sometimes it drove him nearly crazy, thinking about it. How did one find faith? Where was it?

Everything happens for a reason, that is what his father would have said, and his mother, too. Everything happens for a reason. There is good in every bad thing.

He thought he knew what that was, now, the good in all of this. But he did not trust it, had not the faith to believe it was so. To take the chance. But maybe that's all faith was, in the end. Just taking a chance. Not really knowing. Was that it?

He rose and crushed his cigarette beneath his heel and he went to the barn and saddled two horses, and when they were ready, he walked to the house, entering quietly. Helen was asleep already, as she always was after supper now, and so he mounted the stairs and entered the boy's room without knocking. He was sitting there on the bed, rows of rocks and points and shards of coloured glass spread out around him. He looked up in surprise.

"Come with me," Stolanus said quietly.

"Where?"

"Come."

And so the boy rose and followed Stolanus down the stairs and out into the yard and across to the barn. He eyed the two horses, but said nothing, only watched as Stolanus pulled himself up into the saddle and sat waiting.

"Everything happens for a reason," Stolanus said to him.

The boy hesitated, looking confused, fearful. "Where are we going?"

"Get on," Stolanus said, and pinched his eyes shut a moment. "Just get on," he said, more gently, looking away, "and come with me before I change my mind."

———

Helen lay awake on the bed, the curtains drawn tightly on all the windows, the covers up to her chin in spite of the spring warmth. She had heard Stolanus come in and mount the stairs. She had heard them both descend. The quiet closing of the kitchen door. And then the horses, their hooves soft and heavy in the dust, moving past the house, not down the trail and toward the road, but the other way, toward the Sand Hills. And she thought, *So he is taking him to Battleford after all. He is going. He will be gone.* And she felt her throat tighten and ache. And so instead she thought, *Stupid. He should have taken the wagon. Why would he take the horses and not the wagon? But that was like him.* And she thought, *I will not have said goodbye.* And she thought, *Horses, where was the sense in that? Why not by wagon? Why not by car?* Thinking, "*On the mount of the Lord it shall be provided,*" though she did not know why, and she could not place it. Was it from Revelations? Proverbs? But she was tired. And so she did not think long. She closed her eyes and pulled the covers up over her ears and prayed for sleep.

———

The boy rode slightly behind his father, just enough so that his father turned back every so often, to make sure he was there. Neither spoke, though the boy thought that any moment his father would tell him where they were going and why. Once, his father turned and looked as if he would speak, but he did not. Only stared a moment, and then faced forward again and they rode on, across the fields. Before them and to the right, the Hills lay softened with the early evening light. Soon, the boy knew, they would turn violet, as if night came faster in the Hills than on the tableland surrounding them. As if it was always there, just waiting. He wondered if it was to the Sand Hills they were going, if perhaps they were only going to check the cattle they grazed there, as he used to do with Lathias. But he would not think of him, of Lathias, who was gone. He would think instead of Elisabeth, who was alive. Alive, but gone nevertheless. Wasn't she? But still: alive. Yes, he reminded himself of that. She was alive.

When they rode past the Hills and onward toward Krausses', the boy slowed his horse, and when they approached the Krauss place he stopped. His father rode on a few yards and then looked back at him, and he stopped, too, and they sat there like that, just looking at each other. And finally Stolanus nodded and said, "Everything happens for a reason. Remember that." And turned and clucked his horse into motion, and the boy followed at a distance.

They saw Leo before Leo saw them. He sat in a kitchen chair a short way from the barn, or slumped rather, out in the middle of the yard, a flask in one hand, a shotgun across his knees. At the sight of the gun, Stolanus paused, glanced back, and then rode on.

When Leo heard their horses, he started up, the shotgun clattering to his feet in the dust. He gripped the back of the chair to steady himself and bent to pick up the gun and Stolanus turned back and lifted a hand and said, quietly, "Wait here." Then he added, "If he starts to act crazy, you ride home. Understand? I will take care of myself. All right?" The boy nodded. "Wait here," the father said again, and then he turned and urged his horse forward a bit and then stopped and called, steadily, "Leo, *guten tag. Wie geht's?*"

Leo stood there, one hand on the chair, the other clutching the gun. He peered at them, as if he could not quite make them out. Eventually, he nodded, and said, "So. It's you." And nodded again.

Stolanus glanced back at him, but he did not move or say anything and he did not know if that meant he should ride home or not. He wanted to, wanted to go, but wanted to see her also, wanted to look around for her but was afraid to take his eyes from Leo who was stepping carefully toward them.

"It's you," Leo said again. "I thought so. I thought as much."

"Leo," Stolanus said. "I have a favour to ask of you."

Surely then, the boy thought, his father will let him see her, wants them to be friends again. And the boy urged his horse forward a few steps.

"Stay back," his father said to him sharply, across his shoulder. And then to Leo, "I need to see your girl. I—the boy does. For him. I heard—" He faltered. "If she can do what they say. If she can heal, then maybe—"

Maybe what? the boy wondered. Was this about Lathias? But Leo came toward them, then, and his father glanced back at him and he wondered if that meant he should go. But he would not, not until he had seen her, seen that she was alive after all. And where was she, in the house or the barn?

"You think," Leo said, walking forward, "you think after all that happened I would let him near her? Do you think I am a fool?"

"No, Leo," Stolanus said, "I've never thought that."

But Leo was not listening. "That is what everyone thinks, not? Isn't that what they say? You think I don't know? Is that what you think?"

"No, Leo," the father said, shooting the boy a meaningful glance as Leo approached. But the boy would not move. He sat there, staring past Leo, into the yard.

"So high and mighty," Leo went on, "but who has fallen now, I ask you." Leo was right before them, his eyes burning. "I will bring you all low. Now I have something everyone wants. They pay me to see her. They come to me now. And you, too, Schoff. You and your kid, too."

"I will pay, Leo," the father said. "Anything you want. If she can help him. If she can . . . fix it. Anything. Anything you say."

The boy was aware of Leo's presence now, there, a few feet in front of them, staring them down, his eyes red and fierce. But he was not afraid of Leo Krauss. He was not afraid of Leo Krauss. He was not afraid.

"Where is she?" he said, stepping his horse toward Leo.

"Go home now," his father said to him. "I'll see you at home."

"I don't need your money, Schoff," Leo said. "High and mighty. I don't need nothing from you. It's you who needs from me now. Isn't it?"

"Yes."

Leo stared at them a moment, going very still, as if something had just occurred to him. "That's right," he said slowly. "It's you that needs from me." And he nodded and scratched at his ankle with the muzzle of the gun. "I'll think about it," he said. "Not because I need nothing from you, Schoff. Don't you never think that. I don't need a goddamned thing from you. Your high and mighty money." And he looked at the boy now. "But he might do a little something for me. An agreement of sorts. Maybe we can work something out. I'll think about it. Maybe. I'll do that much."

"Can I see her?" the boy said.

"I'll let you know," Leo said. "All in good time." And he nodded and smiled and waved them away. "All in good time."

SIX

Whand his boy rode away, Leo stood in the
yard watching them go. He rummaged the flask from
his pocket and unscrewed the cap, slowly, and drank,
and coughed, and replaced the cap and rubbed his eyes. He lifted
the gun and stared at it and rubbed his eyes again. He had hardly
slept in days, not since the girl had said she would kill him. He had
walked around dazed and bleary-eyed and stupid with exhaustion,
moving just to stay awake, the gun slung across his shoulder. It
gave him little comfort, but he kept it with him anyway, driven by
one thought: he must get Cecilia back. The girl kept the baby out
in the barn with her all the time, now. And Mary was no help, just
as glad to have the baby gone, she had never cared for it. But the
girl had no right keeping her out there. No right at all. And what
was he to do? What had she said? She would kill him.

But the boy, that kid. Now there was something. Get the baby,
he would tell him, and you can see the girl. Get that baby and
the girl is all yours.

In the meantime, his flask was empty and he had all that money,
just sitting there in his pocket. He could use a little something.
Just a little something to keep a man warm.

SEVEN

When he was certain they were asleep, the boy climbed from his bed fully dressed and inched his way down the stairs, shoes in hand, and across the darkened kitchen and out the front door into the mild blue night. The sky was absolutely clear. Crickets sang from beneath the porch stairs. The moon, full or almost full or just beyond full, he could never tell which, cast enough light that he could see quite clearly—the barn, the stables, the granaries, the wagon, the pump, the windmill—all blue and swollen with moonlight, casting shadows on the earth.

But beyond the yard, the prairie yawned darkly. He had not really been out of the house since that night at the river. He sat on the step, just looking, and then he bent and laced his shoes, and rose and walked to the edge of the yard. Beyond lay the Sand Hills, blue also, and he wondered briefly if that was what things looked like underwater, under blue water, lakes, oceans, those Hills there could be at the very bottom of the Pacific, he could be walking on the ocean floor, the water huge above him, miles and miles of dark water, and through that water, stars, the moon. It would not do to be afraid. Lathias had not been afraid, not of anything.

But Lathias was gone. The boy still did not believe, had been wanting all day to go out to the loft, but had not wanted his parents to see him go, for what reason he could not say. But they were asleep now, and they thought he was asleep, too. His mother had come up once, shortly after they had returned from Krausses', they had thought she was already asleep, but she had climbed the stairs and eased herself down on to the edge of his bed and sat there a moment and then she had stretched out beside him, right there on the bed, and he'd had to force himself to breathe evenly so that she would believe he was asleep. She had just lain there a while, he thought she might say something, but she did not; she only rose after a few moments and smoothed the blanket over him and went back downstairs, to her own room, her own bed, his father already there, asleep, he could hear his snores coming up through the iron grate in the floor, a comforting, barnish sound.

Now they were both sleeping; sleeping inside the house and him awake outside of it, and it was night. He crossed the yard and stepped into the barn and stood in the darkness. Something scrabbled past his boots and he stepped back a little.

"Hello?" he said softly, though he knew there would be no one.

He waited some more, then climbed the ladder and felt along the beam at the top for the lantern and he lit it.

Nothing had changed. The rosary there on the wall, the crate Lathias used as a bedside table, the covers on his bed pulled neatly over, the chest where he kept his things. The boy lifted the lid. Lathias's books, books that the boy could not read, a Bible that he could not read either, some photographs of people he did not know, his hunting knife. The boy picked it up.

If Lathias had gone away, as his father had said, he would not have gone without his knife. And not without that rosary either. It made him wonder if his father was telling the truth after all. Had Lathias really gone away? And then, too, he had not said *Gone away*. He had said *Gone*. And that was different. That was something else. He did not like to think about that, about the possibility

that Lathias was not gone away, but that he was gone. And so
he put back the books and the photographs and closed the lid of
the chest. He strapped the hunting knife to his belt. He crossed
himself. He blew out the lantern.

————

The prairie seemed darker than the yard, perhaps only because
there were fewer things upon which the moonlight could reflect:
the earth, some cottonwoods and wolf willow in the slough there,
a couple of stone piles, the far fenceline on his left, and off to
his right, the eerie blue rising of the Sand Hills. Though it was
difficult in all that darkness to keep his course as the crow flies,
he would not, dared not, hug the line of the Hills, as he used
to in daylight. No, tonight he kept his distance from that place.
Tonight it was easy to believe that the stories Lathias had told
him about it were true, the place where the dead walk. He wondered, briefly, if Lathias was there now, his soul. But, no, he
wouldn't think it. He couldn't. It made his heart too heavy, the
grief of it all, the whole sad world. And so he walked on, his feet
sinking softly in the newly seeded fields, and he did not think,
Gone, but only, *Gone away.*

Soon he could make out the Krauss place before him and it
seemed, though it could just as easily have been his imagination—
stirred already by the night and the vast plains and the moon
and the stars—it seemed that the buildings and trees there did
not reflect the moonlight as did the other shapes on the prairie,
but only absorbed it, devoured it, the barn and the shack and the
granaries and the stables, even the scraggly shelterbelt, were not
blue as was the rest of the world, not silvered in the moonlight,
but were rather made darker, as if they were only the shadows
cast by other things. Neither did any light, whether lantern or
stove or candle, shine from the windows of the little shack, nor
any light from the barn, and the boy had the strange feeling, as
he approached, that everyone there was gone, too, that the place

had long been abandoned, that he came fifty, a hundred, five hundred years too late and that everyone had gone; that, as in a fairy tale, he had been sleeping all that time, and now they were all gone, even his parents behind him in his own house, gone, only the dim depressions their bodies had made on their bed, until that, too, was gone.

He stopped and looked about him at the farms in the distance, some with small lights glowing warmly from windows, and he was comforted a little. It was silly, of course, he knew it was, all that life around him, farm after farm, silly to imagine it could ever die out. It could only keep growing, that is what his father always said. He imagined a great city would be there one day, right where he stood, a great city with great tall buildings and roads and cars and trucks and lights, oh, the lights, it could make one dizzy, and all that noise, engines and people, where did they all come from, all those people, walking and riding bicycles and driving in cars and on buses, too, and trains, and calling to each other, and there would be bridges there and big, billowy trees and flowers and parks and ponds with white ducks in them, as he'd heard of in stories, and so many people in that great vast city, oh, the land would be covered with it one day, right there where he stood. He would like that, he thought, all that brightness and bustle. Someday, when he was older. But for now there was only the soft soil beneath his feet and the night around him, the moon and the stars, those stars, how they poured over him in one long bright stream, a river of stars. Lathias had told him the name once, of that celestial river, but he could not now remember it. And thinking of that made his heart grow heavy again. *Gone away.* He looked up at the Krauss place, hunkering before him in the darkness. He thought of Elisabeth.

He had lost her. Then he had lost Lathias. If he could find her again, then maybe . . . But it was too much to think of. For now, he must see her, that is all. He must walk on and on through that dark night, toward Leo Krauss, with the dead walking beside him and the Horseman maybe somewhere at his back. He stopped and listened for that distant rattling of bones. But there was nothing. And so he felt the sheath of the hunting knife at his side for comfort and he walked on, quietly, toward the barn.

When he passed the henhouse, there was a quick stirring and chortling and he stilled himself. If he hadn't felt so afraid he might have thought it was funny, all those hens in there, all ruffled up and bead-eyed, thinking he was a coyote, maybe. He would have liked to tease them a little, give a little growl, sniff at the door. They were funny animals, chickens. Funny, but vicious, too, pecking each other to death sometimes, the weaker ones, the wounded or sick. But they were pleasant when they were out in the yard all feathery white in the sun, peaceful, it was hard to imagine that other side to them, hard to imagine they were capable of eating each other, those mild, pleasant, funny birds scratching placidly in the dust. And he thought of the chickens and it reminded him of the joke Art Reis had once told, about this poor farmer who had three sons, and the first son came to him and asked for a new horse and the farmer said to the son, "No, we just bought a new plow, until that plow is paid for you won't get a new horse," and how, a few days later, the second son came and asked for a bicycle and the father said, "No, your brother won't get a horse and you won't get a bicycle, not until that plow is paid for," and finally, the youngest son went to his father one day and asked for a tricycle and the father said, "No, your brothers won't get anything and neither will you, not until that plow is paid," and how the boy stomped off in a huff and saw a hen come across the yard with the rooster chasing her and when the rooster tried to get onto the hen, the boy kicked the rooster aside and said, "You can walk too until that plow is paid for."

He had always remembered that joke, not because he thought it was particularly funny, but because of the sons—brothers—

and it seemed so wonderful to him, all those boys. And so he had laughed along with the other men, pretending.

The hens fussing in the henhouse because they thought he was a coyote, now that was funny. But then it occurred to him that the sound might wake Leo or Mary who could be sleeping already in the house, and so he whispered, "Shh, shh, quiet now, don't worry, I don't plan to eat you," but that only made them cackle louder and so he moved quickly away and toward the barn.

Now that he was closer, he could see that, in fact, there was a light coming from inside the barn, though the doors had been pulled shut and so he could only see it shining through the chinks between cracked and rotting boards, and it seemed so unbearably bright in all that darkness, it was like the light of God.

Odd that when he was so close, after coming all that way, through all that vast dark prairie, with the ghost of the Horseman at his back, he decided at that moment to turn and go home. Yes, that is what he would do. What did it matter if she was alive or not? What was it to him, in the end?

But it did matter. Of course it did. It was everything.

When they had ridden home from Krausses' earlier that day, he had asked his father what kind of an agreement, and his father had not answered and so he had asked again, and his father had said that it could be nothing good, knowing Leo Krauss. He said he thought he at least knew better than to make any kind of deal with a Krauss. He said at least he knew that much. And when the boy had asked when he could see her, his father had said, "I don't know. Maybe it's better to stay away after all. Maybe that's best." And the boy had said nothing. Had thought, *But maybe there is still a chance. Maybe it will work out after all.* But as they were putting up the horses, his father told him they would send him away, to school, to Battleford, a long way off.

"How long a way?" he had wanted to know.

"Long."

"Can you walk there?"

"No."

"Then how will I get home for supper?"

"You will have your suppers there."

"Every night?"

"Yes, every night. You will sleep there, even."

"Then it is not school."

"Yes, a little bit. It's seminary."

"What is that?"

"A school. For boys. Where they teach you about God."

"Like church."

"Yes, a little bit like church."

"But I can go to church here."

"Well, no, not like church, then. More like church-school."

"What will they teach me about God?"

"Just—I don't know, about the church and God and, I don't know. It's—they will teach you, they will teach you . . . it's more like, how to be a priest."

"A priest?"

"Yes. That is an honour, that is a real calling."

"But I have not been called. Priests have to be called, by God."

"Well, no. Not all of them. Some of them just choose."

"So I can choose?"

"Yes, you can choose to go."

"Can I choose not to go?"

"No. It has already been decided. It will be good. You will like it. You'll see."

"I don't want to be a priest."

"Well, just go and try it. Maybe you will like it, once you are there."

"I don't want to go."

"It has already been decided."

"When will I go?"

"Tomorrow."

And so it did matter. Tomorrow he would be gone, he would never see her. And if Lathias came back? But he would not think of that yet. It only mattered that he talk to her, that he see her. Part of him still believed it must be a mistake. She had drowned. She was gone. But now she was back. She had risen. Like the medicine man's daughter. But, no, she had not risen, that girl. Not at all. Why had he thought she had? And anyway, that was just a lie. He knew that now. It was the Horseman. That's who had risen. Who would rise. Was that a lie, too? He gripped the hunting knife at his belt and approached the barn.

He pressed his eye to a large crack in the boards and looked, but could see nothing, or more precisely, could see no one. Just the stalls and the cribs, some gnawed rope and broken tack hanging against the walls. He moved to another crack farther along, but found the same there. He realized he would have to go around the outside of the barn and look in from the opposite wall and he was just about to do so when he heard a strange sound, an odd animal mewling, and then some shuffling noises inside and the sound grew louder, it was—was it?—but no that wasn't possible, it couldn't be, but for the life of him he thought it sounded just like a baby. He moved quickly around the barn to the opposite wall and peered in again.

There. It was so shocking, seemed so impossible, to see her standing like that, Elisabeth, to see her alive there in the warm light of the lantern, that he almost cried out. But he did not, he only put his hand over his mouth and he looked and looked, he could not get enough of her, and he would not cry, he would not cry, he would not cry. But there she was, wasn't she? There she was, that face, that hair, she was alive, they were right, she was alive. He was so astonished, so mesmerized by the sight of her that it was a moment before he even noticed the baby, though it was crying loudly now, she had it in her arms and was rocking it and cooing and singing a song he vaguely remembered, though he couldn't imagine it had come from his mother, perhaps Lathias, but there it was,

> *"Gentle breezes are now swaying,*
> *Golden Spring begins again;*
> *To distant land my soul is straying,*
> *Hand me now my wand'ring cane.*
>
> *Farewell in thousand blisses.*
> *Boldly ventured is half won.*
> *Full of faith the wanderer parts.*
> *Farewell, my father's house.*
>
> *Farewell I must forsake*
> *My beloved father's house*
> *I must seek my fortune far,*
> *Aloft my eyes are gazing out.*
>
> *Farewell in thousand blisses.*
> *Boldly ventured is half won.*
> *Full of faith the wanderer parts.*
> *Farewell, my father's house."*

He was ashamed, then, of his own hot tears. Tears not for the song, which he had never liked, or even his own leaving or even for Lathias, but because she was there before him and because he had been given another chance, and so he was not to blame after all, for her death, he could not be to blame, because she was not dead, and here was another chance, here she was, he would speak to her again.

"Who is that?"

At first he thought it had been Elisabeth. But the voice came from behind him.

The Horseman.

The boy froze, every nerve in his body on edge, stomach clenched, blood pumping, *Run,* it told him, *run.* But he did not. *The Horseman,* he thought, *come for me, finally, after all this time.*

"Speak up now, who is it?" said the voice. "Turn around so I can see you."

The boy did not move.

"Turn around."

The boy turned slowly and faced the darkness. At first he could see nothing, his eyes adjusting from the lantern light to the night. Then a figure emerged, faceless.

"What do you want? Step forward."

The boy stepped forward and the figure did too.

Leo.

"Well, what is this now?" Leo breathed, coming closer. A rank, yeasty smell wafted from him. He staggered a little as he walked. "Jesus Christ Almighty," he said. "Jesus Mary Mother and Joseph, so you couldn't stay away."

It was only then that the boy noticed Leo was holding something, which he at first thought was a walking stick, was using it to prop himself up against the dirt, balancing on it. But it was not a stick, the boy saw, as Leo came closer. It was the shotgun. On instinct, his hand moved to Lathias's knife at his side.

"I figured you'd come back," Leo said. "Speak up, now."

Though he hadn't asked him anything.

Leo swayed on his feet, planted the butt of the gun in the dirt, leaned heavily upon it.

"Couldn't stay away, eh?" Gesturing toward the barn. "I thought so. I thought as much. And you're worried I will stop you. Well, I won't. You go on and see her. But you do something for me, too. If you'll do it, you can see her all you want. You can take her. Take her for all I care. Take her and throw her in the goddamned river."

His eyes glinting in the moonlight.

"See, I would do it myself, but I can't get at her. The old man tried to warn me, the old grandfather. He warned me but he sent them anyway. And he was right, goddamn it. The old sonofabitch was right." Stepping forward and lowering his voice. "But you could get at her. You could get the baby for me, you could take Cecilia and bring her to me. See? Then the girl is yours. And you could, listen, you could get her down to the river again. Couldn't you. Will you do that? Will you get my baby? And get that whore out of here. I could pay you, I've got all this money." He felt in his jacket pockets, patted, searched. "All this money, see?" He dropped some bills to the ground, bent to pick them up and toppled over into the dirt.

Now, the boy thought. *Run.* But his legs would not move.

Leo lay there, then he started to laugh a little. He propped the gun in the dirt and tried to use it to lift himself but he could not and he laughed again and let himself fall, sitting there in the dirt like a child, the gun across his knees.

"Come here," he said, "and give me a hand up."

Still laughing? Was he laughing? The boy had thought so, but now he was not so sure. Not laughing, but crying. Was he?

Leo lifted a sleeve and wiped it across his face.

"Give me a hand, won't you?"

And the boy stepped forward and moved to hold out his hand.

"What is going on? Who's there?"

It was her. The boy turned. She was there, in the light from the barn door, the baby in her arms.

"Stay back, Jezebel," Leo shouted. "You stay back, you Satan." And he scrambled in the dirt.

"She'll kill me," he said to the boy, "that's what she said. She has my baby, my little girl. I want her back. You give her back to me." Whining now. "You have no right. She wants to kill me. She said it." Then he cocked his head. "Do you hear that?" he hissed. "Christ, can you hear it?" Scrabbling to get up, but falling, falling, stabbing the gun into the ground.

"What?" the boy said, in spite of himself. "What is it?"

"Leo," Elisabeth said, across the darkness, "who is with you?"

"Do you hear that?" Leo said. "Listen. Listen." Scrabbling, the gun in the dust.

"What is it?" the boy said, stepping closer to Leo. "What? The Horseman?"

"Who's there? Who's with you?" Walking toward them now, the baby in her arms.

"It's me," the boy finally said. "It's me."

"Leo?"

"Stay back," Leo yelled. On his knees now. "Give me your hand for God's sake," he cried, "don't leave me down here like this." Stabbing the gun into the dirt. "Here, give me your hand. Christ Almighty, here, she's coming. Here, here. Please."

And the boy reached down.

EIGHT

Later, people would report having heard that shot, and having wondered to themselves whose dog was into whose henhouse now, and some of them confessed to remembering Old Pius Schoff too, that gentle old soul, and Old Krauss, that rotten sonofabitch.

"Remember when Pius Schoff shot Old Krauss's dog?"

"And Pius went over and wrote him that note and left it on the table and that night Old Krauss walked over to Pius's and said, 'Somebody left me a note, but I can't read. What does it say?'"

And they had chuckled together, warm in the light of kerosene lanterns, and maybe they played cards a little, that warm spring night, and remembered the old folks, the ones who had passed on, the ones who had been left behind. And maybe, later, made sentimental with remembering, they would sing some of the old songs, the songs of leaving, and cry a little, maybe—ach, there was no harm in a tear or two, for all that had been left behind, not?—and pat each other's hands, and pray a little, too, together, it was all they had now, before blowing out the lanterns for sleep.

NINE

He walked.

As far as town, with its dead windows, and empty dark streets, and through town and past the community hall and past the convent with its one perpetual light at the front entrance, and beyond, into the dead prairie, and along the Maple Creek trail, to the highway. He walked and walked and walked, until dawn. What else was there to do? He could not stand and wait.

No cars passed in the night, and no wagons either. Nor were there any at dawn. Just when the sun was up over the horizon and the sky was outraged with light, all red and furious, there came the sound of a motor car behind him and he turned and held out his hand, waved. The car came on, passed him, and stopped. He ran to catch up to it.

A man leaned his greased head out of the window.

"Where you going, stranger?" he said.

"Where are you?" he replied, and shook his head. That is not what he had meant to say.

"That's a good goddamned question." The man laughed. "If you mean where am I going, it's all the way to Medicine Hat, that's why I'm on the road already. Early bird catches the worm, they say." The man patted a travelling case on the passenger seat. "Pharmaceuticals man." He grinned. "Not that you'd know what that is. But you're welcome to join me."

He moved the case into the back of the car and pointed to the passenger seat and nodded, in order to make himself understood. These immigrants, dumber than a sack of hammers, they were. But he wouldn't mind a little company for the road. There sure as hell wasn't a goddamn thing to look at. Who the hell would live in that godforsaken place, he couldn't figure out. British Columbia, now, that was the place to be. That was God's Country. Trees and mountains and every damn thing you could want and you didn't have to work too hard to find it, hell, you didn't have to work at all. It was all just there waiting on a man. He wouldn't mind getting his hands on the Jasper circuit someday, and he could, if he played his cards right. It wasn't B.C., but at least there was something for a man to look at. These prairie trips were the worst. One long flat stretch of godforsaken road. What the hell was a man supposed to look at, the sky, a sparrow, a fence-post, the goddamned light, for Chrissakes? No, thank you kindly. Now this one here might be an imbecile, but he'd be good for a laugh or two, pass the time, something to tell the boys when he got back.

"Well, come on if you're coming," he said. "Get in."

Leo got in.

"Rough night?" the man asked.

Leo nodded a little and the man slapped the steering wheel and grinned and ground the car into gear.

"Say," the man said, when they pulled back onto the road, "you look kinda familiar. I think we mighta crossed paths somewhere before. Do I know you?"

But Leo just shook his head and stared out the passenger window. "No," he said, "I don't think."

The man laughed. "You can say that again. That's for damn

sure. Ha ha. Hey, what are you anyhow, Kraut or Uker-anian or Polack or what? Rooshian? I met me a nice little Rooshian girl through these parts once, oh, she wasn't much to look at, but then again, if you don't look, it don't matter, if you get my drift."

He moved to light a cigarette, then he frowned and stared at the man. "Christ," he said. "What . . . Jesus, you ain't crying, are you?"

Leo covered his face with his hands.

"Kee-rist Almighty," the man muttered. "If they don't beat all."

Ten

When Ron Wechter returned from town, he went immediately to the shop where he had put Lathias to work again on the thresher. He was a hell of a worker, that one. Lizzie said he was shady, there was something suspicious about him, because of something that happened over lunch the other day, because he didn't talk much. Could you fault a man for that? And anyway, he'd seen her cluck over him, she liked him well enough. But a woman needs something to complain about. He wondered what she'd say when he told her what he'd heard in town. But that was neither here nor there. It didn't affect her any. He hoped he'd got the name wrong, but time would tell.

Lathias was crouched down in a circle of parts when he got to the shop.

"Hell," Wechter said, "I didn't think you'd take the whole damn thing apart."

Lathias shook his head in bewilderment. He said, "I'm better with horses."

Wechter smiled. "Just make sure that's still a thresher when you put those pieces back together and not a horse."

Then he stood watching Lathias. He opened his mouth to speak, closed it again. Pulled a pouch of tobacco and some papers from his pocket and rolled one for Lathias and one for himself.

"Here," he said, "come take a load off. That engine will make more sense if you let it alone a while. Like a woman, not?"

Lathias rose and walked over and took the cigarette.

They smoked and Lathias said, suddenly, "I need a few days off."

"What's that?" Wechter said. And thought, *So maybe he already knows, then.* "Heading home?"

Lathias nodded.

"Not trouble, I hope?" Wechter said, cautiously.

"No," Lathias said. "I don't think so."

Wechter studied him. Had he heard or had he not? He said, "Something happen?"

Lathias shrugged. "Just a visit," he said. "Nothing in particular."

Wechter nodded. After a bit, he said, "I heard something in town today. Your people, their name wasn't Schoff, was it?"

Lathias looked up sharply. "That's right," he said. "Schoff."

Wechter nodded. "Plenty of Schoffs around, though, I would imagine. That wasn't the Schoffs from over Knochenfeld parish, is it?"

Lathias stared up at him. "Knochenfeld, yes," he said.

Wechter sighed and looked away. "Christ," he said, and stubbed out his cigarette. He looked at his big hands, as if to find something there.

"What?" Lathias said. "What did you hear?"

Wechter looked at him. "A boy of theirs," he said, "I didn't get the name. Thirteen, fourteen years old—"

"Yes?"

"I'm sorry, son," Wechter said. "That boy, he was shot."

———

At first he had not understood. And so when Wechter said, "I guess you'll be wanting to stay home. Take as long as you need. There'll be a job waiting for you, if you want it," Lathias had nodded dumbly and said, "Yah, thank you. Did you hear, how bad is it?" And Wechter had stared at him a moment, uncomprehending, and finally he had laid his big hand on Lathias's shoulder and said gently, "I'm sorry, son. He's dead."

He was grateful that Wechter had left him alone then, in the shop with its smell of oil and gasoline, grateful that he hadn't said, *Was that your brother, then, or a cousin, or what was he to you, that boy that was shot?* No, he had just left him alone, and later, when he was up at the barn saddling his mare, Wechter's wife, Elisabeth, had come with some hot food wrapped up in a clean towel, more than he could possibly eat, and she had squeezed his hand. That was the only thing, he wished she had not done that, because he had to turn away then, shameful, a man his age. He turned away and pinched the bridge of his nose hard, pinched it until his head ached, and still it would not stop, goddamn it, he just could not make it stop.

ELEVEN

No one came the morning Stolanus and Helen loaded up their car with the few things they had decided to take with them. Not Ludmila Baumgarten. Not the Schneider brothers. Not Ma Reis. Not even Mike Weiser.

"Ach," Mike had said to Marian, "what for? What good will that do, seeing them?"

And Marian had looked at him and said, "I've never known you to be a coward."

And Mike had just nodded.

It was not that they did not care, the good people of Knochenfeld parish, only that they could not face them, Stolanus and Helen. And Stolanus and Helen did not want to see them, either, did not want to accept the condolences that, however well meant, could only sound hollow, as condolences always did. There had been a brief investigation, or so, at least, everyone thought. McCready had come out from Triumph to talk to Stolanus and Helen, who would not press charges, at least that is what they had heard, and then over to Krausses', in order to have enough information to file a report. And Leo, he was gone by the time McCready even got there, that is what they had heard. Gone no one knew where.

And good riddance, that is all they could say. And Mary? And that girl? Well, better off without Leo, at any rate.

At the funeral neither Stolanus nor Helen had spoken to anyone, nor even looked about them. Only entered the church alone, and followed the coffin out alone, driven to the cemetery alone where they stood at the edge of the grave and when Father Rieger came to them after committing their boy to the earth, and he laid a hand on Stolanus's arm, Stolanus had only nodded vaguely, and then they had got into their car and driven, not to the community hall for the lunch that the Ladies Auxiliary had worked so hard to organize, but home, leaving everyone to sit and wait for them at the hall, the egg salad sandwiches and slices of kuchen slowly drying in the stale air, the coffee growing cold, until finally they realized Helen and Stolanus would not come and then they ate, though not with any appetite—how could they?—but the ladies had gone to so much trouble, and so they ate and talked, mostly about the weather, about the good crops to come, what else was there to say?

And who could blame them, Helen and Stolanus? Who could blame them for not wanting to sit over their coffees and their sandwiches, nodding dumbly, uncomprehending still, who could blame them? Really, who among them could stand in judgment? They had never liked Helen, no, they would not say otherwise now, but hadn't the woman been through enough? There were some, just an ignorant few, who did not attend the funeral at all. "Well," they said, "and why would we? He was a monster. Did you not hear he had a knife with him? A hunting knife? Going back a second time to finish the job, is what I'd say."

And though the others could not explain the knife, they could not condemn the boy for it, either. And they graciously—one might even say thankfully—gave Helen and Stolanus their space.

Only, the following morning, the morning after the funeral, they, Helen and Stolanus, woke to find a box of food—baked dishes and roasted meats and pies and fresh bread—on their doorstep, and, tied with a long length of white ribbon, a great bucket of flowers: tulips and buffalo beans and the first lilac plumes still tight in their buds. And Stolanus gathered the food and the flowers and brought them inside and set them on the table and he and Helen sat looking at them, and then, without speaking, they rose and began to pack a few things, and carry them out to the car. When it was time to leave they stood a moment in the yard, just looking around, and the spring air was beautiful.

"We should stop at Schneiders'," Stolanus said. "See if they want to get the crop in."

She looked out over the greening fields.

"Leave it," she said.

After a minute, Stolanus said, "Seems a waste."

"Someone will get it in," Helen said. And then she added, "They would not let a crop go to waste."

"Ach, Helen," he said. As he always did.

"Is that it, then?" she said, putting a hand on the car door.

Stolanus looked around the yard. "What about Lathias's things?" he said.

Helen shrugged. "He will come back for them or he will not."

Stolanus looked around the yard again, sighed. Thought of his mother and father who had built the place and who lay now at the old cemetery at Johnsborough and of his daughter there, too, little Katerina, that had been his daughter only long enough to be named, and of his son, who had never really been his son, either, or, at least, not in a long time, his son, committed to the earth now, too, at the cemetery at Knochenfeld.

"I don't know," he said. "We are leaving so much behind, not?"

"Yes," Helen said. "That's how it is. You cannot go anywhere without leaving something behind."

"But, so much?" he said.

And she looked up at her husband and thought, *My God, he*

has aged. When was the last time I really looked at him? When did we get so old? And she almost reached out to touch the lines around his eyes. Instead, she repeated, "Is that it, then?"

And he said, "Yes. That's it."

TWELVE

Mary had sat at the kitchen table all day, and all the previous day, too, and the day before that. Every day since Leo had left. How many days that was, she could not say. Sometimes she stared out the window, stared down the road, as if he might appear there, not knowing for certain whether she hoped he would or she hoped he would not. But he would not. She knew that much now. How could he come back, after what had happened? After what he had done.

"But how did it happen?" she had asked Elisabeth.

"He shot him," the girl had said. "Does it matter how?"

And the boy was dead. And Leo was gone. Now Elisabeth stood in the doorway with that baby and looked at her and said, "I am leaving. I thought you should know."

And Mary nodded and looked away, out the window, past the bottle tree, down the road. What was she to do? Leo had left her nothing. She could not go back home, back to Dakota. Her father would never have her. Would that Leo had taken her with him. She would have gone, God help her. *Take me with you,* she would have said, if there had been time, if he had given her the opportunity. But why would he? Why would he want her? Why would anyone? By the time the shot woke her and she had dressed and gone outside, Leo was gone and there was only that boy lying already dead in the yard and Elisabeth with the baby kneeling over him, the boy's head in her lap, stroking his hair. And she was crying, Elisabeth was. Mary had never seen her cry before, not even as a child. And she had looked up at her, at Mary, and said one word: *Leo*.

And so he would not be back.

"Where are you going?" she said now to Elisabeth, without turning from the window.

"To the braucha's."

"And how will you live?"

"The same way she did. Why shouldn't I?"

"And you think people will come to you? After all that has happened?"

"People will always come."

"And the baby, what about that?"

Elisabeth did not answer, and Mary turned to her. "What will you do with her?" she repeated.

"She is not my child to do something with."

"Oh, you say that now."

"He's gone, isn't he?"

"Because of you." Though she hadn't meant to say it.

"Because of himself."

Elisabeth stood in the doorway a moment longer. Then she entered the kitchen and held out the baby. When Mary did not reach to take her, Elisabeth spread the baby's blanket on the floor and laid her there. Then she reached into her dress and handed Mary some bills.

"Here. I found this outside. In the yard."

"That is Leo's money," Mary said.

"No," Elisabeth said, fiercely. "It's mine." And she put it on the kitchen table and turned to go.

"Elisabeth," Mary said, "you must tell me the truth. I have to know. Was it an accident?"

And Elisabeth stopped and stared back at her. "Nothing is an accident," she said.

———

Later that afternoon, Mary hitched up the mule to the wagon and took the baby and drove out of the yard and down the road to Weisers'. Then she sat waiting in the wagon, staring up at the stained-glass windows. Finally, Marian came to the door, and then Mike, behind her. They looked at each other.

"Mary?" Mike said uncertainly. "But how long have you been waiting? Come, come in. Bring the baby."

Mary tied up the reins and lumbered down from the wagon, the baby in one arm.

Marian stepped quickly forward. "May I hold her a little?" she said.

Mary looked at her as if she were not sure. Marian was the one who had taken Leo's other children, after all. How would he feel about that? But then she handed the baby to her.

"Come in," Mike said, and stood back from the door to let Mary enter.

"Here," he said, pulling out a chair from the gleaming table, "sit down."

Mary sat, and Mike and Marian stood staring stupidly at her.

"Can I get you coffee?" Marian said.

Mary nodded. Marian handed her the baby, and Mike pulled out a chair and sat across the table and cleared his throat and then cleared it again.

When the coffee was ready, Marian poured it out and joined them and they all drank and waited and drank again.

After a while, Mary said, so quietly they could hardly hear, "Have you got a little milk?"

"Milk?" Mike said, surprised. "For the coffee?"

"No," Mary said, "for the baby. She needs to eat a little."

"Of course," Mike said, feeling foolish, as Marian rose for the milk, "how stupid. We should have thought."

"I have money," Mary said, "I can pay."

"Ach," Mike said, "don't insult us. Keep your money."

Marian brought the warm milk and Mary fed the baby and Mike and Marian watched, both of them wondering if this was all Mary had come for, but not wanting to ask.

"So," Mike said, after a while, "how are you, Mary?"

"Ach. Death seeks a reason," she said, shrugging. She wiped the baby's mouth with her dress.

"And," Mike began, glancing at Marian, "and, Elisabeth, how is she?"

Mary grimaced, took a drink of her coffee. "She has gone," she said. "Living at the braucha's."

Mike and Marian exchanged looks.

"What, for good, you mean?"

"Yah, that's what she says." Mary patted at the baby's back. "If she wants to, should I stop her?"

"No," Mike agreed. "She's a big girl. She must do what she wants."

Mary shrugged again, and propped the baby up awkwardly against her belly, and the baby slipped forward and Mary propped her up again.

"And Leo?" Mike said quietly.

The baby began to fuss and Mary shifted her into the crook of her arm.

"Gone," she said.

"You have heard nothing?" Mike said.

Mary shook her head.

Then they were all quiet again.

Finally, Mike said, "Who knows what the future brings?" Then, feeling foolish, he rose to fill his coffee cup.

After a while, Marian said, "And what will you do now, Mary?"

"About what?"

"Well," Marian said, wondering how to put it. "Where do you plan to live? What will you do for, well, for money?"

Mary nodded. "That is why I came."

Mike and Marian exchanged quick looks again.

"Not for money," Mary said, catching the looks.

"Of course not," Marian said, "we didn't think—"

"And not for somewhere to live, either."

"No, no, we never thought—"

"But I don't want to stay out there, out at the farm there. Not by myself, with this baby. And everything. That was never for me, anyway, that place."

"Where, then?" Mike said. "Where do you want to go? Back to Dakota? We will take you in the car if that's what you want."

"No. Never there," Mary said. She seemed ashamed, then, and dropped her head and fiddled with the baby's blanket. "Not there," she said quietly. "Just . . . there is somewhere. Not so far." She looked up at them, uncertain. "I'll tell you. Will you take us?"

"Yes," Mike said. "Of course." And, after only the briefest pause, Marian nodded.

————

It was not a long drive, by car. Mary sat in the back with the baby and a small sack full of her things.

"You will sell that mule for me, then," Mary said, "and the wagon, too?"

"Yah," Mike said, "I think I can get a good price for them, for the wagon and mule together. I wouldn't mind it myself. Could use it, oh, around the farm and such. You'll get a good price for them, I think."

Marian shot him a look, but he ignored her.

When they turned off the road at the edge of town and onto a neat, narrow, tree-lined drive, Mary leaned forward and looked out the window, at the big brick building there, the trimmed lawns and immaculately weeded flowerbeds.

"Yah, and maybe they will not want me," she said, mostly to herself.

Marian turned in her seat and stared at the woman, and at the baby sleeping there on her lap, and for the first time in weeks, and in spite of herself, she softened, smiled a little.

"They will want you," she said.

———

The old nun who opened the heavy wooden door looked them up and down.

"Yes?" she said, sharply, stepping forward a little. "What is it?"

Mike looked to Mary, but she only stood with her head down, the baby against her belly.

So he said, "You must have heard"—clearing his throat—"you must know of, well, what happened last week." He looked meaningfully at the old nun, but she only frowned a little, waiting. "Leo Krauss," he said awkwardly, hoping there would be no need to recount the previous days.

"Oh. Yes," the nun said, waving her hand irritably. "I know about that."

"This here," Mike said, indicating Mary and the baby, "this is Leo's wife, and his child."

"Yes, I am not so old that I cannot see. What is it you want?"

"Forgive me," Mike fumbled, "but I had heard, my wife had said—"

"Will you take them in?" Marian interrupted. "They have nowhere to go."

The nun frowned more deeply, looked at Mary again over the rims of her glasses. Then she reached out and pulled the swaddling blanket from across the baby's face.

"Krauss, eh?"

"Yes."

She replaced the blanket and looked at them sharply again.

"You know we have another Krauss here, an older girl. Magdalen."

"Yes," Mike said. "We knew that."

"Yes, of course you would," she said, eyeing them. "I had forgotten. And what is your relationship to Krausses? You seem to have a good deal to do with them."

"We are neighbours," Mike said.

"Ah," the nun replied, as if Mike had said something deeper.

The old nun stared at him a moment, then she lifted the corner of the blanket again. "Boy or girl?" she asked Mary.

"A girl," Mary said. "Cecilia."

The nun raised her eyebrows. Then she dropped the blanket and nodded. "Well," she said, "come in, then. You're letting in an awful draft."

"You will take them?" Marian said.

"I just said so, didn't I? Do you think we turn people away here? Get their things," she said to Mike, opening the door wider. "We will have to make some room."

Thirteen

When he rode into the yard, he knew at once they were gone. Though everything was as it had been when he left, the whole place somehow carried an air of absolute abandonment. Even the dust in the yard seemed to settle with a heavy finality that belied the lightness of a clear afternoon in late May. Everything—the slow turning of the windmill in the yard, the cooing of the hens beside the barn, the meadowlark on a fencepost, the creak of the front door, his boots on the kitchen floor—everything sounded hollow and lonely. And he realized, only then, that it had always been so. Even when they had all been there, all four of them, the place had already been abandoned, maybe as far back as the death of Old Pius. It was as if there were no heart in it, that place, not anywhere.

He walked through the house once, surprised, and then again, not surprised, either, at all they had left. Dishes and bedding and pots and pans, brooms, lanterns, furniture and cushions, even old coats and hats and mufflers hanging by the door. A stranger happening upon the place might suppose they had only gone into town for the afternoon or to a neighbour's visiting or for a day of fishing at the river. He touched the coffee cups that sat unwashed on the table, and the bucket of flowers wilting there, smelled the rotted sweetness of aging lilacs, pressed his hand against the cold coal stove. He did not go up to the boy's room. Not yet. Not ever, maybe.

He left the house and crossed the yard to the barn, was up in two steps, smelling that old familiar smell of hay and wood and dust and horses. Here, too, everything remained strangely the same, as if he had just come in from a day in the fields. Only his knife was out of its place in the chest and lay, oddly, in the middle of his bed. He had heard what had happened, of course, or at least several variations on the truth at the towns he stopped in on his travels home. The boy had a knife, that was what everyone had said. His knife, he had known that, too. But it was here now. And he knew, too, who had put it there. And why. She had known he would come back. Had meant for him to. He could have taken it another way, that knife there on his bed. But he knew better. As before, there was no accusation. Only a message. This was his place now, as much as it had ever been anyone's. That is what she meant to tell him.

He picked up the knife and handled it a moment. Gripped it in his palm, fiercely. Then he stretched out on his bed and slept.

———

When he woke, he strapped the knife to his belt and descended. He fed and watered the mare he'd left standing in the yard, and went to the kitchen for some food, then sat outside on the porch in the slow silence, eating. Staring out at the smokehouse and the granaries and the chickenshed and the windmill and the pump and the corrals and the barn and the wild rose bushes beyond, tight with dark buds, and the green fields unfurling as far as the Sand Hills in the afternoon light, and the Krauss place there in the distance, as it seemed always to have been, and then the infinite horizon. And he ate and stared and listened. It all felt so inevitable now. It was as if all those years of silence among them had been travelling toward this, as if he must have, how could he not have, known it would all somehow end this way. Knew the boy could not live. Knew that Helen and Stolanus could not stay. Knew that he would end up there alone one day. Had to.

After he had eaten, he rose and rinsed his plate at the pump, and then rubbed water against his face and neck and forearms, and drank. Then he walked to the barn and he saddled his mare again and rode straight for the river.

———

She was there, in a chair by the front door, her white dress falling around her and her bare feet in the rough grass, as if she had known he was coming, as if she had been expecting him. Her red hair was all loose in the sunlight. He had to look away from her, down into the valley, but he could not look there, either, and so he studied his own hands against the worn pommel.

"Where did they go?" he said, after a moment.

When she did not answer, he looked up at her.

She was staring at him, her head tilted to one side. She moved her feet in the grass. "I don't know."

He nodded.

She said, "Do you want something, a drink of water?"

"No," he said, and the mare shifted beneath him.

After a while, she said, "What did you come here for?"

He squinted at her. "See if it was true. I guess."

"What?"

"All of it."

She nodded, smoothed her dress out against her legs. He watched her and she saw him watching and he looked away again, out over the fields.

"You plan to stay here?" he said.

She shrugged. "It's as good as anywhere else." Then she added, "You?"

Lathias looked around him. "There'll be a crop to get in, I guess, come August."

"Nice crop this year."

"That's what they say."

After a minute more, she said, "You been up to the cemetery yet?"

"Not yet," he said.

"I'll go with," she said, "if you want."

"No."

She nodded. He lifted his hand from the pommel, shifted the reins, pulled on the brim of his hat.

"Well," he said.

"Aren't you going to ask what happened?"

"No," he said, "what for?"

"Just to know."

"What would it matter?"

"You think I wouldn't tell you the truth."

"Why would you?"

"I've never lied to you before."

"Yes," he said. "You have."

"So have you," she said.

He stared down at the river. He wanted to say that was not true, either, but he did not. Could not. She was right. And what did it matter, now, what was true and what was not? What did it ever matter?

They sat there, the wind blowing between them, and he thought, *So this is it, then. Her and me. That's all there is, that's all there goddamn is.*

"I kept something for you," she said, reaching inside the pocket of her dress.

She rose and walked over to him and stood there while his horse nudged its muzzle against her, mouthing her blown hair. Then she held it up to him in her palm, a carved buffalo wound with a length of binder twine.

He looked away again, shifted in his saddle, the leather creaking beneath him. After a minute, he said, "That's nothing to me."

She raised her palm higher. "I thought you might want it."

When he did not answer, she closed her fist, withdrew it. He could feel her eyes upon him, but he would not look at her.

"I didn't steal it," she said, "if that's what you're thinking."

"He gave it to you?"

She bit her lip. "He had it. In his shirt pocket. I knew you'd come back, once you heard."

He looked down at her, at her bright, strange eyes, her hair whipping across her face.

"I guess that makes it yours," he said, harsher than he meant it.

She stared at him.

"All right," she said finally. She looked at the buffalo in her palm, slipped it back inside her pocket and pressed her hand against it. "Well," she said. "I might see you sometime, then."

"I don't think so," he said.

He flicked the reins and the mare turned, and she stepped back, her hair in her face.

"I'll tell you something," she said suddenly, her voice cracking a little, had it? Did he imagine that, too? Had he imagined it all? "I'll tell you one thing," she said. "You might not believe me, but I'll tell you anyway."

"Tell me," he said.

"I would have stopped it. If I could. I would have. But I didn't even see it coming. And neither did he. For what that's worth. He never saw it coming."

"No," Lathias said, putting his heels lightly to the mare. "No one ever does."

EPILOGUE

There is a cemetery in a country churchyard—down where the South Saskatchewan River crosses the Alberta– Saskatchewan border—that has almost completely disappeared into the land that holds it, as if, one day soon, it too will be buried.

Oh, the church is still there. No one uses it any more, there are no regular Sunday services, or special ones, either, but if you telephone the caretaker who lives nearby on one of the few farms still occupied (and who, in less than ten years, will be dead too, killed instantly when a semi slams into her truck at the Highway 41 intersection, and buried in the new cemetery in town, beloved wife and mother), she will, with a bit of notice, bring out the key and unlock the church's big front doors and you can look around.

If she's feeling particularly generous and not in a hurry to get back to the housework or the chores, she will let you pull the rope that hangs in the vestibule and ring the bell and you will marvel at the sound of it, ringing out across those fields, as if it would go on into eternity. You will ask if she would like to ring it too, but she will say, no, she does not want to disturb the neighbours and you will look around at the vast barren fields and she will say, a little sharply, "People still live here, you know, it's not dead yet," and you will nod and say, "Yes, of course, I didn't mean—" but already she will have turned away to close the big cupboard that encloses the bell rope.

She will tell you not to miss looking around the old cemetery, it hasn't been used in years, but the wrought-iron crosses there are really something, a real old Russian-German tradition. Beautiful workmanship. She'll walk out there with you, through the long brown grasses and the weeds that no one bothers to cut any more and the grasshoppers that sting your bare arms and legs and the mosquitoes, if it is a calm day, and she will say, "I told Harv he should of sprayed for the hoppers this year, but he said what's the point, so they don't bother the dead? But that's Harv. Can't tell him nothing." And she will say it sure has been a hot one, and the grasses will tickle your bare shins as you follow her, stepping through the wrought-iron gate, into the cemetery.

There are some sixty or so graves. She'll tell you there are others, but that the markers have been lost, rotted, the wooden ones, or blown down or God knows what. "Stolen?" you will say, and she will just look at you like you're crazy.

She will tell you a few records survived the fire in '53, but there's a lot of people down there that history just kind of forgot, she guesses. "Not just here," she will say, "all over. Family plots, unmarked graves." Then she will shrug and wave her hand dismissively out at the endless fields and tell you it would be amazing what you'd find, if you started digging around. "Gone now," she will say. "All gone."

You will wander around a bit and marvel at some of the names—Valentine and Pius and Lucius and Remigius and Aloysia and Kaspar and Balthasar and Emmanuel and Heironimus and Magdalen and Timotheus and Samuline and Barnabas and Leonhart and Balzar and Longinus and Clementia and Franciska and Ottillia and Isidore and Dionysius and Canisia and Benedicta and Hildegard and Bernarda and Florentine and Celestina, these last six being followed by the designation O.S.U. and marked by a small white cross. The caretaker tells you it stands for Order of St. Ursula, the nuns there, from the convent at the edge of town, you will pass it on your way out, you can't miss it. You will remark upon the oddness of the names and she will tell you those were old country names, no one around there is named Valentine any more, that's for sure.

Then you will notice a grave off in the far corner, all by itself, marked by a weathered, wooden cross, and you will ask her about it and she will get a funny kind of look on her face, just ever so slightly, and she will tell you that story would take hours. And you will say maybe you could buy her lunch or at least a cold drink in town. She will touch a hand to her hair and say, "Well, now, that sounds awful nice. I got a stew in the slow cooker but I wouldn't say no to a pop." You will look around once more, at the flat yellow prairie and the dome of blue sky and the white steeple that rises up into it. Then you will walk toward the grave in the corner and the caretaker will follow you and say, "It's kind of sad. All these old souls here. They're pretty much forgot, nobody talks about them any more, families all died out or moved on. A real shame. There's a whole lot of stories buried here." You will step over to the lone grave and say, "I'd like to hear that one." And she will nod and say, "I'll tell you about him, that boy. His name's all scratched off the marker here, always has been, kind of looks like somebody was at it with a knife sometime or other. Shame. Be damned if I can find anyone who remembers it." And she will shake her head, and sigh, "That's a sad story, that one. But I can tell you, if you want to hear."

ACKNOWLEDGEMENTS

I would like to thank the following: my remarkable editor, Phyllis Bruce; Esi Edugyan for her perceptive reading of an early draft; Nita Pronovost and Allyson Latta for their editorial insight; Anne McDermid for her efforts on behalf of this book; Judith Bode and Daniella Gatto for aid in translations; those who cared for my children while I stole time to write, especially Alke Germain; my husband, John, and my mother, Lorraine, as always; and, most of all, Steven Price and Timothy Birch, whose contributions continually exceed friendship.

My thanks also to the Canada Council and the Alberta Foundation for the Arts for making the writing of this book possible.

As this is a work of fiction, I have taken some creative licence with minor geographical and historical details.

Many sources were useful in researching this place and these people. Deserving particular mention are *Paradise on the Steppe* and *Homesteaders on the Steppe* by Joseph Height. I am especially grateful to all those who keep the old ways alive in their hearts and memories.